THE WHITEHALL MANDARIN

Praise for Edward Wilson

'This is an intellectually commanding thriller that does well those things that thrillers are supposed to do, but adds a mordant wit and a poignant sense of the human cost of every move in the game of nations' *Independent*

'An outstanding third novel: an intricate tale of high political drama and deadly action. Wilson is a master at working the history of the period' *Publishers Weekly*

'Brilliant!' *Telegraph*

'It's on a par with John le Carré ... it's that good' *Tribune*

'The professionalism of the novel, so rich in detailed perspectives, its characters so sturdily grounded, enables it to outgrow the spy-thriller's more weirdsome conventions, while delivering strong emotional charges' *TLS*

'Smart, finely written sequel to *The Envoy*' *Publishers Weekly*

'A tense, cerebral, dark story' *Portsmouth Herald*

'The plot is a glorious, seething broth of historical fact and old-fashioned spy story' *The Times*

'A sophisticated, convincing novel that shows governments and their secret services as cynically exploitative and utterly ruthless' *Sunday Telegraph*

'One of the best spy novels I've ever read' *Morning Star*

'The best Vietnam novel ever, which everyone should read' *Independent on Sunday*

'There's no getting away from the book's raw power – highly recommended' *Mail on Sunday*

'Stylistically sophisticated ... Wilson knows how to hold the reader's attention' W. G. Sebald

About the author

Edward Wilson is a native of Baltimore. He studied International Relations on a US Army scholarship and later served as a Special Forces officer in Vietnam. He received the Army Commendation Medal with 'V' for his part in rescuing wounded Vietnamese soldiers from a minefield. His other decorations include the Bronze Star and the Combat Infantryman's Badge. After leaving the Army, Wilson became an expatriate and gave up US nationality to become a British citizen. He has also lived and worked in Germany and France. He is the author of four previous novels, *A River in May*, *The Envoy*, *The Darkling Spy* and *The Midnight Swimmer*, all published by Arcadia Books. The author now lives in Suffolk where he taught English and Modern Languages for thirty years.

THE WHITEHALL MANDARIN

Edward Wilson

ARCADIA BOOKS

First Clown. 'Tis a quick lie, sir; 'twill away again, from me to you.

Hamlet. What man dost thou dig it for?

First Clown. For no man, sir.

Hamlet. What woman, then?

First Clown. For none, neither.

Hamlet. Who is to be buried in 't?

First Clown. One that was a woman, sir; but, rest her soul, she's dead.

Hamlet, Scene V, Act i

For Julia

Wilson

Arcadia Books Ltd
139 Highlever Road
London W10 6PH

www.arcadiabooks.co.uk

First published in the United Kingdom by Arcadia Books 2014

A catalogue record for this book is available from the British Library.

ISBN 978-1-909807-53-2

Typeset in Minion by MacGuru Ltd
Printed and bound by CPI Group (UK) Ltd, Croydon CR0 4YY

Arcadia Books supports English PEN *www.englishpen.org* and
The Book Trade Charity *http://booktradecharity.wordpress.com*

Arcadia Books distributors are as follows:

in the UK and elsewhere in Europe:
Macmillan Distribution Ltd
Brunel Road
Houndmills
Basingstoke
Hants RG21 6XS

in the USA and Canada:
Dufour Editions
PO Box 7
Chester Springs
PA, 19425

in Australia/New Zealand:
NewSouth Books
University of New South Wales
Sydney NSW 2052

London: March, 1957

How strange, thought Catesby, that when you look through a telescopic sight and see another human being fixed in the cross-hairs you end up looking at yourself. It doesn't matter whether it's lens reflection or imagination. You try to concentrate on your target but find your eye superimposed over their eyes. Those other eyes, so blissfully unaware of your unblinking predatory stare, are no longer evil. You feel your hate drop away and realise you can't do it. It was Catesby's most shameful secret from the war: he had never been able to pull the trigger. But he had learnt to since.

'I wish,' said Catesby as he adjusted the telephoto lens, 'that this was a sniper rifle instead of a camera.' He wanted to convince the other two, especially Skardon from Five, that he was hard and of their mind. The third man in the cramped roof space under the eaves of the building overlooking St James's Park was Catesby's boss, Henry Bone.

'I thought,' said Bone, 'that you were fond of Cauldwell.'

'Cauldwell's fine. I like him. He's a professional like us. It's the other one I don't like.'

Skardon frowned. 'He's a scumbag.'

'But,' said Catesby, 'you have to admire Cauldwell and the Sovs. The Russians are consummate professionals. Spying is in their blood, like chess and vodka.'

Bone was coughing. The roof space was full of cobwebs, mouse droppings and two centuries of dust.

Catesby turned towards his boss, 'Are you okay, Henry?'

'You talk too much, Catesby. Keep your eye on that park bench.'

'What's the scumbag doing?' asked Skardon

Catesby peered through the eyepiece. 'He's sitting on the bench looking at his watch.'

'But Cauldwell still no show?'

'Not yet. Tyler seems to be getting nervous.'

'That bastard ought to hang,' said Skardon.

'Did you ask for an arrest warrant?'

Skardon coughed and cleared his throat. 'It's dusty in here.'

Bone shook his head. 'You talk too much, Catesby.'

'How well,' said Skardon, 'did you know Cauldwell?'

'It's in my report,' Catesby replied.

'Remind me.'

'I met him in Germany in the early 50s when I was operating under dip cover as a second secretary in the Cultural Attaché's office. Cauldwell was the same rank in the US Embassy so we met at a lot of functions.'

'And you thought he was…'

'Full of contradictions and too bright to… Hang on, here he comes. Have a look.'

Skardon put his eye to the viewfinder and nodded. 'It's him all right – arrogant little sod. You'd better start snapping.'

Catesby slid back behind the camera – there wasn't room even to kneel – and put his index finger on the shutter release.

»»»»»

In St James's Park the daffodils were in full bloom, but it was a cold day. Tyler had told Euan, his boss at the Admiralty, that he was feeling ill and needed fresh air. Euan always indulged him. Tyler had arrived ten minutes early for the rendezvous and was impeccably dressed. When he had worked in Moscow, the Head of Chancery had always singled him out for his 'first-class appearance and manners'.

Dressing well usually gave Tyler self-confidence, but on this occasion he was still nervous. He didn't know what or whom to expect. He had met the American at a louche party in Dolphin Square. He said his name was Nick Seyton but Tyler had taken that with a pinch of salt as aliases were part of the scene. They later exchanged telephone numbers, but when Tyler had tried ringing him the line was dead. He checked with the GPO and found that no such phone number had ever existed. But Tyler wasn't suspicious. He'd had a lot to drink that evening and must have copied the number incorrectly. Two days later the American telephoned him.

'I tried to ring you,' said Tyler, 'but I couldn't get...'

'Yeah, I know; there's been a problem. Listen, I haven't time to talk. Meet me in St James's Park – tomorrow at eleven o'clock.'

For a second Tyler wondered if he was talking to the same person that he had met at the party. The voice was still American, but crisp and with less Deep South honey.

'That's fine,' said Tyler, 'I'll be there.'

Tyler guessed he would find the American on the Buckingham Palace end of St James's Lake: it was more secluded. He finally spotted him on a park bench partly obscured by a weeping willow. The American was wearing a single-breasted trench coat with a belt, which was casually knotted. Tyler could see that the coat was perfectly cut and expensive.

The American didn't look up as Tyler approached. He didn't even make eye contact when Tyler sat down on the bench next to him. There was a long awkward pause as the American looked out across the lake, his eyes squinting against the lowering sun. Finally, he gave a twisted smile, as if he were inwardly laughing at an unspoken joke. When the words came they were a velvet whisper.

'Did anyone ever tell you that you were pretty when you were a little girl?' The American spoke in the same honeyed accent, a purr of lazy diphthongs, that Tyler remembered from the party. It was the languid Southern drawl of a plantation owner ordering a slave to strip.

Tyler stared across the lake and stayed silent.

'So no one ever told you that?'

Tyler laughed nervously. 'No.'

'Not even your mother?'

'No.'

'What a pity. All little girls should be told they're pretty, even if they're not.' The American paused and gave an inward smile. 'But, of course, John, you are pretty. And I'm sure you want to be.'

Tyler was surprised to hear his proper name. The Dolphin Square gang called him 'Babs'.

'Why,' asked the American, 'do you think I asked you to come here?'

'I think you're playing some sort of game – and not a very pleasant one.'

'Unh, uh.' The American gave a lopsided laugh. 'Oh dear, you sound ever so proper British when you get indignant. Can you do it again?'

'Please don't mock me.'

'I apologise, John. Do you forgive me?'

'Sure.' Tyler paused. 'Now that you know my real name, can you tell me yours?'

The American laughed. 'I don't have a real name. I'm surprised you didn't know that.'

Tyler nodded. 'Okay.'

'Let's get down to business.' The American slipped a hand inside his trench coat and took out a brown eight-by-ten envelope. 'Did you, uh, enjoy your posting in Moscow?'

Tyler stared at the envelope without answering.

'Maybe you can't remember.' The American opened the envelope and slid out the first photo. 'But it certainly looks like you enjoyed yourself – and gave joy to a few others too. Would you like to see the rest of the photos?'

Tyler looked away and shook his head.

'You're lucky, John.'

'How?'

'That it was our guys who were running Mikhailski.'

Tyler knew he had been reckless that evening, but thought he would be safe with Mikhailski because his new friend was a Pole, not a Russian. It seemed at the time, especially after all the vodka, that as they were foreigners, they could do what they wanted and nobody would know. Then later, when a couple of Russians joined in, Tyler was past caring.

'Thank you,' said Tyler.

'I don't understand why you're thanking me.' The American smiled and tapped a finger on the photos. 'You think that I'm just giving you a friendly warning to be more careful in the future?'

Tyler shook his head.

'How's your mother? Does she like the new vicarage?'

'Don't...'

'Maybe she wouldn't mind. She must know what you're like.'

'Keep her out of it ... please.'

'Or there's Euan, your boss. He trusts you so much he lets you call him by his first name. I've heard that you keep a photograph of Euan in his naval officer's uniform in a silver frame on your desk.'

'What do you want?'

'I want you to accept this present.' The American slid a small solid object into Tyler's overcoat pocket. 'It's a Praktina, bigger than the Minox, but I prefer them. Don't let Euan see it.'

Tyler surreptitiously touched the camera. The metal was still warm from the American's touch. 'Why are you giving this to me?'

'Don't be naive.'

Tyler ran his fingers over the camera. 'You said it's a Praktina. That's an East German camera. Why have you given me one of those?'

'They're better quality than ours. And I'm sure you remember how to photo documents from your RAF days. You were trained.'

'What do you want?'

'At first: radar, torpedoes and anti-submarine equipment.'

Tyler felt the Praktina was biting his fingers, as if the camera had turned into a serpent. He looked out across the lake. The water mirrored a shaky reflection of Buckingham Palace. For a second Tyler wasn't sure what he was going to do. Maybe, he thought, it was best to confess everything to Euan. No one would want a diplomatic row with the Americans. There would be a cover-up – and he would receive a quiet reprimand. And what was the point of this spying? Tyler assumed that the Admiralty shared technical information with the Americans as a matter of course.

'I've got another present for you,' said the American. He passed over a bulging envelope. 'Don't worry. The only pictures you'll find in this one are of Ulysses S. Grant and Benjamin Franklin.'

Tyler slipped the money into an inner coat pocket. He was surprised how quickly and thoughtlessly he had done it.

'You like nice clothes, don't you, John?'

'And so do you. It's not a crime to dress well.'

'May I recommend a shirt-maker? His name is Youseff and he's got a shop just off Bond Street. He's a Syrian. You'll find his card with the dollar bills. Youseff is also a good way to find me – and I'm sure you will want to.'

The American got up. He towered over Tyler. His tall body blocked the sun. He stared at the Englishman and smiled – then a second later he was gone.

Meanwhile, a second photographer on the top floor of another building overlooking St James's Park was aiming a long heavy telephoto lens for the last few shots.

»»»»»

Catesby and Bone were walking alone on Birdcage Walk. They were dressed in overalls and carrying long canvas tool bags. They had posed as heating engineers to get access to the roof space.

'Skardon,' said Catesby, 'didn't hang around long.'

'He's in a hurry to get the film developed – and a bit annoyed that he had to use us to get the photos.' Bone was referring to the fact that Skardon's service , MI5, was responsible for surveillance within the UK. SIS were limited by law to snooping abroad.

'Did he argue the case?'

'Vigorously and loudly. But C overruled him on a need-to-know basis. SIS uncovered Cauldwell and we don't want to share the details with the bumbling plods at Five. There are sensitive issues that the retired colonial police inspectors at Leconfield House might not grasp.'

Catesby smiled. Bone's contempt for MI5 was well known in the service: *They're not gentlemen, so you can't expect them to behave like gentlemen.* Catesby looked closely at his boss. 'By the way, Henry, how did we uncover Cauldwell?'

'That, Catesby, is something you don't need to know. Why are you looking at me that way?'

'Because I was thinking how much you look the part in your flat cap and overalls. With elocution lessons, you could pass for a site foreman – or one of those skilled craftsmen who restore the squiggly bits on Georgian ceilings.'

'Actually, Catesby, I have done just that for a friend who has a rather grand place in Suffolk. The fluted cavetto cornices were the most difficult.'

'Who is this friend?'

'You don't need to know that either.'

>>>>>>

It was a busy day for Jeffers Cauldwell and his aliases. For over a year he had been Cultural Attaché at the US Embassy in Grosvenor Square. As a wealthy dandy from the American South, Cauldwell was an unlikely Communist spy – which was why it had been so easy to dupe Tyler and some of the others with the 'false flag' ploy. It was an op whereby a spy pretends to be working for a less toxic intelligence agency, usually an ally's. They thought Cauldwell was a Washington spook, but they were wrong. Cauldwell was a fearless and ideologically committed Communist.

It was a busy day indeed. Cauldwell had a number of chores involving various agents. His next stop was a bench in Green Park. The agent was a Tory cabinet minister who had been spectacularly compromised. The evidence was a Polaroid photo that had come into Cauldwell's possession via an American actor. The photo did not reveal anything illegal, but if made public would ruin the minister's career. The minister was careful not to provide classified information to Cauldwell that would have breached the Official Secrets Act. Instead, he kept the Polaroid out of circulation by providing personal secrets about his colleagues and the upper-class elite. Cauldwell treasured those revelations more than a NATO codebook. He knew that personal secrets were the blackmail levers that could pry open the doors of the Secret State. The bedrooms of Knightsbridge and other posh parts of SW3 were more valuable to a foreign spy than a hidden microphone in 10 Downing Street.

The one thing that Cauldwell had learned during his posting in England was that upper-class society was a sexual circus. The circus hosted a diverse and imaginative variety of acts, which were always performed with aplomb. In fact, participants seemed to prefer performing if an audience was involved. They liked dressing up and showing off. The textbook term was autagonistophilia. Arousal and satisfaction were achieved by displaying oneself as part of a live show or on camera – and probably explained the Polaroid. The lady involved had become sexually voracious after falling down a lift shaft while visiting her Harley Street gynaecologist. But her having the camera in the first place was more interesting than the sex act she recorded with it. At the time the snap was taken, the mid-1950s, the only Polaroid cameras in Britain belonged to the Security Services and the Ministry of Defence

The cabinet minister sent signals to Cauldwell by sticking drawing pins into the park bench. A red pin meant come back in a fortnight; yellow meant they could talk using public phone kiosks; green meant a face to face meeting at rush hour under the clock at Charing Cross. Some agents liked to use drawing pins stuck on the bottom side of the shelf in a phone kiosk as a rendezvous signal, but the pins often ended up covered in chewing gum – and Cauldwell didn't like having to peel off macerated gum. The problem with park benches, as well as public phones, was someone else using them when you wanted to make a rendezvous check. But this time, at least, the bench was empty – and the pin was yellow.

The important thing about telephone rendezvous was split-second timing. You don't dial the number of the other public phone until the person is in place and waiting with phone in hand and finger depressing the cradle. Cauldwell checked his watch and slowly walked to Piccadilly to find an unoccupied kiosk. At the precise second, he dialled the number and the other phone answered immediately with the code name, 'Sholto here.'

Cauldwell gave the verification answer: 'Did you place the bet?'

'Lady Somers is a real runner for the Deputy PUS stakes at Cannon Fodder. The filly has an interesting history.'

'She didn't fall down an elevator shaft by any chance?'

The minister laughed. 'No, you're confusing her with someone else. But I would say that Lady Somers has even *more* interesting history.'

Cauldwell sensed that the minister enjoyed passing on gossip and that the threat of blackmail gave him carte blanche to do it. 'Please tell me more; don't be a tease.'

'No.' The minister brayed an even louder laugh and the line went dead.

Cauldwell hung up and hailed a taxi. He told the driver to take him to 30 Queen's Gate Mews, but that wasn't where he was going. You never tell taxi drivers your exact destination in case the Security Services question them about a curious fare, but it was near enough. Cauldwell settled into his seat and watched London flash past as he worked out the minister's cryptic message. PUS was an acronym for Permanent Under-secretary of State, the highest-ranking civil service mandarin in a White-hall department. So a deputy PUS would be second in rank to the PUS. 'Cannon Fodder' was easy – the War Office. Cauldwell had vaguely heard of Lady Somers. He wondered if she was one of *les grandes horizontales sapphiques* that his cabinet minister sometimes talked about. In any case, Lady Somers, *sapphique* or not, seemed lined up for a pretty big job at War. But what was her 'interesting history'?

»»»»»

It was a quick walk from Queen's Gate Mews to the Hereford Arms on Gloucester Road. Cauldwell used to meet the agent at the Bunch of Grapes on Old Brompton Road, but too many Sovs had started to hang around the Grapes – and that meant MI5 had put the pub under surveillance. But the Sovs were the clever ones. They knew that if you frequented a place, it wouldn't be long before 'watchers' from Five would flock there like wasps to rotten apples. By deflecting surveillance manpower, you could rendezvous more safely at other places.

The Hereford Arms agent was a scientist. He was a difficult agent to run because he was so frightened and fucked up. Cauldwell didn't like meeting him face to face, but there was no other way because the scientist refused to use DLBs – dead letter boxes – or to get the hang of clandestine telephone calls. He also needed a lot of personal support, which was tiresome. The scientist wasn't upper-class – far from it – but he did have his own niche kink. It wasn't, in fact, one that toffs – as far as Cauldwell knew – ever practised. The scientist's kink was paraphilic infantilism, also known as adult baby syndrome. He liked to be dressed up in diapers and to be bathed, powdered and changed. The proclivities split up his marriage. The scientist was talent spotted by the KGB *Rezident* at the Soviet Embassy and his file passed on to Cauldwell – who wondered whether he was worth the bother and risk. He taught at Imperial College and was a specialist in aerodynamics, but his research was inferior to that being carried out by Sov scientists. So what was the point of using him? The point wasn't *what* he knew, but *who* he knew. The scientist was part of the RAF research establishment and also had contacts in the Admiralty Underwater Weapons Establishment at Portland in Dorset. The latter was what really interested Cauldwell.

The Hereford Arms was a Victorian pub painted purple black. It was famous for having been the local of Arthur Conan Doyle – and there were rumours that Jack the Ripper used to drink there too. The current lunchtime crowd was also a bit odd. There were naturalists from the Natural History Museum and arty curator types from the V&A. This worried Cauldwell. He was afraid that one of the V&A crowd might recognise him from his CultAt post. As he ordered a gin and tonic, one of them winked at him. Cauldwell hoped it was flirtation and not recognition. At that moment, the scientist walked in and came to the bar.

'What are you having?'

'A pint of Fuller's.'

Cauldwell ordered the beer and whispered to the scientist: 'Pretend we're a couple of boys about to do something naughty.'

'I don't like that sort of thing. It's disgusting.'

'Not as disgusting as what you do like.' Cauldwell had shifted his voice from American to London spiv. He didn't want to attract attention. 'Sit in the corner, sweetheart, and keep up the act. We need an excuse for talking in whispers.'

Cauldwell took the chair with his back to the bar and the lunchtime crowd. The scientist fidgeted nervously. 'They're staring at us.'

'They're staring at me. You're too dull and boring. Maybe that's why your wife left you, nothing to do with soiled nappies.'

'You're a nasty piece of business, aren't you?'

Cauldwell smiled. 'We all have our faults. Mine is being a completely evil bastard.'

'And that's the reason why I want out now. I've decided to confess.'

'They'll love you at Wormwood Scrubs. Nice fresh boy like you. As soon as they see your face in the newspapers, they'll get out their tubes of Vaseline and warm them on the radiators.'

The scientist turned pale and sipped his beer. 'I still want out.'

'How are you for dosh?' Cauldwell knew that the divorce had cost the scientist a lot of money.

'That's another thing I want to talk about.'

'We can give you more money, but we'll want something in return.'

'But I've already given you everything I had access to when I was at Boscombe Down.' The scientist was referring to an RAF R&D project he had worked on. The information he had passed over was of little value, but the purpose of the op had been to entrap the scientist for the future. And the future was now.

'I don't want information. I want an introduction to your friend from Portland Bill.'

»»»»»

Three days later, Cauldwell was on the last train from Waterloo to Weymouth. The train was nearly empty and the two men were alone in the compartment. Cauldwell was reading a newspaper. The naval officer was in civilian clothes and looked slightly drunk, but not so drunk that he had forgotten his lines.

'I say, is that the evening edition?'

'Yes, it is.'

'Would you mind if I have a look when you're finished? I want to check the racing results.'

'You can have it now.' Cauldwell smiled and handed him the paper.

When the naval officer looked at the sports page, he found the racing results were excellent. A hundred pounds in used notes was pinned to the page – enough to buy the new car he needed.

'And there's more where that came from,' said Cauldwell.

The naval officer needed the money. Booze, women and gambling had drained him. 'We must meet more often, Mr...'

'Hood, just like your battleship.'

'Actually, she was a battle*cruiser*.'

'I should have known that. There's a lot more you can teach me.' Cauldwell could see that the naval officer was going to be a straightforward agent to run. Greed was always easy. But Cauldwell knew he was taking a big risk. The Admiralty Underwater Weapons Establishment at Portland was not his patch. Vasili, his KGB London control, had warned him off it before.

The naval officer slipped the bank notes into his pocket and winked at Cauldwell. 'I'm glad we've met, Mr...'

'Hood.'

'Silly me, memory like a sieve.' The naval officer's voice was now slurred. 'Actually, I was expecting to meet someone else. Have you a colleague called Gordon?'

Cauldwell gave a weary smile. 'There's been a bit of a problem with Gordon, but I can't give you the details.'

'Just a little clue?'

Cauldwell shook his head, then whispered, 'Have you got suspicions about him?'

'I just want to be careful.'

'And this is how you can be careful. If Gordon approaches you, have nothing to do with him. Don't even give him the time of day.'

The naval officer gave a knowing smile. 'He's a nark.'

Cauldwell kept a straight face. 'I'm not saying anything more.'

'*Capisco.*'

Cauldwell stared out the train window into the damp night. He feared he had gone too far. It seemed that Konon Molody, aka Gordon Lonsdale, was already running the naval officer. Portland belonged to Molody – the best Soviet spy in the UK – and messing about with Portland was the most dangerous thing that Cauldwell had ever done. Molody could report him back to Moscow if he heard.

'Bloody hell,' said the naval officer, 'I'm dying for a piss.'

'That's the problem with these trains.' They were in a no-corridor carriage with full-width compartments.

'Yeah, but they're jolly good for having a shag. But I'm bursting.'

'I'll hold the door open for you.'

'Thanks.' The naval officer wagged his finger. 'But promise not to look.'

'Of course not.'

It wasn't unusual for drunken passengers to fall to their death when peeing from such trains. Cauldwell left the empty compartment at the next station.

»»»»»

The next day in London was creepy, dead creepy. Cauldwell had itchy feet and knew something was wrong. He worked late at the embassy doing Cultural Attaché stuff, largely preparing a press pack about Elvis Presley being declared 1A and eligible for US military draft, and keeping a low profile. He took counter-surveillance measures on the way back to his flat that evening but Cauldwell knew something was wrong even before he saw the van. He had just come out of Pimlico underground station. It was a sixth sense, a feeling of eyes boring into the back – and then the tradesman's van at a time of night when no tradesmen would be working. Cauldwell turned into Moreton Street. As soon as the van pulled up beside him, he reached for the Smith & Wesson in his Mackintosh pocket. If there was only one of them, he would put a bullet in the driver and take the van. If there were several, he would empty the clip and run back to the underground station – assuming no one could follow him. The passenger door swung open and Cauldwell aimed at the shadow. And the shadow called out in a hoarse whisper: 'Put that away, Jeffers, and get in. You've been busted.' He recognised the hoarse voice. It was Youseff, the Syrian shirt-maker.

The Admiralty is the finest set of government buildings in London. There is always a mounted horse guard with drawn sword and gleaming breastplate on duty in the Adam-designed arch that leads into a small courtyard off Whitehall. The pomp of the sentinel may be symbolic, but the secrets of the Admiralty are real.

The guarded arch is not an entry for visitors on foot. It would be undignified to squeeze past the stony-faced guard. You would also have to dodge a pile of horseshit. So you go through the narrow pedestrian entrance where a policeman from So1, the Special Protection Branch, will check your credentials and your reasons for visiting. If, however, you are a senior mandarin, the policeman will simply touch his helmet in salute and nod you through with a 'Good morning, Sir X or Lord Y' – or 'Lady Somers'.

It was a warm and sunny day, but Lady Somers was hatless. She had forgotten her hat because she was in a hurry. She was pleased that she didn't need to stop and show her ID. As the first woman ever to become 2nd PUS, Deputy Permanent Under-secretary of State, everyone knew who she was. And now, as she had been elevated to 'acting PUS' owing to her boss's long-term illness, she was in charge. As the duty cop saluted, Lady Somers flashed a quick smile in return and click-clacked across the courtyard on her stilettos. The policeman turned back into the kiosk where tea was being poured by the night rota. He winked and nodded at his off-duty colleague: 'Yeah, I'd give her one.'

'But I don't think you'll ever get the chance.'

Somers was late because a last-minute problem had delayed her. She was a widowed single parent with a difficult daughter. She hated being late and hated it when others used contrived late-ness as a tactic. There was one particularly irritating chap from SIS who always arrived late at the Joint Intelligence Committee juggling teacup, reading glasses and files and never managed to shut the door behind him – despite a balletic attempt to do so with a back heel that he must have learned on the football pitch. He used his late arrivals to disrupt JIC meetings so he could insert his own agendas. It was a tactic that was as successful as it was annoying.

The person waiting for her was an ex-cop with a file full of photos. Skardon had been an inspector in the Met who had transferred to MI5 during the war. It was a good career move. He was now head of A4, the surveillance section, better known as 'the watchers'.

Skardon was waiting in the music room of the building known as 'the Old Admiralty'. He was wearing a trilby and an old Mac and looked a bit out of place amid the eighteenth-century grandeur of gilt chairs and crystal chandeliers. He passed the time by staring at an oil painting of a nineteenth-century sea battle in which one of the ships has capsized and the sea is full of sailors drowning and luckier ones in longboats.

Lady Somers entered the music room, but Skardon continued to stare at the sea battle to show annoyance at her lateness. The ex-cop had a thick manila file tucked firmly under his left arm as if it were his most precious possession. He had spent his working life collecting such evidence. He liked nailing villains. It wasn't a matter of personal satisfaction, but a matter of justice. He believed in public service.

Lady Somers drew level and quoted Kipling as she nodded at the painting, 'If blood be the price of admiralty, Lord God, we ha' paid in full!'

'Someone has to pay.'

'I agree, Jim, but it's an awkward situation.'

Skardon bristled at the first name familiarity that couldn't be reciprocated. He turned to stare at Somers. 'It reeks.'

'It wasn't my decision.'

'Whose was it then?'

'The Prime Minister's.'

'Maybe I should have a word.'

Lady Somers smiled bleakly. 'The PM thinks it's a mistake to arrest this spy for a public trial. His exact words were, "When my gamekeeper shoots a fox, he doesn't go and hang it up outside the Master of Foxhounds' drawing room; he buries it out of sight.'"

Skardon raised an eyebrow. 'Are you saying the PM wants us to kill Tyler and disappear the body?'

Lady Somers shook her head. 'No, no – of course not. It's just his manner of speaking. The PM would never condone that – or any form of state-sponsored assassination.'

'And the cat always gets out of the bag.'

'That too. But the PM – and SIS agree – thinks that we should turn Tyler around and use him as a conduit to pass on disinformation. We've done it before.'

The case in question referred, in fact, to the high-ranking SIS officer who never managed to shut the door behind him. He had been caught red-handed working for Moscow, but was never prosecuted. The case was a long-running sore between MI5 and the Secret Intelligence Service.

'He ought,' said Skardon, 'to have been hung, drawn and quartered years ago. He's taking the mick.'

Somers raised an eyebrow. 'This one is a different situation.'

'No, it isn't.' Skardon gave Lady Somers a long hard stare. 'And you know it.'

'I know that the Tyler case requires special handling. It's not just a matter of using him to pass on disinformation. It also involves the UK's relationship with an ally. There are complicated nuances.'

Skardon handed over the folder. 'It's out of my hands. I'm just a thick cop who can't understand these complex affairs of state.'

'That's not true, Jim. You are the most respected officer in the Security Service. Your advice is sacred.'

'Don't patronise me. Take my advice instead. The best way to stop treason is to hang traitors. Make an example of those deceitful bastards.'

»»»»»

Lady Somers' office overlooked Horse Guards Parade. She had one of the best views of any civil servant in London. She tried not to waste too much time staring out the window over St James's Park towards the palace. Or peeking over the wall into the garden of Number 10. It was a large garden, about half an acre, but not a very nice one. It was mostly grass except for shrubs in tubs and pollarded trees along the wall. It was functional rather than decorative. Nonetheless, on sunny days the Prime Minister sometimes sat alone in the garden in a wicker chair with a book. And on those days, Lady Somers wished that she had a powerful pair of ship's binoculars so that she could see whether the PM was reading Aeschylus or Anthony Trollope – or some dull government report.

There was a knock on the door: a knock that she was expecting and partly dreading. 'Come in, please.'

The man who came in greeted his boss with a nervous smile. He was very timid for someone who had been a senior and well-decorated naval officer.

'You wanted to see me, Lady Somers?'

'Yes, Euan. I hope you have time for a chat.'

'No problem at all. I was expecting you.'

'Would you like a cup of tea?'

'No, thank you.' Euan held a folder in front of his chest as if it were a bulletproof vest and stared out the window.

'Are you all right?'

'Sorry if I appear distracted. I was just admiring the view. It's absolutely stunning – and that's why I worry about these offices.'

'What's your worry?'

'An assassin with a sniper rifle could wreak havoc – especially on Remembrance Sunday.'

'I shouldn't worry about that. The Special Protection Branch make a thorough search of this building whenever there's an event of state. They check everyone and everything – and can be quite a nuisance. But they are necessary.'

'Do you ever, Lady Somers, worry about a police force who are too powerful. *Quis custodiet ipsos custodes?*'

Lady Somers smiled. 'You might even say, "Who guards the guards?"'

'I am sorry if you find my use of Latin pretentious.'

'Not at all, Euan. It was a gentle tease. I suppose the *custodis* you are referring to is Jim Skardon. He was just here.'

'I saw him leave. He didn't look happy. The situation is very worrying – and shocking.'

'It has been resolved – and, to answer your Latin tag, we have overruled the guards. You look relieved, Euan?'

'I don't feel relieved. I feel very sad.'

'About John?'

'Yes.'

'I think you should know everything.' Lady Somers had two files on her desk. She opened one of them and drew out a pack of glossy photos. 'Have a look. I hope you're not easily shocked.'

'I don't need to look. We already knew, about his homosexuality in any case. It was just something that was assumed, but never mentioned.'

'But did you know he was a spy?'

'Not until I read this.' Euan held up the file with two red stripes that he had carried in. 'Of course I didn't know he was a spy. If I had, I would have reported him at once. I thought it was utter nonsense when Five got into a stir about him. I put it down to intolerance and lack of sophistication on their part. Of course, sending John to Moscow was a big mistake. He was too young and too vulnerable.' Euan finally looked at the photos on Lady Somers' desk and winced. 'What happens next?'

'Nothing legal.'

A dark frown came over Euan's face. 'Surely...'

'I meant there will be no prosecution. That's what I meant by overruling the guards.'

'Excuse me, Penelope, but you're talking riddles.'

'Sorry, I'm very tired this morning.'

Euan looked at his boss. She had deep dark lines under her eyes. Lady Somers was usually distant and enigmatic – and never admitted to being tired, annoyed or even pleased. Her eyes, such a dark brown that you could hardly tell the difference between pupil and iris, were blanks that never revealed anything.

Euan decided to risk it. 'How is Miranda?'

'She's fine.' Lady Somers' voice was icy.

'I'm glad.' Euan realised he had stepped over the line and retreated. The daughter discussion was obviously over. Miranda was Lady Somers' only child and, apparently, there were issues.

'To make the deception effective, we have to do more than merely keep Tyler in place.' Lady Somers continued as if Euan's clumsy question about her daughter had been unheard. 'We promote Tyler so he can have a higher security clearance.' She paused and smiled, suddenly looking less tired. 'Now, Euan, you really do look shocked.'

'This is a dangerous game.'

'We've played it before – and it helped win the war.' Somers was referring to 'Double-Cross', an operation in which German spies in Britain were captured and turned in order to send false information to their controllers in Berlin between 1940 and 1945. Among other successes, it had tricked German generals into believing the D-Day landings were going to be in the Pas-de-Calais.

'So we're going to tell Tyler that he's been uncovered – and that he has to do our bidding or else?'

'No, Euan, we're not going to tell him. Tyler is going to be what the spy trade call an "unwitting agent". He will be totally unaware of how he's being used. You look surprised.'

'I'm finding it difficult to take in. It sounds most extraordinary.'

'It was not my decision, Euan. It was made at higher level.'

Euan raised a sceptical eyebrow. 'At what level?'

'At the highest level – and the procedure has been discussed with SIS.' Lady Somers tried to hide her irritation at being questioned. 'There are several reasons for using Tyler as an unwitting agent. He hasn't been trained as a spy and would never be convincing as a turned double. I also doubt his emotional stability – he might panic and run. But most importantly, we will still have the option of prosecuting him for treason in the future.' Lady Somers shrugged. 'We have to stop doing deals that carry a promise of immunity. A lot of people in Five don't like it and they can cause serious problems. I've just had an earful from one of them.'

Euan stared out the window across St James's to Buckingham

Palace. The definition of State was not carved in stone. He suddenly felt Lady Somers staring at him in an odd way. 'There's something else on your mind. What is it, Penelope?'

'Was there anything between yourself and Tyler that you would like to tell me about?'

'Absolutely no impropriety. Certainly nothing involving physical intimacy. John hero-worshipped me – look, there's me already using the past tense.'

'And you felt flattered by his admiration?'

'Yes, in a way. And I didn't want to disillusion him – so I may have embellished the grandeur of the Scottish estate and my war service. It's not unpleasant to be worshipped.'

'I notice that he copies the way you dress.'

'That is embarrassing.'

Lady Somers smiled. 'It's not easy to reprimand someone for that.'

'Or even to mention it.'

'Quite.'

'John is basically a nice lad who is very eager to please.' Euan flushed. 'Sorry, Penelope, my phrasing was unfortunate. But he is very efficient around the office.'

'I suppose he has to be to get all the documents that need photographing.'

'I wish he had confided in me. I could have helped him deal with the blackmail.'

'It's not just the blackmail card. It's money too. Have you heard of MICE?'

'Only the obvious ones.'

'MICE are the options for recruiting an agent: money, ideology, coercion and excitement. In Tyler's case it was M and C. For our Cambridge friends it was all I and E. In my view, Tyler's motives are far more squalid than theirs. But you call him a "nice lad"?'

'John told me that he inherited the money from a distant relative in America.'

'Did you actually believe that, Euan?'

'A lot of us have inherited money – and, in some cases,' Euan smiled, 'that's the main reason why we're here.' He suddenly realised his gaffe and blushed. 'I was, of course, Lady Somers, referring to myself.'

'I'm sure you were, but you have no reason to be self-deprecating.'

'Thank you, Penelope. In any case, I didn't think that a windfall inheritance was anything unusual, so I believed Tyler's story.'

'But MI5 didn't believe it – and that's what set them on his trail.'

'John likes fine things.'

'And that's what gave him away. Five's watchers logged him as having worn thirty-four different suits in one month.'

'I suppose he is a bit of a fop.'

'And you admit he copies the way you dress?'

'Thank you, Penelope.'

'I was teasing again.'

Lady Somers went back to the MI5 file on Tyler and picked out a glossy photo. 'And this one's a smart dresser too.'

Euan regarded the photo with a critical eye. 'But personally, I think the trench coat is *de trop*.'

'Do you recognise him?'

Euan shifted nervously and stuttered. 'He, he does look familiar...'

'Where did you meet him?'

'At a festival concert in Aldeburgh. He has a violinist friend who is part of the Britten–Pears crowd. I then met him again at the US ambassador's 4th of July bash – which was even more *de trop* than his trench coat.'

'Do you remember his name?'

'Jeffers Cauldwell. He's the US Cultural Attaché. Quite a flamboyant figure. No one would ever imagine that Cauldwell is a Soviet spy.'

'That's the beauty of Cauldwell's cover.' Lady Somers leaned back and folded her hands in a way that made her look both regal and feminine. 'In fact, SIS think that Cauldwell may be running a false flag operation.'

Euan looked puzzled. 'I'm sorry, Lady Somers, can you explain?'

'A false flag operation is when a spy pretends to be working for someone else.'

'I know that; it's a traditional naval ruse. But I don't understand how it applies to Tyler.'

'It is likely that Tyler thinks he's stealing secrets for Cauldwell to pass on to Washington, certainly not to Moscow.'

'Why would Tyler think that we have naval and military secrets that would be useful to the Americans?'

'Because we actually have such secrets. Cauldwell knows this – and would surely have explained the situation to Tyler.' Lady Somers lifted a file off her desk and handed it to Euan. 'The Americans want to know how far we've got with our independent H-bomb. It could determine how they treat us an ally – and how much secret technology they share with us.'

Euan gingerly took the file, which bore two red stripes and the UK EYES ALPHA label. He was almost afraid to touch it. 'What do you want me to do with this?'

'I want you to make sure that Tyler sees it – but we'll have to promote him first.'

Euan opened the file and flicked through its contents. He then looked up, his face pale and drained. 'This is madness. We can't let this stuff go to Moscow.'

'It's been doctored. We want the Russians to think we already have an H-bomb. We haven't, but we're getting close. Orange Herald is nothing more than a juiced-up A-bomb pretending to be an H-bomb. It's a ruse. So far our real hydrogen devices have only gone fizz and pop instead of bang and wallop.'

Euan smiled wanly. 'And the thought of little Britain having a tinpot H-bomb is going to make Moscow tremble?'

'Not much, but it makes their strategic planning more difficult.'

Euan went back to the file. There were several pages of diagrams. 'There's something I don't understand.'

'What is it?' Lady Somers' voice had a sharp edge.

'I am sorry if I appear a trifle dense.'

'You're not at all dense – but something seems to be bothering you.'

'I don't understand why we are sending all this technical information to Moscow in addition to the fake test results. Much of this isn't doctored disinformation, but a virtual handbook on how to make a bomb.'

'Letting Moscow get this information is like advising grandmother how to suck eggs. The Russians are so far ahead of us on bomb-making and design it won't give them any advantage in the arms race at all.'

'But…'

'We need to pass on genuine intelligence – but intelligence that's harmless, as I just explained – to convince Moscow that the disinformation is also real.'

'Surely…'

Lady Somers' internal telephone rang and she picked it up. Her faced turned ashen. 'Yes, send him up. I will see him immediately.' She put the phone down and looked at Euan with irritation. 'You'll have to go now. Something urgent has come up. If you have any further questions, please come to see me.'

'Thank you.' Euan turned towards the door.

'And Euan…'

'Yes, your ladyship.'

'Be discreet, but without seeming that you have anything to be discreet about.'

»»»»»

Lady Somers' visitor was a tall, slim figure in his fifties with a pale sepulchral face. He looked like a cross between an undertaker and a Whitehall mandarin. He was dressed in black and had the demeanour of a BBC presenter announcing a royal death. The visitor stood in the doorway with his hat in hand. He looked at Lady Somers, then out of the window over Horse Guards Parade from where the clip-clop of Household Cavalry hooves punctuated his words.

'Everything has changed. Three of them are dead and one is on the run. We hadn't a choice; we had to act quickly.'

As soon as her visitor had left, Lady Somers opened a desk drawer to find the pills. They were in a jade box hidden in a box of tissues. She only took them when she desperately needed them, such as when the back pain she had endured since the operation became unbearable. But this time it was more than back pain. She swallowed the pills with a sip of water, closed her eyes and caressed the jade box as if that too was part of the cure. The hand-carved box had been a wedding present. It was a rare eighteenth-century piece decorated with a phoenix, a dragon and lotus scrollwork. It was priceless. In Chinese culture jade represented beauty, nobility and power. Which were also priceless.

Lady Somers opened her eyes and looked at the wedding photo on her desk. She had been so different then.

Batang Kali, Malaya: 1948

The first rule was never to argue in front of a servant. Guy refreshed his gin and tonic as Penelope told the *ayah* that she was free to go. He listened in admiration as Penelope addressed the servant in fluent Hokkien, the dialect spoken by Malayan Chinese. Penelope could also speak Mandarin and enough Cantonese to make herself understood in Hong Kong. Guy admired his wife and envied everything about her. It was a longing beyond love.

They both listened as the *ayah*'s footsteps padded across the terrace and faded into the night. Guy spoke first, 'You haven't changed your mind?'

'I need a drink.'

Guy listened to the clink of ice and splash of gin. She wanted to calm her nerves for the confrontation. She sipped her drink and then looked directly at Guy without blinking. 'No, I haven't changed my mind. I don't know why you've even asked.'

'Sorry.'

'I'm sorry, Guy. I shouldn't have snapped at you like that. You've been so good, so understanding. A lot of men would have used emotional blackmail – for the good of the child and all that.'

Guy smiled. 'Speaking of which, is Miranda asleep?'

'Out like a light.'

'She is the important thing.'

'Up to a point.'

'I'm not going to argue where that point is. You've already decided that.'

Penelope came close to her husband and put her hand on his. 'Guy, your life has been a lie. We both know that. Now is your chance to change things.'

'I think, Penelope, you might be right.'

'Good, I'm going to bed.'

As his wife turned towards the door, Guy slid open a drawer under the drinks table and took out a Webley revolver.

The shirt-maker's shop was just off Bond Street. With its secret cellar and discreet owner, it was a perfect place for clandestine meetings – and for hiding a spy on the run. But if you weren't a spy on the run, it was a good place to order quality bespoke shirts made from the finest Egyptian cotton. In fact, Vasili used Youseff's shop for buying his shirts as well as for secret rendez-vous. The Russian's sartorial tastes provided cover for his visits as well as his back.

The situation was deadly serious, but Vasili always found the funny side.

'Did you,' asked the Russian, 'really tell him that your name was Nick Seyton?'

'Yes.'

'And Tyler didn't get the joke?'

'No.'

'Ah.' Vasili was bravely trying to grasp colloquial English. 'But maybe it's because the English call him "*Old* Nick"?'

'I don't know and I don't fucking care.'

'You're not happy, Jeffers.' The Russian lowered his voice to almost a whisper, 'And you're going to be even less happy when I tell you what you must do now.'

Jeffers Cauldwell stared into the black shadows of the cellar and sipped his coffee. They were seated at a bare table beneath a bare light bulb with blackness all around them. It had all gone, what the British call 'tits up'. Another colloquialism for Vasili. But the coffee was good. Although Youseff was Syrian, he made his coffee in the Turkish manner. He prepared it in a small pot called an *ibrik* and added sugar as the coffee brewed. The result was black and rich and served in demitasse cups.

There was the distant rumble of an underground train, which shook the pot on the table and made the light sway above them.

Cauldwell lifted the pot. 'Should we ask Youseff to make some more coffee?'

'Not yet. They say that you can tell your fortune by reading the pattern of grinds left in your cup. What do you see in yours, Jeffers?'

'I don't believe in that nonsense.'

'Can I read them for you?' The Russian held Cauldwell's cup in his long fine fingers and stared into it. 'You're going to meet a tall, dark stranger...'

'Very funny.'

'I thought it was. And so, I think, would most British. We Russians have a similar sense of humour to theirs. Perhaps it's the long dark winter nights.'

'Tell me a joke.'

'I'm not going to. Americans never laugh at them.'

'Why are you criticising me for being an American? I've betrayed my country for the Soviet cause. What more do you want?'

'I want to know why you became a Communist.'

'It's in my KGB memoir.'

Vasili suppressed a smile. There were lots of things he wanted to know about Cauldwell's politics. 'Maybe your memoir needs updating. In any case, you'll now have plenty of time to do that.'

Vasili was not just Cauldwell's agent handler; he was also head of the *rezidentura*, the KGB station at the Soviet Embassy. He had the advantage of being a 'legal', someone on the diplomatic list, which meant he had legal immunity. The British couldn't arrest Vasili; they could only send him back to Russia. Cauldwell, as US Cultural Attaché, was a diplomat too. The British couldn't arrest him either, but they certainly could detain him and hand him over to the Americans.

'I want to stay active,' said Cauldwell. 'I'll operate in disguise and under new cover. You don't even need to find a safe house. I'll find my own. I want to continue to run my agent network. I know how to handle them: what buttons to push, what screws to turn.'

'We already have plans to turn your agents over to a new controller. He is excellent, "our man in Portland" – and he speaks English with an American accent. So your false flag ploy with Tyler will still be credible.'

Cauldwell knew who Vasili was talking about. He had just murdered one of his agents. Vasili's 'man in Portland' was indeed 'excellent' and his full name was Konon Trofimovich Molody. Molody's cover name, Gordon Lonsdale, belonged to a supposed Canadian businessman who specialised in slot machines. Cauldwell wasn't supposed to know any of this and discovering it hadn't been easy. Lonsdale's true identity was a trump card he had intended to play when the time was right. But things were fast deteriorating.

Vasili drained his demitasse cup with an appreciative Russian slurp. 'Youseff makes excellent coffee.' He pressed a button and a muffled buzz sounded faintly from above. 'Even if you are not having more, I shall.'

The inside of Cauldwell's head was spinning. The last thing he wanted now was more caffeine. He felt trapped. He wished that he hadn't got into Youseff's van the previous evening. He wished that he had picked up his false passport and headed for a Channel port.

'I know that you are an excellent agent handler…'

The trapdoor opened and Youseff came down the secret stairs with an *ibrik* of fresh coffee. Vasili turned to the Syrian, 'Thank you, my good friend, you are a mind reader.'

Youseff gave a smile that flashed with gold-capped teeth. He picked up the empty pot and departed like a genie. As soon as the trapdoor hissed shut, Vasili continued, 'Although you ran your agents with great skill, you misjudged your former lover.'

'I'm not sure that "love" had anything to do with it. It was your idea.'

'Mr Knowles was a very talented violinist, but would have been an even more talented politician. His decision to give up music for a career in politics was a good one. Who knows,' continued Vasili, 'he might one day have become Prime Minister.'

Cauldwell shrugged. He wasn't sure Vasili's long-term plan would have worked. If Knowles had risen to power, he wouldn't have given in to blackmail. He had principles.

Vasili sipped his coffee and looked closely at Cauldwell over the rim of his demitasse. 'Did you kill him?'

'Who?' Cauldwell was losing the thread.

'Knowles. Who did you think I was talking about?' Vasili smiled and gave Cauldwell an odd look. 'Have you killed anyone else?'

'No.' Cauldwell struggled to look unwitting and innocent. He wondered if Vasili could possibly know about the naval officer on the train.

'But you did kill Knowles?'

'Of course. I had to.'

'Why?'

'Because he found out about me.'

'But you didn't kill him soon enough?'

Cauldwell felt cold sweat begin to trickle down the hollow of his spine. 'What do you mean, "not soon enough"?'

Vasili put his cup down. 'You're busted. Knowles informed on you – and three of the agents you were running.'

'How do you know that?'

'I don't have to tell you.'

'What happened to the others?'

'Two of them are dead. And your American colleague has disappeared.' The Russian stared hard at Cauldwell. 'There are many questions you haven't answered.'

'Then ask them.'

'How did Knowles find out you were a spy?'

'Jennifer Handley told him. It all began last year. She fell in love with Knowles and thought that telling him about me would split us up.'

Vasili gave a mirthless smile. 'It worked.'

Cauldwell frowned. He had suspected from the beginning that the Orford Ness spy ring was heading for disaster. The personalities involved were too unstable. Jennifer's husband, Brian Handley, was head of AWRE, the Atomic Weapons Research Establishment, on the remote shingle spit near Aldeburgh in Suffolk. The couple were a Soviet spy team who had been passing on secrets for years. Cauldwell had callously used Jennifer as a honey-trap *femme fatale*. She would do anything for the Communist cause, but unfortunately she tended to get emotionally involved. Cauldwell had used her to seduce her CIA agent cousin, Kit Fournier, into becoming part of the gang. Fournier fell in love with Jennifer but meanwhile Jennifer fell hopelessly in love with Knowles. The spy ring had become a comic opera of revolving beds.

'By the way,' said Cauldwell, 'I warned you that she was emotionally unstable.'

'There are few spies who are not emotionally unstable.'

'But I'm not one of them.'

'You are, Jeffers, a cold fish. But you still haven't told me how Jennifer Handley got involved with Knowles?'

'She met him when he was playing in a concert at the Aldeburgh Festival – and invited him to an orgy.'

'Were you part of it?'

'Reluctantly. I thought it was a bad idea, but things got out of control.'

'Did you take photographs?'

Cauldwell paused. 'Yes.'

'What happened to the film?'

'I don't know. Someone stole my camera. As I explained, things got out of hand and were pretty raunchy – a lot of booze and drugs too.'

'How unlike you, Jeffers, not to be in total control.'

'I'm not perfect.'

'We know that, Jeffers, we know that. If you were so wonderful, Knowles wouldn't have decided that he loved his country more than he loved you.'

Cauldwell smiled. 'There's no accounting for tastes.'

Vasili shook his head and laughed. 'When I write reports for my bosses in Moscow they never believe me. They somehow imagine that our foreign spies will be drawn from the proletariat and the intelligentsia. When I tell them that our best spies have names like Guy Francis de Moncy Burgess and come from incredibly upper-class families and are frivolous and love other men, they think that I am crazy. And, frankly, my bosses do not like this sort of thing. Despite being Communists, their ideas are very traditional.'

'Maybe you should enlighten them.'

'I try to enlighten the First Chief Directorate on cosmopolitan Western mores. They remain sceptical, but regard England as an exception – a mad country full of unbuckled Lord Byrons running amok.'

Cauldwell looked closely at Vasili. 'And what do your bosses think of me?'

'They think what I tell them about you is true.'

'And what do you tell them?'

Vasili smiled. 'I tell them that you are a talented and valuable spy.'

Cauldwell folded his hands and stared at the table. 'Do you know what I'm thinking?'

'Only if you tell me.'

'The Americans are not going to believe Brit accusations about me being a Soviet spy. They're going to think the lefties in SIS are trying to frame me. No one in CIA or FBI would ever dream that I'm a Soviet spy. In fact, they have me down as a right-wing conservative. My ancestors were plantation owners who kept over a thousand slaves. Okay, my personal behaviour is debauched and unconventional. But old money Southern gentry have a reputation for that. My cover is perfect.'

'I don't think so – and my boss doesn't think so either. He is certain CIA will break you and that you will reveal everything.' Vasili paused. 'But if you think otherwise, why not go back to US Embassy and write a report? Tell them that British are trying to frame you and that you are completely innocent. I dare you.'

'I might very well do that.' The pupils of Cauldwell's eyes turned into pinpoints of black steel. 'But I promise you. If they do arrest me and send me back, they will never break me.'

'I hope that your boast is never put to test. That is why we have made arrangements to make sure it never happens.'

Cauldwell stared blankly into the darkness of the cellar. 'What are these arrangements?'

'You are to leave England for Moscow. It must be done undercover and in such a way that it appears you have committed suicide by drowning.'

Cauldwell remained silent, lost in his own thoughts. It wasn't what he wanted. But he knew there was no other way out. He had to obey orders.

The Suffolk marshes can be among the bleakest places in the world. And even more so when the weather is shit. It was August, but there had been no warm days. A series of Atlantic depressions had brought heavy bands of rain and low temperatures. Cauldwell spent hours looking out of the rain-streaked cottage windows at the sea. It was the waiting time. And he was oddly happy. In some ways he didn't want to see the ship in the offing. He had begun to see the beauty of the bleakness – and to hear it too. When the wind was howling and the sea pounding the shingle he could hear the music of Britten's *Sea Interludes* – played on his dead lover's violin. But the bleak loneliness and the awful weather were useful too. They were the ideal conditions for an extraction by sea.

Cauldwell found it difficult to believe that such isolated places existed within a hundred miles of London. He had taken out a long-term lease on the cottage as a safe house for the Handley gang. The nearest neighbours were miles away. There was no electricity, no phone and no access by road. You needed to pump fresh water by hand. The flint cottage, which was four hundred years old, had been built before the sea encroached. At the time it had been far away and the cottage had been surrounded by rich grazing pastures instead of impenetrable marshes. In coastal Suffolk the earth did not 'abideth for ever' and the churches that preached that untruth tumbled into the sea.

When the fires were lit the cottage was a cosy, homely place. Cauldwell liked eating his supper in front of the inglenook. There were plenty of pheasants in the copse where he gathered firewood. The birds were almost tame and easy to pick off with his Makarov 9mm automatic pistol. He didn't worry about the noise. Gunshots are a normal countryside sound.

Cauldwell had strung the antenna for the R-350 back and forth across the cottage attic. It was a messy job because the attic was a cobweb wilderness full of mouse and rat droppings as well as barn owl pellets. The barn owls were winning the battle of tooth and claw under the eaves. Cauldwell admired the good sense of long-dead builders. They had put round owl-sized holes in the gable ends of the roof space so the owls could get in and keep down the rodents. The owls were like cats with wings – and one of them had even come into Cauldwell's bedroom. It was there, perched on the end of his bed, when he woke in the morning. The owl stared at him for a long while with its head cocked to one side before it flew back up the chimney.

The R-350 was the Soviet Union's newest clandestine radio transmitter/receiver. It was compact and totally secure – provided you used the message puncher and burst encoder. First, you encoded your message using an OTP, a one-time pad. Then you typed the enciphered letters into the message puncher, which punched a pattern of holes on to strips of ordinary 35mm photographic film. (The use of 35mm film was genius. An agent anywhere in the world could buy that film without arousing suspicion.) You then fed the encoded film strip into the burst encoder which read the holes like a player piano does the perforations on a music roll. You press the transmit button – and the entire message is transmitted in a compressed burst of less than a second. It meant that it was nearly impossible for radio monitoring stations to pick up the transmission. And, even if they did, the OTP encoding would be unbreakable.

Cauldwell admired Soviet technology. It was tough, practical and easy to use. And there was always a back-up system if something went wrong. And something had gone wrong. He had used the R-350 dozens of times before, but on those occasions it was always sending and receiving messages from the First Chief Directorate. The First's communication centre was a hub of technology staffed by secret radio professionals. Sending messages to a ship in the North Sea was a different matter. All Soviet merchant ships had KGB-trained radio operators, but their training and the state of their radios varied. The best-equipped ships were IGAs, Intelligence Gathering Auxiliaries, pretending to be fishing trawlers. The IGAs bristled with antennae and radar and were crewed by radio professionals. Of course, no one really believed they were fishing boats. Consequently, the IGAs were kept under close surveillance and it was impossible to use one for a clandestine op like 'ex-filtrating' an agent from a beach.

There was, however, little suspicion attached to the Russian cargo vessels that sailed between Murmansk and East Anglia laden with timber. The timber was imported by a British company, one of whose directors was a former British cabinet minister. The Soviet merchant ships came down the North Sea calling variously at King's Lynn, Lowestoft, Ipswich and ports further south.

Vasili had told Cauldwell that one of the ships would pick him up on her return voyage to Russia. A fast inflatable would come ashore on a moonless night. At first, the plan was for Cauldwell to leave a set of clothes on the beach as if he had gone for a midnight swim. He complained that it was a pretty feeble attempt at a fake death. It was a cliché disappearing act that many had tried before.

Finally, Vasili agreed: 'Okay, don't drown yourself. Just get in boat.'

The first planned rendezvous had to be cancelled because of the appalling weather. Cauldwell had been told not to contact the Soviet Embassy either by telephone or radio because of an increased level of electronic surveillance. The emergency alternative was to ring a public phone kiosk in London from another kiosk at a certain time. It wasn't an alternative that Cauldwell wanted to use. It meant that he would have to break his marshland cover.

The nearest public phone was in a town designated as САУТУОЛД on the Soviet military map. Vasili had given Cauldwell the Russian map to ease communication with whichever ship was sent to pick him up. САУТУОЛД, better known as Southwold, was a coastal resort town with a lighthouse that would be a key reference point for Cauldwell's rescue ship. The map was also intended for use by Spetsnaz commando teams who, if war broke out, would slip ashore to wreak havoc at nearby US airbases. The map's very existence was an awful reminder that Britain was a Cold War pawn teetering on the brink of destruction.

Cauldwell set off across the marshes wearing a black oilskin that he had found among other foul-weather gear heaped on a row of hooks in the cottage. He wondered if he looked too much like a tramp for upmarket Southwold. Or, even worse, the holidaymakers might think he was a local fisherman and ask him questions. Cauldwell could put on a standard English accent, but he certainly couldn't do a Suffolk one. The situation was dire, but vaguely comic too. It appealed to the actor in him.

The rain was lashing in horizontal sheets as he set out across the Bailey bridge that connected Walberswick to Southwold. The River Blyth was ebbing fast with muddy whirlpools spinning towards the harbour entrance. Two women in raincoats and sensible brogues were pounding across the bridge in the opposite direction. Cauldwell had to flatten himself against the railing to avoid being trampled. One of the women acknowledged his giving way with a terse 'Thank you'.

Southwold harbour was called Blackshore. There were jetties with fishing boats and yachts, sheds galore and a pub. The town itself was on a hill surrounded by marshes and sea. It was utterly English. The path to the town from the river rose through water meadows with grazing Frisians. After the cows, the land undulated into a golf course. And then flattened out for tennis courts, cricket and rugby pitches. It had finally stopped raining. There were now breaks in the cloud and streaks of sunlight that made the Suffolk coast look like a Turner painting.

The nearest public phone was outside the Red Lion pub, which was emptying as the landlord bellowed, 'Drink up, please. It's time.' Cauldwell had to wait because a man was already in the kiosk – and the stack of tuppences on the shelf suggested he was going to be in there a long time. Cauldwell looked at his watch; he was going to miss his phone rendezvous. He tapped on the kiosk window, which was fogged with breath and cigarette smoke. The man frowned as Cauldwell opened the door and put on his best English accent. 'I apologise for disturbing you. But I have to make an urgent call to London. My son's been in a road accident and they need my permission to operate.'

The man's face softened. He spoke into the phone, 'Just a sec,

Peg.' Then to Cauldwell, 'Sorry to hear that. I'll get off now.' Then to Peg, 'Ring you later, love. Someone needs the phone.'

Cauldwell dialled the number. It rang ten times. No one answered. Cauldwell pretended to talk to the hospital in case the man outside was eavesdropping. When he had said enough – interlaced with pauses for the consultant surgeon to speak – he hung up the phone and left the kiosk.

The man looked at him, but was too reserved to ask any questions.

'Good news,' said Cauldwell. 'No brain damage, but a broken arm. Thomas won't be playing any cricket this season.'

'Who does he play for?'

'Vale of Eden, it's a local junior team.'

'In London?'

'No, in Surrey.' Cauldwell felt he was skating on thin ice. 'Better get back to tell my wife.'

'Cheers.' The man ducked back into the kiosk.

Cauldwell hurried away. Vasili must have decided the latest phone was insecure. MI5 couldn't tap every public phone in the country, but they did tap the ones that surveillance had picked out as being used by suspicious characters. Spies had to chop and change.

It was raining again as Cauldwell headed back to the cottage in the marshes. The trip had accomplished nothing. He still needed to establish contact; otherwise, there would be no escape. Part of Cauldwell wanted to disregard Vasili's instructions and get out of the country by his own means. He needed, however, hair dye and a moustache to match the image on his false French passport. He had had the forgery done at his own expense some time ago. The KGB did far better forged passports, but Vasili had yet to give him one. When the fires of paranoia were burning, as they often were, Cauldwell suspected that not having been given that passport was a sign of mistrust.

Cauldwell looked out to sea as he descended to the river. There were ferries from Harwich to Holland and Scandinavia. It wouldn't be difficult to dye his hair to become Dubois. And he could simply tell a curious customs official that he shaved off his moustache. Part of him wanted a new life. But he had not yet decided to follow a new direction; it was too soon.

»»»»»

It was a spooky night with gusts of wind flinging rain against the windowpanes. At times it sounded as if someone in the garden was throwing handfuls of pebbles to gain his attention. On one occasion Cauldwell actually opened the casement window and called a furtive 'Who's there?' into the darkness. It was, he thought, like being a character in a Victorian ghost story.

Cauldwell knew he wouldn't be able to sleep. He sat up late into the night wearing the clunky earphones of the R-350 and poised with a pencil and pad to copy. He was desperate for a message. A single candle cast yellow light and grey shadows against the crumbling plaster and oak beams. Cauldwell wondered how many people had been born and died in the bedroom shadows around him. He wondered what those disembodied spirits thought of him. Did they regard him as friend or enemy? Cauldwell wasn't sure what he was. And that was his biggest secret of all.

Finally, there was a faint sound. At first, Cauldwell imagined it was a dead child's finger tapping on the window, but then he realised the tapping was inside his earphones. It was a message in Morse. Cauldwell picked up a pencil and began to copy the letters. He had been expecting the random letters of an encoded message, but quickly realised that the Morse message spelled actual words and not code. The lack of security sent a chill down Cauldwell's spine as he copied the message: NO ONE TIME PAD AVAILABLE EXTRACTION 0115300856 AT 49107308 ACKNOWLEDGE.

It was all Cauldwell needed to know: the time and the place. He quickly checked the grid coordinates on the Soviet map to make sure he had copied correctly. He then replied that the message was received and understood – and turned off the transmitter. There would be no more sending or receiving before the extraction. It was too dangerous.

Cauldwell wasn't unduly worried. Sometimes encryption and

security had to be sacrificed. Under the circumstances, it wasn't odd that the message had been sent in the clear and in English. It was perfectly logical that the replacement ship wouldn't have had the appropriate set of one-time pads. And any radio operator on a Soviet merchant ship sailing in British waters would need to have good English.

»»»»»

The rain had softened to a penetrating drizzle. It wasn't easy to find a way across the marshes to the shingle beach even in daylight. But in the utter midnight blackness it was almost impossible if you had never done it before. Cauldwell looked at the map with a hooded red torch. As the gull flies, the sea was only 400 yards away, but on foot it was nearly a mile of tortuous paths and rickety footbridges. The silhouette of a ruined windmill towered above the reeds like a dark sentinel. Cauldwell followed the footpath towards the mill, but knew from the map he had to turn off that path when he got to a creek. He pushed his way through a tangle of prickly vines. The footing was slippery and glutinous. He hadn't gone far before he slipped from the path into a dank, water-filled ditch and nearly lost a boot. His trousers were torn and he was soaked through. As he regained his balance, there was the cry from an owl that sounded like a cat's miaow. The owl was mocking him. He didn't belong there.

Cauldwell realised he had reached the creek when he heard something plop into the water. It sounded like a clumsy kid doing a belly flop. It was too big to be a rat and too graceless to be an otter. It must have been a coypu. Cauldwell froze and listened to the night. The only sounds were the sough of the sea on the other side of the shingle bank and the piping of oystercatchers. He wondered why the birds were so loud so late at night. But then he remembered they were like that every night. The warning calls were natural. The marsh was a jungle of predators hunting for eggs and chicks.

The footpath rose on to the creek bank. The creek itself was nothing more than a wide ditch that a good long-jumper could have leapt across. But during the early Middle Ages the ditch had been the Dunwich River, where seagoing ships had docked. Cauldwell walked along a narrow slippery bank where carters and sailors and customs officers had once jostled. The medieval river had seen a brisk trade in Suffolk grain and wool exchanged for fine wine, Flemish cloth and Russian fur. The pious rich merchants of Dunwich built sixteen grand churches to thank God for their prosperity. But God did nothing to stop the coastal erosion or to stop His churches from tumbling one by one into the sea. The very last stone of the very last church fell into the sea as the guns fell silent on the Western Front. By then, Dunwich's only exports to Flanders were young men who came back with mangled limbs and blank eyes. Cauldwell felt there was a curse hanging in the damp air.

When Cauldwell got near the shingle bank that kept the sea from the marshes, he felt a sense of exhilaration and release. The reed beds had given way to mudflats and the oystercatchers were piping even louder. There was a lot of noise from a sluice that was emptying water from the rain-sodden marshes. Cauldwell paused and listened to the night noises. There was something sinister in the air. He wondered if he should turn back. At the moment he needed Moscow, but wasn't sure that Moscow needed him. Would he ever get to Moscow? Disposing of his body at sea would be an easy option. The sense of exhilaration had gone.

The only barrier between Cauldwell and the shingle bank was a patch of viscous mud. He decided to risk it. He put a boot forward and sank in, but as he pulled back he lost his footing and found himself flat on his back – covered from toe to head in thick Suffolk mud. When he got up again he found his hand clutching a bunch of samphire. The samphire was the only thing about him that wasn't covered in mud. He bit off a piece. It was lovely, salty and clean – his last taste of Suffolk.

Cauldwell looked around. He now saw there was a firm path to the sea that he had missed. He followed the path and was soon on top of the shingle bank looking out to sea. Cauldwell sat on the bank and laughed. It was kind of funny. When the Russians saw him, they would think they had rescued the Creature from the Black Lagoon. It was also funny because one of Cauld-well's jobs as US Cultural Attaché had been trying to sell the film of the same name to British distributors. A large part of his job had been promoting American 'cultural products' – and *The Creature from the Black Lagoon* was a classic. It had been one of the first 3D films and you needed cardboard 3D glasses with one blue lens and one red lens to get the full effect. Meanwhile, the Soviet Cultural Attaché had been flogging Prokofiev and the Bolshoi.

Cauldwell checked his torch to see if it was still working after being soaked. It was. He needed it to signal to the fast inflat-able that would be coming in to get him. He looked out to sea again – nothing. He checked his watch. He was twenty minutes early. Still plenty of time. Cauldwell now stared south to try and spot the running lights of a merchant ship. There was a flicker of white on the horizon, but he also needed to see the red portside light that indicated it was a ship heading north. He kept his eyes fixed on the light. It finally disappeared; it was a ship heading south.

'Fuck. Where are they?'

Cauldwell suddenly felt very cold. He was sodden from the waist down. He tried running in place to warm himself up, all the time staring at the southern sea horizon. A white light finally appeared – and then a red one. This had to be the ship.

He scrambled down the bank on to the beach. There was only a slight swell. It was as if a month of rain had made the sea too heavy and wet to leap into breakers. Cauldwell took off his rucksack and stretched his arms. The backpack was heavy with the R-350 and his other spy gear. He tapped the deep pockets of his oilskin jacket to make sure he still had his torch and his Makarov 9mm. He took the pistol out of his pocket to check the safety was engaged. He didn't want an accidental discharge to put a hole in a Russian or the inflatable when he hopped on board. You had to remember that 'up' was the safe position and 'down' the fire position – just the opposite of the Walther PPK. Cauldwell looked at the heavy pistol in his hand. He decided it might be a better idea to completely immobilise the Makarov by removing the magazine and the round in the chamber. He didn't want an accident at this point.

Just as Cauldwell was about to put his finger on the pistol's magazine catch, the night exploded into brightness. Not the brightness of a gun discharging, but the brightness of two artificial suns rising from opposite ends of the beach. Cauldwell was centre stage as he had never been before. He was Hamlet with a skull in his hand – his own skull. The blinding beams came from mounted 60-inch searchlights of 800 million candlepower each. Cauldwell waved his gun with one arm and covered his eyes with his other. For a few seconds the only sound on the beach was that of the portable generators powering the giant torches.

'Drop your gun, Jeffers.'

Cauldwell recognised the voice and turned squinting towards the dark shadows from where it had come. As he did so, there was a metallic click.

'Drop it fucking now or I'm going to shoot you in the balls.'

'Is that you, Catesby?'

'It is me. Drop the pistol now. I hate having to shoot people in the balls – the screaming is awful.'

Cauldwell smiled and tossed his pistol. It dropped into the shingle with a hissing thud.

'Good boy.'

Cauldwell stared into the distance, but was too blinded by the lights to make out the other person. 'I can't see you, Catesby.'

'That's good. I've aged a lot.'

'It must be the booze.'

'Or maybe my job.'

Catesby had always suspected that the American had something to hide ever since they had served together in post-war Germany. At the time, Catesby's suspicions had been dismissed and laughed at – and now, finally, he was vindicated. But Catesby felt no sense of triumph. Cauldwell was a mess.

'Bloody hell, Jeffers, what have you been doing to yourself?'

Cauldwell answered with a bleak smile, too exhausted for further banter. He could hear the sound of heavy footsteps running across the shingle and voices speaking in accents from both sides of the Atlantic.

'Don't worry, Jeffers. No one's going to kill you – at least, *we're* not. But we've got to go through legal niceties for your turnover and extradition.'

Two groups of men, six in each, approached like pincers from opposite sides of the beach. The lights behind the men turned them into flat black silhouettes. They looked like disembodied shadow puppets deprived of any human quality. The two largest, and they were huge, were in American military police uniforms. They clanked with handcuffs, batons and Colt .45 automatics as they jogged towards their prey. The first American to reach Cauldwell grabbed his arm and pulled it behind him for handcuffing.

'Not yet, bud,' shouted Catesby.

'My name ain't Bud; it's Hank.'

'Sorry, Hank. You've got to wait a few seconds.'

Everything that happened next was perfectly legal, but totally secret. A UK judge had already approved Washington's request for extradition. Two warranted plainclothes Scotland Yard officers informed Cauldwell of his rights and that he was under arrest. A consul from the US Embassy signed a document accepting custody of Cauldwell under the provisions of the US–UK extradition treaty. Hank was then allowed to handcuff Cauldwell and march him off.

Catesby continued to lurk in the shadows because he wasn't supposed to be there. He was SIS, Secret Intelligence Service. And, as he was constantly reminded by his colleagues in Five, SIS are forbidden to carry out operations within the UK. The argument about who should be handling Cauldwell had rumbled on since the photo session above St James's Park. But SIS had finally won because the Americans wanted Catesby there for 'psychological' reasons. They didn't want violence; they wanted Cauldwell alive. An American 'psych' suggested that Cauldwell was less likely to 'react with violence' if he was confronted by a voice that he knew and respected. And Catesby's voice was the closest they could find.

When he first met Cauldwell, Catesby's diplomatic cover as Cultural Attaché for Film and Broadcasting had been the flimsiest in Bonn and Berlin. Everyone knew that Catesby was a spy. But despite the rough working-class edge Catesby put on, he was a convincing CultAt. He spoke fluent German and was an expert on East German drama. Cauldwell first realised that Catesby was a serious character when he heard him having a conversation with Bertolt Brecht about Schlegel's translation of *Hamlet* – and reciting *sein oder nicht sein* to Brecht's amusement. Cauldwell decided that Catesby might be useful to know – and wondered if he were a potential traitor.

Meanwhile, Catesby decided to open a file on Cauldwell. The American's persona as a social and cultural snob with conservative political views seemed as fake as Mussolini's medals. At first, Catesby thought that Cauldwell's right-wing flag waving was a ruse to cover up his sexual ambiguity. But then he realised that was too simple. In any case, Catesby's reports to London ringed Cauldwell as a potential double. Meanwhile, Cauldwell was reporting the same about Catesby. But not to Washington.

Catesby watched as the Americans led Cauldwell up the beach towards Walberswick. Everything was in darkness again. The giant searchlights had been extinguished and the generators had fallen silent. The only sounds were the fading of squashy footsteps on shingle – and then only the sough of the waves and the piping of the oystercatchers from the marsh. Catesby tensed as he heard something behind him. He instinctively knew it was human and reached for his revolver. He waited and crouched. There was the sound of a footstep on shingle.

'How did it go?'

Catesby recognised the voice and let the gun fall back into a Mackintosh pocket that was well stained with gun oil. 'You shouldn't creep up on me, Henry, especially when I'm tooled up.'

'You shouldn't be so nervous. You knew I was here.'

Catesby nodded to a ship that was passing close off shore. 'And so do the Russians.'

'Did you think I was one of them?'

Catesby smiled. He had, actually, suspected that for some time.

'Don't worry,' said Bone. 'They'll not be coming ashore now.'

As if on cue, one of the giant searchlights reignited and cast a beam against the black hull of the ship. A few seconds later, the ship changed course and veered out to sea.

Catesby turned and looked at the dark shadow of his boss. Henry Bone was everything that he was not: tall, refined, aristocratic and a virtuoso of duplicity. Catesby knew how to be duplicitous too, but his duplicities were simple harmonies compared to Bone's highly structured compositions. Hearing Henry Bone tell lies was like listening to eighteenth-century organ music played by a priest with long fine fingers in the Cathedral of Notre Dame.

Catesby smiled and put on his London voice. 'The Hank geezer promised me I could have a slappy face bash.'

'Speak normal English.'

'I could ask you to do the same, but let's not argue. The Yanks said that I can interrogate Cauldwell provided there's an American present.'

'I already knew that. It was part of the deal we brokered.'

Catesby frowned and kept quiet. He wasn't going to rise to the bait of Henry's all-knowing one-upmanship.

'In any case,' said Bone, 'you still haven't told me what happened.'

'Why weren't you here with me?'

'It's never a good idea to show my face.'

'I agree. To be honest, nothing much happened. It went like clockwork. The American psych was right about my friendly voice being a calming influence. As soon as I told Cauldwell that I was going to shoot him in the balls he dropped his gun.'

'Did he look upset?'

'Not much. In a way, almost relieved to see us.'

'That's interesting.'

'Why?'

'Because of what it says about Cauldwell's relationship with the Russians.'

'Not good, eh?'

Bone shrugged. 'I honestly don't know.'

THE WHITEHALL MANDARIN   47

'Cauldwell isn't like the others. It's almost as if he was working separately, to a different agenda.'

'See what you can find out when you interrogate him. Do you want a lift back to London?'

'No, I'm staying at my mum's in Lowestoft.'

'You love this bleak place, don't you?'

Catesby looked out to sea. 'Can you hear it?'

'Hear what?'

'You're not from here. That's why you can't hear them. They're only whispering tonight.'

'Who?'

'The ghosts, a very old couple. They're trapped down there where the sea meets the shingle and you can hear their voices. They're talking gently tonight, but when the autumn gales come they'll be shouting at each other.'

'What are they saying?'

'I'm not going to tell you, Henry. You're not from around here. What they are saying is family secrets.'

'I'd better leave you.'

Catesby listened until Bone's footsteps had disappeared. Then waited a minute longer listening to nothingness. He felt he had been waiting since that apocalyptic day when the North Sea had finally risen to cut off the last of the land bridge that connected the British peninsula to the rest of Europe. It was too late. That last hunter gatherer, bearing aloft his barbed antler spear and running hard, would never escape the rising tide. Britain was an island.

»»»»»

One of the Americans – Hank-not-Bud – gave Catesby a lift to Lowestoft. Hank wasn't a military policeman. The uniform was a fake. He was a high-ranking intelligence officer. Hank looked surprised when he arrived at Catesby's childhood home. It was a humble terrace house.

'Is this it?' said Hank.

'Yes, we're here, *chez les Catesbys.*'

'Is this where you were raised?'

'Partly. We used to live down by the docks. But we've come up in the world. This house has an indoor toilet and hot water taps. You look surprised.'

'I expected something grand. You sound so upper-crust.'

'That's because you've got American ears. Most Brits can spot my accent as fake.'

'Why then do you talk that way?'

'Are you really interested?'

'Yeah, Limey-Land is a strange place.'

Catesby looked at the American. 'Are you going to put this in my file?'

Hank laughed. 'What file?'

'Good, take notes if you like. I speak like this because I want to fit in. I began to lose my Lowestoft accent at Cambridge. A lot more went when I became an Army officer – and as I rose from grade to grade in SIS, more and more of my origins were chipped away. I'm a little ashamed of it. When I meet my school pals at the pub, I try to speak pure Lowes'toff as if I've never been away. But that voice is more fake than my Cambridge voice – and my mates know it too. When you lose your roots you can't grow them again. Got it? Latest update for the Catesby file.'

'See you in a couple of days,' said Hank. 'By the way, it looks like we'll be doing the Cauldwell interrogation together.'

'I hope so – and thanks for the lift.' Catesby stared nervously at the neighbours' windows. He didn't want any gossip about why he had been dropped off by a big American Ford so late at night.

'See you, buddy.'

Catesby smiled, 'My name ain't Buddy.'

Hank saluted as he pulled away.

Catesby fished the house key out of the letter flap by reeling in an attached string. Every house in the terrace either used letter flap or plant pot. Why not, he thought, just leave the doors unlocked?

Catesby slowly closed the door behind him and took off his shoes. He tiptoed up the stairs avoiding the ones that creaked. He didn't want to wake up his mother, but she slept so lightly she was probably awake in any case. When he crept into his bedroom he found a pair of freshly laundered and pressed pyjamas lying on the burgundy candlewick bedspread. Catesby felt a lump in his throat. Beside his pyjamas was his Ipswich Town scarf. It had gone missing and his mother had found it. The scarf had been a present for his tenth birthday. Even spies had childhoods.

As he stripped and put on the pyjamas his eyes were drawn to a darkened bedroom window on the terrace opposite. There were no back gardens, just small paved backyards with coal bunkers and washing lines. The back passage between the houses was paved with clinker from the coal fires. Catesby stared at the window opposite. He wondered if the girl who had slept in that back bedroom ever came home. Had she split up with her husband?

Catesby and the girl had been in sixth form together, but not in the same classes. She had studied sciences because she wanted to do medicine. They were the only kids from that neighbourhood who made it to the grammar. They weren't close, but sometimes the girl forgot to draw the curtain when she undressed. Was it on purpose?

Although they never spoke, they had always made furtive eye contact whenever they passed in the school corridors. Never a smile, never a word – just a deep, knowing look. In the end she didn't go to medical school, she got pregnant and married a painter and decorator. As she swelled with pregnancy, she never forgot to draw the curtains again. Just before Catesby went off to war, he passed her in Lowestoft High Street. He was so proud of his officer's pips and his parachutist badge.

She was pushing a pram and spoke first, 'Hello, William.'

'How are you?'

She smiled bleakly.

Catesby felt awkward. He didn't know how to say it. 'I was sorry to hear about what happened. Please give my condolences to your aunt. It must be so awful for her.'

The Luftwaffe used Lowestoft as a dumping ground for unused bombs. As England's most easterly point, it was the last bit of land before the bleak North Sea. A single stray bomb had landed at the back of her Aunt Millie's house. Millie was unharmed, but her six-month-old twins were killed. A month later her husband, a trawlerman turned Royal Naval Patrol Service sailor, was lost at sea. It wasn't an unusual Lowestoft story – almost too common to mention. And probably not the best way to start a conversation with someone you longed for.

She brushed a lock of hair from her eyes and stared out over a pile of rubble where a recent German bomb had opened up an unaccustomed view of the sea. 'Aunt Millie's fine. She's resilient.' She looked at Catesby with a mirthless smile. '*Resilient*, that's a posh word for one of us, isn't it, William? But I bet you learned a lot of posh words at Cambridge.' Her eyes glistened with unshed tears.

Catesby gently touched her hand, which was gripping the push bar of the pram.

'You know something, William? I fancied you like mad.'

Before Catesby could say anything, she was on her way up the High Street with her back to him.

»»»»»

Catesby found it difficult to sleep because his bedroom was so cold. In fact, the whole house was always cold no matter how much coal they burned. Being cold was part of living in Lowestoft. Warmth was a luxury like a tot of grog.

The other thing that kept him awake was the Cauldwell business. There were too many missing pieces. It all began with the arrest of British atomic scientist Alan Nunn May in Canada in 1946 for passing secrets – and enriched uranium – on to the Soviets. But after Nunn May's arrest, atomic secrets were still flowing to Moscow. And then four years later Klaus Fuchs was busted, but not the stream of secrets to Russia. One of the things Catesby kept preaching to his American colleagues was that the Russians are chess players. They know how to make pawn sacrifices to protect more valuable pieces. Were the Soviet defectors and doubles who betrayed spies like Fuchs genuine? Or were they tools of a grandmaster in Moscow who was playing a game of sacrifice to protect his rooks and queen? A lot of pieces had been exchanged in the past year.

Busting the Handley gang and capturing Cauldwell was a big success, but it didn't seem complete. Catesby was certain that Handley, Britain's leading atomic scientist, had sacrificed Nunn May and Fuchs to protect himself. Unfortunately, no one had been able to interrogate Handley. He hung himself in the garden shed with a noose made from his wife's silk underwear. Yes, thought Catesby as he turned, sleepless; things had certainly started to get silly. Or tragic, depending on your point of view. Catesby tossed and turned in a cold sweat. He still wasn't sure who had betrayed Cauldwell. Two anonymous typed letters had been posted denouncing him as a spy and giving details, including grid coordinates, of his planned ex-filtration from 'a beach'. One had been sent directly to Dick White, Head of SIS. The other anonymous note had been sent to NID, the Naval Intelligence Division of the Admiralty. The NID note raised even more questions than the one sent to SIS. It had been addressed to Room 39. And insiders, and only insiders, know the unit as 'Room 39'.

The anonymous note to NID had arrived only twenty-four hours before Cauldwell's failed escape and confirmed Room 39's long-held suspicions that there was 'something fishy' about the Soviet merchant ships that plied the timber trade with East Anglia. There was no mention of Cauldwell by name, but ships and ports were named – and radio frequencies to monitor were suggested. It was easy for NID, with its impressive array of electronic surveillance devices, to pick up the un-coded Morse transmission from the vessel sent for Cauldwell and to inform the Security Services of the exact time and place of the extraction rendezvous.

»»»»»

When Catesby came into the kitchen the next morning the kettle was steaming and the toast was under the gas grill. His mother looked up. She was old and tired – and didn't seem particularly pleased to have her son home for a few days. '*Wil je een ei?*' Did he want an egg? When it was just the two of them, she always spoke Nederlands.

The egg question was difficult. There was no right answer. A 'nee' meant a frown of ingratitude; a 'ja' meant a sigh for the extra bother. Catesby decided to go for an *ei* soft-boiled.

His mother began to boil the water. 'There's a letter for you.'

A large brown envelope was propped against the Robertson's marmalade. The address was typed. Something about the letter gave him a chill.

Catesby's mother poured boiling water into the teapot and also into a saucepan for the egg. 'Aren't you going to open it?'

'I know what it is.' Catesby was lying; he didn't know. 'I'll deal with it later.' He changed the subject. 'How's Father Sinclair?' *Mooder* Catesby was a devout Catholic, but she didn't have any problem with her son being an atheist. Catesby found that mildly amusing. It was as if the fate of his immortal soul didn't matter to her any more than whether or not he had an egg.

'He has gout.'

'Who?' Catesby was staring at the letter. It had a North London postmark.

'Father Sinclair; you just asked about him.'

'Sorry, I was elsewhere.'

'Hmm.'

They finished breakfast in the usual silence. Catesby had long since ceased to wonder what had made his mother the joyless widow. Was it the dark secrets of her waterfront youth in an Antwerp bar? Was it the influenza death of his twin siblings? The death of his father in an accident at sea? The twins had died before Catesby was born and he had no recollection of his father. His family had more secrets than SIS. His mother's past as a barmaid on the Antwerp docks was never mentioned. Nor was the series of European uncles and aunts who appeared and disappeared without explanation.

As soon as Catesby opened the envelope in the privacy of his bedroom, he was relieved that he hadn't done so in front of his mother. There was no letter, just a photograph – or part of a photograph. At first glance, it looked like a fancy-dress party about to turn into an orgy. A number of men and women – mostly men – were partially clothed in the dress of ancient Greece. It was a photo parody, a *tableau vivant*, of a painting by Poussin, *The Triumph of Pan*. Catesby recognised the Poussin connection – as would most officers in SIS who knew Sir Anthony Blunt, the spy turned art historian. The photo was a delicious joke, but a dangerous joke. He immediately recognised three of the semi-clad 'Greeks': one was Henry Knowles, who was a leering Priapus; another was Jennifer Handley; and the third, and the only one still among the living, was Jeffers Cauldwell. Mysteriously, about a quarter of the photograph had been roughly ripped away. Catesby knew that the missing part would turn out to be the most interesting. The sender's message was both provocation and tease: 'Who else was there and why won't I let you know?'

Catesby was taking the red single-decker Eastern Counties bus to the airbase at Lakenheath because he still didn't have a car. And it was a long ride too. The scheduled stops were Beccles, Bungay, Harleston, Diss, Thetford and Mildenhall, but the bus would stop in-between for anyone who waved it down. The woman who got on between Thetford and Mildenhall had appeared out of nowhere. There were no houses, no villages: only acres and acres of damp un-harvested wheat bounded by thick dark woods. The woman, who looked to be in her seventies, shook the rain from her umbrella as she spoke to the driver. 'Never seen such weather,' she said, 'it just go on and on, don't it?'

'Not hooly good, that's for sure,' said the driver.

The bus followed the Norfolk–Suffolk border, weaving back and forth across the River Waveney, which separated the two counties. It was a land Catesby loved. He wondered if the woman, the driver and the other passengers on the bus had any idea how lucky they were still to be alive. It was all top secret, but the UK government had demanded a full revelation from the Americans. The previous year, a USAF B-47 had been practising 'touch and go' landings at Lakenheath, but instead of bounding into a 'go' the plane cartwheeled into a bunker full of nuclear bombs. The plane's crew had been killed, but they had nearly taken a big part of East Anglia with them to Valhalla. The US general in charge admitted that it was 'a miracle that one didn't go off'. The incident had caused an enormous row in Whitehall, with some ministers demanding an immediate withdrawal of all US nuclear weapons from the UK.

As the bus approached the airbase, Catesby scoured the sky. He wondered if the US jet jocks were still practising 'touch and go' landings or if they had learnt their lesson. The bus dropped Catesby outside the main gate of the airbase. He waved a 'thank you' to the driver as the bus pulled away in a cloud of diesel fumes.

There was a long line of chain-link fence topped with

concertina barbed wire as far as the eye could see. Although the sign said RAF Lakenheath and a Union Flag waved beside the Stars and Stripes, Catesby knew there would be no British uniforms or personnel inside the gates. He would be all alone. The guard booth was in the middle of the entrance road. A long sign across the roof announced: 3909th Air Police Squadron. Catesby reached for his ID and stepped through the gate.

There were two Americans on duty. One of them straightened his peaked cap and left the entrance booth. He looked like a character from a western who wondered what someone like Catesby was doing in Dodge City. High-ranking British intelligence officers didn't often turn up on an Eastern Counties bus. The American sauntered towards Catesby and then stopped about five paces away. He was wearing an armband that said Air Police and white gloves. He stared flinty-eyed for a few seconds with his right hand resting on his .45 holster. Everything about him was shiny and crisp.

Finally he spoke: 'Good morning, sir. Would you come this way, please?'

It took two telephone calls to confirm Catesby's identity. Five minutes later another crisp member of the Air Police arrived to escort Catesby to Hank's office.

'Sorry you were kept waiting,' said Hank. 'They were expecting someone in an Aston Martin or a Bentley.'

'I prefer to keep a low profile,' said Catesby.

The American laughed and slapped his thigh. 'But a bus!'

'It was too far to cycle. In any case, when do we start with Cauldwell?'

'It's our turn in ten minutes.'

'Whose turn is it now?'

'The medics. They want to make certain he hasn't got cyanide capsules hidden in his molars or up his anus – and that he's healthy enough for the flight back to the States.'

'That's bullshit about the flight. They want to see how much you can do to him without killing him.'

Hank frowned. 'We don't use those methods because they don't work.'

'Maybe you don't do them long enough and hard enough.'

The American shook his head. 'We use psychology.'

'Let's go psycho then.'

»»»»

The interrogation took place in an underground bunker that was a back-up operations centre. It was full of maps, communications equipment and telephones. There were also narrow steel beds, water and food supplies. The bunker was thought to be completely secure against a strike by any known Soviet nuclear weapon.

Cauldwell was seated at a table beneath a neon strip light. He was dressed in khaki fatigues that were army rather than air force issue. He was wearing white sneakers without laces. His hands were cuffed in front of him. There were Military Police wearing helmets and boots with white laces standing on either side of him. They looked a lot fiercer than the Air Police on the gate. Hank nodded at the MPs and they left the bunker.

Catesby looked around at the thick concrete walls – and then at Cauldwell. 'You can't say they don't look after you. If your Russian pals attack, you'll be one of the safest people in Britain.'

Hank was fiddling with a reel-to-reel tape recorder.

Cauldwell gave a crooked smile. 'Who betrayed me?'

Catesby ignored him and looked at Hank. 'Is that thing recording yet?'

'It is now. This interrogation of Jeffers Cauldwell took place on...'

While Hank recited the preliminaries Catesby smiled at Cauldwell. As soon as Hank finished, Catesby said, 'Can you repeat the question, Jeffers? It wasn't recorded.'

'Fuck you.'

'Do you mean fuck me, fuck Hank or fuck both of us?'

'I mean, "fuck you, Catesby", because you're a duplicitous liar. They should be interrogating you, not me.'

Catesby looked at Hank. 'If he's not going to cooperate, there's no point in this interrogation.'

Hank shrugged.

Catesby turned to Cauldwell, 'Okay, Jeffers, can we just have a conversation? I'm here because the British government wants the right to interrogate you before you go back to the States. Actually, we expect to find out fuck-all. I haven't got the time to do the things that might persuade you to say more. In fact, this interrogation has sod-all to do with you and everything to do with UK–US relations. We were nice enough to arrest you and hand you over. So our chat is really a face-saving gesture, a sop to my government – and as an experienced diplomat you know all about such gestures.'

Hank turned off the tape recorder. 'Listen, Mr Catesby, I suggest we erase that bit and begin again. If a transcript of this gets back to London your ass is gonna be in a sling.'

'No, leave it. It's a waste of my time being here and I want them to know it.'

'It's up to you, buddy.'

'Good.' Catesby looked back at Cauldwell. 'You know that Knowles is dead.'

Cauldwell's face remained impassive.

'They found his body on Shingle Street. I thought you should know. It was a difficult one for us and MI5. We got into a scrape with the Suffolk constabulary. Why do you think?'

Cauldwell shook his head. Hank spoke into the tape-recorder microphone: 'Subject shook his head indicating negation.'

Catesby continued, 'Don't play the *faux naif*, Jeffers. The Ipswich plods wanted to interview you, and quite rightly too, as a murder suspect. But we shut them up with a national security D Notice. And they hated it. It's a card we play too often.'

Cauldwell closed his eyes. When he spoke his tone was mild. 'I feel sorry for his parents. It must have been an overwhelming sadness for them.'

'I wish that I could pass on your condolences.'

'Sarcasm doesn't suit you, Catesby. It's your most unattractive trait.'

'If it's any consolation, Jeffers, there isn't enough evidence to convict you of Knowles's murder.'

Cauldwell was stony-faced. He wasn't playing.

'We think,' Catesby continued, 'that Knowles got mixed up with Brian and Jennifer Handley – and that he got to know too much. How did he meet them?'

Cauldwell opened his eyes and sighed. 'The only reason I'm talking to you is because I'm fucking bored.'

'That's fine.'

'It was the Aldeburgh Festival. Jennifer knew everyone from Ben and Peter to Shostakovich. I encouraged Knowles to circulate and accept her invitations.' Cauldwell stopped. 'I don't know what happened afterwards. I didn't own him.'

Catesby was watching Cauldwell closely without seeming to do so. For the first time, he seemed shifty and uncertain. 'Did Knowles ever have sexual relationships with women?'

'Yes, but only in certain circumstances.'

'In what circumstances?'

'When they offered something different or something more.'

'Let's start with "something more". In what way?'

'If the women were important in themselves or offered access to power. Knowles wanted to be Prime Minister – and that's not a secret. It's why he decided to give up his concert career.'

'Can you give me a list of those women?'

Cauldwell smiled and named the most famous. It was a bombshell.

'I'm not surprised.' Catesby lied. He was surprised, but suspected that Cauldwell was making it up to create mischief in high places.

'Should we erase that?' said Hank.

Catesby nodded agreement and waited until the tape was recording again. 'What about the other category of women who succeeded in tempting Henry Knowles?'

'What other category?' said Cauldwell.

'The ones who you said "offered something different". What do you mean by "different"?'

'Usually group sex with another man or men – especially if the men were heterosexual.'

'And that's what Jennifer Handley arranged?'

'Yes, but there was a lot more. Jennifer was a very cunning

minx with her own skills. She was gamine, androgynous and liked to play interesting games with blindfolds and bondage gear.'

'So she was all things to all men.'

'And women.'

'What did you think of her, personally?'

'I never met her.'

'That's a lie.' Catesby opened his briefcase and took out the torn photograph that had arrived in the post.

Cauldwell looked at it, smiled and then laid the photo face down on the table.

'So maybe,' said Catesby, 'you've just got a poor memory.'

Cauldwell leaned forward. 'Or maybe I just didn't know who she was. There was a lot of drink and a lot of drugs at that party.'

'Can you tell me what happened?'

Cauldwell smiled. 'I can't remember.'

'Or don't want to remember; I know the feeling. In any case, when we were in Germany I remember that you were valued as an expert on the visual arts. Part of your job was cataloguing German art treasures so they didn't get looted – or sold by Nazi owners to finance a forged passport and a ticket to Paraguay. Does your mission to Friedrichshof ring a bell?'

'Yes, but frankly, Catesby, I can't see what Friedrichshof has to do with Jennifer Handley or me allegedly being a Soviet spy.'

Catesby smiled and looked briefly at the photo before turning it over again. 'What do you know about Poussin?'

'A seventeenth-century French painter who worked in the classical style.'

'What did the professor tell you about Poussin?'

'You're crazy, Catesby. What fucking professor? You're talking nonsense.'

'Professor Blunt. You were on his team at Friedrichshof. Or I should say, Sir Anthony Blunt, as he was recently knighted. In any case, Blunt is the world's greatest authority on Nicolas Poussin.'

Cauldwell yawned. 'Anthony frequently talked about Poussin, but not obsessively. We were too busy preventing my American colleagues from looting the Hesse family vault.'

'Were you and Blunt good friends?'

'We got along fine. Why don't you ask Anthony?'

Catesby looked closely at Cauldwell. 'I already have.'

'And what,' said Cauldwell, 'did Anthony have to say?'

'You seem to have forgotten, Jeffers, that I'm interrogating you. In any case, it was a private conversation. Just the two of us and a tape recorder.'

'Did he tell you about Michael?'

Catesby pretended not to be interested, but made a deep mental note. He knew that Cauldwell was referring to Michael Straight, an extremely rich and well-connected American who had become a Communist while a student at Cambridge in the 1930s. Why was Cauldwell trying to drop other people – and possibly other Soviet spies – in the shit? It didn't make sense.

'Once again, Jeffers, you're getting our roles confused. Let's get back on course. Have you seen Sir Anthony since Germany?'

'Why should I answer questions when you already know the answers?'

'Because that's the way we play the game.' Catesby sat back and began to fiddle with the photograph. 'Okay, Jeffers, I'm going to tell you some things that I shouldn't tell you.'

Cauldwell smiled. 'You don't have to.'

'Thanks. But I want to because I need your help.' Catesby was copying the interrogation method that Skardon from Five had used so successfully with Klaus Fuchs. You pretend you're a pal on their side and you want their help.

'Cut out the shit, Catesby. That "I'm your friend" crap only works with cretins and emotional weaklings.'

'You're right, Jeffers, it was pretty stupid trying that.' Catesby leaned forward and jammed a finger into Cauldwell's chest. 'But you're going to fucking hear what I've got to say even if you don't want to fucking hear it.'

'Calm down.' Cauldwell seemed to be enjoying himself.

'Thanks, Jeffers.' Catesby picked up the photo. 'This was sent to me anonymously in the post. Now if you were our prisoner, I'd offer a few trades. Maybe three or four months off your sentence for each person in this photo that you can identify – especially the piece that's been torn off.' Catesby glanced at Hank. 'But I don't think your fellow Americans are as corruptible as us perfidious Brits.'

Hank shook his head.

'Let's,' Catesby said, 'just list the characters in the photo that we do know. It must have been a warm day because none of you look particularly cold considering your states of undress. This handsome hunk must be you.'

Cauldwell's face remained blank.

'I'm quite envious, Jeffers. I'm British born and bred and never get invited to these parties, but you, a mere American, appear to have leapt into the country-house orgy circuit in one bound.' Catesby stared a few seconds at the countryside behind the revellers. 'Where was it: Cliveden, Petworth, Waddesdon? I don't often go to those places.'

'I can't remember.' Cauldwell put on a fake English accent. 'One goes to so many of these things they all get mixed up.'

'Jennifer certainly has nice legs, at least the one you can see.' The leg in question exposed to just beyond the stocking tops was draped over a billy goat. The rest of her was held up by Knowles, who was surprisingly well muscled. Jennifer was in a swoon and gazing at Knowles with undisguised lust. 'I bet she converted him.'

Still no reaction from Cauldwell.

'Knowles is obviously Priapus and you seem to be in charge of catering. That's you kneeling on the ground at Jennifer's side with a tray of canapés on your garlanded head. You sly dog. Your left hand is inside Jennifer's skirt.'

'I'm holding her up.'

'Or warming her up for Knowles.' For the first time Catesby noticed a reaction from Cauldwell. It was a slight wince, barely detectable. Jealousy?

'But where is Sir Anthony?'

Cauldwell went stony-faced again.

'I bet he's the one taking the photo. Expensive wide-angle lens too. And, of course, Blunt choreographed it and provided the props. But maybe the pan pipes and that Greek amphora were just lying around the house.' Catesby pointed to the photo. 'I'm sure the one with his back to the camera, helping up the drunk, is Jennifer's husband. He looks like a rugby player going to seed.'

Cauldwell glanced briefly at the picture.

'Thanks. I'll take that for a yes. But frankly, I'm more interested in the identities of those in the missing part of the photo.' Catesby took a book out of his briefcase, *French Artists* by Collins and Liddiment. 'We've got a good library in Lowestoft and I know the guys who wrote this. I bet you didn't know I was a sensitive arty type?'

Cauldwell smiled and nodded.

Catesby opened the book. 'As you can see, there are thirteen humans in the original painting: nine males and four women – and a live goat. This photo shows two of the women and all of the men. The only people missing are these two women.' One of the women wore nothing and the other was bare-breasted and beating a tambourine over her head.

Hank looked at his watch. 'Can we hurry up, Mr Catesby?'

'Sure.'

'What happened later? Who paired off with whom?'

Cauldwell slowly shook his head.

'You put your clothes back on and went to evensong?' Catesby shut the book. 'The problem with you, Jeffers, is that you don't understand where your interest lies. A few minutes ago you were fine. By not cooperating now you're going to make your life more miserable – and, as a result, it will be easier to break you. If you were clever, you would give us a few crumbs – like identifying your orgy pals – and then you would buy a few privileges, like some uninterrupted sleep. That would give you strength to keep the really important stuff secret.'

Cauldwell remained silent.

Catesby turned to Hank and shook his head.

'Listen,' said Hank stopping the tape recorder, 'we're not getting anywhere and I've got to be somewhere else.'

'Can I carry on by myself?'

'You know that wasn't part of the agreement.'

'Who will know? And if they find out, I'll take the blame.'

Hank looked at his watch again. 'I'm between a rock and a hard place. Okay, you carry on, Mr Catesby, and let me know what happens.'

Catesby listened to Hank's footsteps clanging and echoing on the metal stairs. He waited until the thick nuclear-bomb-proof door hissed shut and then turned the tape recorder back on. Catesby noticed that Cauldwell's eyes were closed. He had dozed off. The sleep deprivation routine had already begun.

'Wake up.'

Cauldwell's eyes jerked open. Catesby turned off the tape recorder and smiled. He scribbled a note and passed it to Cauldwell. *Turning off the tape recorder is a CIA ploy to get people to talk more freely. They think they're not being recorded, but the room itself is wired up with hidden microphones. I'm going to see if I can find them.*

Catesby got up and walked around the bunker. The walls were solid concrete, except for grates leading to ventilation shafts. He found what he was looking for and tried to unscrew the ventilation grate with a penknife, but only broke the blade. Catesby then went over to the fuse box. It was locked, but he unlocked it with his broken penknife blade, then reached in and pulled out the fuse. The bunker was plunged into near total darkness. The only light came from the battery-powered EXIT light over the staircase. There was enough light to find the EMERGENCY locker, which was unlocked. Catesby found a battery-powered flashlight.

He shone the light in Cauldwell's face. 'No one can hear us down here. So don't shout for help.' He shone the light on the miked-up ventilation shaft. 'And, since there's no power supply, there's going to be no recording of what happens next.' He focused the light back on Cauldwell.

The American squinted, but seemed otherwise unperturbed.

'I admire your sangfroid, Jeffers. If you have the intelligence that often goes with it, you would realise that it's in your interest to answer my questions.'

'Fuck you.'

'That's a good start. Being in England seems to have worn

off some of your Southern gentleman civility. We have good manners too – and know how to behave at garden parties. Rule number one: don't piss in the punchbowl. But our civility is only a thin veneer. Beneath it we are a hard and ruthless people. Ever seen a fight in a pub? Not something of which we should be proud. And frankly, I am ashamed when I see these traits in myself.' Catesby rested the torch on the table and opened his briefcase. 'They let me keep something of yours as a souvenir. Or maybe I just nicked it when no one was looking. It worked out perfectly. The Americans think we have it – and our chaps think the Yanks have it.' Catesby took a Makarov 9mm pistol out of his briefcase. 'And maybe they'll think there was some colossal cock-up and you managed to keep it.'

There was the sound of dripping water somewhere in the bunker. For a long time it was the only sound. Finally, Catesby pulled back the slide on the Makarov 9mm and chambered a round. 'I know you've been running a network of agents.' He pushed the barrel of the pistol against Cauldwell's left eye. 'You're now going to tell me all their names. And you can start with the two women who are missing from Professor Blunt's snapshot. And if you don't, I'm going to pull the trigger and the bullet's going to go straight through your eye socket and exit from the back of your head taking a large part of your medulla oblongata with it. After a split second of burning shock, you won't feel a thing – which is a pity. I'd prefer to shoot you in the balls and leave you writhing in agony as you bleed to death. But that's not going to look like a fucking suicide, is it?'

Catesby shone the torch on Cauldwell's chest. The American's face looked grey, but impassive, in the semi-shadow.

'I'm not bluffing. No one will believe it was suicide wherever I shoot you, but I don't want to make the cover-up even more incredible than it has to be. British cover-ups are not meant to be convincing; they're meant to be impudent.' Catesby paused. 'On the other hand, I don't have to shoot you. Just give me names.'

'T.S. Eliot, Ezra Pound, Emily Dickinson, Walt Whitman…'

'Well done, Jeffers, you're a fine example of "grace under pressure". Hemingway would be proud of you.' Catesby gave a faint smile, 'But maybe not in every way. In fact, I'm sure Papa Hemingway is hiding something too.' Catesby removed the gun from Cauldwell's left eye. There was a faint red circle on the eyelid from where the barrel had been pressing. Cauldwell opened the eye. It looked weary, despite its reprieve. Suddenly, Catesby grabbed Cauldwell by his shirt collar and jammed the gun hard into his temple. 'Start giving me the fucking names or you're fucking dead.'

The water continued its slow drip from its secret place deep in the duct system.

'It's condensation,' said Cauldwell.

'What?'

'When you shorted the electrics, you turned off the air filtration system and now the air vapour is condensing into water and dripping. I'm surprised you didn't know that. Why don't you just pull the trigger?'

Catesby thumbed the safety of the Makarov down into the firing position and began to pull the trigger. He continued to squeeze the trigger until a loud click echoed off the bunker's walls. 'Don't worry, it is loaded. The Makarov is a very safe heater. It goes to double action for the first shot after you release the safety. That click, as you know, Jeffers, was the hammer cocking. Nice smooth trigger action for a Russian pistol. I'm now going to kill you.'

The water continued dripping. Catesby began to sweat and felt his hand shaking. His mouth and throat were dry. He had failed. He put his left hand on top of the Makarov and pulled back the slide. A cartridge ejected from the breech and landed on the floor with a dull clunk. He continued working the slide until seven more cartridges had flown out. The gun was now empty. Catesby sat down again. It was as if Cauldwell no longer existed. There was no sound of breathing. For a second, he wondered if Cauldwell had died of fright. He picked up the torch and shone it on the American's face. His eyes were open and staring. Catesby still wasn't sure that he was alive. Finally, there was a slight twitch in the corner of the left eye.

Catesby shone the torch on the concrete floor and began to pick up the ejected cartridges. When he had gathered all eight and put them in his pocket, he sat down again. He removed the magazine from the Makarov and clicked all the cartridges back in. He wasn't finished playing mind games. 'I've changed my mind again. I'm going to shoot you after all. But I need a drink first.'

'Stop fucking around and just shoot me.'

'Wait a sec.' Catesby put the gun back in his briefcase and took out a silver hip flask. He took a long swig and kept staring at Cauldwell. The American's face was ghostly grey in the shadow. 'It looks like you need a drink too.' He passed the flask over.

The handcuffs meant Cauldwell had to grasp it in both hands. As he lifted the flask to his lips he looked like a priest raising a chalice. He drank deeply and remarked, 'It's Jim Beam.'

'I thought you might prefer bourbon to whisky.'

'Actually, I prefer vodka.'

'Silly me. That's why you were waiting on the beach.'

Cauldwell handed the flask back.

'Did you think I was bluffing? Is that why you wouldn't spill any beans?'

Cauldwell shook his head. 'Facing death is just another existential exercise.'

'I don't believe that. You knew I was bluffing. It doesn't matter. The Americans will break you.' Catesby paused and stared at Cauldwell. 'Why did you become a Communist? It's an innocent question; you're not going to betray anyone.'

'It's not an innocent question. It's called psychological profiling.'

'Yeah, I know. And all that psych bullshit that we're supposed to use comes from your side of the Atlantic. I was just curious. It might be the last time you have a chance to talk to a friend.'

Cauldwell laughed. 'Why didn't you become a Communist?'

'Because of Stalin. I couldn't stomach his brutality.'

'Typical bourgeois answer, Catesby. But Stalin's Soviet Union was strong enough to defeat Hitler. Nine million Soviet soldiers died in the Great Patriotic War and eighteen million Soviet civilians. No decadent bourgeois country, certainly not the United States, could have endured that sacrifice.'

'Far fewer would have died if Stalin hadn't made stupid mistakes through blind ignorance and arrogance.'

'You can't,' said Cauldwell, 'write alternative "what-if" histories.'

'Sure. In any case, your hero Stalin is dead.'

'I never said he was my hero.'

'You have to say that now. Don't you, Jeffers?'

Cauldwell gave a cagey smile.

'What,' said Catesby, 'did you think of Khrushchev's secret speech?'

'Are you sure, William, that you don't work for the KGB? It sounds like you're testing my ideological commitment, to make sure I'm toeing the latest Party line.'

'I have the impression that you're not a big Khrushchev fan.'

'You're wrong about that. Khrushchev's speech denouncing Stalin was a braver thing than any Western leader has ever done. There's now more freedom for artists and writers.' Cauldwell smiled. 'I detect a faint look of scepticism on your face. You think I'm reeling off Party line propaganda too readily … as if I've practised it to deceive you about my real loyalties in a double bluff.'

'Or maybe a triple bluff.' Catesby shrugged and tried to look bored. He didn't want to show Cauldwell that he had walked into his trap. 'Did your Soviet handler ever ask you to write a memoir for the KGB files?'

'Of course, it's standard practice and you know it.'

'And is your memoir just as full of bullshit?' Catesby picked up the Makarov 9mm and passed it from hand to hand.

'You're getting tedious, Catesby – and I need to piss.'

'Go piss against the wall.'

'Can you undo my handcuffs?'

'Of course not.'

Cauldwell got up and walked to the wall. Catesby listened to the urine splashing and knew the Americans wouldn't be pleased.

When Cauldwell came back to the table, Catesby picked up the photo. 'Who do you think sent me this?'

'I don't know.'

'You ought to know. It was the same person who betrayed you.'

Cauldwell shrugged. 'So what?'

'You're a cool customer, Jeffers, but the Americans will break you.'

The dank bunker now smelled of warm urine. The only sound was the dripping water.

'Would you like another drink?' said Catesby.

Cauldwell nodded and took the hip flask.

'Remind you of the old days?'

'What old days?'

'When you were at the University of Virginia. Tell me about Kit Fournier; he's told me a lot about you.'

Cauldwell shifted uneasily.

'You were in the same class as Kit.'

'Yes, but I didn't know him then. He did political science with a minor in French. I did English Literature and drama.'

'He said you were on the boxing team.'

'That's right. I was the middleweight champion.'

'Under that smooth exterior, you're a pretty hard guy.'

'It's not just being hard.' Cauldwell smiled. 'I had been trained as a ballet dancer. I was so much quicker and more graceful than the brutes, I could easily shrug off their jabs with a casual *épaulement* or a left hook with a *pas de bourrée dessous-dessus*. And then when the clumsy-footed brutes were arm weary...' Cauldwell got to his feet and was throwing punches as well as he could with handcuffed wrists. '*Coupé, degagé; degagé, coupé, coupé!*'

'Did you do ballet with Michael Straight?' Catesby had tossed the bombshell to see Cauldwell's reaction. It was widely suspected in SIS that Straight had been one of Blunt's lovers and had probably worked for Moscow. But no one knew for sure. Those in high places were well protected.

Cauldwell smiled. 'You know everything. Don't you, William?'

'Far from it.'

'You want me to say that Michael and Anthony are fellow Communist spies.'

'Maybe,' smiled Catesby, 'I'm a malicious bastard out to victimise the completely innocent.'

'Michael Straight is completely innocent. He never worked for the Soviet Union.' Cauldwell smiled. 'But you probably think I'm covering for him?'

'You're right; that is what I think.' Catesby paused. 'Funny, isn't it?'

'What is?'

'Michael Straight is a Soviet spy, but you're not.'

'Double bluff, William, double bluff.'

'Why don't you finish the bourbon?'

Cauldwell took a deep drink.

Catesby felt he was getting close to something. The art of interrogation was finding the talk button. But it took time and patience – and you needed to wear the other person down.

Cauldwell pushed back the empty hip flask. He looked very tired.

Catesby gave Cauldwell a long stare and then whispered, 'Tell me about Quentin. Was he a Communist too?'

For the first time Cauldwell's face showed a flicker of surprise, as if Catesby's question was completely unexpected.

'Kit Fournier told me all about it.'

'Kit has a big mouth.'

'Was Quentin your best friend?'

'He was killed in the war. Did Kit tell you that?'

Catesby nodded. The Quentin question had been a stab in the dark. He wanted to put together a full picture of Cauldwell's sexual and emotional past.

Cauldwell yawned and gave a sad smile. 'Quentin was a pilot, but obviously not a very good pilot.'

'Fournier said that Quentin had a twin sister.'

Cauldwell winced.

'And that you used to play a little game.'

'Kit talks too much about what he knows too little about.'

'Can you explain?'

'No.'

'You want to sleep?'

Cauldwell nodded. He seemed almost in a trance.

'But there's one more question on my list.'

'And then you'll let me sleep?'

Catesby nodded. 'What do you think of the situation in Malaya?'

Cauldwell laughed. 'I know nothing about Malaya.'

'And I don't know why they wanted me to ask you.' Catesby looked closely at Cauldwell without appearing to do so. He thought there was a flicker of apprehension on the American's face, but he might have been wrong.

'In any case,' continued Catesby, 'the Communist insurrection in Malaya appears to have failed. Our Asian section would love to know Moscow's view on the situation.'

'I don't know. How should I know?'

'Next time you're in Moscow, tell them the Communist insurrection is failing because it has little support outside the Chinese minority community.'

Cauldwell remained stony-faced.

'You're obviously not an Asia specialist.'

'Is any of that bourbon left?'

Catesby shook the flask. 'There's a trickle. Finish it.'

Cauldwell finished the bourbon and put his head down on the desk. He was soon fast asleep. But it wasn't a long sleep. Ten minutes later, Hank and a pair of military policemen began to clank down the bunker stairs to take Cauldwell away. Catesby quickly replaced the fuse in the fuse box. The neon strip lighting blinked on again.

As Cauldwell was led away, Catesby put the Makarov automatic and the hip flask back in his briefcase. He then picked up the torn photograph and was about to slip it back in its envelope when he stopped and stared. Why hadn't he seen it before? Whoever had torn off the images of the two missing women hadn't done a perfect job. The calf and ankle of one of them was visible just below the tear. The shapely ankle was encircled by a thin silver bracelet.

Henry Bone stared out of his rain-beaded office window at the wedge-shaped building opposite. Bone sipped his tea as if for comfort then sighed. 'I wonder if they find us as ugly as we find them.'

'We're much uglier than them,' said Catesby proudly. 'We're the ugliest building in St James's. That's why they put us here.'

'I think you're right.'

The two buildings in question were 54 Broadway, the anonymous HQ of SIS, and 55 Broadway, the head offices of London Underground. There was, Catesby thought, a certain aptness that the underground and the secret espionage service were neighbours.

'Actually,' said Catesby, 'I rather like their building. But I've never been able to understand why that boy has such a large penis.'

The penis in question belonged to a Jacob Epstein sculpture called *Morning* and was pointing directly at Henry Bone's office. The London Underground building, hailed on its completion in 1929 as 'a cathedral of modernity', also had exterior sculptures by Moore, Gill and Aumonier.

'It has often occurred to me,' said Bone, pointing at the Epstein, 'that the architect planned it thus. He must have been told that we were here; it was his way of pissing on us. He wouldn't have got away with that in Moscow.'

'Doesn't that make us a better society?'

'Would you like another cup of tea?'

'Yes, please.'

As Bone poured the tea from the 'simply ghastly' Spode tea service that he despised, Catesby rewound the tape recorder.

'At first,' he said, 'I was worried about the Americans having a copy of this, but Hank reassured me.'

'What did he think of the interview?'

'Hank said it was all "diddly squat" and a "waste of US taxpayers' money".'

'He wasn't impressed.'

'No.'

'The Americans,' said Bone, 'aren't always as unsophisticated as they pretend. You should be careful what you say around them. I am sure they are going to find your interview very useful. I wish you hadn't mentioned Sir Anthony. You gave away information that may come back to haunt us.'

Catesby tried not to smile. Professor Blunt was a sore point with Henry Bone – and many others in the establishment. Blunt was called 'the untouchable' because he knew where all the bodies were buried. Sir Anthony had been sent to Germany at the end of the war to retrieve personal letters that could have proved very embarrassing for members of the British establishment. It was also believed that Blunt had recruited spies for Moscow at Cambridge University in the 1930s – including Burgess and Maclean as well as the American Michael Straight. But Blunt was untouchable because he knew *too* many secrets. And, Catesby knew for certain, Sir Anthony had a few interesting stories about Henry Bone as well.

'How would you interpret the frankness of Cauldwell's remarks?' said Bone. 'Was he taken in by your ploy?' The interview bunker had, in fact, been wired so that a hidden tape recorder continued to record after Catesby pretended to short the electrics.

'I don't think he fell for it. In fact, I think he relished the idea of being recorded. Part of Cauldwell was performing for posterity. And another part of him was practising his lines for future interrogations.'

'Double bluffs, triple bluffs?'

Catesby nodded. 'Is Cauldwell a fake homosexual? Or a real homosexual pretending to be a fake homosexual?'

'Or simply bisexual? There are persons like that.'

'I don't think it's that simple, Henry. But I feel there is a connection between Cauldwell and a woman who was cut out of Professor Blunt's photograph.'

'You don't have any evidence that Sir Anthony took that photo – or had anything to do with it – and I wish that you would stop suggesting it.'

'*Mea culpa*. In fact, Henry, I have the distinct impression that you don't find that torn photograph very relevant or important?'

'Not particularly; I think it's a red herring.'

'Fine. In any case, Cauldwell's comments about the Soviet Union are fascinating. If there is truth in Cauldwell's words, he weaves that truth into a cloak of lies to disguise what he's really doing.'

Bone laughed. 'You don't think he's a Soviet spy?'

'I'm not sure what he is.'

»»»»

It was Catesby's last day in London. He was only in England on TDY – temporary duty – to help deal with Cauldwell. But now he had to return to Berlin where he was SIS head of station still operating under his feeble cover of Cultural Attaché for Film and Broadcasting. Catesby had a lot of loose ends to tie up before flying back to Templehof. His first stop was Hatchards in Piccadilly. It was the most prestigious bookshop in London and sent books to the Royal Family at Buckingham Palace as well as to Guy Francis De Moncy Burgess in Moscow. As soon as Catesby entered the shop, the manager was at his elbow.

'Would you like a snifter?'

'Thanks, I'd love one.'

'Let's go to my office.'

Catesby had first met the Hatchards manager during the war when he had ordered a complete set of *À la recherche du temps perdu*. At the time, Catesby still had an East Anglian accent and the manager found it difficult to understand why someone who sounded like a Suffolk farm-worker or trawler-boy was ordering the works of Proust in French. He guessed Catesby was buying the books for a more refined and educated fellow officer – and tactfully asked if that were the case. Catesby responded by reciting the opening of *Á la recherche* from memory and in perfect French.

They met again ten years later when Henry Bone despatched Catesby to Hatchards to find out what Guy Burgess was reading. The idea was that his choice of books might somehow reveal the identities of other spies. Burgess's reading preference was mostly recent history. He was also keen on the novels of Anthony Powell, pronounced 'Pole', and always ordered the newest as soon as it was published. As a result, Catesby was sent to Somerset to interview Powell at his modestly stately home and found out that Powell was a high and dry Tory who despised Burgess and his ilk. The author, who had married into the English Roman Catholic aristocracy, was amused by Catesby's name and asked if he had Catholic connections too.

Catesby sipped the manager's whisky and looked at the carbon that he had provided of Burgess's latest book order. As always, the spy's loyal and long-suffering mother paid for the books and shipping.

'I must say,' remarked the manager, 'the number of books ordered has been shrinking.'

'I think the comrade's drinking doesn't leave much time for reading. But it's important that you keep us informed.'

'Do you still read Proust?'

'Not as much as I should.' Catesby had tried to read Proust again, but he was still haunted by a wartime memory. He had been parachuted into the Limousin in the summer of 1943 with SOE. A year later he saw what had happened at Oradour-sur-Glane. The 190 men of the village were machine-gunned in six different barns. And a little later, the 452 women and children, with the sounds of the machineguns that had murdered the men of the village still ringing in their ears, were gathered up and herded into the church. The doors of the church were then locked and the women and children burned alive. When Catesby tried to read Proust again, he no longer saw *la vue de la petite madeleine*, but the flames of Oradour. It was his own remembrance of things past. He regarded civilisation as a lie, a narcotic blindfold. Catesby could never forget Oradour-sur-Glane. For months afterwards he hadn't slept. And years later it still kept him awake in the dark watches twisting in his sheets and waiting for the cold dawn.

Catesby finished his whisky, then slipped the carbon of the book order into his coat pocket. 'Thank you again. It's very good of you.'

The manager led Catesby to the shop entrance. As they were shaking hands, Catesby noticed someone out of the corner of his eye. It was a sudden *coup de déjà vu*, like a Proustian madeleine. She was a stunning woman. He remembered having seen her once before at a meeting of some sort – where even the most reserved of mandarins had stifled wolf whistles and eyed her up.

'Actually,' said Catesby, 'I'd like to have a look around before I leave.'

'Please do.'

Catesby tried not to make it obvious that he was following her. He turned his trilby down to hide his face – and then swivelled his eyes to watch a pair of neatly turned ankles climbing the stairs to the upper level where the art books were kept. The left ankle and its silver bracelet was more than Proust's symbolic madeleine; it was a whole bank of exploding mental flashbulbs. But, thought Catesby, maybe it was just a coincidence. London is full of nice ankles and bracelets that encircle them. He thought about going upstairs to have a closer look, but didn't want to make his interest seem too obvious.

Catesby remained downstairs and flicked through the latest volume of Churchill's *The History of the English Speaking Peoples*. He wondered if the public had any idea of how conflicted, complex and vulnerable Churchill was. Catesby then wandered over to the foreign language shelf and picked up a copy of André Malraux's *L'espoir* – another man of contradictions. Perhaps, he thought, being torn apart inside and trying not to show it was just part of living in the twentieth century. Catesby noticed a Graham Greene book about Indochina that he had been meaning to read. He liked the title, *The Quiet American* – apparently a *very* quiet American – and put it under his arm with the Malraux. He looked at his watch; she was taking a long time. Maybe she had disappeared through a trapdoor in the ceiling and was now running across the roofs of Piccadilly to escape his attention. Catesby continued browsing and stopped at the American shelf. Why oh why was Nabokov *there*? He was Russian. Catesby picked up Nabokov's latest and looked at the first page. It was about lights of life and fires in loin. And, almost on cue, there was the tap of heels on stairs as the woman with nice ankles came back down.

Catesby pretended to be reading, but shifted his eyes towards the woman. She was wearing a purple cloche hat and a purple Mac, but it all looked fine. She oozed the confidence of those who believed they were born to rule. That confidence, and it should be called a 'confidence trick', fascinated Catesby as much as it annoyed him. It was a bubble that needed pricking. But you needed to know where to prick.

The woman passed close on her way to the non-fiction aisle. She had a large art book under her arm: *The Nude: A Study in Ideal Form*. In other circumstances, the book would have provided openings for some cheeky chat-up lines. But, Catesby thought, not now. He put the Nabokov back on the shelf and studied the woman in profile. Maybe he was wrong, but he trusted his gut instincts. The art book tied in with a taste for frolics. He now recalled the meeting where he had seen her. It was JIC, Joint Intelligence Committee, and she was deputising for her boss who was ill.

She wasn't long in the non-fiction section. She soon steamed out as if she had just realised that it was near the end of her lunch break. This was a woman with a job, an important job. Catesby tried not to stare as she passed close by, but caught sight of another book: *The Outsider*, by Colin Wilson. She carried a definite whiff of upper-class Bohemia and weekends at Dartington Hall discussing the works of Rabindranath Tagore.

She was now at the till with the manager. Catesby averted his eyes, but strained his ears. She spoke first, 'Have those books I ordered arrived?'

'Yes ... they came yesterday.'

Catesby noted the brief pause after 'yes'. He understood the manager's dilemma. Do you say 'm'lady' or address her by her forename? It was a difficult question that Catesby never got right.

'Thank you ever so much – and I'll have these too. Could you please get Colin to sign this one for me? But I'll pay for it now.'

As the woman was writing a cheque, Catesby walked up behind her with his own purchases. She smelled exotic: clove, orange and sandalwood. And a note of something strange: a certain pungent scent of incense.

When she had left, Catesby winked at the manager. 'I know that woman, but I can't remember her name. I know that she's Lady Something.'

The manager smiled and toted up the purchases. He seldom broke his duty of confidentiality to his customers, not unless said customers were Soviet spies. Meanwhile, Catesby furtively glanced at the order form next to the till. The title of the book was in Chinese with an English transliteration in brackets. The names of the two authors were also in English lettering: Hao Ran and Chen Duxiu. But there was no name of the purchaser.

'The problem is,' Catesby lowered his voice to whisper the lie, 'I'm going to see her at a liaison meeting with the Asian section tomorrow morning. And I just can't remember her name.'

The manager replied in a low voice without looking up. 'Lady Penelope Somers.'

'Of course, it was just on the tip of my tongue.'

'You should be so lucky.'

Back on Piccadilly, Catesby glanced right and left searching for the purple cloche hat. He quickly spotted it, like a marker buoy riding the tide above the crowds. She was tall. Catesby began to follow her as she turned towards Green Park and had to hurry to catch up. He wanted to introduce himself on the pretext of being a JIC colleague and have a chat but he almost had to run to keep up because she had such long athletic legs. Lady Somers was walking quickly as if late for an appointment. Or did she know she was being followed? The hat changed course in the colonnade in front of the Ritz. She had entered the hotel.

Catesby had been to the Ritz once before, but had been too drunk to take much of it in. The cry at the time had been 'Forget the blitz, let's go to the Ritz.' And that's just what they did. Catesby had just passed out of Infantry OCTU, the Officer Cadet Training Unit, when he'd been led to the hotel by a subaltern he had met during training. His fellow officer had been to Westminster School and Oxford and knew everyone – even the bartender who, it turned out, was a grandson of Sigmund Freud.

Catesby remembered a puce-faced colonel snapping his fingers to be served and young Freud saying, 'Have you lost your dog?' But as soon as he entered the Ritz for the second time, Catesby knew it wasn't going to be as much fun. For a start, Lady Somers had completely disappeared.

Catesby stood in the middle of the foyer, took off his trilby and smoothed his hair. 'Shit,' he whispered, 'where the fuck has she gone?' The words were inaudible, but a liveried concierge at the reception desk was staring with disapproval. Maybe, thought Catesby, they were trained to lip read. The concierge lifted a telephone and Catesby hove out of sight towards the Palm Court. Maybe she was meeting someone for tea. Catesby entered an atrium that seemed to have more palm trees than a rainforest and more chandelier suns than a galaxy. Tea for two at the Ritz. A fantasy escape that cost you a week's wages.

They must have been lying in ambush behind one of the huge potted palms. His voice came first and it was a low bass growl: 'Is that him?'

Her voice trilled a satisfied 'Yes.'

Catesby felt an intense stab of pain. The ex-boxing champion, turned hotel detective, had jabbed a knuckle into the base of his spine. Catesby struggled to stay on his feet. His knees were jelly.

Catesby regained his balance and turned around. Freddie, the ex-champ, was shorter than Lady Somers and looked like a pit bull that had been called to heel. She glared with eyes that were as polished and hard as ebony and snapped 'Don't fucking follow me again' then turned on her heels and clicked towards the Palm Court tea room.

Freddie clamped his huge paw firmly on Catesby's elbow. 'I think you'd better come with me.'

'I saw you fight Harvey at White Hart Lane,' said Catesby.

Freddie smiled.

'I'm glad you didn't hit me as hard as you hit him.'

As the boxer accompanied Catesby to the street he asked, 'What's your business?'

'I'm an art historian at the Courtauld.'

'No wonder you're a perv.'

Catesby limped slightly on the way to the Green Park underground, but otherwise felt good. The Courtauld fib was a lovely
lie.

»»»»

The windows of Henry Bone's office had curtains instead of
blinds. They were thick damask curtains with a simple fleur-
de-lis pattern that muffled the sound of the midnight rain.
Bone hated the faceless sterility of Broadway Buildings and had
imported many of his own possessions to the SIS HQ – including an early-nineteenth-century partners desk of carved oak.
Catesby, on the other hand, felt perfectly at home amid Broadway Buildings' dark warren of plywood partitions, frosted glass
and gloomy rooms with cream painted walls and worn lino lit
by bare lightbulbs. Only senior staff were permitted desk lamps.

Bone looked up from the heirloom desk and stared over his
half-moon spectacles. 'Your best cover story is being a complete
idiot. No one would ever believe that you're one of us.'

'What about Guy Burgess?'

'Precisely. Guy was an idiot too and that's why he got away with
it for so long.' Bone waved a document. 'But this is fascinating.'

'What is?'

'She is. Lady Somers is fascinating. But that doesn't mean
there's any link between her and Cauldwell.' Bone picked up *The
Triumph of Pan* photo. 'Even if the ankle does belong to her. And
I am not, as you requested, going to have our photo-analysis
boffins compare this with existing snaps of Lady Somers' ankle.'

There was something in Bone's voice that made Catesby
suspicious. It was as if he knew more about the photo and the
people in it than he was letting on. 'Why not? A photo-analysis
could provide proof of identity.'

'Because I don't want it to get around that we're snooping on her.' Bone lifted the file on his desk. 'In fact, I had to be
extremely discreet about my own enquiries. I did most of the
work in Registry myself and didn't always initial the document
chits. She's also one of Downing Street's top advisors on Malaya
– their secret gem.'

'Why do you have to be so careful?'

'Because we're Euro/Sov Bloc and the Far East P and T sections don't like us.' A recent reorganisation had created Ps, Production Sections, that collected intelligence and Ts, Target Sections, that decided what was needed. 'They resent the fact that we get most of the money – and it's quite right that we do. Who's worried about Chinese tanks rolling into Western Europe? Far East also think they do a better job with far fewer resources – and that, to be fair, is probably true. Plus I don't get on with Director Far East; he thinks I'm a scheming empire builder.'

'How could anyone think that?'

'Don't be sarcastic, Catesby, it's tedious. Try to learn light irony.'

'You still haven't told me why Lady Somers is so fascinating.'

'It's because she represents so much of our colonial past. Note, Catesby, that I did not say "the best of our colonial past", for I know that would bring on one of your anti-imperialist leftist rants.'

'Don't, Henry, always assume you know what I think.'

'Fair point. In any case, Lady Somers comes from a family of colonial administrators going back to the eighteenth century. Both her father and her grandfather served variously as governors of Penang, the Straits Settlements and Hong Kong. One of her great uncles was knighted for his role in putting down secret Chinese societies that were threatening British rule in the Straits Settlements. Coincidentally, Lady Somers seems to have played a similar role early on in the Malayan Emergency.'

'Did her ladyship prowl the jungles with a Sten gun?'

'I'm sure she did.'

Catesby wasn't surprised. His back still ached from her ambush at the Ritz.

'But,' continued Bone, referring to the file, 'she also speaks fluent Hokkien, which is the main dialect spoken by the Malayan Chinese. Apparently, she was very successful in turning village elders against the Communists. What really happened is all hush-hush.'

'But good news for her family's rubber plantations.'

'Don't be so cynical, Catesby.'

'I'm not the one being cynical. It was the rich rubber barons who insisted that the war be called an "emergency" so they could collect insurance on damaged property that was not covered by wartime activities.'

Bone sighed wearily.

'At least I say what I really think.' Catesby gave Bone a half-smile.

'I don't like your "sly peasant" face. It won't go far in the service. Learn to be inscrutable and hide your duplicities with impeccable manners.'

'As you do?'

'No, Catesby, you need to develop your own style. Your reputation as a lefty is a useful ruse, but please don't practise your ideological rants on me.'

'And what about your ideologies? What are your politics?'

Bone stared into space for a few seconds as if he hadn't heard the question. Then said in soft measured tones, 'My job does not require an openly stated ideological position – and certainly doesn't require sharing it with you.'

'You're the perfect Whitehall mandarin.'

'I would like to think so.' Bone adjusted his reading glasses. 'But the Malayan business is interesting – especially to the Americans.'

'They must be envious. We haven't completely fucked up, like the French did in Indochina or the Yanks did in Korea.'

'To be fair, Korea was a draw. But a Communist guerrilla army has, so far, never been defeated. There's a line of thinking in Washington that it's a mistake to challenge peasant armies led by the likes of Mao and Ho Chi Minh – a sure waste of lives and money. But our experience in Malaya shows it can be otherwise. Therefore...'

'Therefore what?'

'Over to you, Catesby.'

'Henry, I'm not a thick undergrad who needs priming and you're not my tutor. But since you want to play Trinity College capers, could you pass me a flagon of Founder's Port?'

'Would brandy do?'

'It would.'

Bone opened a desk drawer and took out a bottle and two snifters. 'This is twenty-five-year-old VSOP, Catesby, so don't gulp it.' Bone carefully poured a measure and handed it over.

'Thanks.' Catesby warmed the glass with his hands and stared at the amber liquor. The odour was fine and rich, like the closed world inhabited by people like Henry Bone and Lady Somers.

'You've gone quiet,' said Bone. 'I wanted your views on Malaya.'

'I was thinking of something else. But I agree; it looks certain that the British are going to win.'

'You shouldn't say "British" rather than "we" when it's about a policy you don't like. It gives your game away.'

'Fine. The problem with a British victory over the Communist insurgency in Malaya is that it will make the Americans think they can do the same thing in Vietnam – and it won't work for two reasons. One, the Malayan insurgents have little support outside the Chinese minority community. Two, Malaya is geographically isolated from Communist allies who could give support.' Catesby sipped the fine brandy. 'Nonetheless, the hawks in Washington will start squawking "can do, can do". It's the new military mantra of the crew-cut cretins.'

'They must love you.'

'Not greatly.' Strained relations with his US counterparts had been a trademark of Catesby's career. But it was also a cunning ploy. It enabled him to gain the confidence of anti-American Germans and had helped him infiltrate the East Bloc Security Services. Catesby stared into the shadows examining his conscience.

'You've gone all enigmatic, Catesby. What are you thinking?'

'I was thinking that Lady Somers sounds like the bitch from hell.'

'Her life hasn't been all roses. She was nearly captured at the fall of Singapore and her husband died in mysterious circumstances.'

'What were the circumstances?'

'Lady Somers and the family don't talk about it – and because of their influence in Malaya, it's impossible to get a copy of the coroner's report.'

'Sounds like a suicide – or a heart attack in an opium den or a brothel.'

'I do not think, Catesby, that you should even speculate.'

'Does she have any children – or has that been hushed up too?'

'I'm not sure.' Bone picked up the file and flicked through the pages. 'Yes, there's a daughter.'

Catesby wondered if Bone really needed to look at the file. Or was his paranoia about Bone becoming clinical?

'You think I'm hiding things from you,' said Bone.

'Don't read my thoughts.'

'Your face gives them away.'

'I shouldn't be in this business.'

'We need you.'

'Like a knight needs a sacrificial pawn.'

'You're a far more valuable piece.'

'But still a sacrifice.'

'Of course, but only if it's necessary.'

'And what about you, Henry?'

'If I go down, you come with me. And that's never going to change.'

At first, the threat had been light banter. But now it was a deadly truth. They had used each other to protect loved ones and personal secrets. And now they could destroy each other. The only way for both of them to survive, as Catesby well knew, was to blackmail the other not to grass.

Catesby pointed to the *Triumph of Pan* photo on Bone's desk. 'Who sent that to me?'

'I honestly don't know, but your arched eyebrow suggests you think it was me.'

'I think that it's in your interest that I find out more about these people – and do them. But you can't do it yourself because it would risk blowing your cover.'

'What an interesting theory – even if it is a ludicrous one based on paranoia. Sometimes, Catesby, I think that you need a rest. That long walking tour you've always wanted in the South of France beckons.'

'But not yet.'

'No.'

'Okay, Henry, I'll tell you my theory – even though I know you're not going to give anything away with a nod or a wink. I think a lot of toffs in this country have turned rotten. Nothing new there, as Queen Elizabeth I was well aware.'

'And your famous ancestor was one of them.'

Catesby didn't rise to the bait. His name subjected him to a lot of teasing in the service. He frowned and picked up the photo. 'Being in this snapshot doesn't mean you're a Soviet agent. It's merely the upper classes at play. As long as you're part of that crowd, it doesn't matter whether you're a Communist or a Fascist – and it doesn't matter what you do in bed either. This is just a garden party with champagne and Pimms that turned a bit raunchy.'

'And you, Catesby,' said Bone fondling his brandy, 'think that Lady Somers takes part in these, uh, revelries.'

'I...'

'Don't answer; I'm not finished. You are completely wrong about Lady Somers. You obviously fancy her and your pride was hurt, as well as your kidney, when she sent in the Ritz hotel detective to teach you manners.'

'You're wrong about me – and I think you're wrong about her too. You know what I think, Henry?'

'I usually do.'

'I think Lady Hard Face Somers is a dominatrix from the pointy ears of her cat suit to the soles of her leather boots. And no, I don't fancy that sort of thing, but a lot of toffs do.' Catesby pointed at the photo. 'And fancy dress, or undress, parties like this give her a chance to unwind. And, as for her background in Malaya, she's just another high and dry Tory clinging to what's left of the Empire. They're a club within the club. You know the type. They like to wear native dress, know all the customs and are fluent in the local lingo so they can tell the coolies what's expected of them. Why are you smiling?'

'Because your characterisation of Lady Somers is so utterly ridiculous and completely false. You don't know the woman.'

'And you do?'

Bone put on his impassive face. They both knew that kinky toffs had always been security risks. Both of them also realised that, in an ideal world, what a person did in the bedroom had nothing to do with that person's political ideology or loyalty to the state. But they didn't live in that ideal world. Blackmail and honey traps were still the best tricks in an intelligence officer's bag.

Catesby paused and looked at the snapshot. 'I wonder who he is.'

'Who?'

'The handsome young man bearing a basket of grapes. I bet he's a pleb, probably a guardsman. I believe the best tarts come from the Household Cavalry.' Catesby gave Bone a knowing wink. 'But don't think for a moment that I'm being judgemental.'

'May I suggest, William, that there is an element of class jealousy in your makeup?'

'Absolutely none at all. I could fake my way into that world if I wanted to.'

'Why don't you?'

'Maybe I will.' Catesby stared thoughtfully at Henry's curtains. 'Basically, what we want to find out is how far Cauldwell and his gang have infiltrated the gang that run this country.'

'That would be useful.'

'I'm glad you agree. But we will probably find a load of completely unrelated skeletons – that's why they sent Sir Anthony to Germany at the end of the war.'

Bone smiled. 'That's pure speculation, Catesby.'

'I'm tired. Don't you ever get tired, Henry? In fact, I don't think I've ever seen you in daylight.'

'That's not true.'

'You're right. I'm off.'

»»»»»

When in London Catesby shared a flat in Pimlico with his sister and her boyfriend, but they were seldom there. The sister spent the week in Cheltenham, where she was a translator at GCHQ. Her boyfriend, Tomasz, worked on the BBC Polish Service and often did nightshifts at Bush House – or was out gallivanting. The flat was in the basement of a Georgian house that belonged to the family of Catesby's estranged wife. One of the great ironies about Catesby was that he married into the upper classes he affected to despise.

Catesby's wife, Frances, managed to get pregnant at the end of the war when she was seventeen. The Canadian pilot who took her virginity left twin boys in exchange, then fucked off back to Saskatchewan where he had a wife and family. Catesby met her at a Labour Party meeting. He didn't like it when people called Frances and her family 'champagne socialists'. They only drank champagne at weddings and anniversaries. But they could have drunk a lot more champagne if they hadn't given away most of their money to anarchists, suffragettes and other social reformers early in the twentieth century. Catesby loyally defended his in-laws to his lefty friends. What the hell should they do? Hang themselves from lampposts?

Why didn't the marriage work? Catesby didn't know. It annoyed him when people said it was because Frances had married 'below herself'. The reasons were otherwise. Maybe a difference in temperaments and expectations. Catesby knew, in retrospect, that he had come back from France pretty fucked up and needed her. And she had needed him too. The separation was, however, amicable – and sometimes they talked of reconciliation. In any case, Catesby got along well with his wife's family – and hence the cheap rent for the flat. It made him feel guilty but they refused to accept more.

'Bless me, Father, for I have sinned. Except for this sin there is no *ego te absolvo*.' Catesby lay awake and murmuring in the Pimlico flat. He was an atheist, but an atheist who had been brought up as a Catholic. Catesby never got over guilt and the scab-picking habit of examining his conscience. He loathed himself for enjoying the company of refined and educated people. Cambridge had opened a new world for him and he tried to fit in. On occasion, Catesby played the dour working-class card, but he enjoyed the wit and conversation of the glittering world around him. Secretly, and what a dark ugly secret, Catesby wanted to embrace that world and become part of it. At first, he hated himself for that. Then the day came when Catesby realised that, although he wasn't one of them, he was part of their world. That cured him. He no longer desired to be accepted by 'them'. He had seen the machinery behind the stage and realised that the glittering superstructure presented to the audience was controlled by hidden pulleys and wires. But Catesby knew that he couldn't go back to his roots either. On his visits home, he never felt comfortable in the pub and his Suffolk accent was a joke. His deracination was complete. Catesby no longer belonged anywhere. It may have been a lonely fate, but it made him the perfect spy.

While he was growing up, having the name Catesby had never been a problem. Not many people in Lowestoft were aware that one Catesby had been the leader of the Gunpowder Plot. Or that another Catesby had been one of Shakespeare's villains in *Richard III* – and had, in real life, fought beside the crookbacked king at Bosworth Field before being captured and beheaded. The teasing first began at Cambridge – and, later, the irony that an officer in HM's Secret Intelligence Service should bear the name of Britain's greatest traitor was never lost on his colleagues.

Like many working-class folk, Catesby knew little about his family history. He didn't know the full name of a single great grandparent. But he did know that Catesby was not a name typical of East Anglia. Names ending in '-by' are usually from the East Midlands. Catesby later discovered that it was no longer a name in use anywhere. He once wasted most of a day scouring telephone directories as well as British and the voluminous Commonwealth War Records. He wanted to find other Catesbys apart from his local family, but there were none. It was as if the name had been purged from Britain forever. Ironically, there were loads of Fawkes – as if somehow they were less reprehensible. Or that being hanged, drawn and quartered while still alive had made amends. But the only Catesbys were the Suffolk ones perched on England's easternmost extremity. Henry Bone used to tease Catesby with a theory that his ancestors fled to Suffolk to rendezvous with a ship from the Spanish Netherlands sent to rescue them. Night after night they waited in vain on a remote lonely beach, but the promised ship never appeared. When those who remained of the treacherous Catesbys realised that rescue was never going to come, they dropped their fine ways and disappeared into the local peasantry.

Catesby was still alone in the Pimlico flat when he woke with a start at three o'clock in the morning. He was covered in cold sweat. There had been similar dreams before, but this was a new variation. And it had been so real. He actually felt the sand of Covehithe beach under his bare feet and the summer sea lapping around his ankles. Covehithe was unusual for Suffolk, one of the few places where the beach had more sand than shingle. It was Catesby's favourite place. The woods came down to the sea's very edge. At high tide, acorns and chestnuts dropped directly into the seawater from overhanging tree branches. It was a remote place for midnight bonfire parties where no one would bother you. Or a secret place for furtive couplings in the soft ferns while the gentle sough of the sea timed the pace of your lovemaking. In Catesby's dream, he was inside the girl from the opposite terrace, delirious with longing as she stroked his back and whispered how she had wanted him for so long. And then she was gone – a pale nymph disappearing into the wood. Catesby knew it was time to go. He waded into the water and looked out to sea for the signal lights. He had so wanted her to come with him, but it wasn't to be.

When the searchlights came on, it was the reverse of what had happened to Cauldwell. Now, it was Catesby on the receiving end. The first to walk out of the shadows was Henry Bone. He was pointing a revolver, but his face was sad and full of regret. And soon there was a big crowd pointing. Some were wearing bowlers and city suits; others were Tudor gentlemen in ruffs, doublets and hose. Every intelligence officer Catesby had ever known stared at him with hatred and contempt. As always in those dreams, Catesby began to explain that there had been a mistake. He started shouting the names of those who were guilty – and had somehow escaped being uncovered. But he convinced no one and was grabbed by a pair of heavies. In most of these dreams, Catesby shouted aloud and woke up just as they were about to shoot him. But in this dream, they grabbed him and forced his head on to a tree stump. When Catesby looked up for the last time, Lady Somers was striding towards him. She was dressed for a funeral: black hat, black cloak, black stockings, black shoes. She had an axe in her hand. Catesby woke up just as the sharp steel touched the back of his neck.

September, 1958: Aberdeen Proving Ground, Maryland

'You're the ideal guinea pig, Mr Cauldwell. You don't exist. You're already dead.'

Cauldwell laughed. 'But they haven't found the body.'

The testing suite at the Biomedical Laboratory looked almost like a hotel lounge. There weren't, of course, any windows, but there was a two-way mirror that stretched along an entire wall. The suite was painted 'grasshopper green', which was thought to be the colour most calming to psychiatric patients. The walls were hung with watercolours depicting creeks and rivers of the nearby Chesapeake Bay. For a testing suite where experiments involving mental torture were carried out, it wasn't that bad.

The man dealing with Cauldwell was known as Doctor Dirty Trickster. He wasn't a medical doctor, but had a PhD in chemistry.

The Trickster looked closely at Cauldwell. 'I bet you're glad you volunteered.'

'I didn't volunteer.'

'Oh yes, you did – and don't say that isn't your signature on the authorisation form.'

'It's not my signature; you forged it.'

'Unh, uh. That's not the way to be.'

'Okay, I'll try again. I did sign the form. But I did so because I am a loyal and patriotic US citizen who is wrongly suspected of being a Soviet spy.' Cauldwell purred the words in his most honeyed Southern drawl.

The Trickster laughed and slapped his thigh. 'Wonderful. You've already begun to hallucinate and you haven't even taken the drug.'

It was known as Project 112 and Cauldwell was lucky to be there. A previous handler had told Cauldwell, after a particularly uncooperative session, that he was going to be sent to Honduras for the sort of drug experiments that were too radical for the CIA to carry out, no matter how secretly, in the USA. The Honduran Army outfit was called Batallón de Inteligencia 3–16. The Batallón was a way for the CIA to wash its hands of involvement in extreme experimentation on humans – but still benefit from the research. A number of the 3–16 staff were German scientists who escaped trial for war crimes when the CIA smuggled them out of Germany with false passports. The war criminal rat run was called Project Paperclip. There were Paperclip fugitives working at Edgewood too. But, smiled Cauldwell to himself, it was a simple paperclip that was going to free him. He'd found it on the seat of the car that had taken him to the testing lab. It was the sort of simple carelessness that so often compromises security. Some previous passenger in the car must have been reading a document in the backseat and hadn't noticed – or bothered to look for – the paperclip that had fallen off.

The Trickster opened a folder and sifted through a few documents. 'You were interrogated for 549 consecutive days?'

'I don't know. I was submitted to sensory deprivation: no natural light, clocks or calendars.'

'And, as you might not know, your treatment has begun to cause a shit storm on E Street.' Trickster was referring to the CIA headquarters in downtown Washington.

Cauldwell laughed and raised his handcuffed wrists. 'Don't tell me someone thinks your methods are inhumane.'

'Don't be absurd.' In Trickster's accent, absurd rhymed with avoid and Lloyd. 'No, the boss doesn't understand why our methods aren't working. He wants results. So now we're going to try something different.' Trickster picked up a tab impregnated with a pinkish substance. 'You're going to lick this.'

'Maybe I'm not.'

'Don't be so negative – you might even enjoy the experience.'

Cauldwell considered his options – and their options too. The Dirty Trickster might call in the guard and they would try to force him to lick the tab, or Trickster would give up on him and recommend he be dispatched to 3–16 in Honduras. In a way, the

Honduran option appealed to Cauldwell. The gang down there might kill him, but the chances for escape in Honduras might be greater. Or would they? Cauldwell often thought about escaping, but the physical security of his safe house was impenetrable. No windows, concrete floors and no sharp objects to dig or gouge a tunnel. On the other hand, there were few guards. Cauldwell suspected that his detention was a very sensitive secret and there weren't many goons who had the necessary security clearances to look after him.

Cauldwell sighed and looked at the tab. 'What is it?'

'Lick it and see.'

'Is that what you tell your girlfriends?'

'I usually don't have to tell them.'

Cauldwell looked at Trickster and laughed. The chemist was exactly the sort of creepy white male that American girls laughed at. Trickster was a stereotype square who wore white polyester shirts with a breast pocket full of leaking ballpoint pens. He fitted the image so perfectly that Cauldwell wondered if he was putting it on. 'What are their names?'

'Whose names?'

'The girls.'

Trickster smiled. 'I'm not telling. A true gentleman never tells. I thought you knew that, Mr Cauldwell.'

'I do. That's why I've never talked.'

'Touché.' The Trickster winked. 'So your silence involves the reputation of a lady.'

'Lots of ladies.'

'That's not what I've heard.'

'Maybe you've been misinformed.'

'We have psychological tests for that too. Maybe I should recommend you for some.'

'Lick it and see.'

The Trickster frowned, but didn't say anything.

'Have I touched a raw nerve?'

'No, I'm not like you. But I'm not one to cast stones – I don't judge others.' The Trickster paused. 'Maybe if you cooperated, we could arrange some fun. You must be very lonely.'

Cauldwell smiled. 'Arrange the fun first.'

The Trickster lifted the tabs. 'This will be fun. Try one.'

Cauldwell looked at the pink impregnated tabs. There were a dozen of them. 'You only want me to take one?'

'That should be enough.'

Cauldwell glanced at the two-way mirror that ran along the wall nearest them. He wondered how many pairs of eyes were watching. He realised that the observers were not just looking at him, but evaluating Trickster's performance too. Cauldwell also noticed that Trickster had a red panic button to summon the guard. He usually kept the button in his hand – as if, despite their almost polite banter, he expected Cauldwell to go berserk at any moment. Cauldwell wondered if the observers behind the mirror had panic buttons too. Were psychologists such fragile creatures that they couldn't pile in to deal with someone going berserk? But why, then, would Trickster need one too?

'All right,' said Cauldwell, 'I will try one of those tabs. In return, is there any chance you can undo my handcuffs? I've got a pain in my shoulder and my back itches.'

'No, Mr Cauldwell. You're a dangerous man.'

Trickster put the panic button down to pass the drug tray. Cauldwell was ready to pounce. His question had been a ruse. He had managed to pick the lock on his handcuffs with the paperclip he had found on the car seat. The cuffs were off and less than a second later Trickster was lying on his back with Cauldwell's arm pressed hard into his windpipe.

'I know you can't talk, but you can answer my questions by tapping with your hand. One tap means no; two taps means yes. If you answer any of my questions incorrectly I'm going to kill you. Let's start. Is there anyone watching behind the mirror?'

Trickster tapped once.

'Good. Is there only one guard?'

He tapped twice.

'Is that drug an hallucinogenic?'

There were two taps.

'Wonderful – the American Dream at last. Do you know how many doses would prove fatal?'

He tapped once.

'Okay, make an educated guess. How many do you think would prove fatal – or permanently reduce someone to a starry-eyed imbecile?'

'Trickster tapped five times.'

'Good. We might put your theory to the test.' Cauldwell felt Trickster squirm in fear. 'But it might be quicker to joke you, I mean choke you, to death. It looks like the drug's affected me already. But, on the other hand, I might let you live if you help me. Will you help me?'

He tapped twice.

'I think you're lying.' Cauldwell tightened his grip and Trickster's eyes began to bulge and his face to turn purple. 'Can I really trust you to help me?'

The Trickster gave two desperate taps.

'I'm still not completely convinced. I think your consciousness needs to be altered before I can begin to trust you. You are a member of the US military industrial complex – and the life-denying mentality that goes with your job needs changing.' Cauldwell reached for the pink tabs. 'I'm not sure what these are. But I once heard a drunken military attaché talking about the battlefield of the future. He said the atom bomb would soon be obsolete. That one day we would simply spray the battlefield with pink clouds of gentle gas. The gas wouldn't burn the lungs or harm the bodies of our enemies, but would turn their minds from war to universal love. They would throw down their arms and embrace us with bouquets of flowers. And they would still be shouting, "Peace brothers. We love you America!" as we scythed them down with machine-gun and artillery fire.' Cauldwell laughed. 'You ought to get them to dig their graves first. But I was wondering,' he waved the pink tabs, 'if these have anything to do with that peace gas.' Cauldwell peeled one off as he squeezed Trickster's neck tighter. 'Open your mouth and stick your tongue out; we'll soon find out.'

Trickster did as he was told. His tongue looked almost as purple as his face.

Cauldwell pressed the tab on to Trickster's tongue until the pink liquid was absorbed. He then peeled off another tab and did the same again. And then another. Trickster's eyes were dilated with terror. Cauldwell could see that he was counting. He peeled off a fourth tab and pressed it on to Trickster's tongue. 'This is like shoving de-worm tablets down a cat's throat, but I don't suppose you can sick these up.' Cauldwell peeled off a fifth tab and looked closely at Trickster. 'You said that you think five of these might kill the patient. Shall we see if you were right?'

Despite Cauldwell's iron grip, Trickster managed to shake his head.

'Okay, doctor, we'll respect your clinical judgement and stop at four. You wouldn't be much use to me dead.' Cauldwell looked at the wall clock and relaxed his grip a fraction. 'Let's see how long they will take.' He kept a grip on Trickster while he lay beside him like a wrestler too tired to pin his opponent. Cauldwell watched the hypnotic jerk of the second hand as it did its rounds. After ten minutes, he began to feel the stiffness ebb out of Trickster's body. It was as if his former soul had migrated. After another five minutes, Trickster had gone completely limp. Cauldwell wondered if even four tabs had been enough to prove fatal. He relaxed his grip.

Trickster touched his throat and sat up. His glasses were half falling off because one of the arms had been broken when Cauldwell attacked him. Trickster tried to balance his glasses on his nose, but his specs wouldn't stay in place. He finally laughed and threw his glasses away. He stared at Cauldwell with bare dilated eyes and said, 'Who killed the lamb chops?'

'I don't know.'

Trickster sat silent for a few seconds staring into space before he began to cry. 'We all killed the lamb chops – and we're washed in the blood of the lamb.' He wiped his tears and pointed at the wall mirror. 'What's he doing there?'

'Who?'

'Gaspar Lorca. What's he doing down there with the peaches and the housewives?'

Cauldwell began to see a pattern. 'Who else is there?'

'There are whores in the avocados and priests in the tomatoes.'

'Is Shaman there?'

'I don't know, but he must be there somewhere.'

'He wrote the poem.'

'They've all gone. The supermarket must have closed.'

'Do you know Shaman?'

Trickster nodded his head. He was crying again and tears were dripping off his chin. 'Yes. I love him.' Trickster suddenly looked up at Cauldwell with supplication. 'But I love you too.'

'Does Shaman know what you do?'

'Yes, but he is so full of love he doesn't condemn me.' The tears were pouring now. 'I need to love you more and love myself more and repent:

I can't stand the terror in my mind.
When will America…
Go fuck yourself, America, with your bomb.'

'Who really is Shaman?'

'Shaman is a poet priest. He has the power to forgive me, to forgive America.' Trickster tilted his head and looked at Cauldwell with a crazed smile and eyes that were dilated to gaping black pools. The LSD seemed to have kicked his hallucinations to an even higher level. 'I know you. You're the one.'

'Which one?'

'The one *"who preached Communism on Utopia Parkway with your penis in your hand while the air-raid sirens of the Apocalypse wailed you down…"'*

'Yes,' smiled Cauldwell, 'that is me and I've been sent to help you.'

Trickster's face was now ecstatic. 'Then it was you *"who made carnal gaps in infinite Space through ranks of fellating seraphim and trapped the archangel of longing…"'*

'Yes, that is me and you are the archangel of longing.'

'Can we fly?'

'Yes, but we need help. We need the help of the guardian angel.'

Trickster looked puzzled. 'Who?'

'The one outside the door.'

'Anderson. He is one who has not discovered love. He is a nightmare of alcohol and guns.'

'Invite him to join us, but keep it simple. Just say: come in please, we're finished. We'll tell him about love and liberation later.'

There was an internal telephone on the wall next to the door. Cauldwell readied himself on the opposite side of the door as Trickster picked up the phone. 'Hello, Mr Anderson, flap your wings. We are ready to fly.' Cauldwell winced. It wasn't the message that he had suggested, but Anderson probably knew that Trickster was a weirdo at the best of times.

Cauldwell listened as Anderson punched the key code into the lock on the other side of the door. There was a heavy click as the handle turned and the lock mechanism released. Anderson was a big brute in a grey flannel suit. Cauldwell tried to kick his legs out from under him, but Anderson didn't go down. He then tried a karate chop to the neck, but it was like hitting an oak trunk. Meanwhile, Anderson was reaching for his gun. Cauldwell launched his shoulder into the side of Anderson's knee and he wobbled. He grabbed his opposite ankle with both hands and Anderson sprawled sideways, but he now had his gun in his hand. Cauldwell swung behind him. Anderson was back up on his knees. Caudwell whipped a leg around Anderson's ample midriff and trapped him in a figure-four leg scissors. He then pushed forward so Anderson landed on all fours. Cauldwell squeezed his gut hard with his leg scissors then used his fists to knock out Anderson's arms from beneath him. Anderson landed on his face with all of Cauldwell's weight on top of him. He still had his gun in his hand, but was incapable of aiming it at his assailant. Cauldwell put his forearm across Anderson's throat and began to squeeze. 'I haven't decided yet whether or not I'm going to kill you. If you let go of the gun, the decision might be in your favour.'

Anderson let the gun go. It was a Smith & Wesson .38, classic Americana. Cauldwell picked up the revolver with his left hand. 'I was lying. Maybe I'm going to kill you after all, but I'm not going to shoot you. That would be too messy.' Cauldwell tightened his stranglehold and Anderson whimpered. 'Perhaps it would be better to liberate you than to kill you.'

Trickster was smiling benignly at the proceedings. 'But death, Mr Anderson, is a form of liberation too. Except it isn't death; it's entering an endless cycle of reincarnation.'

Cauldwell glanced up at Trickster. 'Can you get the tabs, please?'

Mine eyes have seen the glory of the coming of the Lord:
He is trampling out the vintage where the grapes of wrath are
*   stored;*
He hath loosed the fateful lightning of His terrible swift sword:
His truth is marching on.

Cauldwell had given Anderson five tabs instead of four owing to his larger body size. The result was truly bizarre. Anderson had never read the poetry of Shaman – or any other poet. His cultural references were sparse, but he knew almost every American patriotic anthem by heart. His favourite was the 'Battle Hymn of the Republic'. He sang it in a deep bass except for the chorus, which he rendered in a squeaky falsetto:

Glory, glory, hallelujah!
Glory, glory, hallelujah!
Glory, glory, hallelujah!
His truth is marching on.

By now, both Anderson and the Trickster had taken off all their clothes. Love was in the air. But Anderson was also in the marching mood. Cauldwell found it so delightfully bizarre that he almost didn't want to leave the testing suite. When Anderson wasn't singing, he was shouting parade ground commands: *Present ARMS; Order ARMS; Right step MARCH.* It took some doing to get Trickster to shoulder an imaginary rifle, but he seemed to get some satisfaction from shouting out lines of Shaman poetry as a counterpoint to Anderson's Battle Hymn as they marched around the room in step: '*Them Communists and them Russians and them Chinese are marching too...*'

Which only got Anderson to sing louder: '*I have seen Him in the watch-fires of a hundred circling camps, They have builded Him an altar in the evening dews and damps; I can read His righteous sentence by the dim and flaring lamps...*'

And then Trickster: '*Them Russians want to pee in our swimming pools. Them Chinamens wants to eat our wives...*'

Cauldwell wondered if Trickster was leaving Ginsberg and had become fixated on Anderson. Despite the militaristic words of the hymn, Anderson was now a man of peace for whom marching and patriotic singing had become an expression of love. Each time he marched past Cauldwell he covered him in sloppy kisses.

Cauldwell had kept the door wedged open with a chair. The last thing he wanted was to be locked in with those two when the effects of the drug had worn off and help was on the way. He had Anderson's gun in his pocket; he would need it later. But more importantly, he had found car keys and identity documents in Anderson's discarded clothing. In fact, thought Cauldwell, he would need Anderson's clothes as well.

Anderson shouted, '*Mark time, MARCH*' from the other side of the room and saluted Cauldwell with: '*I have read a fiery gospel writ in burnished rows of steel: "As ye deal with my contemners, so with you my grace shall deal..."*'

Trickster counterpointed: '*The hordes of Asia are rising against us. They want to boil our chickens.*'

And at that moment, Cauldwell picked up the bundle of clothes and left the testing suite, locking the door behind him.

»»»»»

Cauldwell had changed into Anderson's suit, but any guard who looked closely at Anderson's ID photo would quickly realise it didn't belong to Cauldwell. That's where the gun might come in handy. Cauldwell strapped on Anderson's watch. He had lifted that too – convincing the tripping guard that he needed 'to free himself from time to be truly liberated'.

Even though it was past midnight the outside air was still hot and sticky. Tidewater Maryland has a relentless climate. The night was loud with crickets and Cauldwell could smell the dank rotting perfume of swamp and festering river. It reminded him of his own home in the deeper South. But other than the smells and the sounds, the place was completely unnatural. The squat windowless building he had just left was bathed in high-voltage lights. There wasn't a blade of grass, only hard-baked tarmac. It was a high-security facility ringed by a chain-link fence topped with two rolls of concertina barbed wire. The only way out was through a heavy steel gate with spikes on the top that was locked. There wasn't a guard hut, only an MP slumped on a folding chair with a transistor radio pressed to his ear.

Cauldwell got in Anderson's car, a four-door Chevrolet Bel Air sedan painted the olive drab of a US Army staff car. He immediately realised he was going to have to find a different car. This one, in its military livery, was too easy to spot. As soon as he started the engine, the MP got up and began to unlock the gate. Cauldwell took Anderson's revolver out of his pocket and laid it on the seat beside him. He then opened the glove compartment to see if there were any maps. It was full of maps. He found one of Maryland and put it on top of the pistol. He then placed Anderson's ID on the dashboard in front of the wheel, face down because the resemblance was so poor. He drove towards the gate at walking pace. The gate was now wide open and the MP was yawning into a white-gloved hand. The armpits of his khaki uniform were dark with sweat.

As Cauldwell approached the gate, the MP flourished a clipboard with a ballpoint pen tied to it on a string. Shit, thought Cauldwell; you have to sign in and out. On the other hand, you might only need the ID to get into the compound. He decided to pretend he was used to the procedure. Cauldwell stopped the car. He could see immediately that the MP was looking at him with suspicion. He had to act first.

The MP bent down to look in the open window on the driver's side. His right hand was resting on his .45 Colt automatic.

Cauldwell looked him straight in the eye and added a layer of redneck bubba to his usual Southern accent. 'I ain't signed in. Mr Anderson said I didn't have to, but he was in a hurry and I think he was wrong. I don't think you were on duty then.'

The MP's eyes had lost a bit of their flintiness and he was shaking his head. 'Was it this afternoon?'

'That's right.'

'That was Hicks on duty. He's gonna get his ass in a sling for that.'

'I don't think it was Hicks's fault. Anderson was late and didn't want to get his own ass in a sling.' Cauldwell picked up the ID, 'Look, he left his ID in the car.' He then moved the map and picked up Anderson's revolver. 'And he left his fuckin' gun in the car too.'

'Sheeeit. Poor Hicks.'

'Can I have a look at the log?'

The MP handed over the clipboard. The transistor radio was still on and tuned in to WCAO. The music was a twangy guitar piece called 'Rebel Rouser'.

'Turn it up,' Cauldwell requested. 'I like Duane Eddy.'

While the MP fiddled with the transistor, Cauldwell flipped through the pages of the log. 'Look, Anderson was the last one signed in yesterday. There's a space after his name. I can sign myself in now and no one will get in trouble.'

The MP squinted and scratched his head for a few seconds, then said. 'Yeah, why don't you?'

Cauldwell smiled in anticipation at the shit storm he was about to unleash. He was sure that the MP wouldn't recognise the name, but the CIA and FBI certainly would. He wrote the actual forename as well as the nickname and made sure both signatures – signing in and signing out – were easily legible: Harold 'Kim' Philby. He handed the clipboard back.

The MP saluted smartly as Cauldwell drove off. 'Have a good evening, Mr Philby.'

»»»»»

Cauldwell estimated it would only be a couple of hours at most before they discovered his escape. What he needed was another vehicle. When he left the base, he turned left on Route 40, a four-lane highway heading south. There was an overgrown grass strip separating the lanes and diners and gas stations on both sides of the road. A few of the diners were still open. Even more than another vehicle, he decided he needed something to eat and some strong coffee too. The road was straight and he saw the neon beacon warm and welcoming in the distance.

THE NEW IDEAL DINER. The red lights were two feet tall. There was a smaller sign in ordinary white lights underneath: 'Buses and Trucks Welcome!' Despite the glaring lights, the New Ideal looked deserted. The parking lot was empty except for a big Mack Series B truck in the dark shadows of the pine forest that ran up to the back of the diner.

Cauldwell parked the staff car between the truck and the trees so that it wouldn't be seen from the road. He then tucked the Smith & Wesson into his waistband. He was ready for a late supper, but strolled around the Mack Series B before he went into the diner. Mack trucks were one of the few things he liked about his native America. The massive machines had an iconic beauty of raw power set in the stern frown of pure American Gothic body design. The engine wasn't tucked in tight to the cab, but thrust forward with snarling chrome teeth. Cauldwell walked back to have a look at the trailer. It was a massive eighteen-wheeler with canvas lashed over the top. He climbed up on one of the rear wheels and reached under the taut canvas. His hand came out with a fist full of coarse gravel. It was almost certainly aggregate for the new interstate highway. Cauldwell smiled and flung the gravel at the stolen car. An idea was forming.

The only customer in the diner was the truck driver who was polishing off a meal of ribs and grits. He looked pretty happy with himself. He had a shiny round face framed by curls of greasy black hair. Cauldwell knew that type – the class clown who almost always ended up operating heavy equipment in later life. Not just Mack trucks, but bulldozers, pile drivers, rock pulverisers, stump crushers and hydraulic hoe rams. They were the laughing imps who ripped up the wilderness for the industrial warlocks.

When the waitress came to clear the truck driver's table, she stood well away. The driver sat with eyes closed in seeming postprandial somnolence, a toothpick hanging from his moist lips. Meanwhile a surreptitious hand snaked out from beneath the table towards the waitress's thigh. She was more than ready and gave the hand a sharp slap that echoed like a gunshot. 'You behave yourself, Scooter.'

'I was just stretching.'

'No, you were not.'

'Ah, come on, Trixie. You like a bit of affection.'

'You shush. And not when strangers are watching.'

'I wasn't watching,' said Cauldwell.

Trixie gave him a sharp look over her pink butterfly spectacles. 'Don't you encourage him.'

Cauldwell winked at Scooter. 'Got far to go tonight?'

'I ain't going nowhere tonight. I'm sleeping in the cab.' He looked at the waitress. 'Unless'n I get a better offer.'

'Not with your manners,' said Trixie.

'I just been shot down,' said Scooter reaching for his hip flask, 'in flames.'

Trixie was now standing over Cauldwell with an order pad. 'What can I get you, hon?'

'I'll have chicken and sweet potato fries – and plenty of strong coffee.'

Meanwhile, Scooter took another slug from his hip flask and looked over at Cauldwell. 'Would you like some snakebite medicine?'

'That's really nice of you, but I got a lot of driving and want to stay awake.'

'How far you going?'

'Raleigh.'

'You won't get there this morning.'

'I know.'

Scooter got up to pay his bill and whispered something to Trixie that got him another slap. When he was gone, Trixie poured Cauldwell his first coffee. Her eyes had dark rings under them. She was dead tired.

'How long have you been working?' asked Cauldwell.

'Fourteen hours. I'm moonlighting; this is my second job.'

'Why do you do it?'

'So we don't lose our house.' Trixie turned to bring Cauldwell his food.

When he finished eating Cauldwell paid with money he had found in Anderson's wallet. He gave Trixie a five-dollar bill and told her to keep the change, an enormous tip of two dollars. She said, 'Thanks, hon.' And watched him closely as he left. She knew something was up, but she wasn't going to say anything to the cops. Trixie was loyal to kindness; it was too rare.

»»»»»

There were loud snores coming through the open windows of the Mack truck. Cauldwell climbed the steps on the driver's side of the cab and looked in. Scooter was curled up on the sleeping ledge next to the rear window behind a mosquito screen. He was under a light blanket. Cauldwell opened the door and slid in behind the steering wheel. Scooter was still snoring. Cauldwell took the Smith & Wesson from his waistband and prodded the barrel into Scooter's back. 'Wake up.'

Scooter turned and looked at Cauldwell. 'What you doing in here?'

Cauldwell aimed the gun between Scooter's eyes and he stared at the barrel with his mouth open. After a few seconds Scooter whispered, 'Hey, hey, stay calm.'

'I am calm.'

'Hey, listen, you want my truck? You can have her.'

'We're gonna go for a ride.'

'Sure thing. Where d'ya wanna go?'

'Thanks for being so cooperative, Scooter. You're doing just fine.'

'Whatever you want, mister. You don't need to pull that trigger. I'm your man.'

Cauldwell suddenly felt a wave of suspicion. Scooter seemed too practised. 'Has this ever happened to you before?'

'Only once. Had a truckload of National Bohemian stolen. They just wanted the beer. Police found the truck and trailer two days later.'

'Well, this time it's going to be different because I need your help. Sit there.'

Scooter climbed down into the seat next to the passenger door. He was wearing boxer shorts and a singlet.

'Now, I want you to put these on. Just to make sure you behave yourself.' Cauldwell passed over the handcuffs he had been wearing earlier. 'You don't need a key to lock them, just snap them shut.'

Scooter looked nervous. This obviously hadn't been part of his previous experience of having a truck hijacked.

'Put one cuff on your left wrist and then snap the other one on the metal door handle by your right hip.'

Scooter did as he was told. With his left arm locked across his body he felt helpless. He looked at Cauldwell with fear in his eyes for the first time. 'Are you some kind of a sexual pervert?'

'Yes, I am, Scooter. But not tonight and not with you. You're just not pretty enough. So there ain't gonna be any Carolina Chili Dog or Rusty Trombone or Dirty Sanchez – or whatever other games they play in your neck of the woods. I want you for another reason.'

'What's that?'

'I want you to teach me how to drive this thing.' Cauldwell touched a long black stick next to the driver's seat and then a green one alongside it. 'Which one of these is the gear shift?'

'Both of them are. These trucks have got two gear boxes: one four speed and the other five speed.'

'So you got twenty gears, five in each range.'

'But only fourteen of 'em work.'

'Anything else I should know?'

'The steering wheel goes around nine times from lock to lock.'

'Is that a problem?'

'It sure the fuck is on a winding mountain road when you're shifting gears – and one more thing, be gentle with the brakes. They're airbrakes. You stomp on 'em hard, you go through the windshield. This truck can stop on a dime.'

'Let's roll then.'

»»»»»

It wasn't raining, but Cauldwell still had to use the windshield wipers and the window washer to clear the bug splat. Summer night driving in lowland Maryland, and the rest of the tidewater South, means ploughing through hordes of insects attracted to the lights. Some of the bugs are the size of humming birds. Without the wipers and the wash, a windshield is soon covered in a custard-coloured layer of splattered moth, lightning bug, dragonfly and stink bug.

Cauldwell liked the feeling of power as he drove the big Mack truck down Route 40. He imagined he was a comet smashing through the earth's atmosphere as the winged creatures of the night hurled themselves in tribute into the light and engine roar. 'How about some music, Scooter?'

'That'd be nice.'

Cauldwell leaned forward and turned on the radio. He twisted the tuning knob through loud static. The first clear station was a radio preacher: '...*living in the last days of the world. It won't be long before we are in heaven. But we are going to sweat through days of fire and heat before then. The armies are gathering for Armageddon. And meanwhile you must prepare yourself for cleansing. Remember that everybody stinks but Jesus. Keep your mortal body fresh with roll-on underarm deodorant from Congregational Care Products...*' Cauldwell continued tuning until he got a music station. It was Johnny Cash singing 'The Wreck of the Old 97', an engine driver's song about a legendary train wreck. The airbrakes failed at the beginning of a three-mile downhill grade, but the driver stuck with 'Old 97'. In a way, it was a love song.

Cauldwell noticed out of the corner of his eye that Scooter was nodding and tapping to the music. The hijacked driver was a cool customer. 'Do you know this song?' asked Cauldwell.

'Yearp, it's about a train down my way that went off a trestle bridge. The driver and crew were killed, but they repaired the locomotive to run again.' Scooter sang the final verse about how the driver was found with his hand welded to the throttle by the scalding steam. There were tears in his eyes.

Cauldwell smiled and stared at the night road ahead. A deer stared back at the oncoming truck, momentarily frozen by fear in the headlight glare. Cauldwell pressed the horn hard and it gave a doomsday blast like a runaway train. The deer leapt and sprang into the pine forest. 'You know something, Scooter? There are worse ways to go.'

'You mean the deer?'

'No, I mean us and this truck. Are there any trestle bridges near here?'

'No, there ain't. And don't talk like that.'

'Where's the nearest one?'

'In Pennsylvania.'

'Very far?'

'Too far – and it's been shut for repairs.'

'I bet we can bang this rig right through the barriers.'

'Listen, if you want to do that you don't need to take me with you.'

'Hmm, I don't suppose I do, but I like you, Scooter, and I want to turn you into a legend.'

'I don't want to be a legend.'

'Why not?'

'Because I want to stay alive.'

'Are you afraid of dying?'

'Yes, I am.'

'You're not an existentialist, are you?'

'No, I was christened a Baptist, but I don't go to church – it's a load of nonsense.'

'That's good, you're halfway there.'

'Where?'

'To being free. Why are you laughing?'

'Because I'm handcuffed to my fucking truck with an insane fucker driving it who wants to kill us both.'

'Good. That laughter is a sign of freedom. If you were really afraid of dying you would be crying and pleading with me.'

'But since you're crazy it wouldn't make any difference.'

'You got a point there. Your fear of death is normal, but it's not out of proportion to the situation I've put you in.'

'How can I get out of this situation?'

'By not being afraid of what happens. Fear of death takes

away your freedom to participate fully in life. Fear of death and fear of life are related. What do you think?'

Scooter stared at the empty night highway deep in thought. 'When I was in Korea, a lot of the other guys were scared shitless. The Red Chinee just kept coming and coming.'

'Were you scared?'

'Not as much as some, but a lot more scared than the really brave guys. The ones who just didn't seem to give a damn. And you know something?'

'What?'

'Some of those brave guys were really happy – enjoying every minute of it. So were they ... what d'you call 'em?'

'Existentialists. Some of them could have been, but some of them were probably psychopaths – really crazy.'

'Which one are you?'

'I don't know.'

Another Johnny Cash came on the radio. It was about the strange characters you meet in prison, particularly Cell Block 10.

'You ever been in jail?' asked Scooter.

'I just got out. What about you?'

'Not yet.'

'I hope, Scooter, you never have to do time. Have you a road map?'

'Don't need one. It's all in my head.'

'Where's the nearest airport with big planes?'

'Friendship.'

'What do you mean?'

'Friendship, that's the name of the airport.'

'How far?'

'About twenty miles.'

'How much money you got in the truck, Scooter?'

'I got about ten bucks in my wallet, but there's over a hundred dollars in the glove compartment. It's not my money, it belongs to the trucking company and it's for fuel and tolls and such.'

'Good. You can keep your ten dollars.'

'If you want to go to Friendship Airport you got to go through

Baltimore and then get on Ritchie Highway towards Glen Burnie.'

'Good, you direct me.'

The next part of the route was a depressing traverse through black slum housing and white trailer parks with smouldering mattresses and feral dogs. But Cauldwell knew there were other Americas too, the churchy conformity of the white picket fence suburbs and the non-conformity of Greenwich Village. You paid your money, if you had any, and took your choice.

The entrance to the airport was a two-lane road. As soon as they turned on to it, Cauldwell stopped the truck. 'This is as far as you go, Scooter. I'll walk the rest of the way.' The airport terminal and control tower glittered a thousand yards away. 'But first we're going to do something naughty.'

Scooter looked concerned and shrank into himself.

'Don't worry, Scooter; it's not what you think. But your bosses aren't going to like it. And that reminds me.' Cauldwell opened the glove compartment and found the company money, crisp five- and ten-dollar bills. There was also a roll of receipts that Scooter had bound with a rubber band. 'Maybe I should give you a receipt too.' Cauldwell found a piece of scrap paper and scribbled a note: '*Received with thanks, Commandante X. Hasta la victoria siempre!*' He wanted to leave as confusing a trail as possible.

Scooter had begun to look relieved. 'Can I ask you a favour?'

'Sure.'

'You'll find some empty bottles under your seat. Can you pass me one?'

Cauldwell found an empty milk bottle and handed it over.

'Thanks. I'm dying for a piss.' Scooter peed into the bottle and tossed it out the window. 'That's how truck drivers go to the bathroom. Saves a lot of time.'

'Now for the really naughty bit, Scooter. How do you operate the hydraulics?'

'Which ones?'

'The ones connected to the trailer. It's a dumper, isn't it?'

'Sure is. Got two arms that will almost push it vertical.'

'How do you engage it?'

'It's that red knob to the left of the steering wheel. You got to push it right into the slot and then pull it straight out.'

Cauldwell had already noticed that there were steep drainage culverts on either side of the road. It meant that any cop car summoned to the air terminal would not be able to get around the blocked roadway. He smiled as he pulled the knob and heard the wheeze as the hydraulic arms started to push upwards. First there was a ripping sound as the load tore through the canvas cover and then a prolonged hissing whoosh as eighty tons of aggregate poured out of the trailer.

Scooter smiled and slapped his knee, 'Sheee…it!'

'You like that?'

'Always wanted to do it myself – preferably on the car of someone who was hitting on one of my poontang.'

'Maybe next time.' Cauldwell tucked the Smith & Wesson into his waistband. He was still wearing the grey suit that had been abandoned by Anderson the guard when he began his LSD frolic. It was loose around the waist, but otherwise not a bad fit. He also had Trickster's black Samsonite briefcase as a prop. He looked into the rearview mirror to adjust the tie. Cauldwell wanted to look respectable. It wasn't perfect, but he would pass. He opened the door and began to climb out of the cab.

'Been nice knowing you, Scooter. Look after yourself.'

Cauldwell walked quickly towards the terminal lights. He wasn't sure what he was going to do. He wasn't even sure that he would be alive in a few hours' time. He felt lightheaded, but the important thing was he was free. He approached the terminal through a crescent-shaped parking lot that was almost empty. Cauldwell suspected most of the cars belonged to airport employees because it was two o'clock in the morning. There didn't seem to be a lot of flight activity, but he needed to make a move quickly for they would be after him soon.

As Cauldwell walked into the terminal lobby his footsteps echoed on the shining linoleum floor. There were large glass cabinets displaying models of aircraft, a virtual history of aviation exhibition. It was obviously a place to bring your children for a weekend treat. But the only people in the lobby now were an elderly threesome sitting on a bench behind a pillar. Cauldwell felt a shiver; he was in death's waiting room. The impression was reinforced by a huge clock on the main ceiling beam that was held aloft by two winged angels, one of whom was hooded. Cauldwell smiled. The architect who chose that image for an airport departure lounge full of nervous flyers was either very stupid or had a great sense of humour.

The only check-in counter with a member of staff was Eastern Air Lines. The departure board announced a five a.m. flight to Miami. A woman in her twenties was seated at the counter flicking through paperwork and ticking lists. She looked thoroughly bored and made no effort to hide it. Cauldwell approached. She didn't look up.

'Excuse me,' he said. 'I'd like a ticket for the Miami flight.'

The woman frowned, but didn't make eye contact. She finally said something, but Cauldwell couldn't make out the words. She had a Baltimore accent that played havoc with vowels and wiped out consonants. He finally realised she was asking his name and how he was going to pay. Cauldwell began to sign in under the name of D. Hammett; an homage to the crime writer Dashiell Hammett, a Baltimore man who was blacklisted and sent to prison for his left-wing politics. Cauldwell then remembered that Hammett was still living and didn't want his homage to get the writer in even more trouble. He grabbed the form and crumpled it up.

'I got that wrong,' he said.

The woman shook her head. 'Don't you even know your own name?' She was suddenly alert and suspicious. 'Have you got any ID?'

Cauldwell took out Anderson's wallet, hoping there was something without a photo. There was. 'Driver's licence okay?'

'That's fine,' she gave it a cursory glance.

Cauldwell signed in under Anderson's name and paid in the truck company's cash. He glanced at the clock. There was still two and a half hours till boarding. Far too much time to wait around. There were stairs leading to the 'Friendship Observation

Deck'. The airport was definitely a good place for a kids' day out. Cauldwell decided to have a look.

When he got to the observation deck, Cauldwell momentarily froze. He wasn't alone. But he quickly realised that the upright figures were telescopes that cost you a nickel per view. The deck was completely deserted – as was most of the airfield. Friendship wasn't a busy place. And the flat countryside around the airport was sparsely populated too. To the east he could see moving green lights heading south and moving red lights heading north. It was the Chesapeake Bay. Maybe, thought Cauldwell, he should have plotted his escape by ship; maybe he would have been luckier than last time.

Cauldwell heard noises and commotion from the airfield below. He looked over the railing. A four-engine Douglas DC-7 was illuminated in a glare of lights as a tanker filled her fuel tanks. Presumably it was the plane for the Miami flight. The oily tang of avgas tainted the night air. A man dressed in a pilot's uniform was talking to one of the workmen. Cauldwell touched the revolver in his waistband. Maybe buying the ticket had been a waste of the truck company's money. It was a long drop to the tarmac, at least fifty feet. Cauldwell began to look around for a drainpipe. There weren't any he could reach. Meanwhile, something else caught his eye – the flashing lights of a police convoy from the main highway. Someone must have discovered the blocked approach road and talked to Scooter. It had been a stupid stunt. He looked back towards the plane. The fuelling was finished and the empty hose was curling on to a reel at the back of the tanker. The police were closing in. Cauldwell calculated that, even with the blocked road, they would be at the terminal in twenty minutes. He looked again at the pilot. He was still chatting to the tanker driver and seemed blissfully unaware of the unfolding drama.

Cauldwell started running. If necessary, he would shoot his way through the airport lobby to the plane. He wondered if locked doors would be a problem. As he hurled himself down the stairs he noticed a reeled fire hose on the wall. It was his best chance. He grabbed the fire hose and ran back up to the observation deck. The reel squeaked as it spun; there was plenty of length. When Cauldwell got back to the deck he dropped the nozzle over the side opposite the plane. It was a dark unlit area. He kept feeding the hose over the side until it reached the end of the reel and stopped, then he climbed over the deck railing and slid down the hose.

Cauldwell tried to compose himself and think clearly as he ran through the dark spaces in the shadow of the observation deck. When he came into the light on the opposite side, the tanker driver was waving to the pilot and climbing back into the truck. Cauldwell continued running straight at the astonished pilot, and waved Anderson's Security Service ID over his head. The sound of police sirens began to echo in the still air.

The pilot was wearing a short-sleeved white shirt and a tie with the Eastern Air Lines logo. 'What's going on?'

'Security alert.' Cauldwell was breathless. 'There's been a prison escape and the prisoners are holed up in the terminal lobby. We need to move this plane away as quickly as possible.'

'What about the rest of my crew?'

'There isn't time. Let's go.'

The pilot turned and started walking towards the portable stairs that led to a door behind the cockpit.

'Hurry up.'

As soon as they got into the cockpit, the radio was loud with urgent calls from the control tower. Cauldwell whipped out his pistol and pushed it into the back of the pilot's head. 'Do exactly what I say or I'm going to blow your fucking brains out.'

'Is this some sort of joke?'

Cauldwell laughed. 'Depends on your sense of humour. But I'm desperate. Taxi away from this terminal now and take off.' The sirens were so near that their wail permeated the cockpit. Cauldwell's biggest fear was that a cop might get the bright idea of shooting out the aircraft's tyres.

'It's going to be difficult without any crew,' said the pilot.

Cauldwell grabbed him by the collar. 'Get moving or you're dead. You don't need anyone else. I can do the navigating if you're too stupid to follow the coast south to Miami.'

The pilot nodded and smiled. He appeared, in his own way, as resigned to fate as Scooter. He began to flick switches and push buttons. Meanwhile the radio cackled with urgent calls from the control tower: 'Delta Charlie Seven Zero, do you read me?'

'Don't answer,' said Cauldwell, 'and don't send a Morse message by pressing the push-to-talk button either.'

The pilot removed his left thumb from the transmit button which was attached to the control yoke.

'Turn off the radio. We need to take off.'

The pilot pulled back one of the clunky throttle levers and the outboard starboard engine of the Douglas DC-7 began to cough into life. The propeller finally began to turn slowly, like a man awakening with a bad hangover. The other three engines were woken up in turn, but these were quick and alert like young puppies eager for walkies. The pilot took his right foot off the brake pedal and controlled the rudder with his left. The plane began to taxi towards the main runway, but was tracked by a beam of searchlight.

'Turn the radio back on and tell them to kill that light.'

The pilot flicked a green switch. 'Friendship Control, this is Delta Charlie Seven Zero. My passenger requests that you douse the searchlight – and he means business.'

The light continued to gleam. Cauldwell whispered something in the pilot's ear.

'My passenger says that if you don't douse that light and that if any cops get near the plane or try to shoot out the tyres he's going to blow my fucking brains out and then he's going to kill himself. And believe me, he means it.'

The searchlight extinguished. The DC-7 moved into takeoff position at the end of the main runway.

'So are we going to Miami?' asked the pilot.

'Head south, I'll tell you later.'

The pilot pulled back all four throttle levers and the engines revved to a high, deafening pitch. A minute later the lights of Maryland were diminishing into twinkling dots. Meanwhile, Cauldwell opened the navigator's case and was looking at the aeronautical charts. He took out the three WACs – the World Aeronautical Charts – for the southern East Coast of the USA.

'What do we need for landing?'

'You need a Terminal Procedure Plate – we call them "flips".'

Cauldwell rummaged through the case and found what he wanted. 'I've changed my mind. We're not going to Miami. Head towards Columbus, Georgia.'

'Can you work out a bearing? Use a set of parallel rules. They're in the case.'

Cauldwell found the rules and began to juggle them with the chart, which was on his knees, and the pistol.'

'It would be easier if you used the chart table in the navigation cubby.'

'No, thanks. I want to keep an eye on you. Why don't you put us on automatic pilot and do it yourself?'

'Wait till we get to cruising height.'

'How did you learn to fly?'

'In the Army Air Force during the war. I started off flying B-24 Liberators and moved on to the B-29 Stratofortress.'

'Pacific or Europe?'

'Both.' Something inside the pilot seemed to wince, as if there was a sudden pain. 'It's a beautiful night, full moon. I hope you're not a werewolf.'

Cauldwell raised the pistol. 'Pay attention to the flying.'

'I used to be a werewolf, but I'm all right *noooooooooow*.'

'Have you been drinking?'

'No, but I wouldn't mind a drink.'

Cauldwell noticed there were tears running down the pilot's cheeks. 'Stay calm. Do as I say and you'll be all right.'

'Maybe I just don't fucking care. Why don't you just blow my brains out and fly the fucking plane yourself?'

Cauldwell stared out the cockpit window at the moon-bright sky. The cold light was so clear and dazzling he had to squint. Ultimately, you could only control people if they had a fear of dying. Cauldwell wasn't afraid of dying either, but his death would mean the end of the project. It wasn't just about ideology. He wanted his life to be a work of art that changed things – and that self-vision was not even half-finished. This alone made him cautious – and was the only thing that gave his life meaning. Meanwhile the pilot's tears had turned into convulsive weeping.

'What's wrong?'

'My kids loved werewolf jokes. "Mommy, Mommy; what's a werewolf? Shut up and comb your face." But Honey didn't think they were funny. She didn't have a sense of humour at all – she was a greedy, deceitful bitch.'

Cauldwell shook his head. Of all the planes in the world, he had to hijack one with a pilot going through an emotional crisis. He decided to humour him. 'Your wife's name was Honey? Really?'

'Oddly, yes.'

'I assume you're no longer together.'

'She went off with a rich bastard – a businessman in California.'

'And took the kids?'

'Yeah.' The pilot wiped his tears with the back of his hand. 'I wasn't the world's greatest husband – and the drink was a problem.'

'Would you like a drink?'

'I'm dying for one. You'll find the liquor behind the curtain on the port side. There's also a refrigerator with cold beer and ice cubes.'

Cauldwell drew back a blue curtain. There were trays full of liquor miniatures, soft drinks, nuts and crisps set into a trolley. 'What can I get you?'

'Scotch.'

'On the rocks?'

'Just plain.'

'Ring-a-ding okay?'

'What's that?'

'Bell's – that's what they call it in England.'

'You been there?'

Cauldwell smiled. 'Yeah.'

'I flew B-24s out of a base in Suffolk.'

Cauldwell handed the pilot a miniature of Bell's. He twisted the top off and downed the whisky in one.

'I liked Suffolk. Quiet, soft-spoken people – and a gentle

landscape. Kind of ramshackle. You'd see old men ploughing with horses.'

Cauldwell's memories of Suffolk were otherwise. Sex, murder, sex.

The pilot looked at his empty miniature. 'Where did that go?'

'You want another drink?'

'It would calm my nerves.'

Cauldwell passed another whisky miniature to the pilot and opened one for himself. He wondered if he had somehow ingested the LSD that had begun the evening. Things were more than surreal, more than mad. There was something about the night that made him suspicious. It was as if events were being guided by a hidden hand.

'We're at cruising height now.' The pilot tossed back the miniature and eased back the throttle levers. 'You still haven't told me where you want to go.'

'Lawson Field. It's a military airbase in Georgia.'

'I know. Lawson serves Fort Benning.'

'That's right.'

'I'd better put her on autopilot and plot the waypoints.'

While the pilot plotted a course on the chart, Cauldwell scooped up a handful of miniatures from the drinks trolley. If it wasn't LSD, it must have been the danger and adrenaline that made him reckless. The pilot looked up from the chart and sat upright.

'What's wrong?'

'We've got company on our starboard wing.'

Cauldwell looked out the cockpit window and saw the red navigation light of another plane and a sleek silver fuselage gleaming in the moonlight. It was so close that he could clearly make out the profile of the pilot.

'It's a US Air Force Super Sabre. I wish it wasn't so close. A couple of months ago one of them collided with a DC-7 – which is what this girl is – and killed sixty people.'

'Can you raise him on the radio?'

'Shouldn't be difficult.' The pilot flicked a switch and the cockpit was filled with crackling static. 'I'll tell you a trade secret.

If you ever want to talk to another pilot, simply go to 123.45 – easy to remember, one, two, three, four…' The pilot found the air to air frequency and the static vanished. 'What should I say?'

Cauldwell slipped on the co-pilot's radio headset and mike. 'I'll do the talking.'

'Sure.'

Cauldwell thumbed the push-to-talk. 'Super Sabre, this is the DC-7 on your port wing. Can you hear me?'

'Delta Charlie 7. This is Sierra Sierra. I read you five by.'

'Talk plain English, you military asshole.'

'Say again, over.'

'Cut the fucking radio procedure and listen. The pilot is still alive and is my hostage. If my instructions are not followed, he is going to die – and a lot of others too.'

'Can you confirm the status of the pilot?'

Cauldwell passed the mike over.

'Air Force Super Sabre. This is Captain Blanchard of Eastern Flight one zero six seven. Everything that my passenger says is correct.'

'What is your date of birth and your mother's maiden name?'

'21 December 1920 – obviously the darkest day of the year and too near Christmas to get separate presents – and my mom was Marie Aubin.'

'Can you spell the last name?'

'Alpha, uniform, bravo, india, november.'

'I've copied that and will be listening on this frequency.'

Cauldwell turned to Blanchard; the pilot now had a name. 'Let me handle this.' He spoke into his mike. 'Listen up, Super Sabre, and report this to your honchos. If I think there is any risk of an assault on this plane I will immediately kill Captain Blanchard and as many of the attackers as possible before killing myself. On the other hand, if my instructions are followed, no one will be hurt.' Cauldwell removed his thumb from the transmit button. 'Turn the radio off.'

Blanchard flicked a switch and downed another whisky.

'Can you land this thing when you're drunk?'

'Better than when I'm sober. I'm hungry. Are you?'

'No, I dined late.'

'If you look in the refrigerator, you'll find some chicken salad sandwiches with mayonnaise. Could you pass me one?'

'I'm not your fucking servant, Blanchard.'

'Yeah, but we're in this together. If those shitheads – like the jet jock in that Super Sabre – don't do what you say, we're both going to die.'

'How long is it to Lawson Field?'

'About two hours.'

Cauldwell went to the refrigerator, but kept his pistol pointed. He paused for a few seconds and stared at the back of Blanchard's head. He wondered if it might be a good idea to kill Blanchard and try to land the plane himself somewhere safe. It couldn't be that difficult. Cauldwell had already figured out which controls governed which functions. And the instruments – altimeter, attitude indicator and vertical speed – were pretty straightforward too. It might be a rough landing, but Cauldwell was sure he could do it. He lifted the pistol and aimed it at the back of the pilot's head. And then he remembered the werewolf jokes Blanchard used to tell his kids. He hated the sentimentality. By the standards of the US military industrial complex, Blanchard was a damaged human resource. That's probably why they threw him out of the Air Force and he ended up being a glorified bus driver.

'If I don't have to kill you,' said Cauldwell slowly, 'what are you going to do with the rest of your life?'

'I don't know. But I expect it will start with one fucking long FBI investigation.'

'What are you going to tell them?'

Blanchard laughed. 'Anything you fucking want me to tell them.'

Cauldwell suddenly had an idea and lowered the gun. 'Who knows? You might have your uses.' He handed a mayonnaise chicken sandwich to Blanchard. Meanwhile, the Super Sabre kept sentinel.

'I wouldn't mind a beer with this sandwich.'

'Don't push it, Blanchard.'

'A can of Pabst Blue Ribbon would be fine.'

Cauldwell found a tin opener, punched two holes in the Pabst can and handed it to Blanchard.

'Thanks.'

'Have you ever flown a plane when you were drunk before?'

'Only in the Pacific towards the end of the war. The first time was the second big firebomb raid on Tokyo. Can you imagine five hundred Superfortresses packed with incendiaries? LeMay ordered us to fly low, 5,000 feet, to cause the maximum damage. You could smell the burning flesh from the cockpit. They say we killed a hundred thousand, but it must have been more.'

Cauldwell opened himself a beer. He'd commanded a PT boat in the Pacific in the same squadron as Jack Kennedy. He'd liked the excitement – and had got a medal for rescuing downed airmen. 'Did you think it was all necessary?'

'I don't know. But I suspect the atom bombs were pointless; the poor bastards were already beaten. No air force, no navy. They were gonna starve to death if the war went on.'

'Do you know any of the guys who flew the A planes?'

Blanchard laughed and slapped his thigh. 'Shit, I was one of them.'

'Is this the booze talking? Are you making it up?'

'Well, I exaggerate. I didn't fly the plane that dropped the fucking thing. I was flying *Necessary Evil*. Our job was to take photos of the A blast. Our call sign was Dimples Nine One.' Blanchard shook his head slowly. 'I can't understand why we had all these stupid joke names – and naked ladies and cartoons painted on the fuselages. It wasn't a fucking joke. Can you pass me another scotch?'

Cauldwell handed him another and opened himself one too. 'Did you see the bomb go off?'

'No one saw the bomb go off – not the actual fireball. We had to wear black Polaroid goggles – and even with them, I was blinded. And when the shock wave hit us, it was like exploding flak. I thought we were done for.' Blanchard gave a nervous laugh. 'The only thing we saw afterwards was a massive mushroom cloud. You can't imagine how huge the thing was. So unreal. It towered above our plane like a giant genie. It was eight miles high and we could still see it when we were 300 miles away.'

Cauldwell knew that dropping As on Japan was America's darkest moment. It had led to the suicide of a diplomat friend.

The pilot tipped back his head and emptied the rest of the scotch down his throat. 'These tiny bottles are stupid.'

'Have you got a drink problem?'

'My wife thought so. And, to be fair to Honey, she wasn't always wrong about me. I suppose I really started knocking the stuff back just after the war. It wasn't the war that drove me to drink; it was the assholes in charge.'

'Who was the biggest asshole?'

'There were a lot to choose from. Curtis LeMay, Tom Power – but Paul Tibbets probably takes the cake.'

Cauldwell stared into the starry night. Tibbets had been the pilot of *Enola Gay*, the plane that had dropped the bomb on Hiroshima. 'Why was Tibbets an asshole?'

'Because of his arrogant attitude – and his total lack of any remorse or realisation.'

'How well did you know him?'

'Well enough. We were based on Tinian Island. A crappy place, just south of Saipan – all air strips and barracks. They had built special pits for the As on the end of the North Field. Two days before Hiroshima, I remember Tibbets staring into the pit with his hands on his hips. I walked up to him and said, "You looking for your Little Boy" – that was the code name for the bomb. Tibbets didn't answer. Then I said, "Why did you name it that, Paul?"' Blanchard stopped talking and stared into the night.

'What did Tibbets answer?'

'He didn't say a thing. He just turned and walked away as if I wasn't there.'

'Why?'

'Because the worst thing you can do to an asshole is show them that they are an asshole. Tibbets named the plane after his mother, Enola Gay, when the bomb it was carrying, a bomb that was going to kill a hundred thousand civilians, was code-named Little Boy. If Tibbets had admitted the names were a sick

Freudian joke, he wouldn't have been an asshole, just an evil bastard.'

Cauldwell looked out the window at the Super Sabre, a supersonic phallus that was only two wing lengths away. 'How do you know about Freud?'

'My ex-wife made me go to a shrink as a condition of our staying together. We were living in LA at the time and there certainly wasn't any shortage of shrinks. I hated California – too much sunshine and too many rich guys fucking my wife. I think my shrink might have fucked her too.'

'Are you bitter?'

'No, of course not.'

'The drink helps.'

'Yeah.'

The problem with America, thought Cauldwell, was its unreality. But you had to remember that it was all real, that you had really hijacked an airliner with an alcoholic pilot who had witnessed Hiroshima – and undergone psychoanalysis to save a failed marriage. To pinch himself, and make sure he wasn't hallucinating, Cauldwell looked at Blanchard and asked, 'Did you say your shrink was a Freudian?'

'That's right.'

'What did he make of you?'

'He thought I was normal.'

'What did he mean by that?'

'He said that I'd resolved my pre-school oedipal conflicts.'

Cauldwell smiled and passed the pilot another whisky. 'Lucky you.'

'Not that lucky; I sublimated those desires by becoming an obsessive compulsive.'

'Oops.'

'And that I expected my wife to accept my wanting everything planned out and predictable. When I came back from the war, I couldn't deal with any more uncertainty – like being blown to smithereens. I just wanted her to be there when I came home. I didn't give a fuck about meals on the table or the top on the toothpaste tube; I just wanted a home and a woman who was there.' Blanchard began to shake and rock back and forth.

'Are you laughing or crying?'

'I'm laughing.'

'What's so funny?'

'It's not just funny; it's fucking hilarious. I can't stand uncertainty – and look at me now! My wife ran off, I live in a shitty rented apartment – and I'm piloting a hijacked plane with a lunatic waving a gun in my face.'

'Calm down.'

'Okay, I'm calm.'

Cauldwell looked across Blanchard out the port window. The sky was a snowy blanket of moon-silvered cumulus clouds. There were now two Super Sabres. One of them peeled off to the left and was soon out of sight. The new fighter seemed more agitated than the one it had replaced. It flew in close to the airliner. Cauldwell could make out the pilot's head as a dark silhouette that seemed to be staring directly at him. The Super Sabre then accelerated forward. The fighter rocked its wings and flashed its navigation lights.

'Should I make radio contact?' asked Blanchard.

'What do those signals mean?'

'It means we've been intercepted and we're supposed to follow him.'

'Get him on the radio.'

Blanchard flicked a switch. 'Super Sabre, this is Delta Charlie Seven.'

The radio cackled and a sardonic voice answered. 'Thank you for making contact, Charlie Seven. How are you?'

'I'm fine.'

'Good, I'm glad you're fine and everything is going to be all right.'

Blanchard closed his eyes and shook his head.

'Delta Charlie, can you still read me?'

'Loud and clear, Super Sabre.'

'Good. Here's what we're gonna do. I'm going to turn off to port and you're gonna follow me. Won't be long before we're having a nice breakfast of bacon and eggs with plenty of hot coffee. And your passenger can join us. No hard feelings.'

Blanchard depressed the push-to-talk button, but before he could say anything he felt the barrel of a gun pressing into his temple. Blanchard looked at Cauldwell and whispered, 'Okay,' then spoke into the mike: 'Sorry to disappoint you, Super Sabre, but it don't look like that's going to happen.'

'Gosh-darn, that's a bit of a shame. I was so looking forward to meeting you fellas.'

Blanchard grimaced. 'Maybe some other time.'

'There ain't gonna be no other time,' said the Super Sabre pilot. 'If you don't follow me to a safe landing place, I'm going to have to hose you down with 20mm.'

Blanchard looked at Cauldwell. 'I think he means it.'

'I think he's full of bullshit.'

The Super Sabre pilot continued to transmit. 'I'm so close I can see you guys talking. I can't read lips, but I bet you're saying that I'm just bluffing. Well, Captain Blanchard, I can tell you why I'm not bluffing. Your passenger is one high-value dude that a lot of people in very high places would rather see dead than free. Now, if that means your death too, Captain Blanchard, so be it. You've done honourable military war service and you know that sometimes soldiers and airmen get sacrificed for the greater good. And if you can't manage to follow me and land this plane you're going to be one of them.'

Cauldwell turned to Blanchard. 'Is your thumb off the transmit button?'

'Yeah.'

'Good, because I don't want him to hear this…' Cauldwell was interrupted by an enormous bang that shook the airliner as if it were a mouse in a cat's jaws. 'What the fuck was that?'

'The Super Sabre must have throttled back and broke the sound barrier. Look, there he goes peeling off to port.'

'Keep calm, he's trying to scare us.'

'I think he's serious. Those guys are crazy.' Blanchard pointed out the window. 'Look, he's coming back. I swear he's going to do it.'

The sky in front of the DC-7 was suddenly ripped apart by red tracer rounds, as if the night had been slashed by a switchblade.

Blanchard let out a low whistle. 'Shit, that was close.'

'Where's he gone?'

'He had to bank away. Those Super Sabres are so fast they can overtake their own canon fire and shoot themselves down. But he'll be back.'

Cauldwell suddenly felt very sober. The tiredness and alcohol had been replaced by cold clarity. 'Descend now. Fly as low as you can.'

Blanchard pushed the yoke forward and the DC-7 nosedived into the clouds. 'Your ears are going to pop.' The pilot smiled. 'I've never had this much fun with one of these buses. Hope the wings don't come off. But if they don't, he isn't going to find us if he's on visual.'

'But what if he gets a radar fix from the ground?'

'That's the problem.'

'That's why I don't want to stay in the clouds. Listen.'

'What?'

'You can hear him.'

'There's two of them,' said Blanchard.

The radio cackled. 'Delta Charlie, Delta Charlie. You're being a very bad boy. We've got your position fixed. Listen, brother, you've just bought yourself a one-way ticket on the night train to the big adios. You can still get off that train, but it's your last chance.'

Cauldwell thumbed his transmit button. 'Fuck you, asshole.'

Blanchard smiled bleakly. 'You like this, don't you?'

Cauldwell suddenly felt high and elated again on the adrenaline buzz. 'When we get out of the cloud cover, head for the busiest road you can find – a big four-lane highway if you can see one. And try to fly over populated areas.'

Blanchard nodded. 'Okay.'

'He won't risk shooting us down if there are witnesses and the possibility of casualties on the ground.'

'Unless he's really stupid.'

Cauldwell shrugged. 'You never know.'

The DC-7 came out of the clouds. The countryside below was rural and hilly. There were few specks of light – aside from a line of headlights on a straight road that cut a swathe through sleeping farms and woods.

'We're lucky,' said Blanchard. 'That's Route 29.'

Cauldwell knew it well. It was the main road that connected the University of Virginia at Charlottesville to almost every place else. It was a fatal road strewn with the bodies of young affluent Southern men who, drunk on bourbon and youth, sped between university, the women's colleges at Sweet Briar and Lynchburg, and the numerous drinking dens with black jazz bands and more cheap liquor. Quentin's car was one of the wrecks, but he hadn't been in it at the time – he had lent it to a friend. The state cops found Quentin's Pontiac Master Six Coupe, a snazzy car with footboards and windshield sunshades, in a tangle of honeysuckle above the Rockfish River. The University of Virginia had been an odd experience. On one level, a four-year course in drinking, wearing fine clothes and wrecking cars. On another level, it had been a voyage of secret discovery.

'I'm going to level off at about 1,500 feet,' said Blanchard. 'It means we're going to make a helluva racket and wake people up.'

'Good.'

'We're not just an airplane, we're a redneck alarm clock. And pretty soon there will be some big places coming up: Greensboro, Charlotte, Atlanta.'

Cauldwell looked out the window. There was a Super Sabre on each wing, but their intent seemed less hostile.

'Are you disappointed?' asked Blanchard.

'Why should I be?'

'That you're not going to die – at least right now. We've all got a death wish.'

'Freud again?'

'That's right. My shrink said that my drinking was a death wish; I get drunk because it simulates the oblivion of death.'

'Why are you talking about this now?'

'Because I'm both frightened and exhilarated – and then afterwards, if I'm still alive, I'll be exhausted and depressed.'

The drone of the plane engines was soporific. Cauldwell was afraid he was going to fall asleep. He needed to keep talking. 'You were telling me about Hiroshima and Paul Tibbets. Did Tibbets have a death wish?'

'No, he was Oedipus; he wanted to screw his mom. I worked all this out when I did my therapy. In fact, the psych and I spent more time talking about Tibbets than about my marriage – and it was more interesting.'

'But you didn't like him.'

'I hated him – just like Tibbets hated his dad. Did you know that Tibbets had been at medical school?'

'How do you know this?'

'He used to talk about himself; big ego, thought he was impor-tant. In any case, Daddy Tibbets wanted Paul to be a doctor – something useful. But Paul was bored with all the studying. He wanted to become a fighter pilot instead. Daddy didn't like it, tried to stop him.'

'He told you that.'

'No, my shrink did.'

'How did he know?'

'He knew because it all fitted in. You see Enola Gay didn't love Daddy Tibbets – who was also named Paul. She loved her little boy, who was the real Paul, the one she really needed. So she said, "Don't worry, son. It's okay. Drop out of med school and become a pilot. You can't let Daddy Paul push you around – you've got to be a real man. I want you to be a real man."'

'You think she actually said that, or even words like that?'

'The actual words don't matter; maybe no words were said at all. The important thing is the emotional and sexual truth which is hidden in the subconscious.'

Cauldwell stared straight ahead as they plunged further into the night. They were flying so low that the land flew past them like a dark treadmill speeding out of control. He imagined the airliner as a herald angel waking up a sleeping South of shotguns and bibles. He had been cradled in that South and had tasted both its poison and its beauty. And Cauldwell knew this was his last visit. Someone else could redeem the place; it was beyond him and his generation. The mental chains were too stiff and fast. Cauldwell closed his eyes. It felt like he was falling down a long shaft and it was taking forever. Then he really was falling, forward and out of his seat. He woke with a start when his gun hit the cockpit deck with a metallic thud.

'Hey, careful. You don't want that thing going off. Are you all right?'

'Yeah.' Cauldwell shook himself into consciousness and wondered why Blanchard hadn't reached for the gun when he nodded off. Maybe he thought it was too risky. Cauldwell realised he needed to stay alert and awake; he needed to keep talking. 'Tell me about the subconscious.'

'According to my psych, it's a place where we store thoughts and desires that we can't consciously admit we have because they are taboo or unacceptable – like boning your sister or your mom.'

'So Colonel Tibbets wouldn't consciously admit he wanted to kill his father and have sex with his mother.'

'No, that's why he joined the Army Air Corps instead of knocking his dad's brains out with an axe. It's called "transference". It's socially unacceptable to kill your father so Tibbets became a bomber pilot and killed the enemy instead.'

'He transferred his murderous impulses to people he didn't even know.'

'Exactly. But Tibbets gave the game away when he named the Hiroshima Stratofortress Enola Gay. Talk about obvious – but he was too stupid to see it. He put himself in Enola – right in her cockpit – and made her fly like Daddy never could. He rode her hard and good and, of course, he got her pregnant – with nearly five tons of bouncing Little Boy.'

'So the bomb became his own self.'

'Exactly. Little Boy went in her and then came out of her. The biggest bang in the history of the world and a hundred and forty thousand dead. Daddy killed not once, but 140,000 times. And Mama loved it all; she was so proud. Paul showed her that he was a real man.' Blanchard paused. 'I need a drink.'

Cauldwell handed him another miniature of bourbon from the hospitality trolley. 'Death wish?'

'Yeah.'

'One of the Super Sabres has gone.' But just as he said that, there was an ear-piercing wail and whooshing sound. 'He's back.'

'He's diving at us. Hoping he can force us to crash without canon fire. Ignore them; I haven't finished telling you about Tibbets and Oedipus.'

'Go on.'

'Tibbets wasn't Oedipus, not by a long way. When Oedipus found out the truth of what he had done he gouged out his eyes. But Paul Tibbets was no hero and not very bright; he still has his eyes but will never see the truth.'

'But you're okay; you resolved your pre-school oedipal conflicts.'

Blanchard nodded. 'Completely. I get on fine with my mom. She may be a simple, uneducated Québécoise who still works at the sawmill, but she ain't stupid. When I came back from the Pacific she wanted me to say the rosary with her and to go to confession to get absolution for what I had done. But I told her there wasn't no absolution. And then later, she said something interesting.' Blanchard finished his bourbon.

'So what did *maman* say?'

'She said that the Americans would never have dropped those As on the Germans because they were white. But it was okay to drop them on the Japanese because they were the yellow peril, a different race. That's what America does now. Look what happened in Korea – I bet they're going to go after the Chinese next. If you got yellow skin, watch out.'

Cauldwell smiled bleakly.

'I'm feeling a bit drunk. Do you want to drive?'

'You're doing fine. How long have we got to Lawson Field?'

'About forty minutes.'

Cauldwell began to calculate the risk. He knew how bureaucracies worked and he doubted that the people who ordered the Super Sabres to shoot them down would have the time to organise an ambush at Lawson Field.

'Do you want to land at Lawson?'

'It depends if we can contact them by radio.'

'I'll look up the frequency, but you'll have to drive. We're too low for autopilot. Pull the yoke back if you see a mountain ahead.'

Cauldwell put the pistol on his lap and grabbed the yoke wheel with both hands. He tilted it slightly and felt the aircraft respond. The yoke had a solid feel that was firm and smooth. Controlling the power of the enormous mechanical beast thrilled him. It was a night of driving lessons that had begun with an eight-cylinder Chevrolet Bel Air sedan and went on to a Mack truck – and now Cauldwell was at the controls of a four-engine DC-7 airliner. He smiled. He was living the dream of the All-American Boy – and it had its wonder.

Meanwhile Blanchard was leafing through a ring binder titled 'Terminal Procedure Plates'. 'Found Lawson. We get them on 67. Should I try to raise them?'

'Yeah.'

Blanchard selected the frequency and pressed the transmit button. 'Lawson Air Control, Lawson Air Control, this is Eastern Flight Delta Charlie Seven. We're pretty famous. I bet you've heard of us. Over.'

There was a long pause. When the transmission came there were muffled background voices talking to each other. One said, 'Who the fuck is that?' Another said, 'Hey, hey, listen up, Chip. That's that fucking plane that was hijacked.' There was another silence, then the first voice again: 'Delta Charlie, this is Lawson Tower. How can we help you?'

Cauldwell looked at Blanchard. 'You drive. I'll handle this.' Cauldwell thumbed the transmit button. 'Lawson Tower, you can help us. I want two T-10 parachutes with reserves. And I want the guy that delivers them to be stark hairy-ass naked. Your man will approach the rear door of the aircraft completely alone. The parachutes will be attached to a rope with a grappling hook. Your man will toss the hook up into the open door so we can retrieve the chutes. If there's any funny business the pilot gets a bullet in the head. If you do what I say, no one gets hurt.'

'Delta Charlie, I'll have to get back to you. Complying with your request is above my pay grade.' The radio went silent.

'What now?' said Blanchard.

'Do you know those saltwater lagoons behind the outer banks of Cape Hatteras?'

'Sure.'

'The water's nice and calm. You could ditch there and we'd swim ashore.' Cauldwell knew the marshes were an impenetrable wilderness. He reckoned he could escape. It was the iconic landscape of convicts on the run chased by baying bloodhounds.

'I'd better sober up then. Water landings are tricky.'

The radio came to life again. 'Delta Charlie, this is Commanding Officer Fort Benning. I understand that you want to land here and pick up a couple of chutes.'

'That is correct. I don't know whether or not you've been briefed on the situation, General, but I assure you that I am a loyal American citizen and government official who is being pursued by rogue elements of the intelligence services.'

'That sounds highly unlikely.'

'I appreciate, General, why you may think that. But I recommend you contact the following colleagues to ask for verification.' Cauldwell reeled off a list of the highest-ranking army officers he knew. They weren't completely gormless, but he was pretty sure none of them knew about his arrest and incarceration. The US intelligence services were famously at war with each other. The CIA not only despised the FBI and withheld information from them, but also treated military officers with contempt, as if they were dim-witted spear carriers. 'Try Courtlandt Schuyler, CofS SHAPE, George Decker, CINCUNC/COMUSFK, Bruce Clarke, CG CONARC – or the Commanding Officer of the Berlin Brigade.' Even if the Fort Benning CO was unable to contact his fellow generals, Cauldwell was certain that the list of names would convince him that he was dealing with an establishment insider.

When the general's voice spoke again, there was a note of curious caution in his voice. 'What is your ETA at Lawson?'

'In about thirty minutes, approximately 0530 EST.'

'Delta Charlie, stand by for instructions.'

Blanchard looked at Cauldwell. 'What do you think he's going to do?'

'He's going to do what all senior officers do; he's going to cover his ass.'

The radio cackled back to life. 'Delta Charlie, if you are cleared for landing, you will see a green flare. You will pick up your chutes – and leave asap. There will be no further radio contact.'

Cauldwell thumbed the transmit button. 'Much appreciated, General. Message understood, end of transmission.'

Blanchard smiled. 'He's covering his ass. He doesn't know what this is about and he doesn't want to step on his dick in a dark room.'

Cauldwell looked out the window. 'The Super Sabres are still there.'

'They've shut up too; they don't know what to do.'

The two men sat in silence as the plane continued southwards. The bright lights of Atlanta were replaced by darker, more sparsely populated countryside. Cauldwell remembered it as an arid wasteland of red clay, slash pine and scrub oak. It wasn't a land that produced happy people with open minds. There were more bright lights as the plane approached Columbus, a mean garrison town with brothels of the last resort, which serviced you before they sent you to a foreign war to get your balls shot off.

The first sign of Fort Benning was the red warning lights marking the 250-foot parachute towers where trainee paratroopers made their first jumps to practise their landing falls. As Blanchard began to circle the airfield there were the faintest hints of pre-dawn nautical twilight on the eastern horizon, like a young girl stirring from a deep sleep.

'No flare,' said Blanchard. 'Do you think they've changed their mind?'

'If so, it's back to Cape Hatteras.'

Blanchard continued his landing pattern for two more orbits. He made one low pass to check the airfield windsock to ensure he landed into the wind. Meanwhile there was the distant drone of the Super Sabres. There were circling far above.

'Shit,' breathed Blanchard. 'What do you think is happening?'

'Maybe the general's reconsidering his options?'

'There's an ambulance on the runway.'

Cauldwell looked out the window and saw a red cross painted on the roof of an army truck. 'Or a hearse for picking up bodies.'

'Thanks.'

Blanchard continued in holding pattern and made another circuit of the airfield.

'There it is.'

'What?'

'The green flare.'

'Okay. Let's go in.'

Blanchard reached for a lever with a wheel on the end, as if intended to remind the dimmest pilot it was for raising or lowering the landing gear. He pressed it into the 'down' position. There was a loud sound of air turbulence, which increased as Blanchard levered the ground spoilers into position. 'Can you help?'

'What do you want?'

Blanchard pointed to the dial. 'Read the altitude out loud.'

'Four hundred, three hundred...'

'Shit, there's a cross wind.' Blanchard swung the yoke and the plane yawed.

'...two hundred, one hundred, eighty, sixty...

Blanchard pulled back the throttle levers.

'...forty, twenty, zero.' The plane hit the ground on one side with an enormous bump and bounced before it finally landed on all its wheels. The brakes were screaming.

'Is that the best you can do?'

'You try landing one of these when you're drunk as a skunk.'

'Get into take-off position. I don't want to hang around.'

'Good idea.'

Blanchard taxied the DC-7 so that it was facing back the way they had landed.

'Okay, now I want you to open the rear door and leave it open. And remember, I'm going to be right behind you with a gun aimed at your medulla oblongata.'

Blanchard unharnessed himself and stumbled into the passenger cabin.

'You are pissed, aren't you?'

'I've been worse. Follow me, the door's on the port side.'

Cauldwell didn't think Blanchard was going to try to escape, but he still followed him closely down the aisle. When Blanchard got to the door, he pushed down a lever and the door sprang open. Cool, fresh morning air flowed into the plane.

'Remember,' said Cauldwell, 'I want this door to stay open after we take off.'

'Sure. It fixes on to a hook on the fuselage.' Blanchard leaned forward to push the door. It swung wildly and clanged as it engaged the fuselage hook. Blanchard lurched forward and was about to fall out of the aircraft when Cauldwell reached out and grabbed a fistful of his jacket. The jacket began to tear off, but Cauldwell quickly got his hand on the pilot's belt and yanked him back into the plane.

'Thanks, I lost my balance. Phew, it's a long drop.'

'Stand away from the door.' Cauldwell could see the truck with the red cross on the roof approaching the plane. He aimed his pistol at the front of the truck. He wanted to show that he meant business. If they weren't going to follow his instructions, he hoped that a bullet in the radiator would convince the driver to stop. The truck came closer and closer. He turned to Blanchard, 'Rev up the engines, we're going.'

But before Blanchard could move, the truck flashed its lights and came to a stop. It was about forty yards away.

'You want me to take off?' said Blanchard.

'Wait. Let's see what happens.'

The passenger-side door of the truck opened. Cauldwell grabbed Blanchard by the collar and forced him into the open doorway with his pistol clearly pointing at his temple.

'Oh fuck,' moaned Blanchard.

'Stop whining, you're not dead yet.'

A man came out of the truck. He was about fifty years old and had a crewcut. He was stark naked with heavy jowls and a big hairy gut.

Blanchard nodded 'He's a sergeant major; only sergeant majors look like that.'

'Don't relax, it isn't over.' Cauldwell watched the naked man pad to the back of the truck. His gut was firm and didn't wobble, but his enormous testicles swayed back and forth like hairy pendulums. There was the sound of a door creaking open and voices. Cauldwell tensed up and aimed his pistol at the truck. He was afraid he had been tricked and a squad of armed soldiers was about to rush the plane with guns blazing.

'What's happening?' asked Blanchard.

'Shhh.'

The naked man appeared around the side of the truck bearing two large green bundles. There was a rope looped around his shoulders and a grappling hook hanging over his chest. He continued to the plane, half carrying, half dragging the bundles. When the naked man got to just below the open door, he stopped and looked up.

'Here's your T-10s,' he called.

'*Mucho gracias, compa,*' replied Cauldwell. He shifted to English, but spoke with an Hispanic accent. 'Throw the hook up here through the open door. Then go back to the truck and drive away. Go far from the plane.'

The naked man threw the hook into the open door and then walked back to the truck. As soon as the truck sped away, Cauldwell turned to Blanchard. 'Pull the chutes into the plane.'

When the parachutes were safe inside, Cauldwell made a quick inspection. 'Looks good: static lines, reserves. Let's get out of here.'

Cauldwell stowed one chute in the aisle and took the other into the cockpit. As he prepared for take-off, Blanchard asked, 'Why were you talking in a funny accent?'

'Mind your own business. Just get flying.'

The pre-dawn twilight was creeping over the horizon. The control tower was a prickly silhouette against the lightening sky. The only other aircraft on the field were two lumpy C-119s with their distinctive twin tails. They weren't big planes, only two engines, and were used for training paratroopers.

'I hope,' said Blanchard pulling back all four throttles, 'that we've got enough room to take off. This is the only runway and it ain't that long. I bet this baby is the biggest plane that's ever landed here.'

'Why didn't you tell me that before?'

'Because I was too drunk to read the details on the Terminal Procedure Plate.'

Cauldwell looked at the nearest C-119. For a second he wondered if he should grab one of those, but it was too late because Blanchard was already racing down the runway. The chain-link fence at the end of the runway was looming larger and larger as the engines roared. Beyond the fence was a river and on the other side of the river a typical Deep South wasteland wilderness of stunted pine and scrub oak nearly famished by the dry red clay. There was a horrendous metallic ripping sound as the plane left the ground.

'What was that?'

Blanchard smiled. 'We just took out the perimeter fence with our landing wheels. No problem – unless you want to land again.'

As the plane gained height Cauldwell looked at the fast-receding land beneath. The Chattahoochee River hugged the airfield like a sleeping lover. They were now over Alabama, Cauldwell's home state. It was a relentless land; a land of irredeemable division. He came from a white tribe that just didn't know how to change. A few from that tribe, like himself, did change. They weren't rejected or treated unkindly in any way, just stared at with incomprehension as if they were awkward calves who refused to suckle.

'Where do we go now?' asked Blanchard. He had to shout because of the noise of air turbulence from the open door in the main cabin.

'Keep heading south, down the length of Florida and on to the Keys.'

Blanchard glanced at Cauldwell. His lap was full of green silk material. 'What are you doing?'

'Checking the chute.' Cauldwell pulled the rest of the parachute out of its deployment bag. He examined every panel and then he checked all the suspension lines and risers.

'Is it okay?'

'It's fine, so I'm sure the other one will be fine too. If they were going to sabotage them, they'd have done both.' Cauldwell gathered up the parachute and piled it into the corridor behind the cockpit.

'Aren't you going to repack it?'

'Why should I? Won't need it.'

'What about me?'

'Don't worry. You'll be fine as long as you don't do anything stupid.' Cauldwell looked out the window. 'Have you seen the Super Sabres?'

'I think they ran out of gas.'

'Nevertheless, keep flying low. Over main roads and built-up areas.'

'You still haven't told me where we're going.'

'Have you got charts of the Caribbean?'

'Yeah, they're in the box.'

'Pass them over.'

Cauldwell went through the charts. He found one of Honduras and remembered how Trickster had threatened to send him there. He had a vision of himself sedated in a crate being unloaded from a US Air Force plane, but one without identification markings, at a jungle airstrip. Even though the US pilots and air crew were top secret cleared hush-hush operatives, they would have had no idea that the crate contained a human being. They probably would have thought they were handing over secret communications equipment to Honduran military intelligence. Such a rendition was the CIA's trump card. It was the ultimate way to deal with suspects who wouldn't talk. It also left no fingerprints leading back to a US agency. The horror interrogations that followed would have been unspeakable. And yet Honduras was still under civilian rule. Cauldwell wondered if Morales, a liberal reformer, was still hanging on as president while the men in the barracks seethed and plotted against him. Cauldwell put the chart back; it wasn't the place to go. The next chart looked prettier: a sea-wrapped land with mountains.

The ground below was now turning brilliant green in the dawn twilight. The rivers and sea were turning discernibly blue.

They were over Florida and had company again. It was a silver-coloured jet that was smaller and looked more nimble than the Super Sabres.

'The navy's now on the case,' said Blanchard.

Cauldwell looked up from the chart. The new plane was so close that he could read the pilot's name stencilled under the cockpit: LCDR F.P. Tecumseh. For a few seconds Cauldwell thought his tiredness had made him hallucinate, but when he blinked the name was still Tecumseh, the legendary Shawnee warrior chief who had died fighting the Americans.

'It's an A4 Skyhawk,' said Blanchard, 'probably from the navy base at Pensacola.'

Cauldwell continued to stare at the fighter jet. The name of the plane's pilot demonstrated the relentless power of the American empire more than the 20mm canon in its wings. With a name like that, the pilot was almost certainly of Shawnee ancestry, probably a distant descendant of the great chief who had allied with the British in a desperate attempt to save their tribal lands from American expansion. But now he too had fallen into the great melting pot of cultural obliteration.

Blanchard yawned as the sun rose above the sea. 'You still haven't told me where we're heading now.'

'It's a place called La Plata in the Sierra Maestra.' Cauldwell handed over the chart.

'Cuba.' Blanchard studied the chart for a second. 'There's no landing field.'

'We don't need one. What do you think the parachutes are for?'

'Well, you'd better repack the one you unpacked.'

'Don't need it.'

Blanchard felt a chill run down his spine. He looked out the window at Lieutenant Commander Tecumseh. The navy pilot seemed an enigma in silhouette. No radio contact, no visual signals. He was flying almost in formation.

'We'll be over Miami in fifteen minutes,' said Blanchard, 'so if you change your mind and decide to land there you'd better let me know now.'

'Why should we do that?'

'Because we might not have enough fuel left to get to the Sierra Maestra.'

'Might not or won't have enough?'

'It's going to be close – and forget about following the Florida Keys, that's a detour. We'll need to fly over the Bahamas.'

Cauldwell peered at the sapphire morning sea. It looked inviting. He tried to think of another piece of land where he could be sure of a safe welcome. There was none. 'Keep on course for the Sierra Maestra. We'll take our chances.'

They flew in tense silence with the fuel gauge falling. Blanchard knew it was the end. His mind kept jumping between calm resignation and utter panic. He wondered what would happen if he turned around and tried to land at Miami. Would the mad man next to him actually pull the trigger, assuring his own death as well? Blanchard looked at the fuel gauge and calculated the flying distance. In a moment of calm, he did a risk analysis. The chances of running out of fuel over the sea were less than his chances of having his brains blown out if he didn't follow instructions. He was calm again because he didn't have to make a choice.

As they flew out to sea, Tecumseh wriggled the wings of his Skyhawk and flew off. He was, thought Blanchard, probably running out of fuel too. On the port wing, the island of Andros, the largest of the Bahamas, was just visible, an inviting green sliver on the otherwise empty sea.

There was now another plane in the sky, not a sleek jet but a lumpy prop engine job with red, white and blue RAF roundels on its fuselage and wings.

'Don't worry,' said Blanchard, 'I don't think he's got any guns. It's an Avro Shackleton. The British use them for long-distance maritime patrols.'

The radio crackled. 'Hello, DC-7. This is the old kite on your port wing. Are you in need of assistance?'

Cauldwell depressed his transmit button and spoke in a Spanish accent. 'No, thank you.'

'Sounds like you're from around here.'

'I don't want to talk.'

'Fair enough, cheers. But if you want to visit the lovely Bahamas, follow me.'

'No.'

'Righty-ho. But I'm going to keep with you just in case you get in trouble or change your mind.'

Cauldwell didn't answer, but glanced over at the RAF plane. Someone in the cockpit was pointing a huge camera with a telescopic lens in his direction and snapping away. Cauldwell put up a hand to shield his face, but it was too late.

Blanchard smiled. 'I was stationed over there. The Brits are cunning; they always catch you when you least expect it.'

Cauldwell was annoyed at himself for not taking precautions. The American pilots hadn't bothered to take pictures – either because they already knew who he was or hadn't thought of it. Cauldwell hadn't planned his future in any detail. He wasn't even sure he had a future, but having his photo passed around the British intelligence services wasn't going to be helpful.

The Avro Shackleton kept pace with the DC-7 as its fuel gauge began to touch on empty. The British plane finally banked away as the Cuban coast appeared in the bright, sunlit azure sea. There was one final transmission.

'Good luck, old boy. You're now in Cuban airspace and we're handing you over to Havana air control. Cheerio.'

On cue, a P-47 Thunderbolt of the Fuerza Aérea Cubana roared out of the sky, passing only yards in front of the DC-7.

'Shit,' said Blanchard, 'that was dangerous.'

The Thunderbolt was a stubby prop-driven fighter plane that looked like a bulldog with wings. The single-piston engine was enormous and the rest of the plane seemed atrophied behind it; an aircraft that was all head and chest with shrivelled limbs. It was big-band jazz-trumpet loud – the iconic US fighter plane of World War Two.

'Not an easy plane to fly,' said Blanchard. 'The ignition system arcs at high altitudes – and the .50 calibre machine guns are too tightly packed and tend to jam. But they won't need to shoot us down, we're going to crash.'

The DC-7's starboard outboard engine had begun to stutter and finally stopped. The propeller continued to spin in the air flow. 'That one always goes first.' Blanchard's voice had an uncanny calm. 'I'll feather the port outboard to save any drops left. We're flying on fumes.'

'Are we there, at the Sierra Maestra?'

'How the fuck should I know? I've stopped counting the miles.'

Cauldwell stood up and buckled himself into the parachute harness. 'Let's go. You're coming with me.'

'But there's only one chute.'

'You'll have to hang on tight.'

At that moment the inboard starboard engine coughed and stuttered. And a second later the Thunderbolt made a strafing pass and .50 cal bullets the size of courgettes stitched the passenger cabin behind them. Cauldwell pressed the transmit button for one last message: *Hasta la victoria siempre!*

He ripped off the radio headset and pushed Blanchard into the aisle and towards the open door. When they got to the door, Cauldwell wrapped the static line around a luggage rack fitting. They stood in the open door, the wind howling past. 'Hold on tight.'

As Blanchard wrapped his arms around him, the Thunderbolt made another pass and the DC-7's port wing blew into pieces just as they jumped. A moment later there was no engine noise, only rushing wind – and four seconds later the gentle pop of the canopy deploying and then no noise at all.

Cauldwell watched the DC-7 spewing flames and black smoke as it cartwheeled towards the sea. It looked like a 4th of July firework. Meanwhile the Thunderbolt had banked and was heading back towards their parachute. They were only 500 feet from the ground when the Thunderbolt's machine guns opened up. Blanchard looked up as he heard bullets pop over his head. It reminded him of being in the firing range butts as a young recruit, but this time the bullets were louder and there was no protection. A line of holes appeared in the light green silk of the parachute canopy. A complete panel tore out and fluttered in the air; they descended slightly faster and at an odd angle.

The Thunderbolt was now coming back for a final pass as they descended to treetop level. There was once again the sound of machine-gun fire, but it wasn't coming from the Thunderbolt – it was coming from the ground. One of the rounds must have hit a control cable or the pilot. The fighter didn't change direction or come out of its shallow dive. It ploughed into the trees.

Blanchard didn't see the smoke or the flames, for they disappeared into the trees at the same moment. The sound of their feet breaking branches was muffled by the explosion of the Thunderbolt a couple of hundred yards away. They had landed in a pine tree, a *pino de la Maestra*. Their combined weight continued to pull the parachute through the tree branches until they came to a dangling halt about fifteen feet above a granite outcrop. There was the sound of crackling flames from the wreck of the Thunderbolt – and then the sound of ammunition being cooked off in the burning plane and ricocheting off the rocks and whizzing through the trees. Meanwhile, the burning fuel of the downed plane had started a forest fire.

'Shit,' said Blanchard. 'Looks like we're going to have to jump to the ground.'

Cauldwell looked at the ridged granite beneath them. 'And break a leg and get roasted if the fire comes this way.' He pulled the handle on the reserve chute and the canopy and lines spilled out below them. 'We'll slide down on this.'

'Good idea, should...'

'Shh ... be quiet.'

'What?'

'Someone's coming.'

A scruffy bearded figure wearing a beret and carrying a carbine emerged out of the shadow of the trees. He looked at them with an impish smile.

Havana: March, 1959

The revolution had succeeded and the man with the impish smile was now one of the most important men in Cuba. His office was in *La Cabaña*, a massive eighteenth-century fort guarding the entrance to Havana harbour. He kept referring to Cauldwell as Señor Whoever-you-are.

There were only two of them in the office. Cauldwell waited in silence while the other finished coughing. He appeared to suffer from severe asthma.

'Pardon me, Señor Whoever-you-are, these fits just come on.'

'Is there anything I can do to help?'

'You mean with the revolution – or my cough?'

'Either.'

'I would rather you helped with the revolution.'

'How?'

'I think you have your own answer, Señor Whoever-you-are. In any case, we have decided to let you and your pilot friend stay in Cuba for as long as you like.'

'Thank you.'

'But I think you may have your own agendas and plans. Whatever they are, I know that you are a true revolutionary.'

Cauldwell smiled.

Catesby may have wanted a revolution, but he knew it wasn't going to happen. So he joined the Labour Party instead. He contested a seat in the 1945 election. The election was a Labour landslide, but Catesby bucked the national trend by losing miserably. A political career was not on the cards, but Catesby's political allegiances were to prove useful.

The tap on the shoulder was inevitable. Catesby was a talented linguist, a working-class Cambridge graduate and had a good war serving in the Special Operations Executive. His profile and politics were a perfect fit for SIS during a time when the NHS was being formed and the coal mines and railways were being nationalised. But Catesby soon found there was a dark side to his new job. He was expected to spy on his left-wing friends.

»»»»»

'It's a pity,' said Henry Bone, 'that Ralph Miliband doesn't work for us.' Bone was standing at his office window with his hands folded behind his back looking at the Epstein sculptures on the London Underground building opposite. 'Did your friend Ralph know Epstein?'

'I believe they met.'

'Could you ask him if Epstein was influenced by Mayan art? Those figures look very sinister.'

'Is that all you want me to ask him?'

'No, there are other issues.'

'You know, Henry, that I don't like spying on perfectly innocent academics. If you want to find out what Ralph Miliband knows and thinks, you can read his writings and go to his lectures. He doesn't keep anything secret.'

'Don't bark at me, Catesby. You don't even know what we want to know.'

'What is it then?'

'The Sino-Soviet rift. We don't know enough about the

deteriorating relationship between Moscow and Peking. I think things may be getting lethal.'

'Why don't you ask the Americans?'

'They're useless. They think Communism is a monolithic international conspiracy. Any suggestion that there may be conflicts between Communist powers is heresy. As far as they are concerned, all reds are the same and they want to conquer us. We need a more subtle analysis.'

June, 1959: Zhongnanhai compound, Peking

The two men were sitting in matching red armchairs on either side of a rosewood table from the Ming Dynasty. The upper drawer of the table was elaborately carved with two phoenixes facing each other. The mythical birds were poised like fighting cocks ready to battle over which ideological path was the purest way to rise from the ashes. There was a bowl of formally arranged cut flowers on the table, including tiger lilies, orchids, peonies and peach blossoms – which symbolise long life. The flowers were cultivated in a hothouse in the Forbidden City, which was adjacent to the Zhongnanhai compound. One of the men was slim, handsome and had a look and demeanour which, although not altogether Western, was cosmopolitan and sophisticated. He was drinking whisky. The other man had a wart on his chin and a reassuring Buddha-like plumpness. His eyes were warm, but also dark and enigmatic. His teeth were bad for he had never brushed them in his life. He was drinking tea and an aphrodisiac tincture.

The Buddha-like man put on a pair of spectacles to read yet another grim report on the failure of 'The Great Leap Forward'. The plan had begun in 1958 and its aim was the rapid industrialisation of China in order to catch up with and surpass the Soviet Union. The first stage was the abolition of private property and the collectivisation of agriculture. At first, the peasants ate for free in communal canteens, but a year later there was no food to eat for free or otherwise. 'The Great Leap' had been a massive failure. The makeshift backyard blast furnaces intended to produce steel in even the most humble villages now lay blackened and abandoned. The steel they produced proved completely worthless.

The plump man took off his glasses and looked at the cosmopolitan man. When he spoke, it was in Mandarin, a dialect that he wanted all China to learn. 'What do you think, Feifei?'

The cosmopolitan man smiled once again at the nickname that the Buddha-like man had chosen for him so long ago. When they first met his nickname was Daluan, which means 'big bird'. The plump man, who was also slim and handsome all those years ago, began to call his new friend Feifei, Mandarin for 'fly-fly'. For a while the cosmopolitan man was both Feifei and Big Bird – but Feifei was the nickname that stuck. The plump man with the wart on his chin also had nicknames. The most famous was The Great Helmsman, and he was also known as The Girth – but never to his face. Feifei, ever reserved and respectful, only ever called his colleague Comrade Chairman.

'Why are you so silent, Feifei? Has the cat eaten your tongue?'

'I was, Comrade Chairman, reflecting on your question.' Feifei knew that both China and the Chairman had reached a critical turning point. 'The Great Leap Forward' had resulted in thirty million deaths from starvation and widespread discontent. He knew that the Chairman risked being marginalised into a figurehead. Finally, Feifei spoke. He pronounced the words in Mandarin: '*Gan xiang gan gan.*' (Dare to think, dare to act. We can no longer waste time.) They were the exact same words that the Chairman had used to announce the beginning of 'The Great Leap'. Feifei no longer cared if the Chairman spotted his mocking irony.

The Chairman's eyes narrowed and seemed to focus on a distant point. 'I have made mistakes, but I have also rescued a quarter of the world's population from feudalism and grinding poverty. We are still, Feifei, the leading force of world Communism.'

Feifei nodded. He knew that this might have been so, but it was largely owing to his own moderate and pragmatic influence.

Feifei had quietly and covertly begun to import grain from the West to relieve the famine.

'But,' said the Chairman, 'we will never be reconciled with the Soviet Union – even if it means war. Khrushchev is a revisionist dog. When he gave that speech denouncing Stalin, he announced the end of Communism in the Soviet Union.'

Feifei thought the Chairman's pronouncement a little extreme, but he was too subtle to disagree directly. He smiled and shrugged. 'It was a cunning speech. First Secretary Khrushchev is trying to consolidate his power by crushing or isolating the remaining Stalinists who want to dispose of him. In fact, several committed suicide in the days after the speech.'

'It is good that we no longer depend on Russian technology and Russian military weapons. We must develop our own.' The Chairman looked hard at Feifei. 'You know the West so much better than any of us. You must devise a plan to steal the secrets of the West.'

Feifei sipped his whisky and reflected. Following the Chairman's thoughts was often like riding the back of a tiger. But it was possible to jockey that tiger and guide it in the right direction. 'We must, Comrade Chairman, use the West in such a way that the West thinks they are using us.'

'We need spies in the West.'

'We have hundreds of spies, thousands of spies in the West. Many of the overseas Chinese look to us as their homeland.'

'But few of them have access to the great centres of power. Have we spies among the *gweilos*?' The Chairman used the common Cantonese word for Westerners. *Gweilo* literally means 'ghost guy'. It came into use in the nineteenth century because the pale skin of Western sailors led the Chinese to think they were ghosts.

Feifei peered deep in thought at the antique flock wallpaper which depicted a riot of red flowers. Did China have *gweilo* spies? Even one? His musing was interrupted by the tinkle of young female voices from the Chairman's private residence. It was time to leave.

»»»»»

It wasn't easy getting the armchair and sofa up the stairs and into Ralph Miliband's flat. In addition to Ralph and Catesby, there was Isaac Deutscher, another academic. After a lot of groaning, scraped knuckles and cursing in four different languages they finally got the furniture in place.

'Thank you, William,' said Miliband wiping his brow.

'I hope you like them.' The sofa and armchair were from Catesby's flat. 'My sister decided she wanted something more posh. She's a class traitor.'

'And where,' said Miliband, 'is the hidden microphone?'

'It's in the armchair. It activates when you sit in it.' Catesby was joking. As far as he knew, the furniture wasn't bugged. But he did know that Ralph's telephone had been tapped by MI5. The reds-under-the-bed paranoia had leapt across the Atlantic. If you were British and too left-wing your phone calls were no longer private. Catesby blamed the influence of the CIA. The British spies working for Washington were just as subversive as the ones working for Moscow.

'I'll make coffee,' said Ralph.

As Miliband disappeared into the kitchenette, Deutscher asked, 'How long have you known Ralph?'

'Since 1949. We met at a dinner party and discovered that we both spoke French with a Belgian accent.'

'And I believe,' said Deutscher, 'that you work for the, uh, Foreign Office.'

'That's right. I work for the, uh, Foreign Office.'

A rattle of cups announced Ralph's return with the coffee. 'Isaac,' said Ralph, 'is our expert on Mao and Maoism.'

Catesby smiled. 'I wish *we* had an expert on Maoism.'

Deutscher sipped his coffee, then gave a heavy sigh. 'Have you been sent here, Mr Catesby, to spy on us?'

'I don't call it spying,' said Catesby, 'I call it information gathering so that the UK government doesn't make the same stupid mistakes it has in the past.'

Deutscher frowned. 'What do you want to know?'

'Is the split between Moscow and Peking real?'

'Utterly, but the West should not rejoice.'

'Why not?'

'Because Maoism is going to have repercussions for decades to come. It is a force of revolutionary internationalism that is going to spread revolution to underdeveloped countries.' Deutscher paused and looked directly at Catesby. 'And you can tell your colleagues at the, uh, Foreign Office that there is nothing they can do about it.'

'Thanks, I'll let them know.' Catesby smiled. 'Pretend for a second I'm Mao Tse-tung. What advice would you give me?'

'I would warn you of Western powers who might try to play off China against the Soviet Union. Mao must resist that temptation. It could destroy his revolution.'

'You ought,' said Miliband, 'to get your friends at the Foreign Office to read Isaac's biographies of Trotsky. Natalia Sedova, she's Trotsky's widow...'

'I know,' said Catesby with slight irritation.

'Natalia has just given Isaac access to the closed section of the Trotsky archives.'

Catesby smiled bleakly. It wasn't the first time he had become aware that these North London intellectuals living in exile had a better intelligence network than the SIS.

E Street Complex, Washington: 6 August 1960

The DCI, Director of Central Intelligence, was in fine form. He had just got laid after a long lunch at the Quorum Club. He felt he was doing okay for a man of sixty-seven with a club foot – although the foot was something he never mentioned or admitted.

The meeting was far more top secret than the DCI's liaison with a female journalist in a backroom at the Quorum Club. The only others present in the E Street office were the DDP, Deputy Director for Plans, and the Army Chief of Staff.

The DCI spoke first. 'It is irrevocable. They are never going to kiss and make up. It is an opportunity that we cannot fail to exploit.' The DCI looked at the Army Chief of Staff. 'I know, Lyman, that you do not agree – and that's why I've taken you into my confidence.'

The general's trick was to speak in such measured, thoughtful tones that his views, however mad, sounded reasonable. 'Today is an auspicious anniversary. It is fifteen years ago today that we bombed Hiroshima. It is important that the United States maintain the capability to use nuclear weapons against any nation with impunity and with no fear of retaliation. That is essential for a *Pax Americana*.'

As the DCI lit his pipe, he peered over his steel-rimmed spectacles with a playful smile. 'You and Curtis are still disappointed that you never persuaded Ike to attack Russia.'

'It is a window of opportunity that is fast closing. For years the Soviet Union totally lacked the capability to retaliate against a pre-emptive US attack. But it won't be long before Moscow does possess intercontinental ballistic missiles – they might already.'

'So your preferred option…' The DCI paused to deal with his pipe. Safely lit, he continued. 'The pre-emptive strike option no longer exists?'

'That would appear so.'

'Ergo, you might consider other options – such as the one we are discussing today?'

'Possibly, but much depends on the policy of the next President.'

The recent summer conventions had just nominated Kennedy and Nixon.

'Which horse,' said the DCI, 'would you prefer to back?'

The general smiled. 'I would prefer not to say.'

'Very wise. But I assume,' said the DCI, 'that you would give tentative support to our plan?'

The general frowned. 'Yes, but tentative and reluctant.'

The DCI turned to the DDP. 'Over to you, Richard, can you give us an update?'

The DDP's presentation was long and detailed. It included a complex web of false flag ploys in conjunction with disinformation ops. The most important things were discreet channels of communication about which deniability was not just 'plausible', but 'completely and utterly convincing'. The first and last rules were no fingerprints.

When the DDP had finished, the DCI looked at the Army Chief of Staff. 'It's a principle of strategy and statecraft that has been practised through the centuries: *The enemy of your enemy is your friend.*'

Waterloo Bridge, London: 7 January 1961

Catesby felt sorry for Bunty. Reading her file didn't make him weep, but it did make him depressed about the whole business. Bunty was clearly the saddest character in the Portland ring. She didn't know exactly what she was doing. And even if she knew it was wrong, she wasn't doing it for money or ideology. She was doing it because she was lonely. Miss Bunty Gee was the ultimate spinster. Her day job was filing clerk at the Admiralty Underwater Weapons Establishment. Her other job, which occupied every evening and weekend, was looking after her elderly mother – and an even more elderly aunt and uncle who had moved in with her mum. Bunty's life was a hell of lonely desperation. Harry, an alcoholic with a broken marriage, wasn't exactly the best thing since sliced bread, but he was the last chance saloon for a dumpy spinster in her forties.

Harry was an even sadder character than Bunty, but he was too vain to admit it. After serving as a sailor during the war, he joined the civil service and was sent to Warsaw as a clerk in the office of the naval attaché. He became a heavy drinker and dabbled in the black market. He hung around with the wrong sort of people – and there were a lot of wrong sorts to hang around with. He was recruited as a spy by the UB, the Polish intelligence service. Harry liked the excitement and the access it gave him to sex and luxuries. It fed his vanity too – even though, in the hierarchy of agents, Harry was a bottom feeder.

Until that wet dreary January day on Waterloo Bridge, Harry had been one very lucky spy. Years before, his ex-wife had grassed him up as a suspected spy. But the Security Service hadn't taken her claim seriously. She had also complained to the police about domestic abuse even though she had no bruises to show them. Harry was a womaniser and a drunk, but he usually limited his abuse to verbal assaults. The Security Service, which had its own fair share of drunks and bad husbands, dismissed Harry's wife as merely a bitter and twisted woman who wanted revenge. Harry was lucky not to get caught for other reasons. He wasn't very good at operating undercover. He splashed around his extra money in a flashy way with cars and a lifestyle that was far above his pay grade. He was also careless and forgetful when it came to spy-craft skills such as dead letter boxes and anti-surveillance precautions. His handler, Konon Trofimovich Molody, would gladly have dropped him if the intelligence Harry had been getting via Bunty Gee had not been so valuable.

Bunty had been a filing clerk at the Underwater Weapons Establishment since 1950. She was part of the office furniture. No one would ever have suspected Bunt-the-Frump with her broad Dorset accent of being a spy – although she did posh up a bit when she spoke on the phone. Tongues wagged when she started having an affair with Harry, but who could blame her? In fact, and against the odds, Harry treated her pretty well and even talked of getting married. He also taught her how to use a camera to photograph secret documents.

The most secret of these documents pertained to HMS *Dreadnought*, the Royal Navy's first nuclear submarine. They were the details of *Dreadnought's* devices that were used to detect other submarines. It had been part of a shopping list that Molody had passed on to Harry. And, appropriately, the film cartridges were in Bunty's cloth shopping bag as she and Harry descended from the Weymouth train at Waterloo Station.

'I hope,' she said to Harry, 'that Commander Johnson doesn't turn out to be a drowner, because I've taken some awful risks for him.'

Harry patted her hand as they emerged from under the entrance arch into Waterloo Road. 'He's not one of your drowners, Ethel.' Harry always called her by her proper name.

As a child in rural Dorset, Bunty had always been told to keep away from the water meadows when they were flooded. It was because of the drowners. These were beautiful creatures who were neither man nor woman. When the fields were in full flood, the drowners would lay out toys and sparkling trinkets to tempt children to reach into the water for them. And, as soon as they did so, the children would be sucked into the mud to become captives of the drowners and were never seen again.

»»»»»

It was a Saturday and there was little traffic on Waterloo Bridge. This made it easier for Skardon's watchers. They already had Molody under surveillance and were in contact with the cars. It looked like Harry's luck was running out. Meanwhile, Molody had parked his car near Somerset House and was enjoying the river view from Victoria Embankment. He checked his watch and headed for the bridge.

Bunty had first met Molody a few months earlier during another trip to London. Harry had introduced Molody as Alexander Johnson, a commander in the United States Navy, who was a counter-intelligence specialist. 'Johnson' had explained that his job was to check up on how the British handled secret technical information that the Americans shared as a result of the 1958 US–UK Mutual Defence Agreement. It wasn't spying, just a 'verification exercise to build confidence between close allies'. But Bunty didn't know what to believe. There had been times, usually during heavy drinking sessions, when Harry bragged about being a Soviet spy. Bunty hoped it had just been alcohol-fuelled bravado and Harry's constant need to impress.

The view from Waterloo Bridge gave Harry and Bunty a perfect excuse to pause and loiter halfway across the bridge. It was a stunning vista of the Thames sweeping past the Houses of Parliament and included almost every other London landmark. Bunty hugged Harry's arm. She was wearing a fake wedding ring and was looking forward to a night in a luxurious West End hotel. Harry, a Lincolnshire lad, was also dazzled by London but didn't like to admit it. He was hoping they could get tickets to *Fings Ain't Wot They Used To Be* at the Garrick. Bunty, on the other hand, would have preferred *Flower Drum Song*, a musical about wealthy Chinese refugees assimilating into life in the USA. Harry thought it sounded a bit soppy, but would probably go along with her wishes.

The watcher from an observation post on the top floor of Somerset House was the first to signal that Molody was on Waterloo Bridge. For the benefit of the snatch teams in the cars, he counted down the remaining yards to the RV point as Molody nonchalantly strolled across the bridge hands in pockets. Did he have a gun?

Bunty smiled when she spotted 'Johnson'. She found him handsome and utterly charming, but certainly beyond her fondest dreams. For a split second, she wondered if he might be a drowner after all.

»»»»»

Special Branch were in Jaguars and Rovers; MI5 and SIS were in boring Humbers. Catesby and his colleagues were there as invited guests to admire the other Security Services. And they were good. Two Jags and a Rover were the first to pounce as they screeched to a halt next to the three spies. A dozen Special Branch poured out on the footpath, all dressed in identical beige Mackintoshes and trilbies. Why, thought Catesby from the SIS Humber, don't they just wear uniforms? Four Special Branch were waving pistols. Please, Catesby prayed, don't shoot them. Molody took his hands out of his pockets to show that he was unarmed. He seemed the calmest person on the bridge.

The arrest went like a textbook snatch. When Harry twigged what was happening, he grabbed Bunty's shopping bag with the films so that he could throw it into the river. But he was rugby tackled and handcuffed by two Special Branch while the bag was still in his girlfriend's hand. Bunty seemed the most confused and stunned of the three. It must have taken her a while to realise that she was going to be spending the night in a cell instead of a posh hotel. Catesby felt awfully sorry for her as he watched her run her finger over her fake wedding ring in the desperation of lost hope.

The whole thing was over in less than a minute. The Special Branch cars and their prisoners were the first to go. Catesby's driver started the engine, but before he could pull away there was a tapping at the passenger window. Catesby wound down the glass. It was Jim Skardon. Catesby looked at his MI5 colleague.

'Lovely piece of work, Jim. Congratulations.'

'Can we have a chat?'

'Sure, hop in.'

'Why don't you get in my motor? I'm all alone.'

'Sure.'

Skardon drove south over the bridge and parked his Humber Hawk next to a derelict warehouse overlooking a crumbling wharf. The tide was now ebbing fast and carrying with it the detritus of London. Catesby liked being near the river. The sailors in his family always called it 'the London River'. It only became the Thames above London, where deep-sea ships can't go. Catesby's grandfather used to skipper a 'stackie', one of the Thames barges that shuttled Suffolk hay down to London and returned with cargoes of London horseshit to replenish the hayfields.

Skardon spoke first. 'Something ain't right.'

'I totally agree.'

'The whole thing reeks, but I don't know where the smell is coming from.'

At first Catesby wondered if Skardon was being rude about his granddad's stackie, but then realised he was talking about intelligence matters. 'I hope...' Catesby had to be careful. Intelligence between SIS and Five was not always shared. 'I suppose you know there was a tip-off from the Poles. Not the UB, but a military defector. If you didn't know this already, you didn't hear it from me.'

'You're not giving anything away. The Polish tip-off was passed on to us. But it wasn't specific. There wasn't enough information to nail down Molody – or even that pathetic couple.'

'Then how did you know?'

'The information came from a totally anonymous source. The source gave us all Molody's aliases and his London address. Mr Anonymous also informed us that Molody was born in Russia and gave us the details of his Russian family and background – which, of course, we couldn't check. But the source told us that Molody had stolen the identity of a dead Canadian child, the Gordon Lonsdale identity he was operating under. And that's how he came unstuck. We got the RCMP to check the dead kid's medical records in Ottawa. The child had been circumcised and, according to two of Molody's girlfriends, this is certainly not the case with him. We then put Molody under surveillance and tracked him to a safe deposit box he uses on Chancery Lane, under another alias of course.'

Catesby smiled. 'I assume you did a black bag job on the safe deposit.'

Skardon nodded. 'We did the safe box and found tiny one-time cipher pads hidden in a porcelain figurine and microdot copies of secrets stolen from Portland. Then we put everything back just as we found it.'

'Down and dusted.'

'Molody is. But why? Who grassed him and for what reason?'

'What do you think, Jim?'

'I think Molody was a helluva fine agent. One of the best and most dedicated I've ever encountered. In fact, he was just another professional like us, but working for the other side. I respect him. He wasn't a scumbag traitor.'

'But who grassed him?'

Skardon shrugged and looked at the river. 'It must have been the Sovs themselves – and there's only one reason why they would sacrifice one of their best agents.'

'Go on.'

'Moscow Central wants to protect someone who is even more important than Molody. Someone who is running an even bigger spy network that is ripping out the very heart of Britain's most vital secrets. It's scary.' Skardon smiled. 'This business does make you paranoid. I hope I don't sound like an alarmist. But that's my theory. What's yours?'

Catesby told him.

»»»»»

The news of the arrest of Molody and the Portland spies broke two days later. It was a banner headline in every newspaper. Esteban, a wealthy Cuban exile from Castro's revolution, was absolutely delighted. He invited his best girls for a party, but didn't tell them why.

Broadway Buildings, London: April, 1961

Catesby felt lucky to be at the meeting. In fact, he felt lucky to still be in the service. His sister had lost her job at GCHQ because she was deemed a security risk. It was a messy situation involving her duplicitous boyfriend. Catesby had been subjected to months of vetting, but had proved as clean as a disinfected and bleached whistle. There may have been those who still had doubts, but Catesby wasn't going to lie low. He held forth at the meeting, loud and brassy.

'This guy is completely genuine. Not a shadow of a doubt. And how do we know that he is genuine? Because he is totally bonkers. If you don't believe me, call in a psychiatrist. Moscow Central would never use someone who is that unbalanced as a fake double.'

There was a heated debate within SIS and MI5 about whether or not Oleg, codenamed HERO, was a Soviet plant. If HERO was genuine, it would be the biggest intelligence coup that the West had ever scored in the Cold War. The secret inter-agency meeting to discuss HERO had been adjourned in C's office on the fourth floor of Broadway Buildings. It was the only floor of Broadway that wasn't a dingy labyrinth of plywood partitions, frosted glass and grey curling lino. When you emerged from the squalor of the claustrophobic creaking lift you stepped into a magic world of finery. The corridor was covered with thick burgundy carpet and the walls hung with Turners, Constables and Gainsboroughs from the Government Art Collection's VIP vaults – but no Poussins. C's office itself was a serious treasure trove of eighteenth-century joinery. The conference table and the chairs were priceless Chippendale. You sat down very gingerly and didn't rock backwards on the rear legs – or do handstands on the arms of the chair, as had one SAS major to the taxpayers' cost.

The problem with HERO was that he was a 'walk in', an agent

who hadn't been coerced or targeted, but simply offered his services out of the blue. 'Walk ins' were always suspected as plants. HERO was a colonel in GRU, Soviet military intelligence, but even more important was his personal closeness to people at the very top. The two loudest HERO sceptics were from Five. Catesby called them Fox and Ferret because of their pointy faces and demeanour.

Fox retaliated first, 'HERO is sane as well as cunning. If, Catesby, you find his behaviour unbalanced, it could well be an act that he puts on to deceive people such as yourself.'

Catesby gave a weary sigh. 'You're making a *reductio ad absurdum*. Shall I translate?'

Fox was a self-taught engineer in the scientific and technical branch of MI5. He came from a humble background and hated being patronised – especially by someone from an even more humble background. The fact that Catesby had made it to Cambridge and into the 'officer class' enraged Fox. To Catesby's discredit, he loved to rub that fact in Fox's face. They loathed each other. Henry Bone had once described their mutual loathing as 'the rage of twin Calibans seeing their own faces in a mirror'. Catesby knew it was a nasty crack, but laughed. He realised Fox didn't even know what Bone was talking about.

Dick White, the chief of SIS, intervened in his typical emollient way. 'It's not possible, William, to submit HERO to a psychiatric examination, as desirable as that may be.' White nodded to Fox. 'I appreciate your reservations that HERO may be a KGB plant and we take note of the report you submitted.'

Catesby nodded. 'May I continue?'

'Just a second, William.' White gave an admonitory stare. 'I'd like to say something about your comment that HERO is "unbalanced". Betraying your country is almost always the act of an unstable and maladjusted personality. The traitor is often warped by a sense of grievance and desire for revenge.'

Catesby kept a blank face. He didn't want to disagree with the boss in public, but there were many other reasons for turning against your country. White's portrait of a traitor did, however, apply to HERO.

White gave Catesby a softer look. 'Other than Shergy, who can't be here this evening, you've spent more time with HERO than any of us. Can you tell us the latest?'

'He wants to meet the Queen. In fact, he can't understand why the Queen hasn't asked to meet him. He also wants to meet President Kennedy. The Cousins, ever helpful, have promised...'

'Which cousins are you talking about?' interrupted Fox.

'Our CIA colleagues who are jointly running HERO with us.' Catesby gave Fox what Henry called his 'supercilious smile', knowing that Fox wouldn't know what supercilious meant. 'I am sure, Peter, that you know who they are – and that's why Shergy can't be with us. He's dealing with them. As I was saying, the Cousins have promised HERO a meeting with Kennedy if HERO can arrange a trip across the Atlantic. They do make us look mean-spirited for not having wheeled in Her Majesty wearing a crown and ermine. I suggested Lord Mountbatten as an alternative, but HERO wasn't impressed.'

Henry Bone intervened. 'The difficulty in dealing with HERO is that the Americans keep outbidding us in catering to his ego needs and indulging his whims.'

Catesby nodded a thank you to Henry. 'And the photo sessions proved the point. HERO asked to be photographed in the uniform of a British Army officer. So we dressed him up as a colonel in full kit with Sam Browne belt and the bullion lion and crown cap badge of a senior staff officer. I thought he looked the part. But the Yanks trumped us with a brigadier's uniform and a chest full of medals. It was the over the top, HERO looked a right tosser.'

'Don't dismiss the photos, William,' said Bone. 'If HERO ever has second thoughts, those snaps are going to provide a lethal blackmail threat.'

'Good point. But even more lethal is HERO's recklessness. When our session at the Mount Royal Hotel ended it was already past midnight, but HERO insisted on doing the nightclubs. He picked up a girl and didn't get back to his quarters at the Sov Embassy until seven a.m.'

'If he was genuine,' said Fox, 'he would be more cautious.'

'You haven't met him, Peter. You haven't looked into those

mad eyes.' Catesby opened a folder. 'Listen to this. It's from his last interview: "*You need to send me suitcase-size nuclear bombs. You can smuggle them to your Moscow embassy using diplomatic bags. I will then hide nuclear bombs in my dacha. When time is right, I bring bombs into Moscow to destroy Soviet military command in pre-emptive strike.*"' Catesby stopped and took a map out of the folder. 'He even showed us – see the red Xs – where he'd put the bombs. He thinks hiding them in dustbins would be a good idea. He said one or two kiloton should be sufficient and they should be detonated at ten-thirty a.m. to cause maximum casualties. This is a man who has turned against his homeland and wants to kill and destroy everything in it.'

'And I am sure,' said Fox, 'that you're going to tell us why.'

Catesby flashed a flinty smile. 'It is largely because he never knew his father, a White Russian who was killed fighting against the Bolsheviks in 1919 – a dangerous heritage that HERO managed to cover up. One could say that the Soviet State became his hated stepfather – and he managed to keep that hatred secret as he rose through the ranks.'

'Perhaps,' said Fox, 'you should retrain as a psychiatrist.'

'All of us who handle agents should be psychiatrists.' Catesby noted a nod of approval from White and continued. 'But HERO did not rise as high through the ranks as he thought he should. Like many double agents, he has a vastly inflated sense of self-importance. His career began to stall after he was promoted to colonel and never revived. As he became more and more bitter, he began to alienate his colleagues. That's why he was shuffled off into his current job. It's a high-ranking post, but a dead end.'

'Can you remind us,' asked White, 'what that post is?'

'He is head of intelligence for the State Scientific and Technical Commission. Essentially, HERO's job is to obtain technical and scientific secrets from the West. It means he can travel a lot, operate under commercial cover and recruit agents. It also means that he is privy to secrets arriving in Moscow from all other Soviet and East Bloc intelligence sources and agencies. If we've lost it, HERO will find it. In short, this fellow is one extremely valuable agent.'

Dick White looked at his watch. 'I think it's time to end this part of the meeting.'

The Director's words were a signal for MI5 officers and co-opted members of JIC to leave. When the last of the Chippendale chairs had been carefully slid back under the table, White got up to pour tea. Only two of his colleagues remained: Catesby and Bone. It was time to discuss sensitive operational matters concerned with running HERO.

Catesby returned White's glance. 'Thanks. One sugar, please. HERO is a gem. I hope we convinced the sceptics.'

'But,' said White, 'he is a nutter.'

'No coffee for me,' said Bone, 'it keeps me awake at night.'

'A drink?'

'No, I'm fine. The important thing is that we exploit HERO to the hilt before he self-destructs.' Bone lowered his voice to a whisper. 'As I am sure he will.'

'HERO's job,' said Catesby, 'gives him absolutely priceless cover. As an official with the State Scientific and Technical Commission, it means that he can rendezvous openly or clandestinely with our own agents posing as engineers or business people.'

'Indeed, William,' said Bone, 'that is a great advantage.'

Catesby noticed that both Bone and White were giving him the Lord Kitchener 'Your Country Needs You' look. Catesby had seen that look before and knew it meant trouble. The look wasn't a request. It meant: 'This is what is expected of you so just get on with it.' Catesby knew it was pointless to quibble. 'If you want me to go to Moscow to pick up stuff from HERO, that's fine. But I will need to go heavily disguised and with a good cover story.'

'It might not come to that,' said Bone, 'but you would be the contact of last resort if things get desperate. At the moment, we are going to continue to use contacts who have diplomatic cover.'

Catesby knew that if he was sent to Moscow it would be as an 'illegal'. When an SIS agent with diplomatic cover is caught spying, the agent is simply PNG'd – declared persona non-grata – and sent back to the UK. If an 'illegal' is caught spying they go to prison.

'But,' said White, 'we don't, at the moment, want to take unnecessary risks.'

Catesby nodded. The going tariff for Western spies was twelve years in a Sov prison. For Soviet citizens, it was a bullet in the back of the neck. They didn't shoot Western spies because they were a valuable currency to swap for Sov spies imprisoned in the West. Catesby suspected that Konon Trofimovich Molody wouldn't spend a lot of time in Wormwood Scrubs.

'And,' said Bone, 'we'd need to train you up in Moscow Rules.'

Catesby had never been to Moscow, but knew that on their home turf the KGB had no shortage of men and women for surveillance. It wasn't unusual for the KGB to assign as many as two hundred personnel to watch and tail a single target. You had to assume, quite rightly, that you were always being watched.

'Fortunately,' said White, 'our man in Moscow has a wife with a young child. HERO has been briefed on how to pass information into the pram while admiring the baby.' White smiled. 'Don't worry, William. The baby has diplomatic immunity too.'

'The most important thing about HERO,' said Bone, 'is his access to intelligence secrets that undetected Soviet spies in Britain are passing on to Moscow.'

'And detected spies as well,' added White. 'Now that Molody has been arrested, it will be interesting to see if the disinformation that we are feeding Tyler continues to arrive in Moscow.'

'Is Tyler still unwitting?' Catesby wanted to know if Tyler was unaware that he had been uncovered.

'Yes – and we don't keep him under close surveillance because we don't want to frighten off his handler. So we can only assume it was Molody.'

Like his MI5 counterpart Skardon, Catesby didn't like the Tyler arrangement.

'I don't suppose,' said Bone looking at White, 'that Five have had any success in their interrogation of Molody?'

'Of course not. Molody is a complete and utter professional. He is only giving us names that he knows we already know about. And he's spouting disinformation too – providing names, and some very high up names too, that we know are completely innocent.'

'Or maybe,' Catesby added, 'it's a double bluff. Molody knows that we know he's lying so he knows that his accusations are giving a clean bill of health to those who are not so clean.'

'And so on...' yawned Bone. 'You're wandering, William, into the wilderness of mirrors.'

'May we,' said White with a tired smile, 'get back into the reasonably unrefracted light of day. We are certain that a professional of Molody's importance was running a far larger network of spies than the Portland ring. We assume that sometime in the near future these spies will be reactivated and provided with a new handler. HERO will not have access to the identities of those spies or their new handler, but he will see the intelligence they are providing – and, one hopes, pass it on to us.'

'And then,' Catesby said, 'we can trace the intelligence back to its source and uncover the spies among us.'

'Thank you, William,' said Bone, 'for so effortlessly jumping through the hoop of the obvious.'

'You missed the irony, Henry. I don't think it's going to be easy. And I don't think we're going to be running HERO for very long. He is too reckless and unbalanced. I'd give him a year – so I'd better start learning the Moscow Rules.'

Cliveden and Chelsea: July, 1961

Lady Somers had met him through Stephen, her osteopath. His patients included everyone from Winston Churchill to Frank Sinatra. Lady Somers went to Stephen because of chronic lower back pain. He was one of the few people who knew her medical history. He knew how to soothe her back through massage and manipulation – and also provided drugs, including cannabis, to lessen the pain. The problem with Stephen, as Lady Somers ought to have known, was that he had a big mouth.

Esteban was a guest at a little party that Stephen had hosted at his grace and favour cottage on the Cliveden estate. Lady Somers found both Esteban and the cottage a bit vulgar. Esteban wore too many rings and the cottage was the epitome of mock-Tudor kitsch. But its location and privacy, in woodland on a bend of the Thames, were superb. The two things that impressed Lady Somers about Stephen's party were the social mix – black jazz musicians, an Eastern European property millionaire, a government minister, two hereditary barons and a member of the Royal Family – and, most impressive of all, the number of stunningly beautiful young women.

Esteban had swept-back black hair that gleamed like wet coal. He wore a pencil-thin moustache that made him look like a pimp from central casting. He spoke English with a slight American accent. There appeared to be a friendly rivalry between him and Stephen. The two spent a lot of time talking in hushed whispers.

It was a very warm evening and after a while the party spilled out from the garden into the Thames itself. A few of the younger women had stripped off completely and were swimming, their naked bodies glowing like phosphorous in the dark river. Lady Somers had been strolling along the river frontage with a glass of wine when she heard the splashing and shouting. She was trying to avoid the attentions of a stout baron, who was too tactile.

But now she had to turn away from the river. She didn't want to appear to be a voyeur watching the beautiful nude swimmers. As she turned back to the house she sensed someone at her elbow. The distinctive clovey-spicey carnation scent of Malmaison perfumed the air. She knew the cologne well for Euan, her deputy at MoD, doused himself in it. For a second, Lady Somers was annoyed. He was the last person she wanted to meet at the party. She peered into the shadows expecting Euan to bound up like an effete jolly Labrador. But it wasn't him. It was Esteban.

'Were you thinking of going for a swim?' Esteban was wearing a white linen suit and too many rings.

'I haven't brought my swimsuit.'

'Neither have they,' laughed Esteban.

'I don't think my figure would compare favourably with theirs.'

'I am sure you are being too modest. You look like someone who enjoys sport.'

Lady Somers smiled. She would never tolerate such innuendo from an Englishman. 'I play tennis – and I ride occasionally.'

'To the hounds?'

'Sometimes.'

'And you dress up in those red jackets?'

Lady Somers smiled. 'Some people call them "pinks", after Thomas Pink the tailor, but they are wrong and you are right. They should be called red jackets or coats. But I'm a woman so I don't wear red when I'm hunting. I wear a black coat, usually with a flamboyant collar.'

'And shiny black boots?'

'Of course.'

'I bet you look good.'

'I hope so.'

»»»»»

Esteban's visit to Lady Somers' Georgian house in Chelsea was inevitable, perhaps even preordained. She wanted to see what it was like. It had been such a long time since it happened. She wanted to see if she could. It was raining when she let him in. Esteban shook the raindrops from his trilby. She took the hat, brushed it with feminine care and hung it on the hat-rack. She felt his eyes staring at her haunches as he followed her upstairs. She knew that she had good legs.

Lady Somers hadn't expected her daughter, Miranda, to come home that night. They argued on a daily basis and Miranda was out of control. Lady Somers hoped it was a temporary teenage thing, but suspected that it was more serious.

Miranda never came into the house quietly, but at least on this occasion she seemed to be alone and without her druggy friends. Lady Somers turned to Esteban with a finger on her lips as she listened to the footsteps on the stairs. Then the sound of the bathroom door banging open – and Miranda being sick in the toilet. Then the toilet flushing, the shower running and Miranda gargling mouthwash. Lady Somers hoped her daughter was finished and would go to bed. She lay back tense and waiting. Her feelings were ambiguous. Sometimes, on nights like these, Miranda came home full of warmth and needing her. They would sit up and talk for hours like a couple of girls. Lady Somers didn't want that now, even if she longed for it. She waited to hear Miranda's footsteps padding away to her own room. They did for a few seconds, but then they turned back. Lady Somers watched the handle of her bedroom door turn. She flicked on the bedside lamp.

Miranda was wearing a T-shirt that didn't quite cover her pubis. Her eyes were dilated from whatever drugs she had been taking and widened even more when she saw Esteban. Her first reaction was an impish smile. Then she said, 'Oops,' and pulled her T-shirt down in a gesture of mock modesty.

'Good evening, Miranda,' said Lady Somers. 'As you can see, I've got a visitor. I'd like you to meet Esteban.'

Miranda sat down on the side of the bed and extended her hand, '*Enchantée.* Or should I say, *encantada*? Are you a dago or a frog?'

'*Encantado de conocerte.*' Esteban smiled and took her hand. 'I'm a dago.'

'By the way,' said Miranda nodding towards Lady Somers, 'Penelope – that's her name if you don't know – Penelope usually doesn't do this sort of thing. I've never caught her with another man before. She isn't a tart.' Miranda gave a flirty smile. 'I'm the only tart in the family.'

Lady Somers felt no jealousy. She had already proved what she wanted to prove. But she guessed instantly that there was a bond between Esteban and her daughter – and that it wasn't a good thing and there was nothing she could do about it.

Henry Bone paid close attention to the cables from Washington and Havana. A pattern was emerging of Kennedy's presidency – a pattern of ineptness and incompetence. But how much of it was young Kennedy's fault? Bone poured himself another brandy. It was midnight at Broadway Buildings: a good time for quiet reflection. Bone looked again at the decrypted cable from his man in Havana:

> The events of the previous April have proved a complete and unmitigated disaster for US policy. There was no popular uprising to greet the invaders – and more than 1,400 of the 1,500 paramilitaries who landed on the island had been killed or captured within 48 hours. The Bay of Pigs invasion quickly turned from tragedy to farce – and has actually strengthened Castro's rule in Cuba.

Bone smiled. In a way it was good news, very good news. Henry Bone despised Allen Dulles, the US Director of Central Intelligence. He despised him even more than his brother, John Foster Dulles, who had been Secretary of State until a month before his death in 1959. Foster Dulles was not only a sanctimonious shit who had humiliated Churchill and undermined British foreign policy, but also had the rottennest breath of anyone he had ever met. It was as if he feasted on putrefying corpses. In any case, Foster was gone and Allen Dulles would soon follow. Bone knew that it would be impossible for Dulles to remain in post as DCI after the Bay of Pigs humiliation.

The White House: August, 1961

Despite the early reversals in his presidency, Jack was in a buoyant mood. The latest drugs were alleviating his chronic back pain and allowing him to get more exercise. The President's hair was still wet from his morning swim and he had had sex with both the secretaries who had joined him in the basement pool.

DCI Dulles looked at the President and found his face less puffy and 'moony' than usual. He suspected that the doctors were swapping steroids for methamphetamines and increased doses of testosterone. The use of meths was worrying. Perhaps the rumours of Kennedy running naked down the corridors of a New York hotel were true.

The President gave the DCI a boyish smile. 'How are you, Allen?'

'I am fine, Mr President, and thank you for seeing me.'

'First of all, I want to thank you. You have been a remarkable Director of Central Intelligence. You are the founding father of the CIA – and I want you to remain in post until the opening ceremony at Langley in November.'

'But I believe my successor will be taking over from next month.'

'Let's just call it a period of transition.'

The DCI took an envelope from his jacket pocket and handed it to Kennedy. 'In any case, Mr President, I have written my letter of resignation.'

'Thank you, Allen. I accept it with reluctance.'

'There is, however, another reason that I wanted to see you – a very important reason, a matter of the utmost state security.'

The President tilted his head and gave the DCI a cautious look. He suddenly felt an urge to get back in the swimming pool. 'What is it?'

'I don't want the Bay of Pigs to be my final legacy.'

Kennedy frowned. It was the DCI's final legacy, the ultimate intelligence fuck-up.

'There was, Mr President, something in your inauguration address which I will never forget. Your words were: "Let us never negotiate out of fear. But let us never fear to negotiate." Did you mean those words?'

Kennedy nodded.

'I would like to present you with an opportunity to put those words into practice. Even as we speak, the Soviet Union is becoming more and more powerful. Within five years their nuclear arsenal will be more powerful than ours. We both know that there are hawks in the Pentagon who would like us to launch a pre-emptive strike before this becomes reality. But, even if we succeeded, it would mean the destruction of Europe.'

Kennedy folded his hands and looked at the DCI with warmth. He might be a vain bumbling old fool, but at least he wasn't one of *them*. 'It is, Allen, my worst nightmare.'

'There is, Mr President, a way of confronting and weakening the Soviet Union that does not involve NATO tanks and bombers, but does involve top-secret diplomacy. The plan is so secret and sensitive that I have forbidden anyone to write down a single word. Ergo, I can only give you an oral summary. May I tell you?'

'Go on.'

The DCI's presentation lasted fifteen minutes. The President sat stony-faced and noncommittal throughout. He was going to give nothing away. As he finished, the DCI said, 'I suppose there are those who would call this treason.'

The President remained expressionless. He finally got up from his rocking chair and limped over to his desk. The back pain had returned. 'Thank you, Allen.'

'Thank you, Mr President.'

As soon as the DCI had left the Oval Office, Kennedy pressed the button on his desk intercom. 'Evelyn, can you tell Bobby and McNamara to see me as soon as possible?'

London: September, 1961

Henry Bone's celebration of the fall of Allen Dulles was short-lived. The latest cable from his man in Washington signalled new troubles.

It's certain that John McCone is going to succeed Dulles.

McCone is far more competent than his predecessor and a shrewd businessman – and, as such, he doesn't trust anyone and certainly not us. Brits are not popular in this town. I have the impression that something big is happening and we are being excluded. We are no longer consulted or even informed. It is even worse than in the aftermath of Burgess and Maclean when SIS was regarded as the London branch of Moscow Central. At one time Britain was a refined Greece to Washington's brash Rome, but they now look upon us as a bankrupt post-colonial Sodom and Gomorrah. One reason could be the rumours about John Profumo and others. I cannot overstate how damaging these rumours are – nor how well informed the Americans are, or think they are, about British sex scandals. The CIA chief in London must have a very prurient mind and a large team of informants. He should re-title himself as The Tart Finder General. Many of the rumours circulating in Washington are patently false, but there are others that have a ring of truth. The problem is that the puritanical Americans assume that sexual impropriety in high places equates to a security risk. Scratch an adulterous minister and find a Sov spy. I hope that your friend Lady Somers is running a very tight ship at the MoD. The Profumo connection and that other unfortunate business casts a shadow over her department just at a time when Britain desperately needs US military and intelligence cooperation.

Bone put the cable in the burn bag. It wasn't a document that was going to be filed for posterity. He then stared for a long time at his telephone and wondered what he should say to Lady Somers. Bone wasn't happy about one of her recent appointments. Perhaps it could still be reversed. On the other hand, why should he interfere? Whitehall was a bear pit – and when the hounds were let loose it was best to keep your distance from the bear involved. It was called survival.

»»»»»

Euan was pleased that his appointment as acting 2nd PUS at the MoD had finally, after two years in limbo, been confirmed as permanent. It was the same post that Lady Somers had occupied when he had first begun to work with her. In a way, she seemed to be looking after his career, but Euan knew there were strings attached. And one of the strings was named Tyler. Lady Somers had finally ascertained that Euan's involvement with Tyler was more than just a close working relationship within the MoD. And Lady Somers wasn't the only one who knew.

Euan was now part of the Dolphin Square crowd in Pimlico. They were louche and slightly bohemian, a lot more fun than his previous neighbours in Kensington. Euan's new flat was not only closer to Tyler, but also to Whitehall. When the weather was fine he would often walk to work along the Embankment with the Thames gleaming in the sunlight. On this occasion, the weather wasn't fine – but he was still walking, hunched as the drizzle and swirling wind whipped around him. He was also tired and bleary-eyed for he hadn't slept at all the previous night.

Euan kept looking at his watch. The note that had come with the photographs had been very specific. It said he had to be at Vauxhall Bridge at exactly eight-twenty in the morning. It was rush hour and the Embankment was full of cars, buses, bicycles and others on foot also hunched against the drizzle.

The photos of him and Tyler had been taken in a hotel in Brighton. They had spent the weekend there with some Dolphin Square friends who had recommended a nightclub called the Blue Gardenia. The owner had a beard that made him look like a cross between a jazz musician and a beat poet. And a much younger wife who flirted with everyone. It was an anything goes atmosphere.

Euan had been told to carry a copy of *The Daily Worker* tucked under his right arm. He found it embarrassing and hoped no one he knew would notice. In fact, he hid the newspaper until the last possible minute. At precisely eight-twenty he reached Vauxhall. He was waiting for the traffic lights to change to cross over when he heard the voice behind him.

'Don't turn around, comrade, you're working for us now. We know all your dirty secrets.'

As the light changed, Euan felt a hand drop something into his coat pocket. It was a perfect brush pass that no one had noticed. It was now raining harder and umbrellas were sprouting open. Euan was too frightened and confused to try to spot the person who had spoken to him. The voice had been a strange one. It certainly wasn't a British voice – nor an accented foreign one. If anything, it carried a hint of American. Not surprising; the Russians recognised where power had shifted and tended to learn American English.

Euan turned away from the river into Ponsonby Place. There was nowhere to shelter among the perfect Georgian terraces, but he had to see what had been dropped in his pocket. A postman walked past and gave him a funny look. It must have been the sight of *The Daily Worker* under the arm of someone wearing a city suit and a bowler hat. He folded up the newspaper and dropped it in a bin. He then reached into his coat pocket. It was a single typed page folded into four, a shopping list of secrets and where and how to deliver them. There was also a blackmail threat that went beyond sexually explicit photographs. *You were the one who passed secrets on to Tyler. We've got proof of that too.*

Euan found himself shaking and breathing hard. He imagined dozens of pairs of eyes staring at him from the identical Georgian sash windows of Ponsonby Place. Lady Somers had instructed him to promote Tyler and to pass on 'disinformation' to mislead Moscow. But who would believe that? He felt a wave of nausea. Had he been duped? Was Lady Somers a spy?

»»»»»

'Hello, John. How nice to see you again.'

It was a beautiful early evening and Tyler had just crossed Horse Guards into St James's Park. The voice was different and the face was completely different, but Tyler still knew it was him. He avoided eye contact and quickened his pace. 'I don't want to get involved again. It's finished.'

'You are wrong, John. It's never finished – not as long as

you're still on this side of death and Wormwood Scrubs Prison. It wasn't finished when Konon was running you. What did he call himself – Lonsdale or Johnson? You don't have to answer that. It doesn't matter because Konon was busted and is now in jail – as you well know.'

'I'm actually meeting someone in a club in Pall Mall – and I'm late so I'm in a hurry.'

'What has Euan told you?'

'Our conversations are none of your business.'

'Doesn't he even tell you how pretty you are?'

Tyler stopped. 'I must say I'm a bit confused by all this. What do you want?'

'You're in a desperate situation, an extremely dangerous situation.'

'I'm not unaware of it.'

'Does Vasili have any proof that you're passing things on to him? You don't need to look confused. Vasili– or whatever he's calling himself – is the agent who reactivated you after Konon was busted. Vasili is dangerous. We expect that he has been doubled by the British. Do you know what I'm talking about?'

Tyler gave a slight nod.

'A lot of us are certain that Vasili betrayed Konon. You must have no more contact with him. We fear that the British are using him to betray agents such as yourself.'

'What if you're wrong?' Tyler paused. 'Or what if you're lying?'

The other man shrugged. 'I might be wrong, but I'm not lying.'

For the first time, Tyler looked uncertain.

'Things are bad. Our agency is at war with itself. I know for certain that Vasili betrayed me – but I escaped. And now he denies it. You've got to make a choice.'

'What sort of choice?'

'I want you to trust me as your agent handler. By the way, how much has he been paying you?'

'Five hundred pounds every other month.'

The other man laughed. 'He's a cheat as well. He's pocketing half the money.'

Tyler's eyes gave a flicker of interest.

'I'll pay you the full amount – and with any luck Vasili will be recalled to Moscow to answer some hard questions.'

'Maybe you're bluffing. Let's see the money first.'

'Sit on that bench as if we're having a chat. When we get up, you take my briefcase – you'll find a roll of two hundred five-pound notes in it, as well as cipher pads and a new Minox camera – and I'll take yours.'

They sat down. Tyler stirred uneasily. His eyes darted around trying to spot a hidden watcher.

'Just like old times, John. Isn't it?'

'How do I contact you?'

'You don't contact me. I contact you. You'll need the cipher pads to decode my messages.'

They got up, each lifting the other's briefcase. The deal was done.

Brighton: October, 1961

Esteban cut up another lime and added it to the cocktail shaker with the white rum, mint leaves, sugar and ice. He danced salsa steps behind the bar as he shook the cocktail above his head. Miranda clapped her hands and laughed.

After a final rattle, Esteban put the shaker back on the bar. 'Have another mojito, *mi querida*. It is the Cuban national drink.'

Miranda held out her glass. Her pupils were dilated from cocaine and, although it was only the afternoon, she wanted to party. 'I hope you're not going to break Pen's heart.'

'No,' said Esteban suddenly serious, 'you're the only person who can break her heart.'

'Yes, you're right about that – and it's a terrible responsibility.'

'Will she always support you? No matter what you do?'

Miranda nodded. 'Yes – and that's another terrible responsibility.'

'Do you hate being a poor little rich girl?'

'I'm not little – but I hate selfish rich bastards and bullies. And what about you? Do you hate being a rich bastard?'

'What do you know about me?'

'I know that you're a lying bastard. You didn't own a casino, as well as a string of whorehouses and a bank in Havana. And you're not a refugee from Castro's revolution.' Miranda swept her arm towards the faded grandeur of the Regency ceiling. 'And you didn't buy this hotel to make money from dirty weekends and blackmail.' Miranda pointed at the centre of the ceiling. 'By the way, is there a camera lens in that ceiling rose too?'

'No, only those in the bedrooms.'

Miranda smiled. 'It's a good thing those two chaps from Mother's office didn't see me.'

'Your glass is empty. Have another mojito.'

'Why are you trying to get me drunk? You don't want to have sex with me – and I think we know why.'

Esteban smiled bleakly. 'What else do you know about me?'

She told him.

'Since you seem to know so many of my secrets, perhaps you would consider working for me.'

'I wouldn't be working for you; I'd be working for what I believe in – a Maoist revolution.'

'I believe in that too, but our first task is to protect China as the cradle of that revolution.'

»»»»»

At first, Miranda felt sorry for the scientist, but she soon began to despise him and to be disgusted by what he wanted. But she did it because Esteban assured her that he was one of their most valuable assets. The scientist was a specialist in aerodynamics and had been a professor at Imperial College when he was first spotted and compromised by Cauldwell. At the time, his career as a Soviet asset had been short-lived. The information that he was blackmailed into handing over was simply not valuable enough. For more than three years he had been left alone. During that time he had left Imperial College to take up a high security post at AWE, the Atomic Weapons Establishment in Aldermaston. His job involved 'weaponising' nuclear bombs, making them small enough to be shot from rockets – and making sure the rocket was the best aerodynamic shape.

Miranda met him at a party at Aldermaston Court that she easily crashed with her self-assurance and upper-class accent. The manor house had been requisitioned during the war and, afterwards, turned over to a private research company who worked closely with AWE. Miranda pretended to be drunker than she was and 'confessed' that she was actually a CND activist who wanted to convert a nuclear scientist to the cause. At first, the scientist thought she was telling the truth and his ego was so inflated that he didn't realise that Miranda was far too young and beautiful for someone like him to pull. He also reckoned that going to bed with a British CND type wasn't the same as consorting with a Soviet spy. It was an unwise act, but not a criminal offence – or even one for which he could get sacked.

When Miranda asked him what he 'really wanted' and what really turned him on, he shouldn't have told her. And when she readily complied, it didn't take him long to realise that he had fallen into a honey trap. But his need and desire were too strong to back away. He was obsessed. The scientist was trapped in a cage of passion.

At first, the sessions at Esteban's Brighton hotel were a weekly event. But then Miranda began to pull away – and sometimes not turn up at all or refuse to play the game. This made the scientist even more desperate. He knew that he was compromised and he knew there were photographs. He was afraid of blackmail, but he was more afraid of losing Miranda and the pleasure she gave him. He began to take more risks and to provide whatever secrets she demanded.

Miranda hated every minute of it. She had to use drugs and alcohol to deaden her senses so she could go along with the scientist's predilection for being treated like a baby. She had to feed him and also change him and powder him when he had a poo. Sometimes, when he was a good baby, he would lie next to her gurgling and sucking at her breast until he fell asleep. But at other times, he would kick out and throw tantrums – and Miranda began to bear bruises and black eyes. She soon realised that she wasn't being a very good mummy.

Nonetheless, the intelligence from Aldermaston continued to flow. Once every few weeks, at irregular intervals and never in the same place, Esteban would pass on rolls of film to his courier.

»»»»»

Fiona was a waif from Hackney. She ran away from home for good when she was sixteen and her father said 'good riddance'. She had a brief fling with a publican who wanted her to have sex with other men; she stabbed him with a kitchen knife. She did six months in Holloway for the stabbing and began a friendship with a woman who had also stabbed her lover. They called themselves 'the surgeon girls'. The friend recommended to

Fiona that she get a job in a club called Murray's in Soho. 'Pops treats the girls okay and lets you do what you want. He don't ask questions.'

Pops and his son David were both ex-military and Murray's had an air of respectability that was fading fast. There were two jobs for pretty young women. One was dancing fully clothed; the other job was standing bare-breasted and completely motionless in the background. Fiona became one of the bare-breasted girls. She and the other semi-naked girls were kitted out in exotic oriental dress and had to stand completely still. The Lord Chancellor's censorship laws meant that strippers had to pose as immobile statues. During breaks, they covered up so they could become animated again and mingle with the customers. The girls were expected to entice the customers into ordering over-priced champagne for themselves and non-alcoholic fake champagne for the girls. The girls weren't supposed to meet the customers after the show, but the management turned a blind eye if they did.

Fiona met Stephen at Murray's. She was impressed by his wit and charm and the fact that he didn't seem interested in using her for sex. And through Stephen she met Esteban at a Cliveden party. Fiona's head began to whirl. In a few weeks she had progressed from cleaning toilets at HMP Holloway to rubbing shoulders with lords and ladies. She had become someone who mattered.

Miranda became the sister that Fiona had always longed for. They complemented each other and even began to imitate each other's accents and manners. They copied each other so perfectly that it was soon difficult to know for sure which was the posh girl and which the Hackney waif. The way the two could exchange identities became very useful. One of the ugly enigmas of the English class system is the preference of upper-class powerful men, be they hetero or homosexual, for sexual partners from the 'lower orders'.

In a way, Miranda enjoyed pretending she was Fiona during her honey-trap affair with the cabinet minister. She had, in fact, met the man at a country-house party, but the minister didn't recognise her. He probably couldn't see past her fake cockney accent. What surprised her was his kindness. He was probably nicer to her than he was to his wife – and without being patronising. Miranda hadn't expected this; maybe the cabinet minister was an exception. But despite his kindness, she began to realise that his coming to meet her in the Brighton hotel was a form of arrogance. He must have known that he risked being compromised and the risk itself was part of the thrill. But the important thing was proving that he could get away with anything because of who he was. The joy of being a member of the upper-class elite wasn't just power, but total freedom. You could fuck, murder and spy as you pleased – and then lie about it. You were part of an untouchable elite. But the thing that bothered Miranda most of all was the realisation that she was one of them. And, as she rewound the tape that had recorded the minister's pillow talk revelation of security secrets, she realised that she was behaving true to form. Her being caught wouldn't mean prison: it would mean a cover-up.

Fiona had two weaknesses: drugs and wanting to be like Miranda. Esteban was okay about coke and marijuana – and even supplied the girls from his own sources. But he didn't like heroin, which was getting to be a big problem for Miranda, or LSD, which had become Fiona's drug of choice. She felt her transition from Holloway to Cliveden was a weird and wonderful trip and she wanted to heighten that sense of hallucination and exhilaration even more.

But Fiona's wanting to be like Miranda was just as dangerous as LSD. A secret part of Fiona wanted to be posh – which was exactly what Miranda loathed about herself. In a strange way both women were striving to be their opposites, and that striving knitted them ever closer. Miranda was Fiona's role model. Her conversion to Miranda's radical left-wing politics was a far deeper conviction than anything the socialists of her native Hackney could have achieved. Fiona found the Hackney reds boring. Miranda, on the other hand, was bringing down capitalism from the very highest level. Fighting for the oppressed was what posh girls did. It was more chic than anything you could buy on King's Road or Carnaby Street.

Neither of them liked the sex part. But it was something they had to do for the revolution. And it was also an education. Before Brighton neither woman had known the difference between a 'plushy' and a 'furry' – and neither had Esteban, who seemed an encyclopaedia of depravity. It was something they could share a laugh about.

'Furries' were the less complicated of the two. They liked to dress up as furry cartoon animals. The senior civil servant was a plump jolly man who knew all about plutonium handling facilities. He liked to dress up, quite aptly, as Pluto the Disney dog to have cross-species sex with Bambi. The worst thing for Fiona was that they both got so sweaty in the furry suits.

'Plushies' were a difficult target for honey-trap agents. 'Plushies' preferred having sex with inanimate furry objects like teddy bears. And teddy bears and other inanimate furry objects aren't very good at making blackmail threats. The 'plushy' that Miranda was trying to entrap was a top nuclear physicist at the Atomic Energy Research Establishment in Harwell, the same place where Soviet spy Klaus Fuchs had worked. Miranda met him at the Kicking Donkey pub in Harwell. She found him a pleasant boyish man with an air of innocence. Part of her hated the idea of trapping him. They became good friends. Miranda invented an imaginary brother and started dropping hints about his 'strange' behaviour and lack of girlfriends or boyfriends. The scientist opened up like a neglected book longing to be read. He wasn't the only one. At last, he had found someone with whom he could share his dark secret.

He began by leaning over his pint and whispering, 'Have you read *Brideshead Revisited*?'

Miranda frowned. She knew a lot of the real-life people on whom the characters were based. 'Yes, but it's not my favourite book.'

The scientist smiled. 'Ah, but maybe that's because you don't know the book's secret; it's sort of a *roman à clef*.'

Miranda gave a conspiratorial smile. 'But I think I'm starting to guess.'

'The relationship between Sebastian Flyte and Aloysius is deeper than most readers realise.'

'But Aloysius is only a teddy bear.'

'How dare you say *only* a bear!'

'I'm so sorry.'

The scientist lowered his voice. 'In fact, I've got my own Aloysius – and, like Sebastian's Aloysius, he has an ivory-handled hairbrush inscribed with his name that I comb him with. He can't, of course, comb himself. Would you like to meet Aloysius?'

'I would love to.'

'I'll ask him if he'll let you comb him, but I can't promise that he will say yes. He can be very tetchy around strangers.'

Miranda and the scientist began to date in a very chaste way. She eventually visited his house and met, not only Aloysius, but five hundred other furry creatures. His dry cleaning bill, thought Miranda, must be enormous. As they got to know each other better, the scientist began to explain some intimate things – such as that selected furry creatures were equipped with SPAs (Strategically Placed Appendages) or SPHs (Strategically Placed Holes).

As a birthday treat, Miranda threw a surprise party for the scientist at Esteban's Brighton hotel. The best part of the surprise was that the scientist's hotel room was filled with fifty new plush creatures – many of whom were equipped with SPHs. The largest was a five-foot-high teddy with dewy seductive eyes. As the scientist consummated his new relationships, the camera in the ceiling rose whirred away.

On his next visit to the hotel, Miranda tried to convert the scientist from 'plushy' to 'furry'. She realised that Bambi wouldn't work, so she dressed up in a teddy bear suit and spoke in a gruff petulant voice. The scientist spent a long time combing her with Aloysius's hairbrush. She finally managed to get him to do it. It was the scientist's first time with a human being. He was tearful and distraught afterwards and full of guilt.

'Aloysius,' he said, 'will never forgive me – and I used his hairbrush.'

When confronted with the photographs as a blackmail threat to obtain nuclear secrets, the ones that upset the scientist most were the ones of him doing it with Miranda. The scientist seemed more terrified that the photos would be shown to Aloysius and his other plush friends than to his superiors at Harwell. He agreed to cooperate.

Zhongnanhai compound, Peking: April, 1962

The Great Helmsman is no longer at the helm. He no longer takes part in day-to-day decision making, but devotes his days and nights to pleasure and to developing his theory of 'continuous revolution'. But despite his apparent withdrawal, he is still very much in power. The People's Liberation Army will always follow his bidding and remove any opponent.

Feifei still visits him almost every day and continues to show great deference and to hide his growing personal dislike of the Chairman. As the women providing his pleasure grow in numbers, they decrease in age. The Chairman believes he reinvigorates himself by absorbing the life energy of the young. And despite his doctor's pleading, he refuses to take antibiotics for a sexually transmitted disease that he passes on to his young partners. 'If it doesn't hurt me, why should I bother?' And he still refuses to brush his green teeth. 'Has anyone ever seen a tiger brush his teeth?'

The two men sit in silence for a long time before the Chairman looks up from the notebook in which he has been writing. 'The Great Leap Forward, Feifei, is part of a process which is unending.'

'I completely agree, Comrade Chairman.'

'With what do you agree?'

'That our revolution has liberated a quarter of the world's population from feudalism, ignorance and poverty and that it must continue.'

'And what is your role, Feifei?'

'My role is implementing your ideas on a daily basis.'

Feifei cannot say what he really thinks. He cannot explain that he is one of a group of pragmatists who are repairing the Chairman's colossal errors of judgement.

'Tell me, Feifei, when are we going to test our first A-bomb?'

'We are making rapid progress. We hope to have the first test in 1964. Our great technological advances are the direct results, Comrade Chairman, of the wisdom of your Great Leap Forward.'

Feifei was lying. The truth of the matter was the greatest secret of the many secrets that he had to keep from the Chairman.

Broadway Buildings, London: December, 1962

The intelligence community in London were still celebrating the fact that the Cuban Missile Crisis hadn't destroyed their homes and families. The spooks, more than anyone, realised how close Britain had come to annihilation. Bone and Catesby were elbow to elbow in the tiny rickety lift that went to the Director's fourth-floor office.

'If,' Catesby said, 'the public knew what was really going on, there would be a revolution.'

'And that's all the more reason why we have to keep it from them. By the way, William, you are in for a gong in appreciation of the work you did in Havana and Washington. It will be announced in the New Year's honours.'

'I don't want a gong. It's all a load of feudal nonsense.'

'If you don't accept it, you are going to be hung, drawn and quartered. More feudal nonsense.'

The lift door wheezed open and they stepped on to the thick burgundy carpet that led to Dick White's office. There was a famous Turner hanging in the corridor that depicted a red and yellow sunset over London with swirling apocalyptic clouds. Catesby wondered how anyone who knew how close London had come to a nuclear holocaust in the past few weeks could bear to look at the painting.

The green light next to the door flashed on, which meant they could walk in without knocking. Dick White was there to greet them. Catesby was surprised how much the Director had aged since he had last seen him.

'Thank you both for coming,' said White. 'I know it's very late.' It was nearly midnight. 'Events are moving rapidly and not the way we want them to move.' The Director smiled wearily. 'But don't worry. It's not a crisis about missiles being launched – at least, not yet. Please sit down.' White gestured to the chintz-covered armchairs in front of a fireplace where a real coal fire defied Westminster's smokeless zone regulations. 'Tea? Or something more relaxing? I'm having a whisky.'

'Nothing for me,' said Bone.

'I'll join you, sir, with a whisky.' Catesby's 'sir' was sincere. Dick White was one of the few Whitehall mandarins whom Catesby genuinely respected.

'The problem,' said White pouring the drinks, 'concerns either HERO, our crown jewel in Moscow Central, or something more serious.'

'I think,' Catesby said, 'this doesn't come as a surprise to any of us. It's HERO. The autumn gales must have blown the last pan tiles off his shed roof.'

'Perhaps that is the case,' said White nodding and putting on his reading glasses as he opened a manila file with red stripes indicating UK EYES ALPHA. 'Until recently we had a steady backflow of intelligence from HERO indicating the usual level of intelligence gathering by known or unknown Soviet agents in the UK. This seems to have dried up.'

'Moscow,' said Bone, 'is an impossible place to operate. I was never impressed by the use of Vanessa's baby's pram as a DLB.'

Catesby nodded. He knew that Bone was referring to the way HERO used to pass on intelligence during walks through Gorky Park. For his part, he disapproved of the way his SIS colleague had used his infant daughter as an unwitting agent. But at least the baby had diplomatic immunity.

'I agree,' said White, 'but since Giles has taken over as head of station, exchange methods have become much more varied and sophisticated.'

'Such as?' said Catesby.

'Bathroom bleach bottles with false bottoms, toilet cisterns, dead drop spikes.'

'Good,' said Catesby. He was a big fan of the dead drop spike. You pushed it into the ground as you pretended to tie your shoe-lace and did likewise when you recovered one. The agent had to remember to wear shoes with laces.

'In fact,' said White, 'until very recently, the number of dead drop exchanges had been increasing – even though the amount of intelligence contained decreased. HERO was very aware of this and expressed his concern.'

'Did he,' said Catesby, 'fear that he might be under suspicion – and, therefore, temporarily or permanently out of the loop?'

'At first that was what he feared, but then he became aware that his colleagues at Moscow Central were also alarmed at the lack of intelligence coming from their agents in Britain. HERO reckons that three-quarters of the intelligence flow from the UK has dried up – and very suddenly.' White took a document out of the manila folder and stared at it. 'Some of this drying up is probably the after-effects of our busting Molody and the Portland ring, but that wouldn't explain why Moscow's man in the Admiralty has also gone quiet.' White was referring to Tyler, who had been left in place as an unwitting agent to pass on disinformation.

'Perhaps,' said Catesby, 'Moscow Central twigged that Tyler was a plant because he was passing on duff stuff.'

'That is possible,' said White, 'but it doesn't explain why so many other agents – the ones we hadn't identified and were hoping to trap through HERO – have also ceased communication.'

'Maybe they're running scared because of what happened to Molody.'

White shrugged. 'That may well be the case. But we don't know and need to find out. In any case, HERO is certainly running scared. He's virtually disappeared off the radar.' White paused and looked at Catesby. 'We can't afford to lose an agent as valuable as this one.'

'HERO,' said Bone, 'is now refusing to communicate through the usual methods.'

Catesby looked up, displeased. 'So, Henry, you knew about this all along?'

'I didn't know everything until this evening.'

White intervened. 'I asked Henry not to mention anything until now. So, William, if anyone has kept you in the dark, it has been me.'

Catesby felt a chill run down his spine. 'I know what's coming next.'

'I sincerely wish,' said White, 'that there was another way. But please allow me to continue briefing you. HERO sent a very worried and desperate note to Giles...'

Catesby frowned. Giles, as the new SIS man in Moscow, shouldn't have to handle this. He didn't know the vagaries of HERO.

'The note came,' explained Bone, 'via a tin of Harpic bleach with a false bottom.'

'It was,' continued White, 'left in the bathroom of a hotel room, not one of Gile's usual dead drop locations, and passed on to the embassy by a very frightened businessman whom we sometimes use as a NOC.'

'I don't like the sound of this,' said Catesby. NOC was an acronym for a Non-Official Cover spy. If you were spying as a NOC, it meant you had no diplomatic immunity. If you got caught you went to a Soviet prison. Catesby knew that NOCs were the bravest spies in the business – and he dreaded being one.

'By the way,' said Bone, 'the businessman suspected that his hotel room had been searched. It took a long time for reception to find his room key.'

White picked up the document from the UK EYES ALPHA folder. 'This is HERO's note...'

Bone flashed his undertaker's smile. 'It sounds like a last will and testament.'

'I hope it isn't one,' said White, 'but the tone is dramatic. Here it is: "*Dearest Giles, I am very lonely and am desperate to see you, but it is too dangerous. I am sure that I am under constant surveillance. It is impossible to continue to use our usual means of communication. The air in Moscow Central is so thick with suspicion that one cannot see. I fear my own days are numbered, but I remain a loyal soldier of Her Majesty the Queen. I want to perform one last service before I die. But I don't want to die. I want you to rescue me. I can serve you better as a live soldier in London than as a dead hero in Moscow. The best plan is for me and my family to go on holiday to a Black Sea resort and then in the dark of night you send a Royal Navy submarine to pick us up.*

Or Berlin? Or a rendezvous with a fast torpedo boat in the Baltic near Riga?'" White paused and looked over his reading glasses. 'Actually, getting him out is a good idea. And we have a plan in place.'

Bone looked at Catesby. 'Drugged in the boot of a car and over the Finnish border. Will fill you in later.'

'We also,' said White, 'have contingency plans in place for HERO to contact us or for us to contact him in an emergency situation, such as the imminent outbreak of war or a Kremlin coup. It looks as though we're going to have to put one of those in place.'

Catesby nodded. 'And that's where I come in?'

'I am afraid, William, that is the case. It came down to a choice between you and Shergy and you drew the lucky straw. In any case, allow me to finish HERO's letter: "*I fear that something awful has happened in London. But no one knows what it is. The KGB* rezident *at the Soviet Embassy in London was recently recalled to Moscow for consultations. There was, apparently, an angry scene with insults and accusations flying back and forth. There is a rumour that our intelligence operations are in peril because of a traitor at the highest level. A traitor near the top may well be true. But you won't find that traitor in the Kremlin. You will find that traitor in London. One of your very own has betrayed Britain. I still do not know who that person is, but my greatest service to you (and perhaps my last) will be to reveal that traitor's name. Long live the Queen!*"'

Bone looked at Catesby. 'You seem unusually thoughtful. What do you think?'

'I am, Henry, more thoughtful than you realise. I am beginning to suspect, for the first time, that HERO may be a KGB plant.'

'Why?' said White.

'Because that stuff about a British traitor at the highest level sounds like an attempt to throw a hand grenade into the middle of Whitehall – to get us at each other's throats.'

'We've considered that possibility,' said White, 'and that's why we have to send you to Moscow. Other than Shergy, you know

HERO better than any of us. We want you to meet him face to face…'

'And,' said Bone, 'squeeze the truth out of him.'

'How,' said Catesby, 'can we be sure that HERO's letter isn't a KGB forgery?'

'We are,' said White, 'taking a calculated risk in assuming that the letter is genuine.' The Director looked at Catesby with almost parental care. 'But maybe it isn't.'

'Don't worry,' said Bone with a wry smile, 'if things go tits up I'm sure Downing Street will authorise swapping Molody to get you back. If not, it will be a great opportunity to improve your Russian.'

'Thanks, Henry.'

Moscow: 16 January 1963

Catesby was very nervous. He had never had to play Moscow Rules before because he had never been to Moscow. And he knew that he was going to be all alone because no one from the British Embassy would go anywhere near him. Catesby was alone when his Aeroflot flight from Heathrow arrived at Vnukovo Airport. He was alone when he passed through customs in the freezing terminal, alone when a frowning customs official confiscated his copy of the *Manchester Guardian* – you weren't allowed to bring books or Western media into the USSR. (Of course, Catesby knew that, but carried the newspaper to suggest he wasn't a professional.) Catesby felt alone – and frightened too – when he boarded the bus that stank of diesel fumes for the seventeen-mile trip into Moscow. Catesby was alone because all British Embassy staff, especially SIS spies operating under diplomatic cover, were under constant KGB surveillance. If anyone from the embassy had met him, the KGB surveillance teams would have clicked into action and put a tail on Catesby too. Several tails. Manpower was no problem in Moscow.

Moscow was bleak. Almost, thought Catesby, as bleak as Lowestoft – which was nearer to Russia than any place in the UK. It was a connection that made Catesby smile. An even bleaker Lowestoft connection was the Dogger Bank incident in 1904. The Russian Imperial Fleet, en route to the Russo-Japanese war, had opened fire on Hull and Lowestoft trawlers. The Russians thought the fishing vessels were Japanese gunboats lying in ambush in the fog – even though Japan was still another 13,000 nautical miles away. One of Catesby's uncles skippered a trawler that was caught in the line of fire – 'I thought it was a firework display until them shells started landing' – but escaped unharmed. Catesby thought about telling the story to a Soviet soldier to practise his Russian. The airport was full of armed

soldiers – and three of them even came on the bus. The paranoia that caused them to open fire on the trawlers was still there
– and why shouldn't it be? The memory of losing nine million
soldiers and seventeen million civilians in the last war was still
raw in the Russian mind.

Catesby wanted to get the job over with as quickly as possible. He didn't want to hang around in Moscow. He was travelling undercover as an electrical engineer from Birmingham. In
a way, the meeting with HERO need not have been clandestine.
HERO's day job, as an official in the State Scientific and Technical Commission, meant that he could openly meet engineers
and scientists from the West. In the end, however, it was decided
that the rendezvous should be secret. The details had been
arranged by Giles in Moscow. Catesby trusted Giles completely
and admired his professionalism as an SIS head of station, but
following someone else's script in a strange and dangerous city
is a nervous business. In any case, Catesby had learned his lines
and stage directions to perfection.

Catesby asked the bus driver to drop him off at the Yugo-
Zapadnaya station of the Moscow Metro. The request aroused
the curiosity of one of the soldiers who asked to see Catesby's
papers and hotel reservation. The soldier seemed disappointed
to find that everything was in order. He handed back the papers
and reminded Catesby – with a lot of finger wagging – that it
was a serious offence to carry out illegal currency transactions.
Officially, the rouble traded at one to one with the pound. On
the black market, you could get 25 roubles to the pound.

The hotel room was spartan, but clean and warm. The windows
were triple-glazed. There was a radio with a polished wood
veneer that was bolted to a shelf. Catesby saw that you couldn't
unplug the radio, because the wire disappeared straight into the
wall, and you couldn't turn it off either. But you could turn down
the volume so the sound reduced to a barely audible hiss. He was
certain that the radio contained a listening device. Catesby was
tempted to sing to the radio the Lowestoft sea shanties he had
learned from his uncle the trawler skipper, but decided it was
best not to attract attention – no matter how innocent.

Catesby washed and brushed up for the meeting – and trimmed the moustache he had grown as a feeble disguise. He thought that the black moustache and back-combed Bryl-creemed hair made him look more like a spiv than an engineer. On the other hand, his electrical engineer persona was a busi-nessman on the make. Perhaps, thought Catesby, he should have done some illegal rouble transactions to make his 'legend', his cover story, seem more genuine.

Once again, Catesby used the Moscow Metro in preference to a taxi with a driver who would have to report his foreign fares to the KGB. Catesby could easily read Cyrillic so there were no navigation problems. He had to get off at a station called Aka-demicheskaya. It was, as the name suggested, near the Univer-sity of Moscow.

When Catesby disembarked and emerged on to the street, he was, for the first time since arriving in Moscow, utterly impressed. He had known beforehand that the main university building was going to be massive, but not as massive and glit-tering as it appeared in the freezing night air. It was the tallest building in Europe – 790 feet and thirty-six storeys – and broad and muscular too. Catesby found himself gawping like a tourist and wishing that he had a camera – even though carrying a camera always meant trouble. But he didn't have time to hang around, so he got moving.

The rendezvous was on the eighth floor of a Stalinist-era block of flats to the southwest of the university. It was a brisk five-minute walk from the Metro. Catesby decided not to take the sort of counter-surveillance methods that he would have used elsewhere. That would have been a big mistake; it would only make you appear suspicious. In any case, one of the Moscow Rules was that if they were following you, there would be so many of them that you could do nothing about it.

The entrance to the block of flats had a heavy iron door. It looked like the entrance to a tomb and, when it clanged shut behind him, Catesby felt as though he was trapped in a tomb. There was no porter's lodge and no lift. The foyer was almost completely dark; the only feeble rays of light came from a bare low-wattage bulb in the staircase. Catesby mounted the stairs and counted the floors. He stopped when he got to the seventh for he heard low husky breathing from the floor above and smelled cigarette smoke. His first instinct was to retrace his steps and flee. He wanted to run straight to the extra-territorial safety of the British Embassy – but knew that he would never get there. He continued to mount the stairs to the landing of the rendezvous flat.

There were two of them. They were hatted and coated, but not against a cold Moscow winter. They had come by car. Their eyes glowed reptilian from the shadows of their trilbies. Catesby played it straight and naive, as if he really were an electrical engineer from Birmingham – and spoke in the stumbling Russian of someone far less fluent than himself. He recited his cover story to the less Neanderthal of the goons, the one whose knuckles didn't quite reach the floor, and gave HERO's actual name and position within the Scientific and Technical Commission. Catesby wasn't sure how much the goons knew and what their role was in regards to HERO. Perhaps one was a driver and the other was a bodyguard or gofer. After a long pause, the goon opened the door and said, 'Go in. He's waiting for you.'

But when Catesby entered, the room was empty. There was nothing except for a table and two chairs underneath a bare lightbulb. The door shut behind him. Catesby sat in one of the chairs and stared into space. There was the sound of a toilet flushing, but it seemed to come from the floor above. And then he heard an angry voice shouting: 'Why are you here? Get out.' And the sound of feet pounding down the stairs. Catesby suddenly realised the entire building had been cleared for his visit. That wasn't good.

Catesby strained to hear other sounds and stared at the door opposite. He wondered what was behind it. A kitchen? A bedroom? A sheer drop into nothingness? Finally, he did hear something. It was the sound of water running followed by a man coughing – as if he had just taken a pill. Catesby waited and stared. The door opened.

It wasn't HERO, but Catesby had long since given up any

hope of seeing their double agent. But the man was someone he did recognise, even if he hadn't seen him in real life. The man's suit, by Soviet standards, was of excellent cut. He was good-looking and about Catesby's age. The age similarity reminded Catesby that the man had been a helluva lot more successful in the profession than he had. Unlike Catesby, this man wasn't an expendable field operative who got sent on missions abroad under dodgy cover. No, this man was Vladimir Yefimovich Semichastny, the Head of the KGB.

'Welcome to Moscow, Mr Catesby. Excuse me for a second.' Semichastny brushed past and opened the door on to the landing.

Catesby turned away but continued to listen as Semichastny told the two goons to wait for him in the car. He didn't want any eavesdroppers. There was the sound of heavy footsteps pounding down the stairs. As the iron door clanged shut, Catesby felt the barrel of a gun push into the hollow where the top of the spine enters the back of the head.

'Please, Mr Catesby, do not try anything funny or heroic. It would be pointless. In any case, I only want to have a little talk.' Semichastny slipped the Makarov 9mm back into his shoulder holster and sat in the chair opposite.

'I don't suppose Oleg is going to join us?'

'No, Oleg is not going to join us. We find it ironic that you called him HERO.'

'It's a matter of perspective. Is he dead?'

'No, of course not. We are not Stalinists who carry out brutal and secret executions. He will be tried in public in the spring – everything open and legal. But he is guilty and has confessed.'

'He was a very reckless spy.'

'And it was very reckless for your superiors to have sent you here. We were expecting you.'

Catesby smiled wanly. Semichastny, ever the professional, wasn't going to miss an opportunity to stir up suspicions about his SIS colleagues in London. Catesby was now certain that HERO's desperate letter had been written under duress.

'We easily found the Minox camera and the code pads you

had given Oleg when we searched his flat. When we arrested him, he went limp like a wet rag. He couldn't even stand up and walk without help. A most pathetic man – and you call him HERO.'

'To be fair, Vladimir Yefimovich, we British also have a sense of irony.'

'It is something, as well as a love of literature, that our two peoples share. It is, perhaps, ironic that we are enemies.'

'Maybe one day we will share a glass of vodka or Highland whisky.'

'I hope so, but not this evening.' Semichastny gave Catesby an odd look. 'Aren't you afraid of what is going to happen to you?'

'Why? My being afraid won't change anything.'

'That is true. But we are not going to arrest you – even though I was put under a lot of pressure to do so. Many of my colleagues regard you as a valuable bargaining chip for a spy swap.'

'Tell them I am flattered.'

'We are not going to arrest you because you are more valuable as a messenger than a prisoner.'

Catesby stared back at Semichastny. The pieces of the puzzle were clunking into place.

'Oleg's last messages to you revealed that our spy networks in England were producing very little intelligence. At first, we thought this was because of Molody's arrest. Konon, by the way, will never talk. Eventually, we reactivated some of the spies that Molody had been running. We assigned them new agent handlers. For a while there was a flow of intelligence from these sources, but then none at all. Later, we realised that agents who had been very productive in the past – and who were totally separate from Molody's networks – had also ceased all communication. In short, almost our entire intelligence operation in the United Kingdom had ceased to function.'

Catesby knew that it was his turn to give the expected response. 'Excuse me, Vladimir Yefimovich, but my superiors might well think that your remarks are part of a disinformation ploy to induce UK counterintelligence to lower its guard.'

'They may think that, but I can provide you with proof to the contrary.' Semichastny looked very tired and concerned. 'Something awful has happened – something that has put my country in grave danger. And it is also a matter of grave concern to the United Kingdom.' The Russian gave a weary smile. 'As with irony, this is something that should bring our countries together – and that we should be working together to stop.'

Catesby waited. He could sense that Semichastny was sincere and choosing his words carefully.

'Our spy networks in Britain have been taken over by the People's Republic of China. Britain's most important nuclear and strategic secrets are now going to Peking.'

Catesby wasn't surprised. He had known for some time that what Semichastny was saying was true – but he also knew how difficult it would have been to convince his colleagues in SIS and the wider Whitehall establishment. Catesby had kept his mouth shut because he had no evidence. He looked at Semichastny: 'You said you had proof.'

The Russian reached into his coat pocket. What he drew out wasn't a document or a microfilm, but the torn corner of a photograph. He passed it across the table. Catesby immediately knew that the torn edges would fit perfectly into the rest of the photo. At last, the tableau photograph of Poussin's *The Triumph of Pan* would again be complete.

'She is,' said Semichastny, 'a very beautiful woman.'

Catesby looked at Lady Somers in Grecian dress and was inclined to agree. He picked up the torn photo and was about to put it in his pocket when Semichastny reached over and took it back.

'I thought...' said Catesby.

'Then you thought wrong. That photo was for you to see, not to keep.' The Head of the KGB smiled sagely and put the evidence back in his pocket.

Brighton: 17 January 1963

She was completely naked and sprinting towards the sea. Some of the witnesses said she had a knife in her hand with blood on it. It was a freezing January midnight in Brighton – long after the parties had stopped. The second to last person to see her alive was a tramp in Regency Square. He said she wasn't a woman, but a banshee with long hair on fire streaming behind her. The tramp said she was carrying a sword – with blood on it. He saw her race past the war memorial, across King's Road and then into the darkness of shingle beach and sea. The tramp said he heard a hiss when the cold sea extinguished her hair. The cops said he wasn't a reliable witness. The cops weren't allowed to say more. They were told to shut up and get off the case.

In retrospect, Esteban wasn't surprised that it ended that way. Fiona had been going off the rails ever since Christmas. The Christmas holidays were a bad time for her. It reminded her of everything she didn't have, had never had – and never would have. And she certainly wouldn't have it now. The ambulance crew were unable to revive her after the lifeboat crew found her bobbing around near the end of the pier; she was too far gone.

Miranda felt it was her fault and doubled her heroin use to cope with the guilt. It was just before Christmas that she had passed on to Fiona the scientist with adult baby syndrome. Miranda loathed him and found dealing with his needs repulsive. Esteban had agreed to the change because he could see that things weren't going well between her and the scientist. On the other hand, he knew that the scientist was his most valuable agent. He tried to explain it to Miranda, but her eyes just glazed over in a dilated drug haze. He tried to explain it to Fiona, but she just swayed back and forth wearing an LSD hallucinogenic grin.

'What he's giving us,' he said, 'is the most important thing. It's the key to the Freedom Bomb – the shield that will protect the

People's Republic of China from a racist nuclear attack. Look what the Americans did at Hiroshima and Nagasaki. It wouldn't have happened if Japan had had the bomb too.'

But, at least at first, changing girls had been a good idea. Fiona regarded the scientist as ridiculous rather than repulsive. When he was a naughty boy, she would give him a good slap – and Fiona delivered a very hard slap. But when he was a good boy, Fiona did the things he wanted. So, normally, the scientist tried to be good. There was one thing, however, Fiona hated and that was changing him when he had messed himself. He shouldn't have done it that night. For that particular night, Fiona had dropped two acid tabs too many. In any case, she did her motherly duty and tidied him up. On the way back to the bedroom with a fresh diaper, she helped herself to a big glass of vodka and dropped another tab. She was out of it. When Fiona got back to the bedroom, the scientist was cooing and gurgling and lying on his back with his hairy legs waving in the air.

'Oh, little diddums,' she said, 'I know how to make you cleaner and tidier. It happens to a lot of little boys – and not just Jews and Muslims. You need to be circumcised.'

The knife flashed. But it wasn't a circumcision. Fiona held up the amputated penis for a second and looked at it and laughed hysterically. She then threw it in the screaming scientist's face and started running. She was naked and proud. She had won. She wanted everyone to see her triumph as she ran naked and blond through the streets of Brighton with her sacrificial knife held high.

»»»»»

Esteban was the first to discover the body. Fiona and the scientist had been alone in the hotel and there was no one to hear the scientist's final agonised shriek. Esteban stared for several seconds at the pale body on the bloodstained sheet. It was curled into the foetal position with the scientist's hands clasped over his wound. Esteban could see what had happened and swore at himself for leaving Fiona unsupervised. He had known she was a ticking time bomb.

Esteban had to act quickly. The first thing he did was telephone Miranda. He knew she was at her mother's house in Chelsea – and hoped Lady Somers wouldn't answer the phone.

'Chelsea 3765.' It was Miranda's voice.

'Something awful has happened. Don't come back to the hotel – ever again.'

'What happened?'

'Don't ask questions – and don't try to contact me or Fiona or anyone else. Just lie low until you hear from me again.'

'Is that all?'

'You and your mother are heroes. I love both of you.' Esteban hung up the phone.

The next thing he did was pull up a floorboard and take everything out of a hidden metal box. It was the last of the hoard and would soon be on its way.

»»»»»

Hop didn't even blink when he saw how much Esteban had changed. The Cuban now looked almost Scandinavian. There was no moustache and his hair was floppy and blond. Hop, on the other hand, always looked the same. His wire-framed spectacles sank into his fat face like an old piece of barbed wire moulded into an oak tree. His too-small white brimmed hat balanced precariously on his head. His white linen suit draped over his bulk like a loose tent held up by red braces. Hop looked as if he had never left Southeast Asia.

Hop was a Hong Kong businessman based in London who specialised in Chinese traditional medicine. He was a crook and a fraud, who knew that rhinoceros horn was identical to toenail clippings from domestic animals. He collected the nail clippings from a friendly vet and ground them up in a coffee grinder. His tiger penis love potion was indeed made from genuine penises, but not tiger penises. He collected the penises from the same vet whenever the vet had the sad task of putting down a pony or large dog.

Esteban smiled grimly as he handed over the pouch containing microfilms, unprocessed Minox films and miniaturised documents to Hop. He could also have provided Hop something for his tiger penis love potion.

Esteban trusted Hop – and so did the authorities in Britain and Hong Kong. They regarded Hop's medicine business as a ruse that harmed no one and duped the party apparatchiks of Peking out of rare and valuable foreign currency. Hop's exports of bogus cures to the People's Republic of China were always waved through customs at the crossing point in the New Territories without search or query.

Broadway Buildings, London: 18 January 1963

Catesby had just finished briefing Bone on what happened in Moscow. It was the first stage of the reporting procedure. The two of them, mostly Bone, would then produce a slightly sanitised version for Dick White. And then, a rather more sanitised and edited version would go to the JIC and Cabinet Office. The version that would finally wend its way to select Privy Council members in the House of Commons was sanitised enough to be used as a surgical dressing.

Bone peered over his steepled fingers and smiled. 'Semichastny is a consummate professional. Refusing to let you have the torn photo corner, or even a copy of it, was a masterstroke. He knows that a lot of people won't believe you when you tell them it was Lady Somers posing naughty. Semichastny is trying to create divisions between us.'

'You think he's lying.'

'No. I think he's telling the truth, but an unverifiable truth that will cause trouble.'

'And what about his claim that most of Moscow Central's agents in Britain have turned Maoist?'

'I wouldn't be surprised. The Sovs have very little reason to spy on us. In terms of military technology, we're far behind them. The only things we've got that Moscow could be interested in are the secrets we get from the Americans. Britain is a washed-up busted flush.'

'How unusual of you, Henry, to mix your metaphors – and also to express unpatriotic sentiments.' Catesby wondered if Bone had been drinking.

'I am not being at all unpatriotic. I want to see Britain devote itself to sex and depravity, which is where our true strengths lie.'

'You seem in an odd mood, Henry. Has something brought it on?'

Bone closed one eye and gave Catesby a very cryptic look with the other. 'Actually, there are a number of things.'

'Can you share them?'

'The first one is obvious. The Profumo business is about to blow sky high. There's speculation that the Minister for War has been sharing a girl with Ivanov, the Soviet naval attaché – and, of course, there's silly press speculation of a security breach. Total nonsense.'

'What is nonsense?'

'That Jack Profumo would be so stupid as to use post-coital pillow talk about state secrets to impress a mistress. And I'm now doubtful about the Ivanov connection too. But here's another bombshell.'

'What is?'

'Hugh Gaitskell died today.'

'Really? What happened?'

'I don't suppose, Catesby, that you were a big fan of Gaitskell.'

'I wasn't. To be frank, I thought he was selling out Labour and its values – and Gaitskell's foreign policy was too pro-American. Worse than the Tories. But I'm shocked that he's dead – a great pity. I wish the Party had voted him out instead.'

'I am relieved, Catesby, to see that you are shocked and surprised.'

'Why?'

'Because it shows that you weren't part of the plot.'

'What are you talking about?'

'Mad speculation of the most dangerous sort.'

'About Gaitskell's death?'

'Absolutely. Five are splitting from top to bottom with conspiracy theories.'

'You're losing me, Henry.'

'Apparently, Gaitskell's GP contacted MI5 about the illness. He claims that Hugh Gaitskell had a rare form of lupus that is seldom diagnosed outside equatorial Africa.'

'Had Gaitskell been to Africa?'

'No, but he had been to the Soviet Embassy here in London to get a visa for a forthcoming visit to the USSR – which, obviously, he will not now be taking.'

'Are there really people in Five who think the Sovs poisoned him? That's ridiculous.'

'The usual swivel-eyed lunatics who also think that we here are the London branch of Moscow Central.'

'I thought we were.'

'Don't, Catesby, ever, ever make that joke again. In any case, my speculation is that the lunatic fringe in Five are going to claim that whoever replaces Gaitskell as leader of the Labour Party is an undercover Soviet agent who was an accessory to murder.'

'How does this tie in with the Profumo thing?'

'It means our country is about to go through a very dangerous period. When the Profumo business explodes, the government is going to fall. If Labour wins the election and lurches to the Left, the knuckle-dragging press barons and elements of the military are going to be apoplectic. Cue for the loonies in Five to hiss their poison about a Sov plot involving Gaitskell's murder, which might very well provoke the generals to take action.'

'Are you serious, Henry?' Catesby smiled. 'You're pulling my leg. You don't really think there is danger of a military coup?'

Bone replied with his own cold supercilious smile. He picked up a manila folder and handed it over.

'Thank you.' As Catesby leafed through the folder he felt his blood run cold. 'It can't happen here. Not in Britain.'

'Keep reading, William.'

Catesby went back to the file. It contained contingency plans for military exercises around government buildings in Whitehall and at Heathrow airport to practise 'security arrangements' for a 'national emergency'. Finally, Catesby gave a nod and closed the file. 'You're right, Henry. It is serious.'

'Can we now go back,' said Bone, 'to your interesting meeting with Semichastny and his showing you that picture of Lady Somers? What do you think we should do about it?'

'I think Lady Somers has some questions to answer.'

'And whose job is it to ask those questions? Remember, William, SIS are not allowed to conduct operations or interrogations within the UK. Sure, it is a rule that we sometimes ignore. But we can't in her case. Any doubts about her are an internal security matter and the only people who can legally question Lady Somers are MI5. Is that what you want?'

'I see your point, but…'

'No buts, William. The only way to deal with Lady Somers is to do absolutely nothing. Our present situation is too volatile and dangerous. Providing evidence to MI5 that the Whitehall mandarin in charge of defence may be a spy – even if she is not guilty – could pull the final brick out of the foundation wall. I don't want this beautiful house, this Britain, to come tumbling down for the sake of punishing one person.'

Catesby wasn't impressed by Bone's rhetoric. He suspected there were hidden agendas. 'But what,' Catesby lowered his voice, 'if she is a risk to national security?' He paused. 'You know, Henry, it sounds like you might be trying to protect Lady Somers – but I won't speculate why.'

'You don't know the latest, William. If you did you would eat your words. I don't think that Lady Somers was ever a risk to national security, but if she was … she is no longer.'

'Is she dead?'

'No, but two others are. And, if the Maoist spy ring that Semichastny alleged really did exist, it certainly won't be sending any further British secrets to Peking. They are busted.'

'What happened?'

'It began with what the Home Office coroner called a "radical reduction phalloplasty" – medical types have a very dark sense of humour. An Aldermaston scientist, who is suspected of having passed on nuclear secrets, got his cock cut off by a drug-crazed tart.'

The Gaitskell news had shocked Catesby, but Bone's latest revelations were veering into the surreal. For a second Catesby thought Bone had gone mad and was about to start dancing the Lobster-Quadrille as the Broadmoor nurses broke the door down.

'I am not, William, making any of this up.'

Catesby nodded. 'Was what the girl did some form of retribution?'

'Not for passing on secrets. I believe the young woman was

disgusted by the services she had to provide. Sadly, she can't be interviewed because she took her own life. But, in any case, MI5 and Special Branch have been instructed to hush the whole thing up because it involves the great and the good – and, perhaps, some of their own.'

'You've confused me, Henry. If what you say is true, why wouldn't the Security Services keep hush about Lady Somers?'

'They would keep quiet about her, but only until a Labour government comes into power. She would be their surprise trump card, the excuse they are looking for. But at the moment the tipping point hasn't been reached. They want to keep the thing completely hush-hush. They are terrified of press coverage.'

'Echoes of Profumo?'

'Precisely. It all happened in a Brighton hotel run by a dubious Cuban. The hotel provided sexual services of all sorts, no matter how bizarre. It turned out it was frequented by the very finest of the British establishment at play. You couldn't swing a whip without lashing a KCMG and a brace of hereditary barons. So the whole thing is being utterly and completely squashed. The government can't bear another sex and spy scandal.'

Catesby frowned. 'In some ways, I would like the whole thing to be out in the open. These people get away with murder because we cover them in a cloak of secrecy.'

Bone gave a slight smile. 'I don't think you've considered all the consequences and implications.'

'Fine. But tell me, how can you be sure that the Peking spy ring is busted?'

'I can't be sure. I'm only guessing. Esteban, the Cuban who I suspect was more spy than pimp, has done a runner.' Bone paused. 'But here's the interesting bit – and why I'm certain the spy ring is finished.'

'You seem to know a lot about this.'

Bone smiled sagely. 'I have my contacts. The cleaners from Five completely turned over the hotel. They didn't find any nuclear secrets or cipher pads left lying around, but the film was still in the cameras.'

'Which cameras?'

'The ones in the bedroom ceilings. There will soon be a photo file of the hotel's most recent clients and their favourite quirks. And it will be utterly priceless, a crown jewel of blackmail. It won't be long before the confessions come pouring out – usually, I would think, in exchange for immunities from prosecution. The important thing is to keep this thing quiet.'

'Why did Esteban leave the films behind?'

'Good question. Maybe he just didn't have time to empty the cameras. Or maybe he wants us to know who his spies are.'

Catesby shook his head. 'That doesn't make sense.'

'It does if you want to wind up the network and make sure that no one else can use them. Perhaps China now has all the nuclear secrets it needs. Let's see how long it is before Peking tests their first bomb.'

»»»»»

Bone had predicted correctly. The confessions poured forth from all creatures great and small – even from a teddy bear using a human ventriloquist to explain what had happened. There was no point in prosecutions; the damage had already been done. The phrase used over and over again in the top-secret reports was: 'It is not in the national interest to prosecute at this time.'

Buckingham Palace: April, 1963

The Queen was standing on a dais, which made her exactly the same height as Catesby. He gave a nod, what protocol calls a 'neck bow', and avoided eye contact while so doing. He had been coached by Henry Bone on what to do. When Catesby finally glanced at the Queen there was a mischievous smile on her face – as if one of the corgis had just nipped someone she didn't much like. The Queen kept smiling as she pinned the Order of the British Empire Medal on the left lapel of Catesby's morning suit.

'Is it not odd,' said the Queen, 'that a Queen named Elizabeth should be giving this honour to a spy named Catesby?'

Catesby didn't know whether it was proper etiquette to agree or disagree. He simply said, 'I am most grateful, Your Majesty.'

'We ought,' said the Queen, 'to have scheduled this for the 5th of November.'

Catesby laughed nervously.

'Do you detect a whiff of gunpowder in the air, Mr Catesby?'

'No, ma'am.'

'Then it must be my imagination.' The Queen looked directly at Catesby and her smile was now warm rather than mischievous. 'Thank you, Mr Catesby, for your loyalty and service.'

Catesby felt his eyes brim with tears. It was complicated.

»»»»»

The first thing Catesby did after getting his gong was to find his mother and sister. Honours ceremonies were family events – and the Palace officials hadn't demurred at all when Catesby named his GCHQ-dismissed sister as an attendee. As soon as it was all official, Catesby's sister took their mother to Bonds in Norwich to buy a dress and hat especially for the event. It was Catesby's money and his mother had complained that it was too much. She said she would rather have spent the money on coal to keep the house warm for the next winter. But when Catesby wrote her a cheque for the winter's fuel bill, she refused to accept it. In any case, she finally gave in and looked aristocratic in rose-tinged beige with a silver trim.

When Catesby's sister had finished taking photos, he unpinned his medal from his lapel and put it in a velvet-lined box that a courtier had provided. Catesby handed it to his mother without closing it. Her hands caressed the box while she gazed at the medal. The OBE is a silver medal that hangs from a rose-pink ribbon trimmed with pearl grey. The medal bears the likenesses of George V and his wife Queen Mary. Catesby's mother read aloud the medal's motto: 'For God and the Empire.' Catesby didn't believe in either, but his mother did – even though she was Belgian-born.

A tear rolled down the old woman's cheek. It was the first time Catesby had ever seen her display any emotion. She closed the medal box and held it close to her chest. Catesby realised his mother would die before she would let anyone take his OBE away from her. Catesby was ashamed that, at first, he had wanted to refuse the award. But now he realised taking that joy away from his mother would have been ten times worse than betraying his so-called principles.

'Are you crying, Will?' Catesby's sister was at his elbow.

'No.'

'Have a tissue.'

'Thanks.'

'Well,' said his sister, 'shall we go to a pub?'

Before Catesby could answer, he heard distinctive footsteps behind him that he recognised. The man walked with a slight shuffle as the result of a bad crash-landing after his Hurricane was shot to pieces. It was Wingco. At the embassy in Havana he had been known only by his rank. The RAF officer had been UK military attaché in Cuba during the missile crisis. Wingco was also in a morning suit and had received a CBE.

Catesby turned and shook hands. 'How are you doing, Wingco?'

'We're in mufti now, please call me Peter.'

'Great to see you, Peter. And congratulations.'

'Thanks. And warmest congratulations to you as well.'

'I don't know why I got it. I was only a messenger boy.'

Wingco winked. 'That's not the story I've heard.'

Catesby smiled and put a finger to his lips. His role in the Cuban Missile Crisis had been that of a back-channel diplomat shuttling between London, Havana and Washington. It had been tense and nerve-racking.

'What are you doing now?' asked Wingco.

'We're going to a pub – or maybe a Lyon's corner house.'

'Why don't you bring your lovely ladies to my club?' Wingco winked again. 'It would be nice to have a chat.'

»»»»»

Wingco's club wasn't the grandest in London, but grand enough to impress Catesby's mother. It was the most elegant place she had ever been, had ever dreamed about. Wingco's family were all women: an elderly mother, a wife and their three daughters. The club had laid on a reception in honour of Wingco's CBE. It was in a long reception room with crystal chandeliers and spectacular views over Green Park. Catesby realised the club provided a perfect view of the park bench where he often met agents or had confidential chats with Henry Bone. He hoped that none of Wingco's fellow members were lip readers with a powerful set of binoculars.

Wingco touched Catesby's elbow. 'Let me give you a grand tour – and bring your drink with you.' He winked. 'We'll leave the ladies here; they seem to be enjoying themselves.'

Catesby followed the RAF officer up a set of stairs that made his limp more pronounced – and then down a corridor. There was no one else about.

'I think,' said Wingco, 'the library will be best. My fellow members are not great readers, but they can manage a drinks menu.' The room was empty and the curtains drawn. Wingco pointed to an armchair next to a writing desk. When they had sat down, Wingco took a large brown envelope out of his coat pocket and laid it on the desk with solemnity. 'It wasn't easy to get that.'

'But you did.'

'I hope, old chap, you don't think I'm poaching on your territory.'

'It doesn't matter, Peter. I trust you. Trust and loyalty are more important than job description.'

Wingco tapped the envelope. 'This is serious stuff.'

'Go on.'

'I had some home leave just after the missile business settled down. Coincided with a retirement bash here in the club for a former colleague, name of Gerry, who told me a very interesting story.'

Catesby finished his gin and tonic.

'Like another drink?'

'Later.'

'In any case, in the late 50s Gerry was flying Avro Shackletons out of the Bahamas. What a cushy assignment. There wasn't much excitement until one day they were scrambled to intercept a hijacked civilian airliner flying from the USA to Cuba. All available aircrew were beside themselves with joy and everyone wanted to come along – but priority went to an RAF intelligence officer equipped with a camera with a telephoto lens. Gerry did a jolly good job and got right up alongside the hijacked airliner and the intel officer snapped away.' Wingco paused 'The photos are probably ones you already know about.'

Catesby shook his head.

Wingco brightened up. 'Isn't it odd that none of us were told about the snapshots – considering it was our role to be the UK's eyes and ears in Havana?'

'Very odd.' Catesby vaguely recalled reading about the hijack in one of the daily news digests that SIS officers were given, but had forgotten about it. But why, wondered Catesby, hadn't he heard about the photographs?

'I decided,' said Wingco, 'to pursue the matter further because it tied in with rumours about *el loco*.'

'The crazy one.'

'*El loco* is a bit of a dipso who props up O'Reilly's Bar in old Havana. Rumour has it that *el loco* is an ex-American pilot who washed up in Cuba in mysterious circumstances. So when I heard about the hijack photos...'

An erratic line of dots in Catesby's mind was being spot welded together. 'You assumed that the Avro Shackleton's photos might solve the mystery of *el loco*?'

'And they did.' Wingco pushed the envelope across the desk.

Catesby slid out the photos. As soon as he saw who it was, he jerked upright as if the photo was a live cable. 'Good god...'

'You recognise *el loco*.'

'No, the other one.'

'You mean Jeffers Cauldwell?'

Catesby stared at Wingco with sheer wonder. 'How on earth did you find out his name?'

'*El loco* told me.' Wingco smiled. '*Loco* is easy to pump – he trades one secret for each mojito.'

'I'm a bit confused. Did Cauldwell actually reveal his identity to *el loco*?'

'No. A Cuban intelligence officer – who also likes *mojitos* – told *el loco* after Cauldwell left the country. It seems that the Cuban authorities weren't sad to see the back of Cauldwell. They either didn't trust him or didn't like his politics.'

'When did Cauldwell leave Cuba?'

'In early 1961.'

Catesby's head was churning with new scenarios. But there was another unanswered question. He touched the photos. 'How did you get these?'

'When Gerry hung up his flying boots he found himself in command of a large wooden desk in the Air Ministry. When I told him that none of us in Cuba had known about the photos, he assumed there must have been a cock-up. He did the first bit above ground and traced the photos from the Bahamas to the Air Ministry to the Chief of Defence Intelligence, to PUS at the MoD. So if you chaps didn't see them, they must have got stalled at MoD. You're smiling, Mr Catesby, like a very satisfied tomcat who has just caught a very juicy mouse.'

'We'll see.'

'But I know you can't tell me more.'

'How,' Catesby asked, 'did you get copies of the photos if they went AWOL at MoD?'

'The Air Ministry is a belt and braces outfit. They keep spares in case things go missing. It was relatively easy for Gerry to find the relevant filing cabinet – but he was being a bit naughty.'

Catesby put the photos in his jacket pocket – and made a mental note to remember to take them out again before he returned the morning suit to the hire company.

»»»»

Henry Bone did not seem happy to see Wingco's photos. He pushed them to one side of his desk. 'I suppose,' said Bone, 'it would be more prudent to file them than to burn them.'

'You seem,' said Catesby, 'even more unimpressed than usual.'

'What should I do? Grab a set of handcuffs, dash over to Horse Guards and kick in the door to Lady Somers' office? Why are you smiling like that?'

Catesby didn't answer. The image of Bone, handcuffs and Lady Somers was as piquant as it was ridiculous.

'In any case, nothing is going to happen, nothing at all, William – no matter how damning the evidence. This government cannot and will not bear another scandal.'

'But it would be interesting – treason prosecution or not – to see what happened to the hijack photos after they were sent to MoD. Maybe it was a clerical error.' He paused. 'Or maybe Lady Somers got rid of the photos in order to protect Cauldwell, who seems to have reinvented himself as Esteban the Cuban Maoist pimp.'

'How did you work that one out, William?'

'It's a guess based on trends. The Sino-Soviet rift seems to have found its way to Havana. Che is pro-Mao and Fidel still prefers Moscow. It also ties in with what Semichastny told me in Moscow about Peking having stolen his spies.'

Bone took off his reading glasses, massaged his eyes and yawned.

'You're tired, Henry.'

'I need a break. I wouldn't mind a couple of weeks in Italy with my sketchbook and watercolours.' Bone swept his arm around the office. 'To get away from this sordid ugliness.'

Catesby didn't say a thing. It was unusual to hear Bone express such personal emotions. Maybe, he thought, you needed at least an OBE to be privy to them.

Bone put his reading glasses back on and picked up the photos. 'Yes, we will file them – and I will make a note of what you reported.'

'And then stash them away under the hundred years rule.'

'No, William, I don't think it will be that long.'

Catesby noted a slyness in Bone's voice and manner.

London: 22 November 1963

The shock still hadn't drained away, but there was work to be done, no matter how numb the senses. Henry Bone knew that he would be in his office till well after midnight. The cables from Washington were flowing in thick and fast and the cipher clerks were bleary-eyed. The death of a king means no courtier or ambassador can sleep. Bone's desk lamp at Broadway Buildings would not be the only one burning late into the Whitehall night.

Bone glanced at the wall clock. There wasn't much time. He had an appointment with the Prime Minister, but there was still one more cable to read and evaluate.

More bad news. It appears that the suspect, Lee Harvey Oswald, defected to the Soviet Union and lived there for nearly three years. The hawks at the Pentagon and elsewhere are rubbing their hands with glee. If they can find or fabricate evidence that Oswald was acting under orders from Moscow it will give them an excuse for war. They wanted to attack last year during the Cuban Missile Crisis, but Kennedy blocked them (just). There are also rumours that Castro may have ordered the assassination. Once again, utter nonsense. It does appear, however, that Oswald was a member of the pro-Castro 'Fair Play for Cuba Committee'. The mood in Washington is dangerous and volatile. There are also rumours that Oswald was not the assassin and that what happened in Dallas was a right-wing coup d'état.

My Soviet counterpart is extremely nervous and keeping a low profile. He actually fears for his life. He kept saying, 'We had nothing to do with this. We are not crazy. Our killing an American President would be suicide for the Soviet Union.' He did, however, come up with one conspiracy idea that was 'crazy'. He thinks that China might have staged the assassination in such a way that the Americans would think it was Russia and then attack Russia in revenge. Too much vodka methinks. In any case, if war breaks out America may survive, but the UK would be completely destroyed. Sleep well.

The Pentagon: 25 November 1963

President Johnson was dressed in the solemn suit and black tie that he had worn to the funeral. He still hadn't moved into the White House because he didn't want to disturb Jackie Kennedy and her children during a time of grief and mourning. This also meant that he couldn't use the Oval Office or other White House facilities. The meeting, therefore, had been adjourned in the office of the Chairman of the Joint Chiefs of Staff. At first, most of the National Security Council had been present, but now only three remained – the President, the Chairman of the JCS and the Director of Central Intelligence – to discuss a matter of extreme secrecy.

The DCI spoke first. 'This is, Mr President, a policy that I inherited from my predecessor and that was approved by President Kennedy. I can see its merits and logic, but there are strategic risks involved.'

The JCS Chairman, still in full-dress uniform, nodded towards the DCI. 'It is a daring policy that was devised by John's predecessor.'

'You mean,' said the President, 'the one who fucked up the Bay of Pigs?'

The DCI smiled bleakly. 'It wasn't our brightest moment. But it is a policy that has already been acted upon and there is no turning back.'

'To be fair,' said the general, 'it is based on a principle of solid military strategy that has served leaders through the centuries: *the enemy of your enemy is your friend.*'

The DCI explained the policy in detail, including what had already been done.

The President's face turned white.

Catesby wanted out. The war in Vietnam was the final straw. He found it impossible to work with his American intelligence colleagues. But to be fair, some of them secretly agreed with Catesby's anti-war views.

Catesby's first act of defiance was to write articles under a pseudonym condemning the US war in Vietnam as a crime against humanity. He was careful not to give away any classified secrets – Catesby didn't want to go to prison – but he didn't mind if his bosses found out that he was the author. His anonymous journalism could be construed as gross misconduct – and Catesby wanted to get sacked while he was still young enough to start another career. But instead of sacking him, they promoted him. The message was clear: once a spy, always a spy. Catesby had become a member of a priesthood that protected and tolerated its members – even if you were completely off the rails and outrageous. Guy Burgess had proved that. In fact, Burgess, Maclean and Philby had never been sacked. The only way they managed to get out of the business was by defecting to Moscow. And Catesby wasn't going to do that.

In the end, Catesby decided to accept his situation because there was nothing he could do to change it. If, say, he turned up at the next JIC meeting wearing a Red Army uniform and shouting anti-capitalist slogans, he wouldn't be dismissed. It would be assumed that he had had a nervous breakdown owing to pressure of work. He would be given time off to recover. In any case, Catesby also began to realise that his ideas did matter and that he had greater influence as a respected spy than he would as a journalist or lecturer.

10 Downing Street: July, 1967

In the end, Catesby didn't turn up at JIC wearing a Red Army uniform – just a lounge suit and a tie. The meeting had, in fact, turned into a very awkward one because of the Foreign Secretary and Catesby's help was needed. The Foreign Secretary was a working-class Londoner who had left school at fifteen to help support his family. He didn't hide his resentment of those who came from more privileged backgrounds. He also liked a drink. He wasn't Catesby's favourite Labour politician, but Catesby was better able to deal with the Foreign Secretary's aggressive questioning than the other JIC members. The main topic of the JIC was China. The Foreign Secretary was exasperating everyone by asking the same question over and over again. He wanted to know how Washington was likely to react to the growing rift between Moscow and Peking – and he wasn't satisfied with any of the answers he was getting.

In the end, it was obvious that Catesby was the only person at the JIC meeting who could deal with him. He looked directly at the Foreign Secretary and put a bit of South London into his voice.

'The Americans don't even know the difference between a Tankie and a Trot. They only speak their own language and don't understand that the goons in Moscow Central hate other Communists even more than they hate capitalists. That's why the Yanks are fucking up in Vietnam – sheer ignorance. I don't want us to make the same mistakes.'

It seemed at last to be an answer that satisfied the Foreign Secretary. The meeting was able to move on to the next agenda item. The CGS, Chief of the General Staff, coughed assertively and stood up to make his presentation.

Catesby smiled with anticipation. It was fun, like being in a film. The Indian-born field marshal was an upper-class Brit straight out of central casting. He was respected in Whitehall for his implementation of the 1966 Defence White Paper, but even more admired for having played first-class cricket and having been a member of the Egyptian national team as well. He was a fast–medium offspin bowler. Catesby noted the long, strong spin-bowler's fingers when the CGS uncovered the flip chart for his talk. He also kept an eye on the Foreign Secretary, expecting to see proletarian resentment, but the cabinet minister seemed just as impressed by the field marshal's cricket credentials as everyone else. Sport is the glue that keeps Britons together.

'As you know, gentlemen and your ladyship, the People's Republic of China detonated a hydrogen nuclear bomb on the 17th of June, less than three weeks ago. The remarkable thing about this successful test was the short period of time it took China to advance from fusion to fission. Fusion, of course, is the process that causes an atomic bomb to explode and the far more complex fission process is the way one detonates an H-bomb. A fission device is, as you know, ten to a hundred times more powerful than a fusion device.' The general flourished a pointer at his chart:

FUSION TO FISSION
France = 105 months
United States = 86 months
Soviet Union = 75 months
United Kingdom = 66 months
People's Republic of China = 32 months

'I am sure you realise,' said the CGS holding his pointer on 32 months, 'that this is an utterly remarkable technological and scientific achievement.'

Catesby sneaked a glance at Lady Somers. Her face was attentive, but expressionless.

The Foreign Secretary looked at Dick White, as well he might, for the SIS was directly accountable to the Foreign Office. 'Well, Sir Richard, this is your patch. Can you explain how China managed this?'

Catesby listened with admiration as White spoke intelligently, articulately and informatively for nearly twenty minutes without revealing a single thing. Dick White ended with a master stroke: 'I am sure this question is also being asked in Washington, Paris and Moscow – and I am also sure that their intelligence services have much more to account for than we do.'

Catesby thought he detected a faint smile on Lady Somers' face. But he might have been wrong.

Century House, London: July, 1968

The Director looked more tired than Catesby had ever seen him. In fact, everyone looked tired. The move of SIS HQ from Broadway Buildings to Century House, a modern glass tower block in Lambeth, still rankled. It was as if the intelligence service had been relegated to a lower league and sent across the river. Change and uncertainty were in the air. Catesby had been in his new post, DD-R/Eur – Deputy Director Requirements Europe – for less than a month. It was a big promotion, but Catesby was already missing the dangerous and less well-paid life of a field officer. A number of his colleagues resented his promotion. They thought Catesby was put in the post as a sop to the Labour government.

'I've asked to see you, William, to share with you something personal – and in some ways painful.'

Catesby was startled. The tone of voice was so unlike the usual cool and reserved manner of Sir Dick White.

'I've handed in my resignation and I will be leaving the Intelligence Service in the near future.' White looked at Catesby and smiled. 'No, I haven't done anything disgraceful – at least nothing they know about. It is simply that I feel it is the time to retire. It's not public yet. You are only the second person I've told.'

'I will, sir, respect that confidence.'

'But, William, as you probably have guessed, that is not the only reason I asked to see you.' White laughed. 'In fact, you might not even be here for my leaving party.'

Catesby smiled. Beneath his mild exterior, White had a wicked sense of humour. 'Am I being sacked?'

'Of course not, William, but you are being reassigned on temporary duty to R/FE.'

'Asia?'

'That's right.'

'Somewhere warm?'

'Very warm. You're going to Vietnam.'

It was Catesby's turn to laugh, but he didn't. He knew it wasn't a joke.

'I suppose I'd better fill you in and give you some background.' White opened a file on his desk that contained photos and documents. 'By the way, you'll need to get fitted with a disguise and a false passport or two. You're going undercover.'

'I will, Sir Richard, refuse this assignment if it involves helping the Americans in any way in their ghastly and immoral war.'

'No, William, it will not. You'll be undercover as a journalist – and will be going to Vietnam entirely for British interests.' White paused. 'It's a matter of unfinished business that needs clearing up. I don't want to leave this matter for my successor.'

Catesby glanced at a photograph that had spilled out of the open file on White's desk. 'Who is that attractive young woman?'

'The Right Honourable Miranda Somers – Lady Somers' daughter and only child.'

'I've heard that she's a bit of a wild thing.'

'You heard correctly. I suppose you know that she was part of the Brighton honey-trap ring that was blackmailing Aldermaston scientists for nuclear secrets?'

'I did know, but I thought it wise to keep my mouth shut about it.'

'You were very wise to do so. In fact, Miranda Somers and her mother were the only suspects who were not interviewed.'

'Too establishment and too sensitive?'

'It's more complicated than that.'

'I'm not surprised.'

'In any case, William, Miranda decided it best to disappear after the Brighton ring was busted. She enrolled as a student at the Sorbonne where she did postgraduate work in drugs, sex and radical politics.'

'Was she part of last May's demonstrations?'

'Not very much. I don't think she found the Paris protests sufficiently left-wing or radical.' White paused and picked up the photo. 'So Miranda decided to go to Vietnam instead. She wants to help the Viet Cong and the North Vietnamese fight the Americans.'

Catesby shrugged. He didn't disagree with her idealism, but it wasn't something you could shout about in SIS's headquarters at Century House. The change to a modern glass tower didn't include a change in attitude.

'You look puzzled, William.'

'I'm not sure what you want me to do.'

'I want you to find Miranda and interview her about her mother's involvement – or lack of involvement – in the passing of nuclear secrets to Peking.'

'Why would she tell me?'

'Because you are a persuasive interrogator – and you are also authorised to grant her complete immunity from any future prosecution when she comes back to the UK.'

'Why don't we cut out the middleperson and go straight to Lady Somers?'

'Indeed. There are a lot of questions we want to ask Lady Somers,' White flashed a sly smile, 'but we want to know the answers to those questions before we ask them.'

'Of course.'

White picked another photo out of the file. 'We also need to flesh out your journalistic cover story. This man is First Lieutenant Francis Lopez. He is a Special Forces officer who is suspected of having betrayed his camp to the Viet Cong – and then to have deserted to fight on their side.'

'With Miranda?'

'We hope so. Trying to find Lopez would be perfect cover to track her down.'

'So I'm going to be a Fleet Street hack trying to score one of the biggest scoops of the Vietnam War?'

'Exactly.'

Catesby smiled. 'Can I file the story? It would help my retirement fund.'

'It wouldn't be wise. There are bigger issues – such as the future of British democracy.'

'Are the rumours true?'

'Yes, there is a plot to stage a military coup to overthrow the Wilson government. But to make sure it will never succeed, we must resolve all the questions concerning Lady Somers. Evidence that the first female head of the Ministry of Defence was part of a plot to pass nuclear secrets to China would provide the plotters with lethal ammunition.'

Saigon: October, 1968

The CIA man in Saigon wouldn't have recognised Catesby even if he hadn't been in disguise. Their paths had never crossed because the American was a 'Third World' specialist who had never been to Britain or Europe. At first, Catesby had reservations about the way the costume section at Broadway Buildings had changed his appearance. He was supposed to be undercover as a journalist, but felt he looked more Carnaby Street than Fleet Street. Catesby didn't much care for the Ringo Starr moustache and shaved it off. But he rather liked his hair dyed surfer blond and grown to collar length. The disguise was irrelevant for the CIA guy, who was so whacked out on drugs and Jim Beam that he didn't give a flying fuck whether Catesby was a journalist, SIS, KGB or a front man for The Rolling Stones.

Catesby offered the CIA man his passport, press credentials and the ID issued by the US Department of Defense – all were in the name of Easton, James. The ID was identical to the one carried by US soldiers except Catesby's status was 'non-combatant' and his rank and branch were 'British Correspondent'.

The CIA man opened the stiff blue passport, looked at the back of the front cover and smiled. 'You guys are something else: listen to this, "Her Britannic Majesty's Secretary of State requests and requires in the name of Her Majesty all those whom it may concern to allow the bearer to pass freely without let or hindrance…"' He handed the passport back. 'What's Her Britannic Majesty gonna do if I don't let you pass freely?'

'She'll probably have your balls cut off and roasted on a spit in front of you. A Royal Navy gunboat with a contingent of marines is now hove-to off the Mekong entrance waiting to hear if you're going to cooperate.'

'Really?'

Catesby nodded.

'Sheeee…it. Well, I'd better help you then. What do you need?'

'I want help in finding someone. One of your lads who did something naughty.'

The CIA man fixed Catesby with a wary look. 'Who are you talking about? Which branch of service?' An alarm bell had rung and the mood of light banter was gone.

'The tabloid rags I work for are mostly interested in tits and football – soccer in your speak. But they also like war stuff and spy stuff if it's sensational enough. In any case, they want me to investigate a rumour about a Green Beret officer who is supposed to have defected to the Viet Cong.' Catesby laughed. 'It's probably all bullshit – but I've got to come up with some copy that justifies the expense of sending me here.'

The CIA agent flashed a smile that was as bleak as it was insincere. 'You're right. It is bullshit. Sounds like a dragon story to me. This war is full of myths – that's why we call this place Disneyland East.'

Catesby noted the American's relaxed expression. He seemed relieved to be off the hook. But Catesby spoiled it by pulling a brown envelope from the pocket of his safari jacket – the Brits in Vietnam dressed like they were plantation owners in Kenya. 'There is, however, evidence that the Green Beret defector story is true.' Catesby spilled a photo from the envelope and handed it to the American. 'At first, I thought your rogue SF officer was another Vietnamese, but then someone pointed out his features are Hispanic. I can see the difference now, but he does blend in.' The CIA man's face had turned, to paraphrase the song, 'a paler shade of fish-belly white'.

There were three other photographs and a copy of a news clipping. The American studied each photo closely. In one of the snaps, the Green Beret deserter and another Westerner were surrounded by smiling Vietnamese wearing black pyjamas and brandishing Kalashnikov AK-47 assault rifles.

The CIA man pointed to a tall plump middle-aged man. 'Who's the fat round-eye?'

'His name's Wilfrid Burchett. He's an Australian journalist of very left-wing persuasion.'

'Is Burchett a friend of yours?'

'I've never met him.' Catesby was telling the truth.

The American tapped a finger on Burchett's image. 'We know about this fucker. And we'd like to waste the son-of-a-bitch. He keeps trying to pretend to be an American and to call in air-strikes on our own troops. But our guys are wise to him because he doesn't sound like an American – they think he's some kind of Englishman.' The CIA man looked closely at Catesby. 'And how the fuck do you know Burchett?'

'I said I didn't know him.'

'You said you'd never met him.'

'Okay, I'll explicate. I've never spoken to him, written to him or communicated in any way. My editor gave me those photos and all the details about Burchett and your rogue Green Beret. My editor is a cowardly fuck who wants the story, but doesn't want to get his arse shot off getting it. So he uses an alcoholic hack like me to take the risks. And, by the way, it's well past gin o'clock.' Catesby reached into a deep pocket of his safari jacket and pulled out a hip flask. 'Would you like a snifter? It's not gin; it's whisky – the sort you call scotch.'

The CIA man's face softened. 'Let me find a couple of glasses.' The American went to a cabinet that obviously had its own drink supply and returned with two heavy-bottomed glasses that were none too clean. He held up one of them to the fading sunlight.

'The hooch girl does a lousy job. I inherited her from George.' The American shrugged and put the glasses on the table. 'But I think your scotch will disinfect the dysentery bugs.'

Catesby unscrewed the top of the silver hip flask that bore the coat of arms of an ancient and noble English family. The costume section had decided it was a useful prop to impress Americans. While being coached for his undercover role in Vietnam, Catesby had been tasked to invent a back story to explain how he came into possession of the heirloom hip flask. His first invention was a tale about having nicked it at a country house party that he had crashed. The thief option was rejected and replaced by a story that the flask was a present from a toff who had an unrequited crush on Catesby. The idea was to tick as many US-held British stereotypes as possible. The CIA man looked at the hip flask with envy.

'Have you ever met Queen Elizabeth?'

Catesby shook his head and lied: 'No. But I've seen her on television – my mum always watches the Queen's Christmas broadcast.'

'You guys have Christmas?'

'Oh yeah – and then we go foxhunting on Boxing Day.'

'What's Boxing Day – you have fights?'

Catesby explained and feared that he was laying it on too thick. But after all, this was Disneyland East and cartoon images were the ones they understood. The graceful brown people they were burning and blowing apart were not human beings, but brainwashed robots controlled by an evil international conspiracy.

The American pushed the smudged glasses forward. 'Aren't you gonna pour some of your scotch?'

Catesby noticed the company logo for the first time. There was a horizontal red diamond on each glass with DOW inscribed in block white capitals. Catesby realised he was not just in Disneyland, but at a forward control centre of the Military Industrial Complex. Perhaps the glasses were dirty because the Vietnamese housekeeper hadn't wanted to touch them. Dow Chemicals was the company that produced napalm and Agent Orange. Catesby hesitated before pouring. It seemed wrong to pour good honest malt into those glasses, but he finally flashed a Judas smile and decanted two fingers of whisky into each.

The American sipped. 'Tastes funny. Are you trying to poison me?'

'No, I'm not. I'm told poisoned whisky tastes faintly of almonds. This stuff comes from Laphroaig on the Isle of Islay and their water is flavoured by the peat bogs. Maybe it's an acquired taste.'

'Expensive?'

'Over twenty dollars a bottle.'

'Then maybe I'll get used to it.'

Catesby gestured at the photos on the table. 'Getting back to Lopez...'

'How did you know his name was Lopez?'

'You haven't looked at the news clipping. We weren't sure until we matched up Burchett's photos with one that appeared in the *Baltimore Sun*, your Green Beret's hometown.'

The CIA man picked up the clipping. It reported that First Lieutenant Francis Lopez of the Fifth Special Forces Group (Airborne) had been reported Missing in Action following a battle at Nui Hoa Den, where a remote Special Forces outpost had been overrun. There were no American survivors and a massive search and rescue operation had failed to locate the missing officer.

The CIA man frowned. 'The USARV press officer stepped on his dick when he briefed that newspaper. He should have checked with us first.'

'How did you want Lopez reported?'

'BNR.'

'What's that mean?'

'Body Not Recovered. It's not like MIA. It means the fucker is definitely dead, but there were no bits to shovel up and bag.' The CIA man finished the whisky and Catesby recharged the Dow glass. 'The idea was that if Lopez popped up, we could say it wasn't him but some other greaseball pretending to be him. Maybe a Cuban who spoke good American.'

'Are there Cubans fighting with the Viet Cong?'

The CIA man smiled. 'Don't we wish. Catching one of those bastards in South Vietnam would be the Holy Grail. It would give us an excuse to nail Castro once and for fucking all. We got Che last year. He was an absolute shit guerrilla. He hadn't done his homework and didn't speak Quechua. Our guys did.'

'Were you there?'

The American's smile turned enigmatic. 'Let's get back to Lopez.'

'I bet you would like to establish some link between Lopez and Cuba.'

The American leaned forward and stared hard with undisguised menace in his eyes. 'Who the fuck is Lopez? What's this shit about Cuba?'

Catesby wondered if this was the CIA man's way of saying that his previous remarks were off the record. Or maybe the American was completely mad.

'Let's have some more of that scotch.'

Catesby emptied the rest of the hip flask into the American's glass.

'You still haven't told me how you got those photos of Burchett and that other piece of shit.'

'I already explained. My editor gave them to me.'

'How did your editor get them?'

'He wouldn't tell me. Investigative journalism is a bit like working for an intelligence agency. You only tell your underlings on a need to know basis – and you never reveal your sources.'

'And I'm getting pissed off with you because you're not telling me even the little bit you do know.'

Catesby stretched out his hands. 'Okay, I'll spill the beans. But most of my beans are only guesses. My editor has connections with the British intelligence service that go back to the war.'

'Which one? SIS or the Security Service?'

Catesby was impressed that the American knew them by their less popular names. 'Both, but mostly SIS. In fact…' Catesby gave the editor's name, 'actually worked for them during the war.' He wasn't giving away anything that wasn't already in the public domain, but the American took it for a crown jewel and scribbled it in his notebook.

'So what happened?'

'I can only speculate. I suppose ASIO were involved – know them?'

'Australian Secret Intelligence Organisation, something like our FBI.'

'Maybe a bit better. In any case, ASIO are out to get Burchett. I've heard a rumour that a member of the Australian Communist Party and a close confidant of Burchett is an undercover ASIO agent and managed to get those photos.'

'How did he or she manage that? The Australian government won't issue Burchett a passport. Ergo, he can't visit his homeland. He gets around on a North Vietnamese travel document.'

Catesby smiled. The CIA man knew his stuff. 'The ASIO agent didn't get them in Australia. He met Burchett at a Black Sea resort in Bulgaria.'

'Your speculations sound very detailed.'

Catesby shrugged. 'But maybe they're wrong.' And they were wrong. The photographs had been obtained in a black bag op. Burchett's hotel room had been burgled.

The American leaned back in his chair. 'What I can't understand is why Burchett has never published the story. It would be a big fucking scoop.'

'Yeah, I don't understand it either. It must be that Burchett is afraid that publishing could endanger Lopez and his new comrades. Maybe he puts his ideological commitments before his journalism.'

'But you haven't got such scruples?'

'None. I'm a journo whore.'

The CIA man looked closely at Catesby. 'Let's do a deal. I'll put gas in your tank and point you in the right direction. But if you find the little shit, you report back to me – every detail – before you file the story.'

Catesby shook his empty hip flask.

The American smiled softly. 'You want a drink?'

'Maybe I'd prefer to shoot up. Got any heroin?'

'If this is your idea of a joke, you are one sick fucker.'

'I could put you in contact with some London dealers. Would you like that?'

'Get out of here, asshole. You're a crazy...'

'Not so fast,' Catesby reached into a breast pocket – the safari suit was full of pockets – and took out three pages of a flimsy carbon copy document and spread it on the table. 'And don't pretend you don't know what I'm talking about.'

The American reached for the pages.

Catesby pulled them back. 'I want to explain things first.'

The American stared. His eyes were dilated and fixed. Catesby suspected that the CIA man was feasting on a diet of uppers and downers. The booze and the downers made him vague and hallucinogenic. The uppers – probably amphetamines and bennies – made him sharp and aggressive. It was a lethal combination that often led to psychosis. Catesby knew he had to be careful.

He raised his hands in a gesture of peace. 'I'm not judgemental. I think you guys are great. You may have made some mistakes of political judgement, but your core business is great.'

The American got up and walked over to the cabinet. He pulled out a record, placed it on a hidden turntable and turned up the volume loud. He had his back to Catesby and was reaching for something else as music flooded the room. It was a Buffalo Springfield song about guns and paranoia. The situation was turning surreal. Later, Catesby remembered that the CIA man had acted in perfect harmony with the music, as if he had choreographed and practised the scene.

The gun pointed in Catesby's face was a 9mm Browning automatic. He knew the weapon well and could see that the safety was in the off position and that the CIA man had already begun to squeeze the slack out of the trigger. Buffalo Springfield's lyrics and the electric guitar were pounding hard into the now too cool air. The air conditioners were on full blast, but their background hum was obliterated.

Catesby was thinking very clearly. The purpose of the loud music was to mask the sound of the bullet that was about to enter the left side of his forehead and then exit behind his right ear, taking out a piece of skull about the size of a tennis ball. He closed his eyes and whispered, 'I love you.' It was a pointless romantic gesture because Catesby knew she was long dead and couldn't hear him.

Catesby opened his eyes to the American's braying laugh. CIA still had his finger on the trigger, but was slapping his thigh.

'What's so funny?' said Catesby.

'You are. You said you loved me. You think that if you drop your pants and let me cornhole you that I'm not going to kill you. You bitches from Limey-land are sure enough strange critters.'

'I wasn't talking to you.'

The American relaxed the pressure on the trigger. 'Who were you talking to then – your mommy?'

'Just pull the trigger and leave me alone.'

'No, I'm not going to kill you – just yet.'

Catesby was still finding it difficult to get used to being

alive – and wasn't certain that it was all that pleasant a sensation. 'You don't know anything about me.'

'I know that you're one pathetic sick puppy.'

Catesby shrugged and watched the American waving the gun in time to the music and the lines about paranoia hitting deep and twisting the conscious. Catesby was sure the room was bugged. The high-volume music was intended to cover words as well as gunshots. He pointed to the carbon copy typed document. 'Have you looked at this?'

'Enough to get the gist.'

Catesby decided it was time to play his hand. 'The Green Beret deserter story isn't the big scoop I was sent here to get. Every insider with half a functioning brain knows the truth about you. CIA isn't an intelligence agency, that's just your cover story. In reality, you're the world's biggest drug cartel. You've turned US foreign policy into a racket. Fantastic, you've followed our example. British India was an opium factory – and China was our biggest customer. That's why we fought the Opium War. The Dowager Empress started to cut up rough about her subjects being whacked out all the time so we had to send in gunboats to teach her a lesson. So don't think I'm trying to be a morally superior Brit.' Catesby pointed at the carbon copy on the table. 'Even if I fabricated some moral shock and outrage in that article.'

The American picked up the carbon and started to read.

'And just to let you know why shooting me would be a bad idea. That article hasn't been filed yet. But if I don't get back this evening, my very loyal stringer is going to telex it straight to London. I see that you're enjoying it. When you get to page two you will notice your own name mentioned. But my favourite bit is the way your guys in the mortuary unit at Da Nang Airbase shove condoms full of heroin up the arses of dead GIs to smuggle the stuff back to the States. And the syndicated news agencies will spread this story all over America from sea to shining sea. You will be famous.'

The American sighted along the pistol. 'Sounds like I haven't got anything to lose.'

'Pull the trigger and you will lose. Let me live and we can do a deal that will benefit both of us.'

'Put your cards on the table and don't deal from the bottom of the deck.'

'I can spike the drug story easy. It will never see the light of day.'

'How can I be sure?'

Catesby nodded at the carbon copy. 'Even if I double-crossed you, you've now got your own copy. You would have forty-eight hours to wipe your fingerprints off every dead GI heroin mule. You can drop all your helpers and contacts deeply in the shit and cover yourself in rose-scented cologne. It might be a good idea to clean up your network in any case. A lot of the guys working for you have big mouths and no loyalty – otherwise, I wouldn't have been able to write that article. You could say I've done you a favour, but I haven't done it for free.'

The American put his gun down and stared. 'How much?'

'You're lucky. I'm cheap – thirty thousand US dollars. And not that funny monopoly money MPC shit, but real greenbacks.'

Catesby was referring to Military Post Currency. It was illegal to hold genuine US currency in Vietnam: a court martial offence for US troops and a criminal offence for Vietnamese. The idea was to stop corruption and to prop up the South Vietnamese currency, the dong, at an exchange rate that was ten times higher than the market reality. US personnel were issued MPC instead of real dollars. They could use MPC to buy drinks in American military clubs and goods from US PXs, Post Exchange shops. MPC made its way into the Vietnamese economy via prostitutes and drug dealers, but it was a risky currency to hold. Every few weeks, on an unannounced and secret date, a new series of MPC was issued and the old MPC became completely worthless. Only valid holders of MPC, US personnel, were allowed to exchange the old MPC for the new MPC. If you were a Vietnamese with a big wad of MPC, you were out of luck. But despite the risks, a Vietnamese black market involving MPC deals flourished. No one wanted the low-value dong.

The American looked at his gun, now lying on the table, and then at Catesby. 'It's a lot of money. I don't think you're worth it.'

'You're haggling over peanuts. You know if you take a walk down Tu Do Street you'll find a dealer before you've gone fifty paces. If you're stupid, you pay fifty dollars MPC for a bag of pure heroin. But you can bargain him down to twenty dollars for the bag. Now, how much would you get for that same heroin on the streets of New York? Three thousand, even five thousand bucks? Don't haggle when you're sitting on a pile of gold – or you could lose it all.'

The American looked thoughtful. 'Come back in three days. I'll give you half the money then – and explain what you've got to do to get the other half.'

As part of his preparation for Vietnam, an SIS South East Asia specialist had told Catesby to read Conrad's *Heart of Darkness*. 'That's what it's like. It doesn't make any sense – and if you try to make sense of it, you will go just as mad as Kurtz.'

It didn't make sense – and Catesby realised that it was impossible to do what he had been sent to do. There was no direct route to Miranda Somers – only detours and dead ends. He was sure all the stuff he had gone through with the CIA man about Lopez and Burchett and drugs was pointless. Catesby was ready to cable London saying that he had failed and was returning to England. But before he sent that cable, he wanted to make one more contact – his last chance to find Miranda.

The best place to meet hacks in Saigon was at the Rex Hotel during the 1700 hours press briefing by the US command – colloquially known as 'the five o'clock follies'. Catesby had been told to look for her there – and easily found her. She seemed thoroughly bored as a US lieutenant-colonel wittered on about the successes of 'Vietnamising' the military effort. She was a French female journalist who had known Miranda in Paris. The information had come via the SIS man in the French capital.

Catesby didn't know whether or not the Frenchwoman had been told his real identity, so he kept up his journalist cover. He told her that he wanted to visit the 'Iron Triangle' northwest of Saigon.

The Frenchwoman smiled and said, 'It's so boring.'

'What is?'

'This war. But if you want to go there, I take you.'

»»»»»

The trip, as she had warned, was neither dangerous nor exciting. The Frenchwoman's open-top Peugeot 403 cabriolet was sandwiched in a convoy of US Army two-and-a-half-ton trucks, what the Americans call 'deuce and a halfs'.

'They have these convoys every day,' she said. 'But they only go
to the 25th Infantry Division at Cu Chi. That is as close as anyone
can safely go. If you want to see war, you need a helicopter.'

The tarmac eventually gave way to a long straight road of red
clay. The convoy threw up clouds of orange dust. The countryside
was completely flat. The only trees that could have provided cover
in an ambush were a great distance from the road. The Americans
waged war with bulldozers and defoliants as well as bullets and
bombs. The Frenchwoman had red hair, probably dyed, which
Catesby thought went well with the clouds of red dust. He only
spoke to her in English. He knew that his fluent French, with a
hint of his mother's Belgian accent, wasn't particularly compati-
ble with a cover story as a journalist from the East End of London.
But the Frenchwoman possessed all the shrewdness of a Parisian concierge and clearly knew that Catesby wasn't what he pretended to be, but she also had the grace not to admit it.

The drive to Cu Chi wasn't completely uneventful. In retrospect, Catesby thought the sound of the explosion had been
oddly muffled considering the size of the bomb. A few seconds
after it went off a grey plume rose over the road ahead and the
convoy ground to a halt.

The Frenchwoman yawned. 'Happens all the time, so stupid.'

'Boring?'

'Yes.'

Eventually, Catesby heard someone shout an order from
further up the column. A tailgate clanged and a squad of US soldiers jumped down from the truck in front of them and deployed
on either side of the road with weapons at the ready. Catesby
was surprised there wasn't a more coherent contingency plan
for such a situation. The troops in many of the trucks stayed put,
some simply smoking and joking. Others stood up and peered
towards the front of the column to see what had happened. The
troops who had deployed to form a defensive perimeter didn't
seem sure what they should be doing. A few peered into the
distant tree line before they got bored and slouched down on
their backsides to light cigarettes. The air soon became loud
with the clatter of helicopter blades.

'We could be here a long time,' said the Frenchwoman.

'I think I'll have a look.' Catesby slung a camera around his neck.

'Of course – you're a journalist.'

Catesby felt a frisson of excitement as he set off up the road. It was why boys went to war; but they soon learned. He walked alone for 400 yards before he came to a flurry of activity. A half dozen US soldiers wearing flak jackets were scouring the side of the road with mine detectors. Behind them a group of Vietnamese soldiers were putting body parts into bags. There were also motor vehicle parts scattered over the side of the road – notably an axel and a gearbox. Three helicopters had landed and another helicopter was firing rockets into a distant tree line. Catesby walked over to a helicopter where an American in his forties, about twice as old as everyone else, was directing things like a scoutmaster. His collar bore the oak leaf insignia of a lieutenant colonel. His voice was decisive, but mildly annoyed.

'The ARVN were supposed to have cleared this road. Tell the *thieu ta* at district to get an armoured personnel carrier up here asap.'

Catesby turned towards another officer with black-framed spectacles who wore the twin bars rank insignia of a captain and seemed mildly amused by the incident. 'What happened?' said Catesby.

'The ARVN didn't do their job,' said the captain. He was referring to the Army of the Republic of Vietnam. 'The *Quan Canh* jeep escorting the column ran over a booby-trapped bomb and got blown to fucking smithereens.'

'Any American casualties?'

'None so far, just the white mice.'

The *Quan Canh* were the Vietnamese military police, but they were also called 'the white mice' because of their distinctive white helmets and gloves. Catesby thought he had better take a few snaps to prove he was a journalist, but felt he was disrespecting the dead. Meanwhile, he heard the US lieutenant colonel demanding another Vietnamese escort, an ARVN APC, before the column moved forward again.

Catesby turned to the captain. 'Would it be fair to say that you use the Vietnamese as human mine detectors?'

The captain shrugged. 'I'm not sure about the "human" bit. But it's their country, so if it blows them up it's tough shit.'

On cue, a Vietnamese Army armoured personnel carrier began to clank up the road to take over from the blown-up *Quan Canh* jeep. Catesby had seen enough and walked back to the car. The Frenchwoman, oblivious to the drama, had smeared sun cream on her face and was lying back in the driver's seat as if she were on a sun lounger in Saint Tropez. She stirred as Catesby got in the car. 'Interesting?'

Catesby shook his head. He wanted to get away from the squalid war and talk about something else.

The Frenchwoman gave him a funny look. 'Were you in the war?'

'I was too young. I was only sixteen in 1945.' That was what the date on his false passport indicated, at any rate.

'You look older.'

Catesby smiled. 'Thank you. I've had a hard life.' The weakest part of his cover identity was the fact that his fake IDs were for someone six years younger than himself.

'That makes you only thirty-nine. I can't believe you are one of those vain men who can never admit they've passed forty.'

'I look older because of what I've been through. It's a hard life in the East End of London. I was once nailed to the floor by a gang of villains who thought I was a grass. They cut off all my toes with a pair of bolt cutters and then worked their way upwards.'

'What's a "grass"?'

'*C'est un mouchard.*'

'So you know a bit of French?'

'Just schoolboy stuff.'

'Is it not strange that your school taught you French underworld slang?'

Catesby smiled. 'It was the East End of London. They were hardly going to teach us Proust.'

'I think you are a big tease.'

The truck engines in front of them began to grind to life in a cloud of red dust and diesel fumes. 'It looks like we're starting to move.'

The Frenchwoman started the engine, which gave a high-pitched whine compared to the heavy American trucks. 'When are you going to start to tell the truth?'

'You wouldn't believe me if I did.'

'Then I will have to make up my own stories about you. And, by the way, I was in the war and I was only fifteen when it ended.'

'What did you do?'

'I carried messages for the Maquis and counted German vehicles – child's play. Now, some truth from you? Why are you here?'

'I would like to report on this war from the other side – to see what it's like to be with the Viet Cong and the NVA.'

'It is possible, but not easy. The North Vietnamese never trust you.'

'How can you get them to trust you?'

'It helps if you are a woman – but maybe if those London gangsters got high enough with those bolt cutters…'

'I'd rather not talk about it. Have you had any experience with the Viet Cong?'

The Frenchwoman shrugged. 'It is difficult to say.'

'Even in French?'

'Even in French. Because I do not trust you.'

'Why not?'

'Because you're trying to hide what you are really doing.'

Catesby stared out at the countryside. For some reason it reminded him of Thetford Forest. A part of him always wanted to be in East Anglia – and images of home always made him think more clearly. Catesby was now certain that the French-woman had talked to the SDECE man at the French Embassy – and that's why she had so readily agreed to give him a lift. The French intelligence agency, Le Service de Documentation Extérieure et de Contre-Espionnage, ran a good-sized station in Saigon. The SDECE mission was not just to gloat over the Amer-icans' difficulties, but also to be in a position to reassert French interests when things completely fell apart. Catesby imagined that the SDECE man had probably treated her to a few drinks and dropped a secret or two in an attempt to get his leg over. It's the way they operated.

'You mentioned,' said Catesby, 'that it's easier for a woman to make contact with the Viet Cong.'

'In most cases – and you should know that.'

'And how should I know that?'

'Because that's why you've been sent here.'

Catesby looked at the distant tree line and tried not to show his annoyance. It was likely that the SDECE man was already plotting ways to drop him in the shit. 'I don't understand what you're saying. You're talking riddles.'

'You're not a journalist.'

'Wrong.'

'You work for a very wealthy and aristocratic British family.'

Catesby laughed. The SDECE man had either lied to her or got it wrong. Or the Frenchwoman was lying about what she actually knew. Bluff and double bluff. 'Actually, that would perfectly describe the owners of one of the newspapers I write for.'

'Don't treat me like a fool. Everything about you is fake.' '

'Who am I then?'

'I don't know.'

Catesby sensed she was telling the truth. 'In that case, tell me more about this aristocratic family.'

The Frenchwoman gave a very coquettish smile. She was enjoying the drama. 'They are almost royalty.'

Catesby smiled. 'Good work, you've rumbled me – *ça veut dire démasquer*. I've been sent here to recover a valuable family heirloom that disappeared from a château after the fall of France.'

'The family heirloom that you are seeking is a human one. Her name is the Right Honourable Miranda Somers.'

Catesby was now certain that his meeting with the Frenchwoman was no accident. It had been set up. But he decided to play the game. 'Don't you know her other names? She has quite a string of them – just like your French aristos.'

The Frenchwoman sounded put out. 'Regardless, Miranda has disappeared and there is a rumour that she has come to

Vietnam to work for the National Liberation Front in their struggle against the Americans.'

'How did you hear about her?'

'I met her in Paris last May, during *les événements*.' The Frenchwoman was referring to the May 1968 demonstrations that had brought down de Gaulle's government.

'Were you part of it?'

'Of course. I didn't have my head split open, but I was teargassed.' She lowered her voice. 'I am a member of the French Communist Party. I argued that we should have occupied the Élysée Palace, the National Assembly and all the ministries. Then they would have had to send in the army to retake them and there would have been a revolution.' She shook her head and sighed. 'But in the end it all came to nothing. It fizzled out and the Gaullists came back into power – and that's why I came here.'

A helicopter gunship flew low overhead. Catesby laughed. 'Listen, they've come to get you.' When the clatter of blades faded, he asked. 'How did you meet Miranda?'

'It was at a meeting of the Sorbonne Occupation Committee. There had been bitter battles with the police all day. I remembered her leading a group that were overturning and burning cars in the rue Gay Lussac. She was ecstatic.'

'Did she speak at the meeting?'

'Very briefly and in very stilted French. She said that what had happened that day had not been a "true proletarian revolution", but a "Dionysian ritual of release".'

'How did that go down?'

'The Stalinists booed, but a lot of others shouted support. The feeling was mixed. In any case, I decided I must interview her. You should understand that I wasn't just there as a protester, but also as a journalist. Revolution or not, I still had to pay my rent and earn the radishes...'

'It's "earn some bread".'

'In any case, we became very friendly and spent two weeks together.'

'What did you find out about her?'

'She had such a beautiful name, Miranda. And she was BCBG.'

It was Catesby's least favourite French phrase. It was an acronym for *bon chic bon genre* and meant smart and classy.

'Miranda had such wonderful clothes and a pair of boots that I would have died for. It was obvious that she came from a good family. Why are you laughing?'

'The revolution appears to have got stalled in the fashion pages.'

'Miranda would have agreed. She hated her upper-class background, but knew she couldn't escape it. She liked nice things and never pretended to be a proletarian.'

'Pity, I could have given her lessons.'

'She was, like so many aristocrats – how do you say, "a wild child"?'

'In what way was she wild?'

'She drank a lot and I am sure she also took drugs – and she had lots of sex. A new man or two every night. One time I even caught her doing it with a *flic* in a doorway. I tried to get her to say that the policeman had raped her, but she said that she had seduced him.'

'Was she wearing the boots?'

'I believe she was.'

'What about her drug taking?'

'I think she took cocaine and amphetamines. They were drugs that made her hyperactive and she would go days without sleeping – and then sleep for fifteen or sixteen hours.'

'Did she enjoy the sex?'

'I don't know.' The Frenchwoman paused. 'I think that she enjoyed the ritual more than the act itself.'

'As in Dionysian rituals of release?'

'There is a part of Miranda that is very aesthetic. She told me that she studied art history.'

'A lot of girls from her background do art history. It's useful for valuing mummy's and daddy's collections.'

'Miranda did say they had some nice things. Her favourites were two Poussins that a family friend had helped them get at a very low price.'

An imaginary camera in Catesby's head began to click. 'Tell me more about her family Poussins. He's one of my favourite painters. Why are you laughing at me?'

'Because you're only pretending. You're not the sort of man who likes Poussin.'

'How little you know about me.'

'I bet you only want to know about the Poussins so you can burgle the house and steal them.'

Catesby stared at the back of the two-and-a-half-ton US Army truck in front to remind himself where they were. The bumper was stencilled in white lettering: 25th INF DIV. Two helmeted soldiers in flak jackets were reclining against the tailgate and laughing, the barrels of their M16s swaying to the rhythm of the truck. Catesby felt his stomach lurch. This wasn't the world of Poussin: it was Salvador Dalí fading into *Guernica*. The real morphed into the surreal and then into madness.

'What's wrong?' said the Frenchwoman. 'Have I offended you? I was only teasing.'

'Now, about those Poussins I want to nick.'

'*Comment*?'

'*Faucher*.'

'I don't believe you're really a thief. In any case, Miranda said they weren't paintings, only rough charcoal studies for other works.'

'Which ones?'

'Are you really interested?'

'Very.'

'One of the studies was for a painting hanging in the Louvre. When Miranda found out about it, she almost dragged me there. I had to use my press pass to get through the police barricades.' The convoy slowed to a halt. 'Damn, I hope they haven't found another mine. It will be very bad if we don't get to Cu Chi before dark.'

'Which one?'

'It could be any sort of mine.'

'I meant which was the Poussin in the Louvre that Miranda so wanted to see.'

'It was called *Et in Arcadia Ego*.'

A chill went up Catesby's spine and his sweat turned to ice. 'Do you know what it means?'

The Frenchwoman shrugged. 'Pfff, Latin wasn't my best subject, but it's an easy phrase. It means "And I am in Arcadia," a sort of rural paradise.'

'You don't know what it means.'

'Are you going to tell me?'

'No.'

Catesby smiled bleakly and continued to shake his head. It was a memory that had nothing to do with the spy game. Something that never left him, part of growing up. The classics master at Denes Grammar had been Captain Pearse, an unmarried man who dressed well and lived beyond his means. *Et in Arcadia Ego* was from Virgil. When Pearse asked the students to render it, everyone gave the same answer as the Frenchwoman.

'The problem,' boomed Captain Pearse, 'is that you don't know who is the "I" of "I am".'

Catesby put up his hand and Pearse nodded. Catesby stuttered, 'Th-the "I" is Death. It means that even if you are happy in Arcadia, Death is still present.'

Captain Pearse stared through Catesby. His eyes were total blanks with no points of reference. A month later the ghosts of Passchendaele proved too much for Captain Pearse. He collapsed in a heap during a Latin lesson. Catesby remembered Pearse curled up on the floor with chalk dust on his gown, his eyes mad and gleaming with tears, talking to a ghost: 'I loved you, I loved you...' They never saw Captain Pearse again.

The trucks in front shifted into gear and the convoy started moving. Catesby looked at the soldiers. A handful were certainly marked for death, but would any of them ever experience the enormity of the Somme, of Verdun, of Stalingrad?

'They're different from us,' he said.

The Frenchwoman nodded. 'Yes, they are different. And, by the way, I know what *Et in Arcadia ego* really means.'

'And what did it mean to Miranda?'

'It was something that she had to act out.' The Frenchwoman smiled. 'And that was very strange.'

The camera in Catesby's brain had begun to click again. The Frenchwoman kept looking at him with an ironic smile. Catesby felt her look was stripping away every layer of deceit.

'Since,' he said, 'I'm a common ignorant prole, can you tell me about Poussin's *Et in Arcadia Ego*?'

'You're not ignorant.'

'Thanks, but I've never seen the painting.'

'The setting is rustic and there are four shepherds gathered around an ancient tomb. Three of the shepherds are male and one is female, except…'

'Except what?'

'One of the shepherds has a man's body, but a woman's face. I don't understand why and Miranda wouldn't explain it.'

'Maybe you're wrong about the woman's face. Shepherd boys can be very pretty.' Catesby gestured to the truck in front. 'Look at that soldier – he looks about fourteen.'

'Perhaps you are right. In any case, Miranda seemed to prefer pretty boys.'

'What happened? You said she acted it out.'

'We took the train to Fontainebleau and had a day out in the forest and a picnic on the banks of the Seine. She wanted me to record it with a camera – which I found a little sordid. And, of course, we all had to dress as Greek shepherds – even myself who, I must tell you, did not take part.'

'In the Dionysian rituals?'

'Correct.'

'Who were the others?'

'Three young men. The Congolese was the oldest and the tallest. I think he was about twenty-five. The Algerian boy was about nineteen or twenty. But the Vietnamese boy was the youngest. He must, however, have been at least eighteen, because he was a university student. But he looked fourteen and so innocent – and almost feminine.'

Catesby gave a weary smile. He had reached an age when he had begun to find young people as vulnerable as they were predictable. There was nothing you could do to stop them from pressing the self-destruct button. His own youth had been a struggle to escape the grinding poverty of a depression-era fishing town. There were few choices and the only self-destruct buttons were drink and crime. Rich girls like Miranda had the option to choreograph a much more artistic and fashionable self-immolation.

'And remind me,' said Catesby, 'what exactly were you supposed to be doing at this acting out?'

'I was to record it with two cameras: one to take stills, the other a 16mm cine camera.'

'And how did the young men feel about this?'

'They weren't aware. I hid in the bushes to film and photograph.'

Catesby laughed. 'You were Actaeon and Miranda was Artemis. You were lucky you weren't transformed into a stag for peeping and torn to pieces by your own hounds.'

'You certainly are not the uneducated man you pretend to be. Miranda did mention the parallel – but the scene which ensued was certainly not that of a virgin bathing. The Congolese and the Algerian were satisfied first and simultaneously – and then swapped positions for a second round. Meanwhile, Miranda stroked the Vietnamese boy, who looked terrified. When it was his turn he required some coaching. Miranda eventually took him in her mouth with both passion and tenderness. Then spat his semen into her hand and spread it over her breasts.'

'Did she explain the symbolism?'

'Yes, but it was pretty obvious. Miranda comes from a family of white rich imperialists and it was her duty to offer her body to the world's poor and oppressed as compensation for the crimes of her ancestors and her own personal wealth.'

'It's the least she could do.'

'Don't be sarcastic.'

'I wasn't being sarcastic.'

'Unfortunately, the poor of the earth, at least the older two, weren't just satisfied with Miranda. They found me in the bushes – I made a noise when I got stung by a wasp – and then they wanted me too.'

'They turned into Actaeon's hounds?'

'Almost, but the Vietnamese boy saved me. He turned on his companions and was surprisingly fierce. In fact, he saved both Miranda and me for the mood had turned ugly. I don't want to say anything else, but Miranda insisted that we deserved anything they wanted to do to us.' The Frenchwoman frowned. 'And that infuriated me, because I come from a humble family of socialists.'

'Did they hurt you?'

'No.'

'I'm glad. What happened to the film in the two cameras?'

The Frenchwoman smiled. 'Miranda wanted both cameras and all the film. But I managed to shoot an extra roll of .35mm which I hid and kept for myself. I am, after all, a journalist and have to make a living.'

'If they censored the pics, it would be a superb front-page story for *Paris Match* – but I suppose you would feel more comfortable writing for *L'Humanité*.'

'I do both.'

'Was the orgy by the Seine the last time you saw Miranda?'

'Yes, it was.'

'How did you know that she went to Vietnam to fight with the Viet Cong?'

'Because she always talked about doing so. And who can blame her idealism? It is the great anti-imperialist struggle.'

'But we all talk about doing things we never do. I often say I'm going to drink less and become a nice person.'

'You are a nice person, but you won't admit it.'

'How little you know.'

'I must stop the car now and get out my violin so I can accompany your self-pity.'

'Thanks.'

'You and I,' said the Frenchwoman, 'have something in common, a shared interest.'

'What?'

'Miranda.'

'What other evidence, proof, is there that Miranda has come to Vietnam?' Catesby wanted to be sure he wasn't on a wild goose chase.

'The Vietnamese boy...'

'From the orgy?'

'I wish you wouldn't call it that.'

'Sorry, just tell me.'

'His name is Huynh. Miranda sent him to tell me that she had gone to Vietnam to fight. I am sure that Huynh has connections with the NLF in Vietnam and he may have helped Miranda come here, but he wouldn't say when I pressed him.'

'Is that all the proof you have that she is here?'

'No, a few weeks later she sent me a photo of herself wearing a North Vietnamese Army helmet and sitting on an anti-aircraft gun.'

'What did you think of that?'

'A little bit vain, a little bit silly. Miranda likes dressing up and posing. But you must remember how young she is and how guilty she feels. She wants to be genuine.'

'She's not like us.'

'No, we are what we are.'

Catesby looked closely at the Frenchwoman. If she was telling the truth about her age, she was a worn thirty-eight-year old who could have passed for forty-five. He was prematurely aged too. Catesby was a forty-five-year old who looked fifty. And here, he thought, were the two them chasing an errant child through a war waged largely by unformed young men slowly uncurling from adolescence. War was a form of child abuse. But children weren't innocent, at least not in the way that most adults defined innocence. The film of Miranda's frolics by the Seine would put paid to that illusion. But children were naive beings who trusted others, often the very ones they shouldn't trust. Catesby didn't trust anyone, including the woman next to him. He knew you could only trust someone when you had drained every hidden corner of their consciousness and memory so there was nothing left to conceal. This was the art of the interrogator – to return an adult to the innocent dependency of a child. Catesby couldn't do that to the Frenchwoman, but he wanted a lot more answers from her.

'What,' she asked, 'are you going to do when we get to Cu Chi?'

'I'm going to march straight into the G2's office and tell them all about you.'

The Frenchwoman blinked as if pretending she didn't understand.

'You know only too well, my little sweetheart – G2, division intelligence.'

She gave a brittle laugh. 'Why would you denounce me? And after I've been so open and honest with you.'

'Because you are trying to use me and you haven't told me the whole truth.'

'Then I will go with you into G2 and denounce you as well.'

Catesby laughed. He was back at Roman Hill Primary: it had degenerated into playground taunts. 'Yes, but the Americans already know what I'm doing.'

She stared silently at the back of the truck in front of them. Catesby could see that she was rattled. It was clear she wasn't an intelligence professional – she was too naive and untrained – but he suspected she might be an 'unwitting' tool of someone who was.

'Okay, fine,' she said, 'do what you want.' She then told him to do something extremely obscene in French.

Catesby laughed. 'I suppose you want to film that too.'

'No one would be interested – not even perverts.'

'Let's stop exchanging insults. I want to help you – and I will, if you tell me a few things.' Catesby paused. He wondered if she genuinely believed the story that he was working for Miranda's family. 'How did you know about me?'

She shrugged. 'An editor in Paris told me and showed me your photo.'

'I don't think you correctly heard my question. Try again.'

'Someone at our embassy told me.'

'The one here in Saigon?'

She nodded.

'And I bet it wasn't the ambassador.'

'No.'

'Do you still call it the *Deuxiéme Bureau*?' Catesby referred to the French secret intelligence service by its old name. The Bureau had ceased to exist with the fall of France in 1940.

'The older ones do. It's a lot easier than SDECE, Service de Documentation Extérieur et de Contre-Espionage.'

'Who did you speak to?'

'He didn't tell me his name, but he was in his fifties and had black curly hair. He looked hard and military, probably a bit of a *facho*, and spoke with a slight Corsican accent.'

Catesby tried not to smile. She was describing Antoine Savani, who still called himself 'Captain' from his time in military intelligence. Catesby remembered Savani from the early 50s in Marseilles. Savani had worked hand in hand with the CIA to replace the Communist dockworkers with the Corsican mafia. The Americans saw it as a straight swap. The drug dealers were less harmful than the Communist trade unions. Heroin is always better than Marxism.

'What,' asked Catesby, 'did he say about me?'

'He said you were an adventurer and a mercenary who had connections with the criminal underworld.'

Catesby smiled at the irony.

'But that you were trusted by the British upper class to do their dirty work – and that's why you're here trying to find Miranda.'

'Did this SDECE man try to seduce you?'

'A little bit. He took me to dinner and tried to get me drunk, but I pushed him away.'

'And he took "no" for an answer?'

'Yes.'

'Then what was in it for him?'

'What do you mean?'

'Why did he give you information about me for nothing in return – unless you really did…'

'No, I wasn't interested. You don't know about me.'

'You're not telling me the whole truth.'

'About myself?'

'No, about what the French intelligence bloke told you. He wants something out of this, he did a deal.'

The Frenchwoman went silent, then said, 'I don't know what you're talking about.'

'I'm talking about my own survival. I don't like French secret intelligence using someone like you to put a trail on me. If you want me as friend – and not as a dangerous enemy – tell me everything now.'

The Frenchwoman took a deep breath. 'The SDECE have agreed to help me with a *Paris Match* – or a *Figaro* or wherever it appears – story about what he calls "Mi'lady Miranda". It's a reaction to what happened last May. They want to make the Left look silly and immature – and there's also the British angle. It's the Poussin connection.'

Catesby's brain started to whir and click like mad.

'The art historian who helped Miranda's family obtain the Poussin studies is an ex-British intelligence officer named Sir Anthony Blunt. The SDECE man confided that he is certain that Sir Anthony was a Soviet spy. He is certain that Miranda can help uncover this fact.'

'But Miranda is a woman of the Left, a Communist. Why would she want to betray a fellow comrade?'

The Frenchwoman smiled like a card player about to lay down a winning hand. 'Don't you understand? Don't you see why Miranda dismissed last May's demonstrations and strikes as a mere "Dionysian ritual of release"? Don't you understand why she gave her body to those young men from Africa and Asia?'

Catesby knew the answer, but shook his head to pretend he didn't.

'Miranda is a Maoist. She hates the Soviet Union and all its works.'

Catesby despised Savani's ideologies, but had a grudging respect for his professionalism and flair. The Miranda story would further exacerbate the ideological rifts within the French Left – and a rich English girl playing radical politics would also be delicious. And, as a bonus, a cross-Channel exposé of Anthony Blunt to rubbish the British intelligence services. So, thought Catesby, Savani wants to play games. He smiled. He had an absolute gem about SDECE to pass on to CIA. The wonderful thing about espionage wasn't what enemies did to each other, but the way allies stabbed each other in the back. His thoughts were interrupted by the sound of a propeller plane at low altitude.

'Cover your mouth and don't breathe in.'

The plane was flying over the distant tree line of an abandoned rubber plantation and spewing out a cloud of yellowy-orange chemical.

'What's that?' said Catesby.

'Agent Orange. It kills trees – and everything else.'

When the plane had finished its business, Catesby turned to the Frenchwoman. 'There are still loose ends that need clearing up. You mentioned that Sir Anthony helped Miranda's family get two Poussin studies. One was *Et in Arcadia Ego*. What was the other one?'

The Frenchwoman smiled broadly. 'Oh yes, that one. It was much larger and more ambitious – and Miranda wanted to act that one out too. But she would have needed quite a crowd.'

'Can you remember what it was called?'

'The something of Pan … ah, the *Triumph of Pan*.'

'What is it like?'

'A triumph of sensuality and abandon.'

'What role did Miranda want you to play?'

The Frenchwoman suddenly looked puzzled. 'She said she wanted me to be her mother, that she needed a mother. I was a little confused, but when I found a copy of the painting I understood. There are two females next to each other, one of whom is larger and more mature.'

'Have you children of your own?'

'What has that to do with anything?'

'Sorry, but there is one more thing that I don't understand.'

'There are many things that I don't understand.'

'You look familiar – and I think I know why.'

'There are many frumpy women like me in the world.'

'You're not frumpy – you're nice looking.'

'Don't get personal.'

Catesby could tell she meant it. 'Okay, this is what I don't understand. You said that it was easier for a woman to make contact with the Viet Cong than a man.'

'Sure, women seem less threatening.'

'Not always. But assuming that's true, why haven't you made

an attempt to go over to the Viet Cong yourself and try to find Miranda. Why do you need me?'

The Frenchwoman looked at the haze of yellow-orange smoke that still hung over the tree line. 'I hope the wind doesn't blow it this way.'

'Are you trying to avoid answering my question?'

'Not at all. I know that it is easier for a woman to contact the Viet Cong because I did so myself. I faked a car breakdown on the coast road north of Hoi An just before dark – I siphoned out the petrol. It was a dark moonless night and I did not have long to wait. In any case, I had arranged the rendezvous through an intermediary.'

Catesby realised that he had seen the Frenchwoman before. The dullest job of an intelligence officer is going through endless document files. Before leaving for Vietnam, Catesby spent three weeks – three hundred working hours – sifting through files, press cuttings and photos. His eyes ended up bleary and bloodshot, but a good intelligence officer never forgets a face. In the press photo, she was wearing a conical hat and black pyjamas. Catesby was surprised that her story had merited so little column space. Perhaps the media had grown weary of Vietnam.

'But,' said the Frenchwoman, 'it didn't work out as I had hoped.'

'What happened?'

'A US Marine patrol found my abandoned car the next morning. I had expected this, but I didn't expect the huge reaction that my disappearance triggered – not being an American, only an obscure French journalist. That very same day the area was flooded with American troops – two whole battalions of US Marines.' She smiled. 'I never thought I would have over a thousand young men chasing me. And the sky was full of helicopters too. Not what I wanted.'

'Did they find you?'

'Fortunately not. It might have been a bloodbath if they had. The search went on for five days. Our hiding places were cramped, but completely undetectable. The National Liberation Front commander instructed the regional cadre and the guerrillas to lie low and not to engage the marines. You know, of course, that the NLF follows Mao's guerrilla war doctrine. "When the enemy attacks, we retreat. When the enemy with-draws, we attack." Their discipline was perfect: no movement and total silence. I shared a cramped bunker with six guerrilla fighters, two of whom were women. It was so small, not more than a metre in height. On two occasions, we heard marines moving through the seemingly deserted village overhead. The second time they came there was an explosion when an Ameri-can tripped a booby trap. We heard the helicopter that landed to pick him up. The loss of a comrade made the marines search the village more thoroughly than they had before. We heard them thrashing around only feet away, but they didn't find us. During that time we lived on a ball of rice and a cup of water a day. We had to pee in bottles – and could only go out to do the other late at night.'

'I bet you weren't very popular. The search was your fault.'

'They never showed any resentment. At first, they said my being there was a good thing because it relieved pressure on the 2nd NVA division in the mountains and allowed them to resup-ply. But at the end of the fifth day, they said I must go back. I was so disappointed. I had come so far – and done the most dan-gerous and difficult things. And how I wanted to find Miranda – not just for the story, but because I loved her. I pleaded, but they said that I must go. Perhaps they did not trust me. Late that night one of the guerrillas blindfolded me as they had when they took me there. They must have feared that I might lead the marines back to their hiding place.'

Catesby knew the blindfolding had nothing to do with distrust. It was a standard procedure. The Résistance group he worked with in the Limousin had blindfolded their own mothers before they led them to a hideout. Guerrilla warfare was a ruthless vocation in which no one could be expected to withstand torture or death threats to other family members without talking.

'In the end, I was taken back to the road where I had left my car. The car was no longer there, but when I got it back the marines had serviced it and filled it with petrol. It was absolutely gleaming. But I never saw my clothes again. The Viet Cong had dressed me like a typical peasant woman. When day came there was a lot of traffic from the big base near Da Nang, but it was a while before an American realised that I was a round-eye woman, even though I was frantically waving them down.'

'What happened next?'

'They replaced my black pyjamas and sandals with Marine Corps fatigues and boots. I was surprised they had my size. I also had a lovely hot shower and washed my hair – and they fed me an enormous breakfast with gallons of coffee and orange juice. It was very pleasant.'

'And that was that.'

'No, they interrogated me for two days. But because I had already concocted a story of being captured after my car broke down, I decided not to fabricate an elaborate escape adventure. I told them that the Viet Cong had released me because I was a French journalist and that the Viet Cong did not want to create bad feelings with the French government – and the last bit is true.'

'How did the Americans take that?'

'They continued to treat me well – and said that I wasn't responsible for my government's errors. By then, of course, I was pretending to be in love with everything American. And I was a bit taken – I adored those hot showers and they even gave me a basket of cosmetics. After the intelligence types had finished with me, I was handed over to a press officer. He was very disappointed that I hadn't made a dramatic escape after being raped and beaten by sadistic guards, but I couldn't change my story. And then, of course, the newspapers came with their pencils and cameras – I had to put on my black pyjamas again for the photographers. There were some articles about me in the international press.'

Catesby nodded, but didn't admit he had seen one.

'So, I can't do it again. Neither the Viet Cong nor the Americans would believe me nor treat me as well. You cannot fake being captured twice. I have – how do you say – blotted my reporter's notebook.'

'Copybook. But I prefer the American equivalent.'

'What is that?'

'He stepped on his dick.'

'A dick is a … ah, yes.'

'That's right.'

'And I haven't got one … and how could one, unless one was an acrobat or it was impossibly long?'

Catesby could see that the Frenchwoman had a very literal mind and didn't take it further. 'Did you ask the Viet Cong about Miranda?'

'Yes, but only one of them spoke good French and he said that he would have to pass my question on to someone else.'

'It sounds like he didn't have the authority to deal with it.'

'Exactly.'

'If I find Miranda, I promise that you will have your *Paris Match* front-page scoop.'

'Don't make my mistake. The Viet Cong guerrilla units near the coast in Quang Nam are under too much pressure and too much surveillance. They are very gallant, but haven't the time to deal with people chasing a rich Western girl like Miranda. You must go further inland, into the mountains, where you will find the regular North Vietnamese Army divisions. That will be more difficult and dangerous because there are no civilians to help you and no passable roads.' She hit the steering wheel of the Peugeot cabriolet. 'At least not for a car like this one.'

'You mentioned a contact. Could he help me too?'

'It's a she. Her name is Truong Thi Nhung and she lives in Da Nang. She comes from a bourgeois Catholic background and teaches languages at a convent school in Da Nang. You may find it hard to win her trust. She is a very complex woman who can be hard and ruthless.'

»»»»»

Catesby found the infantry division's base at Cu Chi completely bizarre and surreal. It was a town of 20,000 inhabitants sprawled over a treeless expanse of bulldozed earth. The land was so flat there were no vistas beyond the endless rows of regimented huts and footpaths lined with rocks painted white. Even though there were military trucks and jeeps and helicopters the war seemed a remote possibility. Soldiers wore baseball caps instead of helmets and no one inside the base itself carried a weapon. And there was no trace of whatever had been Vietnam. It was a null space where nothing connected with nothing. Catesby felt overcome by nausea and wanted to get out.

The opportunity came in the form of a helicopter ride to a 'sweep and destroy' operation. Catesby spent a day with an infantry company. Not a shot was fired except by American troops into tree lines and bamboo thickets. It was called 'reconnaissance by fire'. The idea was that enemy troops would reveal their presence by shooting back – if, presumably, they were really stupid. But they can't have been stupid – or there at all – for no one fired back. Nothing happened until late afternoon when a rifleman managed to step on a mine and get his foot blown off. Catesby managed to hitch a lift back on the medevac helicopter and was in Saigon the next day.

»»»»»

The CIA man wasn't in a better mood, but he seemed saner and more sober. At least this time he wasn't playing loud music and waving a pistol in Catesby's face.

The American began first: 'You spiked that article, didn't you?'

'You know I did. If I hadn't spiked it, I'd be floating face down in the Mekong River.'

The American nodded.

'And it doesn't matter what I write now because you've covered up your tracks and wiped off the fingerprints.'

'Once again, you're talking through your ass.'

'I lost a lot of money by spiking that story – so where's my 15,000 dollars?'

'Tell me again why you're worth it.'

'As I said before, I'm going to help you nail Lopez, your rogue Green Beret, and maybe you can get Burchett, the Australian commie, at the same time.' Catesby paused. 'But I'm feeling generous, so I'm going to give you a bonus prize.'

'It better be a good one.'

'How well do you know your counterpart at the French Embassy?' Catesby was going to enjoy this. It was payback time.

'Not very. I've met him once or twice. His name is Guerini or something like that. He's a sleazy greaseball, looks like a wop.'

'His name isn't Guerini.' Catesby smiled. It was interesting to learn the SDECE man had taken the alias of a Marseilles gangster he had collaborated with. 'It's a good story, but I'm not going to tell you more until you hand over the money that you already owe me. I got you out of a lot of trouble.'

The American went over to a grey iron box bolted to the floor. He came back with a thick brown envelope and pushed it at Catesby. 'Do you want to count it?'

'Don't need to. I trust you.' Catesby put the envelope inside the pocket of his safari jacket without looking inside. He would later drop the cash off at the British Embassy and get a signed receipt. Times were tough and the dollars would be a welcome stash for SIS to pay off agents. 'Guerini can't use his real name because of something that happened here in Saigon in 1955. Does the name Antoine Savani ring a bell?'

'A tiny tinkle.'

'You obviously weren't here in '55 because if you had been, that bell would have rung so loud your ears would be bleeding.'

'That was before my time.'

'Antoine Savani was French chief of station then, just as he is now under his new name. It was quite a daring move sending him here considering his history. It suggests that SDECE hasn't completely given up the business.'

'What business?'

'Your business, heroin.'

The CIA man's face turned pale and hard. 'I think we've had enough of that shit.'

'Sure, but maybe Savani hasn't. 1955 was a bad year for the French intelligence service. They fucked up at Dien Bien Phu and lost the war and all of Indochina – and quite rightly their funding was slashed. The only way they could survive in the lavish style to which the SDECE was accustomed was Operation

X.' Catesby looked closely at the American. 'You guys might want to learn a lesson from their book – but I think you already have.'

The American remained unblinking and expressionless.

'In any case, despite French losses elsewhere, Antoine Savani still maintained a fiefdom in Saigon and the Delta. It was the best gangster empire in Southeast Asia. Savani controlled the Hall of Mirrors, the world's biggest brothel, and the Chinese Triads in Cholon – no mean feat. But the jewel in the SDECE's tarnished crown was the heroin trade. The opium still poured down from the Golden Triangle via the hill tribes of Laos.' Catesby smiled. 'But then you guys messed it up for Savani. Your new puppets, Ngo Dinh Diem and his gang, wanted to take over. A bit funny considering that Diem was a devout Catholic who only wanted to be a priest, but the rest of the family were more practical. You know about the gun battle, don't you? It's part of secret CIA legend – not something you tell the new guys.'

The American nodded.

'It must have been a very impressive fire-fight. It was the only time in history that two Western intelligence services faced each other in open combat. Savani's SDECE colleagues fought side by side with Vietnamese river pirates, dealers, pimps and a handful of Corsican mafia flown in especially for the event. But somehow the CIA and the Ngo family prevailed. It must have been your finest hour; pity you weren't there. I wonder if CIA called in some Chicago mafia to help? In the end, there were more than five hundred dead. Ngo Dinh Diem was the best Vietnamese leader you guys ever put in the ring. You shouldn't have had him murdered.' Catesby paused and looked at the American. 'Were you part of that?'

The CIA man stared through Catesby, his eyes like cold blue bullets.

'I'm sure the gangsters you replaced Diem with also have their merits, but I'm not sure that fighting to the death is one of them. Still, I'm not here to lecture, I'm here to do a deal. Warning you about Antoine Savani is a friendly service – take it as such.'

The American's eyes softened.

'As Savani and his river pirates fought a rearguard action in the tangled mangroves of the Rung Sat Swamp he offered a reward for the head of Lansdale, the CIA chief of station. Not just his head; he wanted Lansdale's body gutted and filled with dirt – and his sex organs shoved down his throat. Take care, my friend, for Savani's contract may now have your name on it.'

The American sat back. 'How the fuck do you know this stuff?'

'I dug it up while I was investigating the article you just paid me to spike.'

'I haven't paid you to do anything – and don't you forget it.'

It was turning into a 'through the looking glass' conversation, but Catesby played along. 'Sure, I must have been mistaken.'

'And now I want to give you some help – concerning a matter of mutual interest. That camera of yours is too big.' The CIA man was referring to the .35mm Nikon Catesby carried in a bag as part of his journalist cover. 'It's too conspicuous.' CIA opened a drawer and took out what looked like an Olympus Pen Double E camera. 'It's smaller, but you get only three shots – and they're just .22 calibre rounds. It's best to aim straight into an eye.'

Catesby picked up the camera and looked at the American through the viewfinder: 'Bang.' He shook the camera and put it down on the table. 'Shit, it wasn't loaded.'

'I bet you were the class clown at Eton.'

'How did you know I went to Eton?'

'Because all Limey assholes go to Eton.'

Catesby laughed. 'Well, you certainly got that one right.'

The American looked back in the drawer and picked up three cartridges. 'Here, you'll need some rounds. And here.' He scooped in the drawer again. 'Have three more. You ought to practise using it before you go.'

Catesby put the camera and bullets in the pocket with the banknotes. It was quite a haul. 'Who do you want me to kill?'

'First on the list is Lopez. He's worth 40,000 more gringo dollars. And you'll need a real camera too, because we'd like to see some photos showing his sorry-ass dead body.'

'Like Che in Bolivia?'

'Exactly.'

'Were you there?'

'You ask too many fucking questions.'

'And who's next on the list?'

'Burchett. But he's only worth 20,000 bucks – hey, but maybe you ought to ask your colonial friends in Canberra to throw in some Australian bucks if you nail his entrails to a tree.'

Catesby was impressed. The American actually knew the capital of Australia. 'And what about the third bullet?'

'Just take out the highest-ranking gook you can find and submit an invoice.'

Catesby frowned. 'But I've got to get there first.'

'Your itinerary begins with a flight from Long Binh airfield. You can get a lift there on the embassy bus. Then you need to find your way to the northern sector – that's where Special Forces send all their crazies, like Lopez, the ones they don't want to see again. The person who will point you in the right direction is Bucksport the Sailor. He'll love you.'

»»»»»

Catesby was the only round-eye on the embassy bus. It was used for transporting the Vietnamese cleaners and cooks. Catesby sat next to a shy young woman who hid her face behind long silky hair. The driver went out of his way to drop Catesby at the Long Binh base. The bus wasn't, however, allowed through the gate. Since being attacked during the Tet Offensive, 'indigenous personnel', usually called indigs or slope-heads or gooks, were not allowed on the base unless they had a special pass and a round-eye to vouch for them. But Catesby wasn't high-status enough to do the vouching.

Catesby's trip north began with a C-130 flight to the base at Cam Ranh Bay. All the other passengers packed into the cargo plane were replacement soldiers wearing green fatigues that were crisp and still unbleached by the sun. They looked tired, confused and resigned to being herded from place to place. At Cam Ranh, Catesby was picked up by a three-quarter-ton truck with 5th SFGA stencilled on the bumpers. Catesby could see that the soldiers on this truck were a different breed from the young livestock on the plane. They were older, harder and wore twisted cynical smiles under their green berets. The truck followed the coast road for thirty miles to the Special Forces headquarters at Nha Trang. No one spoke to Catesby – and they didn't say much to each other either. A sergeant sitting opposite Catesby drank can after can of beer with slow deliberation. At one point, he stood up and hurled a half-empty can at a Vietnamese woman walking beside the road with baskets balanced on both ends of a stick, shouting 'Have a drink on me, slopehead.'

When they got to Nha Trang a captain with a clipboard ticked off the names of the replacements. When they had dispersed, the captain came over to Catesby. 'Slimeball said to be expecting you.'

Catesby assumed Slime-ball was the CIA officer.

'He says I've got to put you on a Blackbird heading up to the SOG FOB. You'll be sharing the plane with a load of CCN replacements. Don't talk to them – and don't go with them when you get to Da Nang. Someone from C Company will pick you up. Got that?'

Catesby nodded. The very earth of the 5th SFGA compound oozed testosterone. They were headed for Command and Control North, the Forward Operating Base for the Studies and Observations Group unit that operated illegally in Laos.

The Blackbird was a C-123 painted with dark night-operation camouflage. There were no identification markings, as if that would disguise the plane's origins if it went down in a place where it shouldn't be. The eight replacements wore jungle hats dyed black instead of berets. They were very quiet. Catesby sensed an aura of death so intense that their bodies seemed already to swell and putrefy.

It was dark when the plane arrived at the huge airbase south of Da Nang. The officer sent to fetch Catesby had a brief chat with one of the CCN black hats, then motioned that Catesby follow him to a jeep.

'I used to be with them before I got wounded, but now I've got a Mickey Mouse job at the C Team.'

'Not badly wounded, I hope.'

'Bad enough. You're British?'

'More or less.'

'One of my cousins is the Duke of Edinburgh – on my mother's side. She's Greek.'

'Can you speak Greek?'

The officer launched into Greek and sounded very fluent, but Catesby didn't know the language so he couldn't judge. 'Have you ever met the Duke of Edinburgh?' asked Catesby.

'No, but my mother has. She's from Corfu.'

Once again, Catesby felt as if he had stepped through the looking glass.

»»»»»

Bucksport the Sailor was actually a lieutenant colonel commanding the C Team on China Beach and all the Special Forces camps in I Corps. The colonel bore an uncanny resemblance to Humphrey Bogart and had a similar voice and manner. Catesby and Bucksport were sitting in the commanding officer's quarters, which were sparsely furnished. The only decoration was a framed watercolour of an oil tanker on the plywood wall. Bucksport pointed to it.

'That was my ship. She was torpedoed on the Murmansk run in early '42. Only two of us survived.'

'Is that why they call you Bucksport the Sailor?'

'It's also because I come from a place called Bucksport in Maine, a tiny place on the Penobscot River. Can I top up your whisky?'

'Yes, please.'

The room was dark. The only light was a desk lamp pointed at the lower wall.

'There wasn't much to do in Bucksport other than go to sea. I went when I was fourteen. I've been all over your country: Liverpool, Glasgow, Portsmouth, London. I liked it.' The colonel paused. 'Listen. Can you hear the sea?'

It was a quiet night, but the compound was practically built on the beach. Catesby listened and could just detect the surf murmur of the South China Sea. 'Yes.'

'After getting torpedoed, I decided I'd had enough of being a sailor so I joined the Marines. That was a mistake, but at least all the bad things that happened to me happened on land. The worst was Tarawa, but I survived. Forgive my being so talkative.' The colonel looked at Catesby. 'But there is a reason for it.'

Catesby nodded and kept eye contact. He didn't know what to say. Bucksport wasn't completely mad, but it was obvious that he had lost a few marbles. At least, thought Catesby, he knew the marbles were missing and was willing to look for them.

'I think,' said Bucksport, 'they are sending you to me as a provocation. And if you understand who I am you might understand what they are trying to do.'

'Who are "they"?'

'Everything that is brainless, pointless and evil about this war.'

Maybe, thought Catesby, he wasn't mad at all; in fact, he could be the first sane American he had met. But that must make you pretty lonely in the asylum. Catesby felt comfortable with Bucksport. The American was another working-class kid, a wharf rat like himself, from the other side of the Atlantic. And the two of them had risen to some rank in the business of killing and spying.

'You need more whisky,' said the colonel, 'and so do I. It's Canadian rye.'

'What happened next?'

'They patched me up and sent me back for more. After the Japanese surrendered, I came back to the States and married my childhood sweetheart. I had changed, but she understood that. I got a job as an insurance salesman in Bucksport, but I wasn't any good at it and began to drink too much.

'When Korea came along I joined up with the Marines again. They were desperate and made me – a kid who left school at fourteen – an officer. In December 1950 we were sent up north to the Chosin River. Things were going fine until the Red Chinese Army crossed the Yalu River, but the biggest enemy was the cold. It got down to minus 37 degrees Fahrenheit. It was so cold the medics had to put morphine syrettes into their mouths to defrost the morphine before they could inject it into the screaming wounded

– and frozen plasma was, of course, useless. Our weapons mal-
functioned because the cold was so intense that the springs on
the firing pins would not strike hard enough to fire the round.'

Catesby sipped the rye whisky. He knew that Bucksport's
story was part of a pattern. But you had to ignore the human
suffering to see where the dots connected.

'Most of my platoon died of cold when we were cut off during
the retreat. Not a glorious way to die. When the Chinese overran
our position I hid myself beneath a pile of my marines' bodies.
But they dug me out and found me.' The colonel laughed. 'Not a
glorious way to be captured. I was a PoW for nearly three years
and that was an education too.' The colonel refilled both glasses
and looked at Catesby.

'What did it teach you?'

'It taught me that heroism only works on the day and only if
your side is lucky and you win. The first few months were pretty
bad. We were in a camp run by the North Koreans. More than
half the Americans in my barracks died of frostbite or disease.
No medicines, little food. I had dysentery, scurvy and was
covered in lice. Yeah, I know the joke – but otherwise I was fine.
Then we were sent to a Chinese camp and things were much
better. They dressed us in Chinese quilted uniforms, which were
warmer than our American ones. The food wasn't bad and when
the weather got better they even gave us baseballs and basket-
balls so we could exercise. Naturally, there was a reason for all
this better treatment – and the reason was what they were telling
us in the daily political lectures. Not exactly brainwashing, but
it was indoctrination – sometimes very subtle. I didn't resist,
but didn't succumb either.' The colonel smiled and looked at the
warm amber glow of his whisky. 'But your man did.'

An alarm bell went off in Catesby's brain. He knew exactly
who Bucksport was talking about. 'I didn't know I had a man
in Korea.'

Bucksport gave Catesby a searching stare. 'I'm surprised you
didn't know him. He was an Englishman like you.'

Catesby winced. 'An Englishman like you' was uncomfort-
ably close to the mark. He had known the PoW turned Soviet

spy very well. They had worked together in Berlin and some-times chatted in Nederlands, their common language. That was a mistake because it aroused the suspicions of their SIS col-leagues. Years later, after the spy was uncovered, Catesby had been submitted to long hours of interrogation. In retrospect, he wasn't surprised that he hadn't spotted his colleague's treachery. He had always been so honest, so sincere and morally earnest. But maybe that was what had turned him.

Bucksport wasn't going to let Catesby off. 'You must have known him. You're a journalist and it was in all the papers.'

'Of course I knew about him. But I thought you were asking if I knew him personally.'

Bucksport looked shifty. 'I must have been misinformed.'

'Who informed you?'

'I run the best network in Southeast Asia and that's why they're out to get me.'

Catesby shrugged. He was sure they would come back to that later. 'You were talking about indoctrination sessions?'

'It wasn't just Red Chinese indoctrination. There was a Catho-lic priest in our PoW camp who was a professor before he became a chaplain. He used to give lessons about books to educate us ignoramuses – and the guards didn't stop him. One of the books he talked about was by Cardinal Newman, an Englishman. The book was called *Apologia Pro Vita Sua*. I didn't much like the book, but I liked the title. Of course, I never learned Latin. The priest told me the title meant "a defence of my own life" – well, I thought, "an apology for my own life" would be a better one.'

Bucksport sipped his whisky and stared into the darkness. 'That's what I'm trying to give you, if you've got time to listen – and I won't blame you if you don't. An apology for my life.'

'I've got the time.'

'In the end, I got pretty bored with the priest's lessons. It was all about angels fluttering around on top of a manure heap and arguing about whether it was bread and wine or an actual body they were eating. I, being a simple man, wanted to learn more about the manure heap. Why was it there and who owned it?'

Bucksport laughed. 'I think the priest and his nonsense did a better job of making me see the Red Chinese point of view than the Chinese did. More whisky?'

'Yes, please.'

'You sound very hoity-toity with all this please and thank you. Your English spy friend would have called you bourgeois.'

'He wasn't my friend.' Catesby smiled. The spy had, in fact, often called Catesby 'bourgeois'. At the time, long before the spy's arrest for treason, Catesby thought the bourgeois taunt was teasing. But now he saw he really meant it.

The colonel topped up Catesby's glass. 'One day something odd happened at the camp. Things got a lot better – especially the cleanliness and the food. They seemed to want to clean us up and fatten us up too. Then we found out why. One day a bunch of photographers and reporters turned up. One of them was an Australian called Wilfrid Burchett. Of course, we were grateful for the visit because it made things better. The Chinese even issued us swimming trunks and took us for a swim in the Yalu River. Propaganda stunt or not, it was good. Afterwards, Burchett interviewed a group of us and said the camp was "like a holiday resort in Switzerland". I quickly put him right and told him about the months of lice and dysentery. The Chinese didn't like that much. And Burchett, to be fair to him, apologised for the Swiss resort remark.'

'Did the Chinese take it out on you?'

'No, on the contrary; they made even more of an effort to convert me to the cause. I ended up assigned to a Marxist study group with that Englishman you never met – and found out he wasn't an Englishman at all, but half Dutch and half Egyptian. But that, I suppose, made him an even better spy.'

Catesby realised, once again, that if he hadn't had a Belgian mother and learned languages he would never have become an intelligence officer. Spies were cosmopolitan.

'And,' said the colonel, 'that's where it all started to go wrong.'

'What happened?'

'I'm not a very good student. I don't like being preached at.' Bucksport paused. 'And I was missing my wife. It happened during a talk about class structure. I must have looked bored and the Chinese group leader asked if I had fallen asleep. Nothing nasty, it was meant in good humour. But I turned nasty. I said, "I'm bored because you're not telling me anything I don't already know. I was born into shit poverty in a shithole. My pay as a merchant seaman was stopped by the capitalist shipowners the minute my ship was sunk by a Nazi submarine. So don't you tell me about capitalist oppression and inequality – I know more about it than any of you will ever know." Then I shouted, "Now you're oppressing me. Why don't you send me home to my darling Harriet?" Then something must have snapped in me. I picked up the book we were studying and threw it at the Chinese leader. I regretted doing that. It knocked his glasses off and they broke. Pity – he wasn't a bad person and couldn't see a thing without his specs. I shouldn't have done it.' Bucksport stopped and looked at his whisky.

'What happened next?'

'Another Chinese piled in and knocked me to the ground. Now, I was a pretty tough kid. I didn't like being hit. The red mist descended. I managed to get an elbow into the Chinese guy's face and split his nose open. Then I got on top of him and started choking him to death.' Bucksport sipped his whisky and laughed. 'I don't think I would be here to tell the tale if I had done that in a Jap PoW camp or a Nazi one. But the Chinese still got pretty mad at me. I was bruised and bloody when I woke up in a cage. They decided I didn't appreciate the pleasures of Pyoktong – that was the name of the camp – so they transferred me to Pukchin Mining Camp, which the other PoWs nicknamed Death Valley.

'The worst part was the trip there. They put my cage in the back of a truck and we could only travel at night because of the American bombing. When we stopped they turned me into a circus attraction. Villagers used to come to gawp at me and I would rattle my cage bars and make noises like an ape. I used to throw shit at them if they got too close. The Chinese liked my act. They must have thought it proved that Americans were barbarians – but I was doing it to show that if you treat someone like an animal, they act like an animal.' Bucksport paused. 'Then we got to Pukchin and that was that. Conditions weren't that much worse than Pyoktong – and I realised that the reason they moved me wasn't to punish me, but so that I wouldn't contaminate the other prisoners with my attitude.'

'Did you ever see the Englishman again?'

'No, but I would like to.' Bucksport smiled. 'I'd like to apologise to your English friend for damaging his book. It was the one I threw at the Chinese guy: Karl Marx's *Theories of Surplus Value*. And the funny thing was that I was beginning to like it.'

'I think he lives in Moscow. You could send him a replacement copy.'

'Maybe you could do it for me?' The colonel looked at Catesby darkly. 'Who do you really work for?'

'You can believe what you want. But does it matter?'

'I suppose it doesn't – but I'm not going to tell you more than you need to know regardless of who you are.'

'What do I need to know?'

'I haven't finished my story.' For the first time Bucksport sounded a little slurred.

'Go on.'

'I was released from Pukchin PoW camp on 19 September 1953. After medical checks by the UN authorities, I was turned over to the Americans. More medical checks and debriefings then back to the USA and my beloved Harriet.'

'How did you end up in the US Army?'

'I had had enough of the Marines – I wanted to do something different. But I wanted to stay in the military because that was the only life I knew. And I didn't want to give away the surplus value of my labour in a civilian job.'

'Is that a joke?'

'Yeah. But it wasn't a joke I could tell anyone. I got into Special Forces when the unit was just starting up. I started off as a sergeant, but a few years later they gave me a direct commission as a captain and made me an A team leader. We were supposed to be parachuted behind Soviet lines in Eastern Europe if the Cold War ever turned hot. Our job was to rendezvous with partisans and blow up Russian supply lines. I suspect that we would have been rounded up and shot within a couple of hours after we landed, but I kept my mouth shut about that because I wanted to play the game and work my way up through the ranks. I had Harriet and two daughters to support. So I kept getting promoted – and here I am now, *el supremo* for the northern corps. But you know something? They've never trusted me. That's why that CIA bastard sent you up here.'

'Can you explain?'

'First of all, they don't really trust anyone who has ever been a PoW in Korea. They think we're all some kind of Manchurian candidate who has been brainwashed to kill the President. CIA hate Special Forces. They want to run the whole spook business themselves. And they also think I'm a maverick who needs cutting down.'

'Why?'

'Lots of reasons. In particular, because I won't let Program Phoenix, their assassination squads, operate in any of my AOs. So here's the drill. They've sent you up here chasing Lopez because they want to see me fuck up. In fact, they blame me for the whole Lopez mess.'

'How well did you know Lopez?'

'Enough to know that he was a fucked-up kid with lots of brains. He'd been educated in France and then went to Harvard.'

'Why was he fucked up?'

'Because he didn't know who he was. I think his mother was a Tijuana hooker who didn't even know who the father was. She must have given him away to this rich family back East who adopted him. His stepparents were not only rich, but prominent and powerful liberals – real American aristocracy. So you have this guy, Lopez, who had all the manners and ways of an old money East Coast preppy, but the face of a mixed-race *mestizo* – the sort of urchin you'd see rooting through the garbage in a Juarez dump. I don't know what made him snap and do that awful thing.'

The story that Catesby had heard was that Lopez had helped the Viet Cong overrun a Special Forces outpost in which all the Americans had been killed. 'Do you think he's still alive?'

'We've had confirmed sightings from captured VC and NVA – and also from two of our agents. What's the slimy bastard in Saigon want you to do?'

'He wants me to kill him.'

'You'd never get out alive.'

'I know, but as an alternative he wants me to provide intelligence if I get behind enemy lines – and he also mentioned your old Australian pal, Burchett.'

'Two birds with one stone.'

'Or maybe three.'

Bucksport suddenly looked cautious. 'Did CIA tell you there might be someone else?'

'No, I've heard a rumour from elsewhere.'

'A young Western woman?'

Catesby nodded.

'I wish that kids wouldn't get mixed up in this mess, but most of our soldiers are kids too.' Bucksport stood up and drew a curtain, which revealed a map. 'If CIA wants me to "render you all assistance", as the Eyes Only message instructed, I'd better put you in the picture.' Bucksport pointed to a mountainous area directly on the Laotian border. 'Lopez was last sighted in this grid square. The easiest way to get there is to hitch a ride in a Russian truck from Hanoi. That's what CIA ought to have told you, but it's not easy from this side of the border because there aren't any roads. What that bastard in Saigon would love me to do is give you a lift in one of my helicopters – preferably with me in it. In the unlikely event we didn't get shot down, he would then accuse me of running unauthorised intelligence operations outside my AO. SOG can go in that area – and further west towards Tchepone too – but I can't. And the reason why SOG goes there is to pick up Golden Triangle heroin. It's the safest operation those poor bastards do. They fly them in Korean War-era Sikorsky choppers they must have got from the helicopter museum. The North Vietnamese know what it's about as soon as they see those ancient choppers so they don't shoot at them. The heroin that doesn't go up the veins of live in-country GIs goes up the asses of dead GIs awaiting repatriation back to the States in the I Corps mortuary at Da Nang airbase. If CIA really wanted to help you he would have sent you to the SOG FOB, which is just down the beach.'

'So there's not much you can do?'

'Don't worry. I've got a few tricks up my sleeve that Saigon doesn't know about.' Bucksport pointed to the map. 'There's a leper colony here at Thuong Duc run by Australian Bible Society missionaries. Ever heard of them?'

Catesby shook his head.

'The mission of the Bible Society is to translate the Bible into languages where there is no translation. Most of the patients at the leper colony are Katu montagnards. The Katu not only have no Bible, they have no written language to write it in. The missionaries at Thuong Duc are first-class anthropologists and linguists and are trying to create a written language for the Katu.'

'What's this have to do with my finding Lopez?'

Bucksport sipped his whisky. He had turned a corner and seemed more coherent, the more he drank. 'I'm surprised you haven't spotted it. The answer's Wilfrid Burchett. The Bible Society leper colony is immune from attack or harassment by the VC and NVA – and I suspect it's because of Burchett. He isn't that bad a man and must have a soft spot for his fellow Australians.'

Bucksport pointed to the map. 'Now what I can do is put you on a helicopter for the leper colony. That's no problem because we've got an A camp just the other side of the river – and we sometimes drop in relief supplies to the lepers.' He paused. 'And I'll tell you another secret. I'm sick of war. I got two months more to do and then I go back and retire. Now, if you're lucky, you might be able to contact Burchett at the colony. But make sure you've been taking your dapsone; you don't want to become a leper.'

'Thanks.' Catesby looked into his whisky. 'But what if the rendezvous with Burchett doesn't come off?'

'If Burchett doesn't show, you've got to make your way up this river.' Bucksport pointed to a blue line that writhed like a serpent through the coastal plain. 'It's called the Song Thu Bon and empties into the sea at Hoi An. Go up past the marine base at An Hoa. You might check out the coal mine at Nong Son. They also seem to have worked out a deal with the VC and NVA. But you want to stay on the river till this place.' He pointed to a narrow gorge. 'The NVA buy rice and food supplies in the Que Son Valley and ferry them across the river here then porter them up into the mountains to the 2nd NVA Division. But you need to be careful and lucky; that river crossing is bombed to fuck. Needless to say, I never told you any of this. But even if I did, my ass is still covered for your job is to waste Lopez so I was only helping you, as were my instructions.'

'Where do you think I'm most likely to find him?'

'Probably across the border in Laos in one of the five base areas. Forget about the Ho Chi Minh Trail as being a mass of barefoot peasants acting as human pack animals or pushing heavily laden bicycles. And only Americans call it the Ho Chi Minh Trail; its real name is the Truong Son Strategic Supply Route. It's a web of roads, some paved with gravel, and the supplies are carried in trucks. The trucks shuttle the logistics between waypoints where the supplies are trans-loaded on to the next truck relay.' The colonel laughed. 'The people who think we're fighting a guerrilla army have got their heads up their ass. One of the engineer regiments maintaining the Truong Son has twenty bulldozers, eleven road graders, three rock crushers and two steamrollers. If you get there you will find oil pipelines, underground supply depots, barracks, communication centres, classrooms and hospitals. This war is America's Stalingrad. And just like the Germans, we believe our own propaganda of invincible power and have grossly underestimated the enemy.'

'Anything else?'

Bucksport shook his head. He suddenly looked very weary.

'I hope you have a good retirement.'

'It won't be good. My wife died last year.'

'Sorry.'

'But you've got to soldier on. Maybe I'll go to college and try to learn something.'

'I think you could teach them more than they could teach you.'

»»»»

Catesby spent the night in the transient officers' billet. It was an old French beach house built of grey weathered clapboard with a wide veranda facing the beach. He lay awake under a mosquito net listening to the gentle sough of the sea. Once again, Catesby realised that he didn't know what he was doing or why he was doing it. The Americans didn't know what they were doing either, so they just threw around money and bombs. Catesby understood he had now become immersed in the pointless waste and brutality that swirled around him. He could see that the CIA man regarded him as a passing pest who had to be shut up with either bullets or dollars. Bucksport, on the other hand, was a lone voice in the wilderness.

Catesby lay awake sweating into a not very clean sheet. He wasn't going to give up and tried to focus on why he was there. Why had Her Majesty's Secret Intelligence Service sent him to the middle of a mad Asian war to find and interview the daughter of a Whitehall mandarin? Why was her mother's role in a hushed-up spy scandal still important? The loss of secrets was now irrelevant. So why was he there? It wasn't a matter of an external threat to the UK; it was a matter of an internal threat. Catesby had seen their mad eyes gleaming with resentment. They hated Harold Wilson's government and they hated the way Britain was changing. They were looking for an excuse, any excuse. Catesby saw his job clearly. He had to find out what had happened – and then bury the whole mess where the plotters could never find it.

»»»»

In the morning Catesby waited for the Thuong Duc helicopter with the Greek-speaking officer who had met him at the airbase.

'It shouldn't be a bad ride,' said the officer. 'Thuong Duc isn't taking any incoming at the moment. The old man said you want to do a story on the leper colony. We'll land at Thuong Duc camp first, then drop you off. The leper place is just across the river.'

'I might be staying there a while. How do I get a lift back?'

'There's a radio link with the camp. Just call them up and say you want a ride.'

The rest of the conversation was drowned out by helicopter noises. The flight was a dog leg over the sea to avoid anti-aircraft fire, then high over the coastal plain. Catesby made out the river, the Song Thu Bon, and a tributary that twisted north to Thuong Duc. The countryside was a mixture of steep mountains and soft paddy fields. The Thuong Duc camp was a sand-coloured rectangle at the base of a mountain with almost vertical slopes. Catesby turned to watch the two teenage helicopter pilots as they calmly guided the helicopter through a series of feints to avoid ground fire as they approached the camp. Their cool competence seemed the only sane thing in Vietnam.

The chopper quickly offloaded personnel and supplies on a dusty square, then made the short hop across the river to the leper colony and landed on a grassy rise. A bespectacled middle-aged woman, who held a bush hat to protect her face from the whirling dust, was waiting.

»»»»»

The bespectacled Australian woman was Mildred. Years in the sun had turned her skin leathery brown and made her intense blue eyes all the more piercing. She looked like everyone's stereotype of a Sunday school teacher, but her manner was softer. 'My parents,' she said, 'were members of the Bible Society and I suppose that's how I got involved.'

It was late at night and all the staff and patients had gone to bed. The only sounds were an occasional moan from the sleeping wards or the rumble of distant artillery. Catesby and Mildred were sitting on opposite sides of a table with a single guttering candle. The electricity generators were off for the night. The thing that had immediately impressed Catesby was the cleanliness and utter tidiness. The building, red shutters and tiled roof, looked like a villa in the South of France.

'Have you been taking your dapsone?'asked the woman with a maternal look.

'Yes, religiously.'

'Good. But you probably don't need it; 95 per cent of the pop-ulation are naturally immune – as I most certainly am. There are so many myths about leprosy.'

'Like your limbs falling off?'

'They don't fall off, but they do become deformed as you probably noticed today. Secondary infections cause cartilage to be absorbed into the body, which is why many of our patients have fingers and toes that are so badly misshapen.'

'Are you are a doctor?'

The woman smiled. 'I'm a doctor on two accounts. I'm a medical MD and a PhD in anthropology.'

Catesby was mildly abashed. 'Are you very religious?'

She smiled again. 'I knew you were going to ask that ques-tion. I'm religious in that I believe all human beings are the same family and come from the same source – whatever that is.' She shrugged. 'And I believe the Bible is evidence of our common ancestry. Muslims, Christians and Jews all claim to be descend-ants of the tribe of Abraham. And the Greek Prometheus, nailed to a mountain as punishment for giving fire to mankind, is awfully close to Christ. Would you like me to pop you another tinny of Fosters before they get warm?'

'Yes, please.'

'Good, I'll have one too.'

As the Australian fetched the lager from the now silent fridge, Catesby felt once again that he had been catapulted into a world as surreal as Dali's lobster telephones. He and Mildred had begun the evening discussing the recent Ashes tour to the background noise of American artillery fire pounding a nearby ridgeline. As the shells fell, Catesby was pleased to discover that England had scraped a series draw in the fifth test when Under-wood had taken seven wickets.

'The fascinating thing,' said the woman as she sipped her Fosters straight from the tin, 'is the way that creation myths overlap.'

Once again, Catesby felt the surreal boat of Vietnam surf down another wave.

'We've managed to complete an oral translation of Genesis into the eastern Katu dialect.'

Catesby had already learned that the 50,000 Katu montagnards spoke three different dialects that were not mutually comprehensible.

'The Katu,' the woman continued, 'simply love the story of Noah because it's so close to their own creation story.'

'They built an ark?'

'No, but there was a flood. The Katu tried to escape by fleeing up the tallest mountains. In the end, all the mountains were covered by the flood waters and every person and every land animal had drowned – except for one Katu and one dog who had found safety on the highest peak.'

'Was the dog's name Adam?'

'Don't be rude and drink your beer. But it's interesting that you say that because the Katu was a young woman – which reflects their being a matriarchal society. In any case, the woman had sex with the dog and her children became the forebears of the Katu tribe.'

'A very modest creation myth.'

'And the Katu are a very modest and gentle people. They not only believe that every living being is sacred, but the very earth itself and every rock. You must only take and use what you need to survive. Otherwise, the spirit of the tree or the river will be angry with you. I was so angry when the Americans tried to recruit the Katu as soldiers, but the colonel who sent you here put an end to that. He is a good man.'

'And he knows that you have contact with Wilfrid Burchett?'

'Yes, and you must keep that a secret. We call him Ong Wilfrid. Ong is Vietnamese for uncle. Wilfrid has helped us with the North Vietnamese and the Viet Cong. They will never interfere with us here and they have agreed not to use the Katu as porters or labourers – and Wilfrid, in his turn, writes good stories about the North Vietnamese.'

Catesby nodded at the radio set. 'How can you communicate with Uncle Wilfrid without being listened to by the Americans or the Vietnamese?'

The Australian woman smiled. 'Wilfrid has a young Katu assistant called Joseph. I speak to Joseph in eastern Katu dialect. There are no Vietnamese or Americans who can understand what we are saying – then Joseph, a fine linguist, translates for Wilfrid.'

'What's the situation now?'

'It would be too dangerous for you to meet them. The trails between here and the NVA base areas are being heavily bombed. There is also a large number of American-led reconnaissance teams in the area.'

'Is it because someone knows I'm here?'

'I hope not; it could be because the Americans fear the North Vietnamese are massing for an assault on the Special Forces camp.'

»»»»»

The next night there were rocket and mortar attacks against the camp, which appeared to confirm what the Australian woman had said. Catesby sat in a deckchair on the veranda of the villa with a tin of Fosters in his hand and watched the action. It may have been lethal, but it was also a rather pretty fireworks display. The steep mountainside near the camp sparkled with the back-blasts of rockets being launched. They reminded Catesby of flashbulbs going off from the terraces during an evening football match. Meanwhile the whole area was bathed in the greenish-white light of illumination flares slowly descending on their mini-parachutes. And at ground level there was a fierce criss-crossing of red tracer rounds from the camp with green tracer rounds from the attackers. But the best show was when the helicopter gunships turned up and bathed the mountain with streams of mini-gun fire that looked like solid lines of light. It was clearly not a good place to go rambling.

In the morning Catesby listened as Mildred spoke eastern Katu to Joseph over the radio. There were occasional delays of a minute or two when no one spoke. Catesby assumed that Joseph was translating to someone else, presumably Ong Wilfrid, before speaking again. At one point Mildred wrote something down. Catesby could see worry etched on her face.

He waited until she had finished the transmission then asked, 'Things are not going well?'

'Wilfrid says it's too dangerous to send a scout to lead you to the NVA base area from here. He has, however, given me the name of someone in Da Nang who might be able to help you. But I will have to decode the name first. Joseph and I have devised a code using the book of Genesis and the Katu alphabet. It will only take a minute.'

Catesby watched as she added a copied set of letters to a copied passage from Genesis. He could see that Mildred was using the polyalphabetic trigraph, the securest code imaginable. The Noah story was her decryption key. This was a country where even missionaries had to use spy-craft. Mildred copied something on a scrap of paper and handed it to Catesby.

'This,' she said, 'is the name of your contact in Da Nang and where you can leave a message for her.'

Catesby read the decryption. It was the very same name the Frenchwoman journalist had passed on to him on the road to Cu Chi.

»»»»»

The bicycle repair shop also dealt with motorbikes and scooters. You found it by going up a dark alleyway off Hoang Dieu Street. Once again, Catesby was given a lift by the Duke of Edinburgh's cousin.

'Da Nang's off limits to US troops,' said the Greek American. 'They think it's too dangerous. We're allowed to tool around the town because we tell the MPs that we have to liaise with our Vietnamese counterparts – which is bullshit. But you'll be all right because you're a *nhà báo*, a journalist.'

'Thanks for the lift.'

'By the way, the best way to get on with the Vietnamese is to trust them. If they think you don't trust them they will mess you up. If you do trust them they will look after you. At least, it's worked for me and I've survived five years here.'

'Thanks for the advice.'

'And next time you see Prince Philip, tell him that cousin Theo sends his best wishes.' The American ground the jeep into gear and disappeared in a cloud of petrol fumes.

As Catesby walked up the alleyway to the bike repair shop he kept repeating 'trust them' as a mantra. Not much else he could do. He was alone in a war-torn country where he hardly spoke a word of the language. The door to the bike shop was open so Catesby walked in. There didn't seem to be anyone around. The shop was dark and smelled of grease and cooking spices. Most of the pushbikes were French, but practically all of the motorbikes were .50cc Hondas. There was, however, a looming presence in the shop. It was under a tarpaulin spotted with grease stains. Catesby could only see the bottom few inches of the motorcycle wheels so he couldn't be sure what it was. But somehow it beckoned like a lost lover from the dark shadows. Catesby knew that whatever lay beneath that tarpaulin was part of him, part of his heritage. It seemed to pulse: *home, home, I've been waiting for you*. Catesby needed to see her, to touch her. He lifted the tarpaulin and there she was – a gleaming hunk of England, a perfect BSA 441 Victor motorcycle.

Catesby would have caressed the bike if he hadn't felt a hand touch his shoulder. It wasn't a harsh touch, but it wasn't a gentle one either. And whoever was there had entered the shop in complete silence. Catesby turned slowly to face a Vietnamese man dressed in a T-shirt and black shorts. He greeted him with '*Chào, anh*', a phrase he had picked up which meant 'Hello, older brother.'

The Vietnamese, a lot younger than Catesby, answered, '*Chào, ông.*' Hello uncle.

Catesby pointed to the bike and then to himself. He wanted to show that he was British like the BSA Victor, but the Vietnamese word for British was *anh*, the same as older brother, and trying to actually say it would just make things more confusing.

The Vietnamese stared at Catesby without blinking. It was time to come clean, to explain why he was there. Catesby had practised the name of the Vietnamese woman with Mildred and knew he had it right: 'Truong Thi Nhung.'

There was a brief flicker in the eyes of the Vietnamese, but otherwise his face remained blank.

Catesby pointed to the motorcycle again and said, '*Tôi người Anh.*' I am English people.

There was a flicker of understanding in the eyes of the Vietnamese.

Catesby then pretended he was kicking a football and said, 'Manchester United.'

The Vietnamese beamed a broad smile and said, 'Your Bess.'

Catesby nodded and repeated, 'George Best.'

The Vietnamese held up his thumb and said, 'Numbah one.'

Catesby wanted to get on the case again. He pointed to himself: '*Nhà báo.*' Journalist.

A look of recognition crossed the face of the Vietnamese. He pointed to the motorcycle and said, '*Nhà báo Anh.*' He then made a gesture with his hands of someone taking photos with a camera.

The BSA Victor had been explained. The bike had belonged to a British photojournalist. Catesby strung together a question with his limited Vietnamese. He wanted to know how to find his fellow Brit to ask about the BSA Victor. '*O dao nhà báo Anh?*' Where is the English journalist?

The Vietnamese said something that sounded like 'my buy' and made helicopter noises to show what the word meant. He gracefully gestured with his hands to show a helicopter flying along, shouted 'Bang!', then made sad hand gestures as the helicopter fluttered to earth.

Catesby now understood how the big British bike had ended up reigning over the bicycles and tiny Hondas. He also understood that in Vietnam motorcycles were safer than helicopters. He wanted to get back on track and asked about the woman contact, '*O dao Truong Thi Nhung?*'

The face of the Vietnamese turned serious. He pointed to a chair near a simple wooden table in a dark corner. Catesby realised he was being asked to sit down and wait. A second later the Vietnamese had disappeared as silently as he had appeared, despite his having a pronounced and obviously painful limp.

Catesby tried to restrain his spy instincts to have a look around, but they were too strong. He was soon up and snooping. Catesby could see it wasn't just a workshop, but the mechanic's home. On a shelf near the table was a plastic washing-up basin with china bowls, chopsticks and cups – and neatly rolled up on the floor beneath was a sleeping mat. The shop was very well equipped with tools – including a power lathe. During his snoop, Catesby discovered that the tools had a dual purpose. The mechanic did a good job of clearing up, but not a perfect job. Catesby found the spiral-shaped valve spring underneath the workshop table. It was worn and probably had needed replacing. The mechanic, with his limp, probably found it difficult looking for tiny dropped parts under the table. Catesby wondered what had happened to the soldier who had carried the AK-47 rifle that had once housed that valve spring. Catesby put the spring in his pocket as a talisman – just as he became aware that he was no longer alone.

In her yellow silk *áo dài* and white trousers she looked out of place among the tools and detritus. Catesby's first impulse was to tell her to be careful not to get grease on her clothes, but she was practised at keeping an *áo dài* clean and wove gracefully through the shop. She spoke in French that was fluent, but had the slight rising and falling lilt characteristic of the Vietnamese. It gave the totally false impression of a birdlike fragility.

'I had,' she said, 'been expecting you, but didn't realise everything about you. Cuc said that you used to play football for Manchester United. You are an extraordinary person.'

Catesby smiled. Cuc must be the name of the Vietnamese in the bike shop. 'That was a complete misunderstanding. I have never been a professional football player.'

'Oh, Cuc will be so disappointed.'

Catesby made a mental note for a request. He was sure that George Best would sign a photo. SIS had done far more for less deserving agents. 'But trust me to make up for it.'

Nhung looked at Catesby. 'I have been told that you are a journalist who is sympathetic to our cause.'

Catesby nodded.

'I have also been told to help you make safe passage to the Vietnamese People's Army base areas near the Truong Son Strategic Supply Route. I cannot personally take you there, but I know someone who can help. It will be a very dangerous journey for you, but it will be worth the risk.'

Catesby looked at Nhung. At first, he had thought she was barely out of her teens, but now he realised she was a mature woman. When she frowned there were lines around her face and eyes – and a look of pain too.

'The first part of your journey will begin here and Cuc will help you. You will eventually meet Huynh, who speaks fluent French and very good English. He will guide you the rest of the way.'

The name rang a bell. 'Did Huynh used to live in Paris?'

'Yes, until very recently. Huynh is a new fighter.'

»»»»»

The BSA 441 Victor was well suited to Vietnam. It had lots of ground clearance and was just as good off the road as on. Catesby could see why the dead photographer had chosen it. But the 'Beezer' Victor is a temperamental beast too. If you don't treat her right, she shows her contempt with a shudder, a cough and a stall. And she needs lots of skilful foreplay to get in the mood. All 441cc are in one big thrusting cylinder. So you need to be strong as well as graceful. The trick is to gently flood the carburettor with not a drop too much petrol or a drop too little. Then you have to make sure her piston is exactly dead centre, engage the valve lifter and finally jump down on the kickstarter with a long, smooth and firm motion that would test the butch-est male dancers of the Bolshoi Ballet. By now, of course, you've released the valve lifter and are expertly twisting the throttle to her needs; otherwise she will stall. But if she doesn't, the engine roar is glorious and throaty and you are in for one hell of a ride.

The road south of Da Nang was flat and straight. The only elevation was Marble Mountain, which stuck out of the coastal plain like a rotten tooth. There was a lot of traffic, both Vietnam-ese and American. What Catesby enjoyed most was accelerating past lumbering convoys of US Marine armoured personnel car-riers. Compared to the lumpy marines in flak jackets, Catesby felt like a creature of freedom – he wasn't even wearing a crash helmet. He was far too old to be a rocker or a mod, but the rockers were more his style. Catesby also preferred The Rolling

Stones to The Beatles, but it wasn't the sort of thing he often discussed among the pinstripes at senior SIS meetings in Century House. His colleagues would have told him to act his age. There was a clear stretch of road ahead. The only traffic was conical-hatted Vietnamese on foot or on bikes, but Catesby restrained himself from going full throttle to get the Victor up to 80: 'Act your age, William, act your age.'

Just north of Hoi An, Catesby had to turn off Route One, which had been good and fast moving. The road inland was unpaved and insecure even in hours of daylight. Most of the traffic was US Marine supply convoys heading to their big base at An Hoa. The marines called the area 'the Arizona territory'. Maybe, thought Catesby, it was because there were a lot of Indians in Arizona. In any case, the marines looked far more alert and vigilant. Each truck was armed with an M60 machine-gun. No one sat idly. The machine-gun crews, as well as the marine riflemen with M16s, peered into the bleak and blasted countryside. But no one paid attention to Catesby as he bounced along on the BSA Victor.

It wasn't until Catesby reached Liberty Bridge on the Song Thu Bon that anyone noticed him at all. The bridge was heavily guarded because it kept getting blown up. The guards looked very tired and nervous. Two of them approached Catesby in a queue of vehicles waiting to cross the river. Their uniforms were so bleached by the sun that they had lost their camouflage. One of the marines had used a black marker pen to draw a peace symbol on his helmet liner and below the symbol it read: 'I'm not a tourist, I live here.' The message on the other marine's helmet liner was less serene: 'These people aren't people.'

The peace symbol marine spoke first as he stroked the Victor's petrol tank. 'Where'd you get this? Wow, you're really groovy. Cool.'

'I borrowed it from a friend in Da Nang.'

'Has he got any Triumphs? I'd love a Triumph Bonneville.'

'No, just this one.'

The other marine spoke. 'British bikes are shit. You ought to get a Harley.'

The traffic was moving again. Catesby revved up the Victor. 'See you guys later.'

The peace symbol marine smiled. 'Is that bike a Victor Charlie?'

Catesby smiled bleakly at the joke alluding to the Viet Cong as he crossed the bridge to the south bank of the Song Thu Bon. The marines on the trucks and armoured personnel carriers seemed even more tense and alert. There was evidence of heavy fighting on both sides of the road, including burnt-out tanks and torched villages. It was slow and dusty. After ten more miles, there were guard towers visible in the distance and the marines became less tense. A few took off their helmets and lit up cigarettes. They had run the gauntlet without any losses.

After the marine base at An Hoa, there were no more Americans and little traffic of any sort on the road. It was a rural and deceptively peaceful Vietnam. Peasants in black pyjamas and conical hats trudged along the road with baskets of produce, including live squawking chickens, cantilevered on shoulder poles. Catesby ran the motorbike at slow speed and low revs so as not to disturb the tranquillity or announce his presence.

The road finally ended at a river landing where three boats were pulled up on the bank. There was also a squad of South Vietnamese soldiers lolling about under a canopy.Their weapons were not at the ready. Catesby had sussed enough of the order of battle to realise these were RFs, Regional Forces. They were not the fiercest of Saigon's warriors. The Americans called them 'ruff puffs'. The sergeant in charge greeted Catesby in English: 'Hello, good morning' – even though it wasn't morning.

'Is it far to the coal mine?'

The sergeant smiled warmly and broadly, but didn't understand a word.

Catesby tried again in French and added Nong Son to coal mine.

The sergeant nodded, '*Oui, oui, oui.*' But didn't give a distance.

Catesby looked at the boats. None of them seemed sturdy enough to carry the Victor. There was a broad, well-trodden footpath along the riverbank, which continued where the road ended. Catesby pointed to the path and asked, '*Nong Son?*'

The sergeant smiled and nodded.

'*Beaucoup VC?*'

The sergeant tilted his head and looked thoughtful, then said, '*Pas beaucoup.*'

Catesby decided to risk it and got back on the Victor. It wasn't easy to start because dust was clogging up the air filter. But after the fourth try the motorbike roared into life and echoed up the river valley – which was no longer coastal plain but lush green mountains. The Vietnamese onlookers cheered and applauded.

The riverbank path was an easy one for the Victor. The area was largely under the control of the Viet Cong, but Catesby felt no sense of menace – only rural tranquillity. He knew the tranquillity was deceptive and that at any moment a squad of hard-looking men carrying AK-47s could appear from nowhere. And, if they did, Catesby had no idea how he was going to explain why he was there. Nhung had warned that it was impossible to give him a *laissez-passer* that would be recognised by every guerrilla in Quang Nam province. They were rightfully paranoid and suspicious of strangers. They had been bombed too much.

It was late afternoon when Catesby arrived at Que Son. It was the largest village since An Hoa. He knew that it was safe when he spotted a pair of RF soldiers milling about in the market-place – who looked even less combat-ready than the previous ones. Catesby dismounted and wheeled the Victor to the river landing, which was a wide expanse of firmly packed sand. He had reached the rendezvous and could see a man on the opposite bank shouting and gesturing. The man wasn't in black pyjamas, but was wearing blue overalls and beret like a French worker.

The coal-mine barge was a French navy landing craft that had been left behind in 1954. Indeed, the entire village and mine looked as if they too had been transported from France. Catesby had a weird feeling that he had stepped into a time–space hole and been mysteriously transported to Picardie or the Pas-de-Calais. The only things that weren't like northern France were the Vietnamese workers and the Buddhist temple. Everything else, from the football pitch to the red-tiled workers' cottages to the concrete electricity poles to the heavy 1930 Renault trucks to the Café de la Paix with its 'baby-foot' table, belonged to a different era and a different place.

»»»»»

Catesby regretted that he hadn't brought a change of clothes to dress for dinner. Although *le directeur du mine* wasn't wearing evening dress, he did look elegant. *Le directeur* spoke absolutely fluent French without a trace of Vietnamese accent. He was an ageless man who could have been fifty-five or seventy-five – and he certainly wasn't self-effacing about his status and achievements. The villa was hung with diplomas and photos of *le directeur* with famous men. Among those Catesby recognised were André Malraux, the writer, Saint-Exupéry, the aviation pioneer, and Robert Schuman, who'd pretty much founded the Common Market. There were also numerous photos of his daughter in and around their home in the rue du Faubourg St Honoré.

The food was elegant and simple, the wine was complex, but had a supple finesse. It was a dinner for three, but the conversation was entirely between *le directeur* and Catesby. Huynh sat silent for most of the meal and only spoke when asked questions – a well-behaved young man. Catesby behaved himself too and didn't make any references – coded or otherwise – to Huynh's tryst with Miranda on the banks of the Seine.

'I'm looking forward to examining your splendid motorcycle in the morning. I don't suppose,' asked *le directeur*, 'that you could take me for a spin?'

Catesby looked at Huynh, who frowned. 'I would love to,' said Catesby, 'but we might have other…'

'Ah, yes. I remember now that you have other business that needs your attention.'

'But,' Catesby lied, 'when that is finished I promise to give you a ride on the Victor.'

'Good. I love machines, particularly fast machines. I once piloted my own aeroplane.'

Catesby now realised that the slight figure muffled up in flying gear in the photo with Saint-Exupéry was *le directeur*.

'You know,' said *le directeur* gesturing to the Saint-Exupéry photo, 'he loved good wine.'

'Then I am sure he would have loved this one. It's superb.' Catesby held the Burgundy up to a candle flame. 'Most English think that Bordeaux is the best French wine, but they are wrong.'

Huynh stirred uneasily and made a rare intervention. 'But I am sure the wines of *Monsieur le directeur*'s château in Bordeaux would prove that most English are correct.'

Catesby smiled bleakly and realised once again why he wasn't a Foreign Office diplomat. But *le directeur* was a natural diplomat and rode to his rescue. 'No, Huynh, I agree with monsieur. My château is just a hobby. The great estates are in Burgundy, but I like the sea air.'

In any case, the wine made Catesby's brain spin and accentuated the surreal irony of the situation. He was making stilted conversation at a dinner party with a man who was almost a parody of the Parisian *haute bourgeoisie*. The other dinner guest was another Parisian of Vietnamese descent, who had recently dressed up as a Greek shepherd to participate in an orgy with an upper-class Englishwoman in a *tableau vivant* of a Poussin painting. The young Vietnamese had, Catesby assumed, decided to follow the woman to Southeast Asia to fight alongside her as a fellow comrade in a Communist army. And yet surrounding them in *le directeur*'s dining room were the icons of capitalist wealth refined by a patina of culture and good taste: fine wines, Sèvres porcelain, Louis XV candlesticks and an early Miró painting.

The mood was broken by the rumble of artillery, which was not very distant. The candles flickered and the shadows swayed. *Le directeur* ignored it and rang a porcelain bell. An elderly Vietnamese woman in a formal high-collared *áo dài* appeared. For the first time, *le directeur* spoke Vietnamese. Until then, Catesby hadn't been certain that he even knew the language. The woman disappeared and a moment later there was a whiff of alcohol mingled with the scent of something rich and sweet burning. The woman returned bearing some *crème brûlée*.

'Would you like brandy and coffee with...' *Le directeur*'s

words were lost in a deep thunder roar of artillery impacting. The windows were open and the sky above the palm trees flashed white.

'Yes, please.' Catesby shouted to make himself heard above the bombardment. He reckoned it was big stuff, maybe eight-inch, and was probably landing six or seven hundred yards away. Catesby assumed the shells were targeted at the ridge line, which rose up sharply behind the coal mine. He remembered from Bucksport the Sailor's map briefing that a spur of the Ho Chi Minh … *no*, the Truong Son Strategic Supply Route, ran along that ridge line. In any case, he wasn't going to say anything about the artillery. Mentioning the shelling, or anything about the war, was obviously a breach of etiquette at *le directeur*'s dinner table.

Le directeur served the brandy and the coffee himself. He then attacked his *crème brûlée* with such ravenous delight that it seemed it was the dish he had been waiting for all evening. *Le directeur*'s eyes were so full of bliss that Catesby thought about offering him his own *crème brûlée* as well.

Le directeur shook his head, as if he had read Catesby's thought. 'You must forgive me. As I get older, and I can't see how much older one can be, I love sweet things more and more, but I must control myself.'

There was now a racket of small arms fire from across the river. Catesby remembered an RF outpost on the edge of Que Son village near where they crossed the river. He guessed that the post was now being attacked. The rattle of small arms was joined by heavy machine guns and the thump of RPG rockets. Catesby was seated at right angles to a window facing across the river. Out of the corner of his eye he could see red and green tracer flying in opposite directions and occasionally ricocheting off rocks towards *le directeur*'s villa. It was difficult to maintain the etiquette and not watch the battle. Catesby sipped the VSOP brandy and finished his *crème brûlée*.

Meanwhile, *le directeur* stifled a yawn and rubbed his eyes. He looked at Catesby: 'Have you read Proust?'

Catesby quoted the opening of *Remembrance of Things Past*.

The lines where the narrator recalls that when he was young, he 'used to go to bed at an early hour'.

Le directeur looked slightly abashed, as if realising Catesby was more than a rosbif prole on a fast motorbike. 'How apt,' said le directeur. 'But how ironic. Now that I am old I need to go to bed early – but when I was young I wanted to stay up forever. The world was a new fresh place to discover. In any case, you must excuse me. I will leave you and Huynh with the brandy and coffee.'

Catesby watched le directeur pad into the shadows. He was sure that the real reason for the old man's early night was to leave him alone with Huynh so they could plan their next move. Le directeur was obviously a man who never said anything directly – the ultimate diplomat. Catesby glanced at Huynh, whose face was a blank, then poured more coffee. It was going to be a long night.

It was obvious that what Nhung and Bucksport the Sailor had said about the coal mine was true. The mine and its village were neutral squares, Vietnam's Switzerland. They were immune from the war that swirled around them because both sides wanted the mine left intact as an economic resource when the war finally ended. The coal mine had its own uniformed and armed gendarmerie, but they never took sides.

The battle continued to rage on the other side of the river. At last, Catesby was free to look out at it. After a few more minutes, the green tracer began to dominate. Then the red tracer disappeared altogether. There were a few more rocket thumps and a gradual diminuendo of rifle fire. Then an eerie silence, but not a real silence at all for the night was now pierced by the moans and cries of the wounded and dying. And the sound of a boat being paddled across the river. Catesby poured himself a brandy.

'I believe,' said Huynh, 'that you have met…' He said the name of the female French journalist who had given Catesby a lift to Cu Chi.

'Yes, she spoke very fondly of you. You were, I believe, a student at the Sorbonne.'

The sound of moaning was now much louder. There were footsteps too and people talking in hushed voices.

'Yes, I was studying architecture.'

'But you decided that being here was more important.'

'It was a difficult choice. I had to accept that Vietnam was my country and not France.'

Catesby decided to be direct. 'Did Miranda help you make that decision?'

Huynh shifted uneasily. 'No … well, perhaps in part. Maybe Miranda made me think about things. But maybe I would have come here in any case.'

Catesby suspected that Huynh was besotted with Miranda. That was good news for Catesby, who needed Huynh's help to find Miranda, but maybe bad news for Huynh. 'Have you seen Miranda since you came here?'

'Yes, I have.'

The elderly woman came back into the room to clear the *crème brûlée* ramekins. She had changed out of her traditional *áo dài* and was wearing a starchy nurse's uniform that must have dated from World War One. Catesby remembered that the coal mine had its own infirmary. As the old woman left the dining room, Huynh stood up and said, 'Excuse me,' and followed her.

Catesby was left alone for nearly half an hour. He passed the time by drinking brandy to calm his nerves and looking at the bookshelves. There were two signed first editions by Malraux, *L'espoir* and *La Condition Humaine*, and one by Saint-Exupéry, *Vol de Nuit*. All the titles were apt in the situation.

When Huynh came back he was nervous and agitated. His arms were laden with clothes. 'We need to leave tonight, very soon.' He put the clothes down on a chair and picked out a pair of black pyjamas. 'Here, you'll need to put these on. I hope they fit.'

'Who won the battle?'

'We did,' said Huynh, 'but at a cost.'

»»»»»

There were two people in the narrow boat nearest the landing, but only one of them was alive. There was another boat of the same size waiting further up in the shadow of an overhanging bank. There were three people in this boat, but only one of them was able. The third was heavily sedated. Not so much to ease the pain, but to keep him quiet.

Huynh led Catesby to the boat with the dead body. The corpse was lying flat in the bottom of the boat as if he had had too much rice wine at a Tet celebration and fallen asleep. There was no place to sit. The boat was built to carry cargo so Huynh and Cateby had to squat at either end of the body. Catesby was struck by the smooth, graceful beauty of the boat. The planks had been laid lengthwise and tapered upward to curved double ends. He rubbed his hand along the smooth flawless wood and knew that the fishermen of Suffolk would have been impressed by the craftsmanship.

It was a dark moonless night and the boat with the wounded Viet Cong set off first. The oars were mounted on posts in the stern of the boat and the oarsman rowed standing up and facing forwards. There was a low mist over the river so that only the upper body of the person rowing was visible. The rowing motion had an unearthly grace and the oarsman looked like a ghost dancing on a watery cloud.

The boat with Huynh, Catesby and the dead VC followed close behind. Both boats clung close to the shadows of the bank. For the first half a mile the river ran under sheer granite cliffs and their cover was perfect. The steep banks then gave way to marshes, sandbanks and low river walls with paddy fields beyond. They were in the last basin of the Song Thu Bon before the river twisted into the mountain gorges. The mist drifted away and the boats became exposed and vulnerable. There was no moon, but the stars had begun to glow fiercely.

Catesby remembered that Bucksport had mentioned a Special Forces outpost on a mountain that dominated the river basin. He wondered if they had night-vision devices. Just as that thought flickered through his mind, the champagne cork pop of a mortar shell leaving the tube echoed over the river valley. The Viet Cong boatmen were well drilled. In the few seconds before the illumination round reached the top of its parabolic flight and ignited, camouflage netting woven with river flotsam was stretched over both boats. Even the most beady-eyed observer would only see detritus from the monsoon floods.

There were more illumination flares during the next few minutes and the river valley was bathed in a creepy unnatural phosphorescence that was as bright as day. Catesby began to hate the illumination rounds. He imagined their phosphorescence was refined from the decaying souls of the war dead. He then realised that his hand was resting on the face of the dead Viet Cong. He raised it, sticky with blood.

The illumination rounds ceased when a thick mist rolled in over the river valley. The camouflage netting was rolled back and stowed and the boats set off again. Catesby washed his hand in the river. The problem now was not concealment, but navigation. Visibility was down to less than five yards, but the boatmen appeared to recognise every foot of the riverbank. The rowers pushed with renewed vigour. There were soon disembodied voices from a riverbank that was lost in the mist. They had made it.

The village was called Phu Gia. It was base to a company of Viet Cong guerrillas, but it was also a staging post for supplying the 2nd NVA division in the mountains to the west. North Vietnamese purchasing agents went into the Que Son valley to buy rice at twice the going market price in South Vietnam. It was dangerous for the farmers to do this for they risked retribution at the hands of a CIA Phoenix team, but high profits and high risks go hand in hand. Catesby remembered the old Marxist saying: 'The capitalist will sell you the rope that you use to hang him.'

Catesby helped carry the dead man to a hut in the village where he was laid on a hard earth floor. His name was Quoc and he was a native of the village. A woman threw herself on Quoc and started keening in a wail that pierced Catesby to the quick. He was suddenly back in Limousin in 1944, and he had never wanted to go there again. A minute later a young man, Quoc's brother, arrived and started crying. Catesby left them to their grief.

Outside the hut a debate was raging about what to do with the wounded man. Huynh tugged at Catesby's sleeve and said, 'We have to be going.'

Catesby gestured towards the wounded soldier. 'But what about him?'

'He's too ill. They are going to take him to a field hospital in Tien Phuoc, not far from here, where he will recuperate – or die.' On cue, a cart pulled by a water buffalo arrived. 'Come on,' said Huynh, 'we must hurry or it will be too late.'

The next part of the journey was by river again, but only a short distance to the gorge where mountains blanked the now clear sky on either side. The boatman took them to a landing where there were other boats and a lot of activity. It was the crossing point on the river where the rice from Que Son made its final journey to the 2nd Division base areas in the mountains along the Laotian border. The portering was mostly done by men carrying bulging rice nets on their shoulders, but there were also heavily laden bicycles. Here, at least, the logistics were labour intensive. And, as far as was possible in the starlight, Catesby could see why. The land leading to the river crossing had been completely 'craterised'. There was literally nowhere that wasn't part of a bomb crater. The craters overlapped with each other like grotesque Olympic rings. Catesby watched a dark line of porters stumbling across the moonscape.

'At one time,' said Huynh, 'there was a village here. A very pretty village. The B-52s came one night and there were no survivors.'

Come with me, my dearest, to visit green Truong Son.
We will travel the road of history as it changes day by day.
Sing with me, my love, the song of Truong Son, the road
of the future...

Catesby didn't know what the words meant until Huynh translated them. They had first appeared on a poster pinned to a tree alongside the trail.

'Is it a poem or a song?'

'It is both,' said Huynh.

Catesby was surprised by the number of posters along the trail, but most of them were pointing the other way to greet the soldiers coming south. His favourite showed women fighters firing AK-47s at American soldiers. The caption read: 'The Southern Female Guerrillas are Truly Gutsy.' Catesby suggested that 'fearless' or 'courageous' might be a better translation than 'gutsy', but Huynh disagreed because it was more 'visceral'. They had begun to speak English at Huynh's insistence. Catesby wasn't sure why. Perhaps it was because Huynh thought the NVA officers would find it more difficult to eavesdrop on English than French. Or, more likely, Huynh wanted to practise his English so that he could talk more easily to Miranda.

The trails improved as they got closer to the border with Laos and they started to meet powered vehicles. The first was a Chinese-built motor-tricycle that was grossly overloaded with .122 rockets and tins of Russian mackerel. And a day later there was a three-wheel Chinese truck carrying a howitzer. If Catesby ever got back to London he knew he would be expected to give an intelligence report on what he had seen. But he would refuse to do so unless he had a cast-iron guarantee that it would not be shared with the Americans. It was going to be a delicate situation. But the gist of any report would be that the bombing wasn't working. The North Vietnamese logistics network was too large, too hidden and too dispersed.

Catesby could see that Huynh genuinely believed he was a journalist sympathetic to their struggle. It was a cover story Catesby needed to keep up. His journalist cover meant he was treated as a celebrity by the NVA officers. It would be a good idea, Huynh tactfully suggested, if Catesby started calling the NVA by its proper name, the PAVN – the People's Army of Vietnam.

As they travelled further north and west the number and variety of propaganda posters increased. But as they now travelled mostly at night, Catesby only saw them in the camouflaged rest areas where they slept and relaxed during the day. Catesby was surprised by the large number of women fighters who featured on the posters – but almost all the PAVN soldiers he encountered were male. He asked Huynh about it.

The young Vietnamese shifted uneasily. 'Most of the soldiers you see are going to die. Have you not seen the tattoos that many of them have on their arms?'

Catesby had noticed the tattoos. 'What do the words mean?'

'"Born in the North to die in the South." It's important to keep up their spirits, so we make them believe that their mothers and sisters are fighting and falling too. And,' added Huynh, 'many of them are.'

Catesby remembered a poster depicting a family: 'A mother and her children fight the Americans together!' It had sad echoes of the bereaved family in Phu Gia.

Two days later they reached the Laotian border. There were no border markings other than signs on the trail welcoming the PAVN to the South and large posters exhorting: 'Devote all our souls and strength for our southern kin!' Catesby noticed that many of the posters now bore images of Ho Chi Minh looking much younger and healthier than he actually was. There were images of Ho reading a newspaper, of Ho speaking to a microphone and saying: 'Nothing is more important than freedom and independence.' Catesby decided to sound out Huynh about the political situation.

The cooking fires in the waypoint rest areas were never lit until nightfall. But the mess halls were getting larger and larger. They were under thatched roofs where the camouflage was changed daily as soon as it wilted. The mess hall where they had eaten their midnight lunch was, during the day, divided into classrooms where the incoming soldiers learned infantry tactics and weapons familiarisation. After Catesby had finished his rice and Russian mackerel – Moscow had sent millions of tins of the fish to Vietnam – he asked Huynh if they could have a chat without the PAVN political officer listening in.

'It doesn't matter,' said Huynh. 'This one hardly understands a word of English.'

'Yes, but he might recognise some of the names we use – and then ask you to translate.'

Huynh looked around furtively to see if anyone was listening. 'What do you want to talk about?'

'The political succession in Hanoi. Ho isn't getting any younger – and I am a journalist. But I assure you my reportage will be favourable to the cause. Let's have a look at the anti-aircraft battery. It appears pretty impressive.'

'The crew will be asleep. They lay their bed rolls in the ammunition bunker.' Huynh smiled. 'They say if it takes a direct hit they won't wake up.'

The anti-aircraft battery consisted of three Soviet-manufactured ZPU-1 guns. They weighed half a ton each, but could be broken down into 170lb sections for transport by pack animals. Catesby already knew this from innumerable SIS training sessions on Warsaw Pact weaponry. Weapons usually bored him rigid, but these had recently brought down three US helicopters trying to insert SOG reconnaissance teams. The political officer had gloated when he told Catesby the story. The PAVN had no military secrets when it came to broadcasting their successes to the world. They realised it was a war for public opinion as much as military objectives.

Catesby settled himself into the gunner's seat of the nearest ZPU-1 and took a bead through the sight. He had never been popular with the Cousins. Catesby knew that the CIA suspected he was a working-class version of Burgess and Maclean covertly passing NATO secrets to Moscow Central. They were wrong. Catesby regarded himself as a loyal Briton – and it was this loyalty that made him advise Prime Minister Harold Wilson to keep the UK out of Vietnam. But what would happen, Catesby wondered, noting the ZPU-1 was loaded and ready to fire, if he actually shot down an American bomber or helicopter? Advising Wilson not to send UK troops to Vietnam was one thing, but this...

'You wanted to talk to me?'

In his fantasy about being a PAVN anti-aircraft gunner Catesby had almost forgotten Huynh. 'Sorry, I was dreaming.'

'You wanted to talk about politics?'

Catesby nodded. He suspected he was going to have to walk a tightrope in the next few weeks and wanted advice on how to keep his balance.

Huynh paused, then spoke in a whisper. 'It is no secret that Ho Chi Minh is old and unwell. The two Le's – Le Duan and Le Duc Tho – are effectively running things. In my view, Le Duan is the more powerful and the more radical. He is determined to liberate the South at all costs through military victory.'

'How do you feel about that?'

'I support his views, but it isn't an easy decision. There are others – such as Ho himself – who favour a negotiated peace. They think that the puppet government in Saigon is so corrupt that it would soon fall like a rotten fruit. But who can be sure when the Americans have so much money and power to back them up?'

Catesby stared thoughtfully into the dark night. Ruling a country at war is drinking from a blood chalice. You are walking into the unknown and each false step – and there will be many – will cost thousands of lives. Catesby looked at Huynh, who was a dark, diminutive shadow.

'And what about you? Why have you come back and what is your role?'

'I have already said. I am a Vietnamese patriot who wants to fight and suffer alongside my people. And as a student of architecture I have practical engineering skills. I have been offering advice on road building.'

'And what about Miranda? Have you followed her back here because you love her?'

'She is part of the reason, but not all of the reason. She is a very strong-minded woman. Her views may get her into trouble.' Huynh sounded almost angry.

'Are your differences with Miranda political or personal?'

'Political. She doesn't understand the limits of Vietnamese nationalism and independence. She wants our war to be part of an international peasant revolution.' Huynh shrugged. 'Miranda is a fanatical…'

The jigsaw pieces were falling neatly into place. The thing that annoyed Catesby about the Americans, and many of his SIS colleagues too, was their ignorance about Communism. The best intelligence officers were merely stupid; the worst were rampaging cretins on a crusade. None of them grasped the gaping theological differences between Communists. The inner-sanctum high priests of Moscow and the theologians of Peking hated Communist heretics more than they hated the capitalist Satan.

Huynh began to walk away.

'You didn't finish,' prompted Catesby. 'You said Miranda was a fanatical something.'

'She's a fanatical Maoist. And she doesn't realise that China is Vietnam's historical enemy. We admire their culture, but fear their power.'

'But you accept China's help. Most of the ammunition and explosives I've seen coming down this trail have Chinese markings on the boxes.'

Huynh patted the anti-aircraft gun that Catesby was sitting on. 'Most of the heavy weapons and the trucks are Russian.' Huynh smiled. 'Our leaders are playing a duplicitous game; they have to. We want to play Moscow and Peking off against each other. We want Russia and China to compete for our allegiance, to bribe us with guns and food.'

'In the end, which way will you jump?'

'Personally, I want Vietnam to be independent of both of them. But I suspect that Le Duan and most of the leadership are secretly pro-Moscow.' Huynh smiled. 'I know for certain that General Giap is pro-Russian. He drives around in a Russian limousine.'

'And what role is Miranda playing?'

'She is helping with our propaganda effort. And her insights into the British ruling class and your political system are very valuable.'

Catesby smiled. She certainly had tons of salacious gossip to pass on. 'What about her Maoism?'

'She certainly argues a good case long into the night. And no one can condemn her for being pro-China. But I think the situation is turning awkward.'

'Is she in danger?'

'I hope not. In any case, you will meet her in a few days.' Huynh laughed. 'Provided a B-52 bomb doesn't meet you first.'

»»»»»

Two days later they came to a paved road for the first time. The crushed gravel surface looked bluish-grey and Catesby remembered the rock crushers and bulldozers that Bucksport had briefed him about. The heavy Soviet ZIL trucks travelled in convoys of six from waypoint to waypoint – about 20 miles apart – where they were offloaded. On the return journey north, the trucks were mostly empty except for sacks of letters and badly wounded or very ill PAVN soldiers. As an honoured journalist guest, Catesby rode in the cab of a truck with the driver. Perhaps they didn't want him to report tales of the horror that the mutilated soldiers lying as cargo had experienced.

There was a delay of nearly two days when the road was closed because of a B-52 bombing raid which took out a bridge, caused a landslide and killed a number of engineers and road workers. Catesby had been close enough to hear the air being sucked into the fireballs of the bombs before he was rushed to an underground bunker. Considering the massive amount of damage, the road and bridge repairs were carried out quickly and efficiently. An entire battalion of engineers appeared as if by magic. A PAVN press officer showed him an oil pipeline pumping station that had been unscathed and was up and running.

Catesby knew that posing as a journalist was a natural cover for a spy. The two jobs are similar. You asked a lot of the same questions because both professions were seeking the same underlying truths. One of the PAVN transport officers had bragged to Catesby that US bombing interdicted only 3 per cent of the supplies heading south. Catesby kept a tally of the wrecked trucks and road damage he had seen and reckoned the figure was accurate. The camouflage discipline and the ingenuity of the PAVN were impressive. He particularly liked the hidden river bridges, which were built just below the surface of the water. Trucks splashed happily across the rivers while the bridges were completely hidden from aerial reconnaissance.

But it wasn't going to be an easy victory, even though the North Vietnamese were harder and more disciplined than their

southern compatriots. It was obvious that the Saigon government was corrupt and unpopular, but the popular uprising in
the South that Hanoi was hoping for had not happened – and
might never happen. Catesby realised that the PAVN was in for
a long and bloody war.

»»»»»

Tchepone is a Lao town with thatched houses on stilts, which
straddles Route 9. It is on a fast-flowing river with rapids and
surrounded by mountains. The PAVN military base near Tchepone was a massive hidden city that sprawled over several
square kilometres. There were mess halls, hospitals, communication centres, an airstrip, classrooms, a theatre, surface-to-
air missile batteries and massive underground supply depots.
Catesby was given a guided tour by a French-speaking PAVN
colonel. He was impressed by the medical facilities. The big
problem wasn't trauma wounds from US bombing but malaria,
which killed three times as many soldiers as the Americans.

Catesby liked the Wild West atmosphere of Tchepone. The
only rationale for the town was Route 9. Tchepone was a stopover
point for travelling traders and soldiers. The French had built the
road to link the Vietnamese coast with the western extreme of
their Indochina empire at Savannakeht on the Thai border. Tchepone was the halfway point and had everything a weary travel-
ler needed: bars, chop houses, opium dens and brothels.

The town was also a good place for Catesby to shake off his
PAVN minders and have private chats with Huynh. He got the
impression that Tchepone was off limits to the military. The res-
taurant was a relaxed place where you sat on reed mats around
a raised platform woven out of rattan. The low platform served
as a dining table laid out with a variety of food that you could
eat in any order. Catesby didn't trust the water so he ordered Lao
whisky, which they sell by the bucket. There was also French '33'
beer, which everyone called *ba moùi ba*.

'*Ba moùi ba,*' said Huynh, 'is Vietnamese slang for being lech-
erous. It means you've had too much "33" and have lost your
reserve.'

Catesby was surprised to hear Huynh say that. It was the first time that he had referred to anything even vaguely sexual. Huynh always seemed shy and puritanical. Seducing him must have required all of Miranda's skills. 'Are the Laotians more hedonistic than the Vietnamese?'

'I wouldn't say hedonistic; I would say more relaxed. The French used to say: "The Vietnamese plant rice; the Cambodians watch it grow; the Laotians close their eyes and listen to it grow."'

Catesby gestured at the table. 'But this food is excellent and prepared with great care.'

'The French colonists made racial assumptions that were not true.'

'What is that called?' Catesby pointed to a spicy mixture of marinated meat.

'*Larb moo.*'

'So it must be beef?'

'No, it's pork.'

'But pigs don't go moo.'

Huynh didn't get the joke.

They ate with bare hands as was the custom. Catesby noticed that the Laotians only used chopsticks to eat noodles. He began to understand why SIS and FO Asia types go native. When they come back to London they don't always adjust and seem to have contempt for the people around them. He wondered if that was the key to understanding Lady Somers – or at least part of it.

'Does my English,' said Huynh, 'sound more British or American?'

Catesby smiled. Huynh's English was heavily accented and sounded neither, but he wanted to be kind. 'You definitely sound British.'

'Good. That's how I want to sound.'

'But try not to say "gotten" or "restroom".'

'Thanks.'

'And how good is Miranda's French?'

'Not as good as my English.'

'I am sure you are right – and I'm looking forward to meeting her.'

'Then you can judge for yourself.' Huynh paused. There was a faint note of suspicion in his voice. 'Your French is good – awfully good for an Englishman.'

'Thank you.' Catesby paused and wondered if Huynh knew more than he was letting on. 'It's a pity we haven't met Miranda yet. Is she near here?'

'I believe she is.' There was something dark in Huynh's voice. 'And I believe there are going to be meetings this evening.'

Catesby helped himself to sticky rice and a large portion of *moo*. Something told him that he needed to eat up, even though he had lost his appetite.

»»»»»

There was an East German tape recorder on the table. Catesby assumed the three PAVN soldiers seated around it were officers because of their age and demeanour, but none of them wore badges of rank. There was a fourth person wearing a PAVN uniform, but he clearly wasn't Vietnamese although his skin was just as dark as theirs. He didn't really look like any of the photos Catesby had seen. He looked older, more tired – and much harder. His eyes and cheekbones clearly belonged to the indigenous peoples of Mexico and Central America, but there were also traces of Spain and other European countries as well as hints of African swarthiness. Lopez was the classic Latin American *mestizo*, the mixed-race progeny of centuries of slavery, rape and colonisation. He stared at Catesby with blank expressionless eyes.

The oldest of the PAVN officers spoke in a stilted singsong French. 'We are pleased to introduce you to Captain Francis Lopez. As you know, Captain Lopez witnessed at first hand the brutality of the US military in its war of aggression against the people of Vietnam. Captain Lopez made the heroic decision to change sides to fight with the oppressed people of the world against US imperialism.'

Catesby wasn't sure whether to address Lopez in French or English. He knew that Lopez had been educated at a *lycée* in Paris, but decided that English would make his journalist cover less suspect. 'It is a privilege to make your acquaintance, Captain

Lopez. Thank you for meeting me and, I hope, you will agree to be interviewed to tell the world your story.'

There was a long pause before Lopez spoke, but when he did the discrepancy between the *mestizo* face and the East Coast patrician voice could not have been greater. The voice of Lopez was the product of generations of old money polished to perfection by expensive prep schools and Harvard. It wasn't a voice you could buy with elocution lessons. You either had it or you didn't. The Roosevelts had it, the upstart Kennedys did not. Gore Vidal and Katharine Hepburn had it too. It was never condescending, but often supercilious and languid. The Lopez version, like Vidal's, was soft and had a faint hint of the American South.

'If I were handing out prizes for platitudinous bullshit insincerity, you would be first in line.'

Catesby smiled. 'I apologise if that's the way I sounded.'

'Maybe it's just the way you are.'

'You're probably right. I can't do social niceties without sounding like I'm taking the piss. I'm just a hack reporter trying to get a scoop.'

'What newspaper do you represent?'

'I write for two papers.' Catesby named them. Both had proprietors who were friends of C and more than willing to cover for SIS.

'I don't think either of those newspapers could be described as anti-imperialist.'

Catesby nodded agreement. Lopez knew his stuff. Both papers were conservative-leaning. 'But they have big circulation – and I want the British public to realise that the Americans are waging a brutal and senseless war.'

Lopez looked at the French-speaking PAVN officer and spoke to him in what sounded pretty fluent Vietnamese. The only word Catesby picked up was *thieu tuong*; the guy Lopez was talking to was a general. The conversation lasted a minute or two with another PAVN officer joining in. This one was addressed as *dai ta*, colonel. All three of them made gestures in Catesby's direction that didn't seem complimentary. The conversation ended and Lopez stared hard.

Catesby could tell that the room was used for meetings and briefings. There were maps on one wall and the red flag with yellow star of the Democratic Republic of Vietnam stretched across another. High on the wall behind Lopez was a portrait of Ho Chi Minh. Catesby reckoned that Uncle Ho's eyes were looking at him with more kindliness than anyone else in the room. Even though they were in an underground bunker, Catesby could hear the pounding of the monsoon rain echoing down the stairs and corridor. The *thieu tuong*, the general, finally broke the uneasy silence and said something to an officer seated in the back of the room. Catesby heard the officer get up and leave. There were footsteps on the stairs and then the flap of the tarpaulin that stopped the rain coming in and the light getting out. The only sound other than the rain was the steady hum of an electricity generator.

Lopez looked at Catesby with the cold expression of an Aztec priest about to raise the execution blade – an Aztec priest who had been to Harvard and the Sorbonne. 'Basically,' said Lopez in his bored, languid voice, 'you are a lying piece of shit.'

Catesby folded his arms and shrugged. He looked up at Ho Chi Minh, trying to work out how he had been rumbled. It was most likely the French intelligence service. The SDECE wanted to ingratiate themselves with the Vietnamese side, who were most likely to win, and dropping Catesby in the shit was a good way to do it.

The tarpaulin flapped again and there were two sets of feet coming down the stairs. Catesby stared down at the table in front of him. He didn't want to give the newcomer the satisfaction of seeing him turn around out of nervous curiosity and fear. Catesby was frightened, but he wasn't going to show it. He only looked up when the new arrival spoke, recognising the voice only too well.

'You've aged a lot, William. And dyeing your hair blond doesn't hide the fact. It's a pretty silly thing to do for a man your age. Your face is far too tired and gaunt for a man who claims to be thirty-nine – and the drink hasn't helped your looks either. But I suppose dyeing your dark tresses was part of your feeble attempt to pass as a cool, hip war reporter ten years younger than yourself. Even the Vietnamese, who believed your lies, thought you were a ridiculous character.'

'Six years younger,' said Catesby with a defiant smile.

The PAVN general said something in Vietnamese. He appeared annoyed. The newcomer turned to the general and replied. His Vietnamese sounded halting; he obviously wasn't as fluent as Lopez.

'I've just told him, William, that you are definitely Catesby, the British spy.' The newcomer smiled and took something out of his pocket. 'Would you like me to take your picture?' He was holding the fake Pen Double E camera that the CIA man had given to Catesby. The newcomer aimed at Catesby through the viewfinder. 'Don't worry, William, I'm not going to shoot you. While you were in Tchepone having dinner we went through your belongings. We wanted to find out what you were photographing. But when I opened up the camera to take out the film, I found these instead.' He held up two bullets. 'Who were they intended for?'

Catesby wished he had ditched the camera-pistol in a river or handed it over sooner. Why had he kept it? One idea had been to present it to a high-ranking PAVN intelligence officer as an example of CIA treachery and to prove his own bona fides. Another had been that it might have come in useful if he ever got in a jam. But ditching it would have been the sensible solution.

'You still haven't answered my question,' said the newcomer.

Catesby slowly shook his head.

'You're making things difficult for yourself, William.' The newcomer nodded towards the Vietnamese. 'These guys will play a lot harder than you did with me during your pathetic interrogation at Lakenheath. How long ago was that? Twelve years? But I knew that you were bluffing. All that pistol waving didn't scare me at all.'

Catesby smiled at Cauldwell. 'You haven't aged at all, Jeffers. And you look good in that Mao suit.' Cauldwell was wearing a high-collared Chinese tunic. 'But aren't you giving away too much of your politics?'

Cauldwell smiled back, but it was a frigid smile that didn't completely hide the worried frown.

»»»»

Catesby wasn't alone in the cell. The other prisoner was an American pilot whose F-4 Phantom had been shot down. The American had broken his left arm ejecting from the stricken plane and was in pain. The Vietnamese had strapped the pilot's arm to his body, but not given him any other treatment. Catesby couldn't do much to help because his hands were chained, but the American was pleased to have someone to talk to. 'Talking keeps my mind off the pain,' he said.

'What happened?'

'We got hit by a SAM. I managed to eject, but Wayne didn't – at least I didn't see his chute.'

'Who was Wayne?'

'The Weapons Support Officer, the guy in the backseat. What part of Australia are you from?'

'Sydney.'

The pilot didn't recognise Catesby's accent. He thought he was a captured Australian soldier.

The conversation was interrupted by someone shouting in Vietnamese through the overhead grid. Their cell was a hole in the ground with a locked iron grid that sealed off the entrance. The shouting Vietnamese shifted to limited English: 'No talk, no talk.'

The pilot shouted back. 'Fuck you, Ho Chi Minh.'

'No talk, no talk.'

The grid was unlocked and moved aside. A ladder was stuck down the hole and a pair of hands reached for the American.

'Maybe they're moving you to a hospital?' said Catesby.

'Fat chance,' said the pilot.

The Vietnamese kept shouting: 'No talk, no talk…'

Catesby ignored the guard and said, 'What's your name?'

'Norman Phillips.'

Catesby made a mental note of the name so he could pass it on to the Americans if he ever got out of the mess.

'What's your name?'
'Ned Kelly.'

»»»»»

Catesby was left alone that night with the monsoon rain pouring through the uncovered grate. He curled up wet and cold on the damp earth floor. The rain stopped just before dawn. After a freezing morning mist, which was even colder than the night rain, the sun came out – and the prison turned from damp hole to airless oven. There was no water to drink. Catesby lay still and licked his own salty sweat to keep his mouth moist. They came for him at noon. They dragged him out of the hole and bound his arms with rough twine that cut into his wrists and made them bleed. Then everything changed.

At first, Catesby thought he was being taken out to be shot. If he had been in their position, Catesby would have recommended execution as the easiest way to solve the problem. The Democratic Republic of Vietnam was not at war with Britain and, indeed, the Prime Minister Harold Wilson had stood up to enormous pressure from the White House to send even a token British military presence to Vietnam – 'Come on, Harold, just one Black Watch piper would be fine.' So on one hand, Catesby knew that the Vietnamese didn't want to create a diplomatic incident by executing him. On the other hand, why was a British intelligence officer snooping around behind PAVN lines in a sensitive base area? The US and the UK were, of course, still close allies. Had London worked out some sort of deal to appease Washington by providing covert intelligence aid? Catesby knew these were questions his Vietnamese captors had no way of answering. The simplest and best solution was a bullet in the back of the head, then bury him in an unmarked grave and never admit that any of it had happened. And there was no way London would say a word. The SIS was hardly going to admit they had sent a spy to Vietnam. As Stalin used to say, 'No man, no problem.'

Therefore, Catesby was more than a little surprised when they took him to a sanitation area where there were ditch latrines and washing facilities. One of the guards cut his bindings and pointed to the latrine. For a second, Catesby thought they were going to throw him in the shit and shoot him there. He then realised they were asking if he needed to defecate and urinate.

When Catesby had finished his business, they bound him again but not as tightly. Next stop was a bamboo hut with a thatched roof. They took him inside to where a man of about his own age was seated at a wooden table drinking tea. The man, like the others, was wearing a green PAVN field uniform without badge of rank. Although clearly Vietnamese, he bore an uncanny resemblance to Jean-Paul Sartre. He said something to the guards in a soft voice and Catesby's bindings were cut. He then addressed Catesby in perfect French, 'You must be hungry and thirsty.' Before Catesby could answer, the man said something in Vietnamese and one of the guards hurried away. The man smiled at Catesby. 'Please sit down; we can talk and eat at the same time.'

As an intelligence professional, Catesby recognised the inter-rogation game that was being played. He also knew that it was a waste of time and pain not to go along with it because you only got beaten up until you finally decided to play the game – or they got fed up and shot you. The food arrived. It was noodle soup with pieces of pork and Catesby was ravenous.

They ate in silence for a few minutes before the Vietnamese asked, 'Are you a Catholic?'

'I was brought up as a Catholic, but I lost my faith as soon as I found my brain.'

'Ah, there's an answer to that. God is infinite, but your brain and its understanding are finite. You cannot understand God for the same reason that a water buffalo cannot understand Max Planck's Second Law of Thermodynamics.'

'Are you a Catholic – or a physicist?'

'At the end of his life, Max Planck was both. He criticised atheists for the way they derided religious symbolism without understanding the complex anthropological origins of those symbols.'

If, thought Catesby, he ever ran a dating agency, he was going to link up this guy with the Australian woman at the Thuong Duc leper colony.

The man folded his hands, almost as if in prayer, and looked closely at Catesby. 'I was trained as a priest, a Jesuit. But, even though I've parted from the Church, I am still a priest.'

'Once a priest, always a priest.'

'That is correct. And because I am a priest, I think this may be a good opportunity for you, Monsieur Catesby, to confess your sins.'

'But, Father, as I explained earlier, I am no longer a practising Catholic.'

The priest smiled. 'But you are still a practising spy – and that is what you need to confess.'

It was so smoothly done that Catesby almost wanted to stand up and applaud. He knew what was coming next.

On cue, the priest turned from being interrogator to being enforcer. He placed a canvas pouch on the table, took out three documents and handed them to Catesby. 'You can,' he said, 'easily understand the ones in English and French. I assure you that the Vietnamese version is a true and accurate translation. If you like, I can provide a dictionary so that you can check.'

'Thank you.' Catesby quickly read the English version. It was a full confession of his 'activities' as a British intelligence agent acting in 'full collaboration' with the Americans in support of the US war effort. The confession would be a diplomatic bombshell that might even bring down the Wilson government.

'I hope you realise that signing these documents is a mere formality. It is highly unlikely, almost unthinkable, that they would ever be made public. It is – how should I say – a mere gesture of good faith and friendship. At a later date, I suppose, you could even claim that your signature was forged – or extracted under duress.'

'But what if they were ever made public?'

'Which is as good as impossible – so you have no reason for not signing. And the sooner you sign, the sooner you will be free to go.'

Catesby laid the documents on the table. 'How stupid do you think I am?'

The priest smiled. 'Perhaps I was pushing the cork in a little too far.'

'Or putting too many eggs in the pudding?'

'Ah, your English equivalent is better.'

'You are an intelligent man, Father.'

'It's best that you not call me that when the others can hear. Call me major, *thieu ta*, instead.'

Catesby was confused. He wasn't sure whether the Vietnamese was sincere or taking the piss. In any case, it was a good interrogation technique for it kept the 'subject' off balance. Catesby decided to respond with sincerity – and truth. 'It would not be in the interest of your government for me to sign these confessions. And if you give me a chance, I can explain why.' Catesby lifted the documents. 'And, speaking as an intelligence professional, it is rather premature to have me sign a fabricated confession before you've even interrogated me as to why I'm here.'

The priest arched his eyebrows and gave a Gallic shrug like a *maître d'hôtel* dealing with a complaint about the plumbing. 'What you say has a certain logic.'

»»»»»

For the next three days Catesby was kept under guard, but not in a cell. His room was part of a barracks complex and must have been used as the private quarters of a senior officer. Catesby hadn't been asked again to sign the confession; in fact, no one spoke to him at all. The conditions weren't bad, but Catesby found the silence eerie.

Early on the morning of the fourth day, Catesby was roughly shaken awake by a guard. He was allowed to toilet and wash under strict guard and given a change of clean clothes – white civilian shirt, black trousers, sandals. It was still a dark misty morning when he was taken to the briefing bunker where he had met Lopez and been unmasked as a spy. Catesby was shivering and wished they had given him a jacket.

There were eight people in the briefing room. All were dressed in PAVN uniforms, except for one man who was in a white civilian shirt. And once again, Catesby found that the warmest and most sympathetic eyes were those beaming down from Uncle Ho's portrait. As usual, none of the PAVN wore rank insignia, but a wizened man who looked well into his fifties, maybe sixty, wore a red shoulder patch like a unit insignia. The gold lettering at the top spelled *Quan doi Nhan dan Viet Nam*, which Catesby had already sussed meant People's Army of Vietnam because he saw it everywhere. He wasn't sure about the words in bold at the bottom of the insignia, *Bo Tong Tham Muu*, but guessed they meant General Staff because this guy seemed awfully important and wanted others to know it.

The wizened man said something in Vietnamese to the man in the white shirt who then addressed Catesby in good English. 'Who are you?'

Catesby began with his full name and date of birth. He explained that he spoke French because he had a Belgian mother. He described his poverty-stricken childhood on the backstreets of Lowestoft and how he escaped via grammar school and Cambridge University. Catesby told them about his time as an SOE officer with the *maquis rouge*. He was straining to establish his credentials as a comrade, but could tell it wasn't what they wanted.

The wizened man finally interrupted his flow. The white shirt translated: 'We'll take down your biographical details later. But now tell us why British intelligence sent you to Vietnam as a spy.'

It was a difficult one for it meant walking a tightrope over a dangerous political crevasse. It was the same tightrope that Vietnam walked between Russia and China. It wasn't a matter of telling the truth or lying; it was a matter of telling truths and lies in a way that the Vietnamese could accept. 'For some time,' Catesby said, 'we have been aware that British military and intelligence secrets have been passed on to … foreign powers. In the early 50s it was obvious that the recipient of these secrets was the Soviet Union. Many of the spies involved either fled to Moscow or were arrested. We were aware, however, that spy rings were still operating in London – but not all of them were controlled by the Soviet Union.'

The wizened man tapped on the table and spoke. The translation came: 'Are you saying that your intelligence service believes that Vietnam is spying on Britain?'

'Absolutely not.' Catesby smiled. 'But if you are, your spies are doing an excellent job for there is not the slightest suspicion that Vietnam is involved in espionage in the UK. That is not why I've been sent here.'

There was an uneasy silence around the room. When the wizened man finally spoke again he stared hard. The translator took a while to render the words. 'You are talking in riddles. You keep avoiding telling us why you are here.'

'If it sounds like I'm talking in riddles it's because I'm trying to solve a riddle. The disappearing British secrets were passed on via our Ministry of Defence. The head of that ministry is Lady Penelope Somers. She is the first woman ever to have held that job – and a lot of people in the MoD have old-fashioned ideas. They don't think a woman should be in charge of defence.' Catesby looked around at his exclusively male audience and wasn't sure that the point had sunk in. 'In any case, there are rumours, almost certainly false, that Lady Somers may have something to do with the leak of secrets. The only reason I am here is to interview Lady Somers' daughter, Miranda, and, I hope, to clear her mother's name.'

There was a stir of confusion around the table. Once again the wizened man spoke through the interpreter. 'Can you tell us what you know about her?'

'Miranda Somers is a very idealistic woman who rejected the wealth and privilege of her background to become a socialist.' Catesby was careful not to say what sort of socialist. 'She has embraced your struggle against US imperialism and has come here to help. And the only reason I have come here is to interview Miranda. My presence has nothing to do with Vietnam. If Miranda were in Timbuktu, I would be there instead.'

The wizened man spoke again, but this time no translation followed. He remained seated with eyes cast down as the others filed out of the room in silence. When their footsteps had finally faded, he looked up and spoke in French. 'You are in a very difficult and dangerous situation, Monsieur Catesby.'

'Why are you telling me that?'

'To sharpen your mind. The risks and complications of letting you live appear greater than those of killing you. It's a simple mathematical equation.'

Catesby tried not to smile. His last interrogator was a fan of Max Planck. This one seemed to prefer Blaise Pascal. Being on death row was an education.

'Perhaps,' said the wizened man, 'you can change that equation.'

'It's about China, isn't it?'

The man gave a barely perceptible nod.

Catesby continued. 'You've lived in awe and fear of your giant northern neighbour for thousands of year. Your love of China would be undiluted if the Chinese lived on a different planet or continent, but China is too close. You prefer their calligraphy to the written language that the French forced upon you. And I bet that you, personally, would rather speak Mandarin than French.'

The wizened man spoke sharply, as if Catesby had touched a raw nerve. 'I do not need you to give me a lesson on my country's culture and history.'

'I apologise, but I'm trying to save my life. China is now a nuclear power. The Americans aren't happy about it, but the Russians are even less happy because that's where China's bombs are aimed. There's a big mystery about how China got her nuclear weapons so quickly. The Soviet Union stopped giving China technical and military aid in 1959, but China still managed to test an atomic bomb five years later in 1964. But the biggest and most frightening mystery is what happened afterwards?'

The eyes of the wizened man sharpened into tiny black pinpoints. 'Go on.'

'It took the United States seven years to successfully test an H-bomb after they managed to make the As that obliterated Hiroshima and Nagasaki. The Soviet Union took almost as long, six years, to go from A to H-bomb. But China made it from A to thermonuclear hydrogen bomb in three years. We'd love to know how they did it. And to what extent stolen British nuclear secrets were involved. And that is why I want to interview Miranda Somers.'

'Why should we permit that? Why is it in Vietnam's national interest?'

'It is in your country's interest to stop China from acquiring advanced military technology that China might very well use against Vietnam in a future war.' Catesby wondered if he had gone too far, but it was too late to stop. 'And I'll tell you another thing, China doesn't want this war to end. It's in China's national interest to keep Vietnam weak and dependent while keeping the United States drained and politically divided about the war.' Catesby paused. 'Foreign policy is a dirty, vicious, cynical business.'

The man's eyes looked unconvinced and sceptical. He reached forward to switch off the East German tape recorder that had been running throughout the interview. 'I'll have to write a report as well as get everything translated and transcribed. I'm not sure Hanoi will be convinced.' The wizened man then put a canvas folder on the table. He looked at Catesby with bored annoyance, like a form tutor dealing with a recalcitrant pupil. 'Do you know what this is about?'

Catesby nodded.

The man took the confession statements out of the folder. 'Your refusing to sign these is absolutely pointless. They are worthless documents that will never see the light of day, but it is a procedure that my superiors in Hanoi insist upon.' He nodded at the tape recorder. 'You've already made statements that are far more compromising.'

'But those statements are true.'

'You are being tedious. Truth is relative.' The man paused. 'I don't want to submit you to the indignities of force, after which you will sign in any case. But I will offer you an incentive. If you sign these documents, I will strongly recommend to Hanoi that you be allowed to interview Mademoiselle Miranda.'

Catesby knew that the promise was worthless, but he knew that the threats were real. In any case, the worst that the 'confession' entailed was an admission that he had been working for the Americans – which, although repugnant to Catesby personally, was not an admission regarded as a high crime in many parts of Whitehall. 'Pass them over.'

As soon as Catesby had finished signing the documents, the wizened man picked up a landline telephone and said something in Vietnamese. A few seconds later the guards arrived to take him back to his cell.

»»»»»

The outcome wasn't the one Catesby had expected. Once again, there was a wait of three days. There was no ill treatment. The guards simply treated him as a non-person – a domestic animal that required regular feeding and toileting. The only problem was the boredom. There was no reading matter in the austere room other than a worn and tattered Russian-Vietnamese dictionary. Catesby's Russian wasn't fluent, but it was pretty good and he was able to use the dictionary to learn some Vietnamese. He no longer had to use sign language to the guards to indicate that he wanted water or a trip to the latrine. But when he asked for paper, so he could practise writing phrases, the answer was a firm *khong*, no. When Catesby asked the guards if they would like to learn Russian, there was a flicker of interest before their faces turned stony again. Little did Catesby know that he was hoisting himself by his own petard.

Catesby knew that his imprisonment was going to come to an end one way or another. He still hadn't discounted the possibility of 'a stick of brass candy' – Vietnamese slang for a bullet. If Catesby were in their position, that's what he would do. So he wasn't going to whine. It was a tough game – 'big boys' rules', as they said in Belfast.

But when the end came, it was unexpected – especially the bottle of Stolichnaya vodka. The bottle and the news of his release arrived via the Jesuit who looked like Sartre. 'The most difficult thing,' he said, 'was getting it chilled. Our hospitals have refrigerators for certain drugs, but only one of them has a freezer and the *bac si*, the doctor in charge, required some persuasion. I know that it is early in the morning, but shall we drink to your release?'

The fact that Catesby was still bleary with sleep made the dawn meeting even more surreal and incomprehensible. 'I am surprised,' he said rubbing his eyes, 'that you store vodka in the camp.'

'Oh, this vodka isn't from our camp supplies. Far too much of a luxury. It's a present to you from your comrades in the Soviet Embassy in Hanoi.'

'What the fuck!' Catesby had lapsed into English.

'Pardon, I didn't understand.'

'Sorry,' he went back to French, 'it's all such a surprise.' But Catesby knew that disinfo ops should never be a surprise.

The Jesuit lowered his voice. 'We have to be very careful. We can't let it be known that Moscow put our government under pressure to release you. Many of us are pro-Russian, but we don't want to offend the Chinese as we still need their supply lines. And I also know that it is essential that you keep your cover as a loyal British intelligence officer. The Soviet Embassy made it clear that we must treat the matter as top secret, but that we must render you every assistance in your interrogation of Miranda and Jeffers Cauldwell.'

Catesby's brain was now fully awake and clicking like a telex machine spewing out encrypted reports that needed decoding and evaluation. The Hanoi *rezident*, KGB head of station, must have been overjoyed to hear that Catesby was tracking down Miranda Somers and had infiltrated behind PAVN lines. The *rezident* was certainly running his own Vietnamese agents – the Jesuit might be one of them – who had passed on news of the mission. The KGB *rezident* had then concocted a plan with Moscow Central to try to kill three birds with one clumsy rock. The bird they wanted to kill most was Jeffers Cauldwell. He had started out as a Soviet double agent and then defected to China – and took his London spy ring with him. Miranda needed neutralising too. The Aldermaston scientists, politicians and MoD officials that she had honey-trapped had provided – and might, as far as Moscow knew, still be providing – strategic intelligence to Peking that could damage the Soviet Union in a future conflict. And then there was Catesby. Normally, starting a rumour that one of the other side is working for you was a crude disinformation ploy. But when intelligence agencies were as uptight and paranoid as the CIA and SIS had become during recent years, these false rumours could be lethal. The intelligence world was as incestuous as an East Anglian village and spewed out just as much gossip. If some Neanderthal pinstriped blimp stood up on his knuckles and accused Catesby of being a Sov spy, Catesby could only hope that his signed confession to being a US poodle would also surface.

'I think,' said Catesby, 'we should taste this vodka.'

The Jesuit smiled and poured as if it were communion wine.

»»»»

Cauldwell wasn't wearing his Mao suit; he was wearing a Pathet Lao uniform. It was a compromise between Chinese and North Vietnamese influence. The peaked soft cap with its leather visor was definitely Chinese, but the green tunic with two breast pockets and side flaps was definitely North Vietnamese. Catesby wasn't sure about the trousers. They weren't baggy like the standard PAVN ones that had straps at the bottom so you could fasten them around your ankles. Maybe, he thought, Cauldwell had them especially tailored.

Catesby smiled. 'You always look good, Jeffers. Back in London, in the old days, I remember your ambassador describing you as a perfectly turned-out diplomat. His exact words were *comme il faut*. In contrast, I've always been a bit of a mess.'

'But you're real, William, you're real.'

'How little you know about me.'

It was Cauldwell's turn to smile. 'How very true, William. You are a very complex person. I knew that when I first met you.'

'Are you taking the piss?'

Cauldwell smiled.

They were sitting in Catesby's quarters, which had improved since his recent change of status. There were books, writing paper, bright propaganda posters on the walls and changes of clothing. Normally, Catesby would assume there were hidden microphones, but the earth floor and bamboo walls seemed incapable of hiding listening devices. And maybe the North Vietnamese intelligence officers simply didn't care what they talked about.

'Thank you for having lunch with me,' said Catesby. 'There's caramelised fish in that clay pot.'

'They're treating you like a celebrity.'

'It's just the normal hospitality I should expect as a representative of Her Majesty's Government.'

'Are you still sticking to that line?'

'Yeah, because it's so easy to remember.'

'I think you're telling the truth, William. You're not a Sov spy.'

If, thought Catesby, the Vietnamese were listening to the conversation, they would find it an incomprehensible game of chess where an admission of truth meant checkmate. But if anyone could understand that, it would be the embattled and ambiguous Vietnamese. They weren't merely walking a tightrope between Moscow and Peking; they were doing pirouettes on it.

'Nor,' continued Cauldwell, 'does Lopez think you're a Moscow man.'

'I'll ask him personally.'

'Good. He'd like to have a talk.'

'How do you and he – fellow Americans as it were – get along?'

'We have our differences.'

'He comes across as more sincere than you.'

'How little you know, William.'

'Have some Lao whisky. They only sell it by the bucket and I'm trying to use it up.'

Cauldwell held out a porcelain cup painted with mountain scenery and Chinese ideograms. 'The characters mean happiness and long life.'

'Well here's to both for both of us. Have you started to learn Mandarin?'

'I am taking lessons.'

Catesby sipped his drink and stared at Cauldwell.

'Why are you staring at me like that?'

'Because I want to strip off your outer layers and reveal your soul.'

'Very funny, William.'

'I'm not being funny. England has changed and I've changed with it.'

'Is that why you've grown your hair long?'

'You've never understood me, have you, Jeffers? You've never realised that I'm a bit of a rebel.'

'Your feeble attempts at rebellion, William, are the products of your bourgeois mind.' Cauldwell smiled. 'You remind me of Tony Hancock in that film, *The Rebel*.'

'I'm impressed by your knowledge of popular British culture.'

'You are a ridiculous character, William. You're self-deprecating, but narcissistic at the same time. You've always been so lonely – by the way, I always recommended you as ripe for sexual entrapment.'

'I'll tell you something, Jeffers; your sexual practices aren't going to be very popular in Chairman Mao's Cultural Revolution. All that stuff is bourgeois decadence.'

'You're right. Romance and sexual obsession are symptoms of bourgeois decadence. England, by the way, is the world's most sex-obsessed society. That's why it's so easy to recruit English spies.'

'And you did a fine job of that.'

'When it comes to spreading the revolution, the use of any form of vice is permissible.'

'Are you being ironic?'

'No.' As he spoke Cauldwell got up and walked over to the bookshelf where there was a writing pad. He picked up the pad and took a biro out of his pocket.

'It sounds as if you are a true believer in the cause.'

'I always have been. I explained that to you all those years ago when you beat me up in that bunker at Lakenheath Air Base.'

'You were a loyal Soviet spy in those days.'

Cauldwell smiled. 'Maybe I wasn't – perhaps I was getting fed up with Khrushchev's revisionism.'

'You preferred Stalin the monster?'

'He had his faults, but not as many as those who followed him and completely sold out the revolution.' While he was speaking Cauldwell was writing something on the notepad on the table between them. *In case we are being bugged, I wouldn't want to further embarrass our Vietnamese hosts by making them privy to this list of names. All of these are Brits who have worked for the Sovs.*

'You know,' said Catesby ignoring Cauldwell's scribbles, 'that the Sovs betrayed you. Their head guy in London set you up for us – but at the time we didn't know why.'

'And you've since asked your friends in Moscow Central?'

'But you just said that you're sure I don't work for the Sovs.' Catesby smiled.

'Nice food they've given us.' But instead of picking up his chopsticks, Cauldwell was writing furiously. *None of these is working for China or double dipping and working for both.*

Catesby read the list as he spooned caramelised fish on to boiled rice and seasoned it with *nuoc mam* sauce. It was depressing reading. The list contained the names of a few who might have been Soviet agents, but it also contained names of people who were either totally innocent or simply indiscreet in their activities. Cauldwell was doing a disinformation exercise. He wanted to cause trouble for both Moscow and London. The highest profile name was that of the Prime Minister himself. Cauldwell had written next to the PM's name: *the KGB put this guy in Downing Street by assassinating his predecessor, Hugh Gaitskell. They poisoned him with a rare form of tropical lupus, administered in a biscuit, when he visited the Soviet Consulate for a visa.*

'I wouldn't mind some of that Lao whisky,' said Cauldwell.

'Help yourself, there's half a bucket left.' Catesby winked at Cauldwell, folded the list and put it in his pocket. He knew what he was going to do with it – and then he would scatter the ashes in the latrine. The allegation that Harold Wilson was a Soviet agent was a tired chestnut that had been bouncing around London for ages. But it was also a toxic chestnut that right-wingers kept passing from media owners to military chiefs.

Cauldwell took a long swig of the whisky and looked at Catesby. 'It's a pity, William, that you're not bright enough or brave enough to be one of us.'

'I'm getting fed up with your insults.'

'I shouldn't have said that.' Cauldwell smiled. 'You don't win people over by insulting them.'

'That's right, Jeffers. Come over to us. We'll send you on an interrogation course. You become the subject's best fucking friend.'

'You must have flunked the course, William. You never manage that.'

'Oh, I don't know. My way of being someone's friend is not always obvious.'

'How long have we known each other?'

'Early 50s in Germany. About eighteen years.'

'You used to go undercover as a Cultural Attaché. At first, we thought it was joke of miscasting. But you really are an arts man – you know your stuff.'

'I wish I knew more about Poussin.'

'Maybe you'll soon find out.'

'Are you going to tell me?'

'We'll see.'

'I've never been able to understand where Poussin ends and Moscow Central begins.'

'Maybe,' smiled Cauldwell, 'they're completely separate and always were.'

The garden party for arty toffs that appeared to have turned into an orgy was something Catesby had still not worked out. He was pretty certain that the *tableau vivant* of Poussin's *The Triumph of Pan* was a booze-fuelled jape that had been inspired by Sir Anthony Blunt. And he knew at least half the semi-dressed 'Greeks' had been involved in espionage. But maybe it had had nothing to do with playing games for Moscow. Or blackmail or honey traps. Maybe it was just the upper classes at play on a warm summer's afternoon. And maybe there were deeper secrets involved than merely spying for foreign countries. The secrets of the ruling elite belong to them and them alone.

Cauldwell stared with a wry half-smile. 'You don't know what to do about them. You don't know whether to hang them, spy on them or embrace them. You must have been awfully confused when the Queen gave you the OBE.'

Catesby smiled.

'You said, William, in a joking way I'm sure, that you wanted to strip off my outer layers and reveal my soul. Maybe I'm now doing that to you.'

'Perhaps you are. On the other hand, there's a lot that you don't understand about me – or yourself. You were born in an absurdly rich country into an obscenely rich family. You quickly got bored with fast cars, yachts and social snobbery so you decided to play with political ideology instead – the ultimate toy for the spoilt rich. I grew up in poverty, but I saw a lot worse poverty around me. I love those people and want to protect them.'

'There are big differences between us. But we have one thing in common.' Cauldwell smiled. 'We are both traitors to the class we were born into.'

It was Catesby's turn to smile. 'That's not very original, Jeffers. It's what Chou En-lai said to Khrushchev.'

Cauldwell was a little taken aback. 'And it's just as true in their case.'

'If Chou and Mao had been in charge in the Kremlin during the Cuban Missile Crisis the people of Moscow would now be radioactive ash. Your first job is to protect your people.'

'Mao saved a quarter of the world's population from near starvation and feudalism.'

'And then starved thirty-five million of them to death during the Great Leap Forward between 1958 and 1961.'

'About 3 per cent of the population.' Cauldwell flashed a cold smile. 'Your own government's policies starved a million Irish during the potato famine – 12 per cent of the population.'

'You're a little bundle of point-scoring facts aren't you, Jeffers?'

'Those facts are real lives and real human pain.'

'Yeah, I know.' Catesby filled their cups from the Lao whisky bucket. 'But Mao has made mistakes!'

'Of course.'

'You're not a blind devotee?'

'No, but I believe in discipline.'

'So, Jeffers, what's your future?'

Cauldwell looked into his cup. 'I don't know. It depends on how the Party wants to make use of me.'

'I've heard that the Cultural Revolution has spawned an anti-Western atmosphere in China. You might not be welcome.'

'I think you've been misinformed. But even if that were true, I can always go back to Cuba.'

'Are you sure they would have you?'

Cauldwell shrugged.

'I couldn't do it,' said Catesby, 'even if I was a true believer.'

'Do what?'

'Live a life of exile – never being able to come home.' Catesby realised that the conversation had moved on. They were no longer playing spy games. Whether or not the Vietnamese were recording was irrelevant. They were two middle-aged men trying to make sense of their lives.

'Back in the German days,' said Cauldwell, 'most of my American colleagues were convinced that you were working for Moscow – but I believed they were wrong. You weren't subtle enough. Were you ever tempted to work for Moscow?'

'No.'

It was Catesby's turn to stare into his cup. He wondered if the answer was completely honest.

'What are your politics, William?'

'I'm a democratic socialist. I don't like violence – other than the odd punch-up. We didn't need an armed insurrection to establish the National Health Service and to nationalise the mines and the railways. But that's the way we do things in Britain. In other countries it's different – and I sympathise.'

'It doesn't sound as if you're going to be joining us?'

'No, Jeffers. In any case, I don't like the Cultural Revolution. It's Mao turning into King Lear.'

Cauldwell laughed. 'You are one helluva revisionist!'

'I feel sorry for you, Jeffers. You don't have anything to fall back on – you've never had a personal life.'

'No.' Cauldwell smiled. 'In any case, it's bourgeois decadence.'

'I think there are other complications.'

'You're right. The revolution doesn't respect different forms of sexuality. It's just a sacrifice I have to make for the greater good.' Cauldwell looked momentarily wistful. 'If it mattered that much, I would stay here. The Laotians don't mind – and the Vietnamese simply don't talk about it and pretend it doesn't exist. I did have a lover – his name was Thien – but he died of malaria. I miss him.'

'You're easier to deal with, Jeffers, when you're a monster.'

'Oh, I can be that too.'

'By the way,' said Catesby, 'when I was interrogating you at Lakenheath, you didn't finish telling me about your pal Quentin.'

Cauldwell's face darkened and he stared into his cup. 'He betrayed me.'

'And you never forgave him.'

'I didn't have the chance; he was killed in the war.' Cauldwell smiled. 'But it was an absolutely masterful betrayal.'

'What happened?'

'You have to imagine the University of Virginia on a warm spring midnight when I was a student before the war. What we call The Lawn is a grassy Italianate piazza with colonnades and pavilions on each side. It's a very romantic place – especially with a tease like Quentin. We used to play a little game acting out a poem called "Piazza Piece" by John Crowe Ransom. It's about an old man, obviously a metaphor for death, trying to seduce a beautiful young girl. You think it's silly?'

'No.'

'Good. You might learn something. In any case, we dressed up for the game. I pretended to be the old man and put on a grey wig with an eighteenth-century frock coat and buckled shoes. Quentin would wear a hooped party dress, heels and a wig of black ringlets. We would weave in and out of the shadows of the colonnades passing a bottle of bourbon between us. Sometimes we would have a little audience – or someone playing a harpsichord in one of the pavilions. We usually stopped to polish Icarus's balls.'

'Pardon?'

'Icarus; he flew too near the sun and his wings melted.'

'I know the story, but I didn't know you had to polish his balls.'

'This Icarus was a bronze statue of an aviator, a memorial to Quentin's uncle who been a pilot in the Lafayette Escadrille.'

Catesby nodded. He knew the Escadrille had been a group of American volunteers who fought for France in World War One while the United States was still neutral. They were mostly Southern and mostly rich.

'My father flew with them, but unlike Quentin's uncle, my daddy survived.'

'Why did you polish Icarus's balls?'

'We shouldn't have. It wasn't our job. The ball buffing is supposed to be done by the first-year girls at Sweet Briar College. Visiting Icarus at midnight with a tin of Brasso is part of the Sweet Briar initiation. As a sophisticated Englishman, I am sure you find this somewhat absurd.'

'We have our own rituals. And Quentin was in drag as one of those girls?'

'That was the idea – and he polished Icarus's balls with relish. When they were dry and shining he caressed them and licked them – and gave me knowing glances as he progressed. Quentin was a cunning vixen – a master of deception and double bluff. Do you know what he did?'

'I'm starting to see a pattern.'

'What is that pattern, William?'

'You never really know who anyone is.'

Cauldwell gave a bleak smile. 'You are clever. We were alone – or so I thought. I was deep in the shadows of the colonnade. The night was scented and dankly warm. I took a big swig from the bourbon bottle and put it down next to a Doric column to deliver my lines about being a dirty old man in a coat of dust. Quentin then delivered his line about being a young beauty waiting for her true love. For the first time there was real yearning in Quentin's falsetto – and yet something different too. I walked forward – and was immediately reproved and pushed back.'

'What a tease.' Catesby looked at Cauldwell. 'By the way, are you sure this hooch isn't bugged?'

Cauldwell smiled and nodded his head. 'I went back to the bourbon bottle – and took another deep drink. At that age, I needed courage. When I looked up again, the white skirt had parted to reveal gleaming thighs above high black-buttoned boots. I ought to have known then. The voice came again, but far less of a falsetto – a voice of absolute longing and abandon.'

'And you obliged.'

'It was too late to stop. I unbuttoned my flies and went forward to meet my fate. As soon as I put my arms around her I knew for sure that Quentin had betrayed me.' Cauldwell smiled. 'Laetitia had been after me since I was sixteen.'

'His sister?'

'Twin sister, in fact. She wanted it so much, was so hungry. We did it standing there in the colonnade. She wrapped her legs around me so that she was completely off the ground, but still managed to pump and grind as if she were a well-oiled machine on high revs. She clawed at me. Her passion was frightening. But the odd thing, the oddest thing, was that her real femininity was less feminine than Quentin's fake femininity. And that, Catesby, is how I lost my virginity.'

'Why have you told me this?'

'To help you solve a riddle.'

'Thanks.' A flashbulb had popped in Catesby's brain and briefly illuminated the missing woman from the Poussin – a veiled enigma in the mist.

There was the sound of approaching footsteps and the door curtain twitched. Lopez entered and addressed Cauldwell. 'Your transport is going to be ready soon.'

Catesby studied the two Americans. Both came from wealthy privileged backgrounds and both had rejected their country to become Communists of one form or other. But despite that, there was a coolness between them. Lopez was much younger and seemed an edgy man of action. They both were killers, but Lopez wore the lethal persona more easily.

Cauldwell stood up, turned to Catesby and shook his hand. 'Thanks for lunch, comrade. When you find the path to democratic socialism, please let me know – but I won't hold my breath.'

'Next time you organise an orgy at Cliveden, can you get me an invite?'

'It wasn't at Cliveden. It was in Suffolk – a little patch of wood-land overlooking the River Alde.'

Another red snooker ball whirred across the baize and clunked into its pocket. The mystery was getting clearer.

'Look after yourself, Jeffers.'

'You too. I'm sure we'll meet again.'

Lopez stuck his head out of the door and shouted something in Vietnamese. Two PAVN soldiers appeared. They were more smartly dressed than most, with pith helmets bearing the enamel gold star on red insignia, and packing Makarov 9mm automatics in leather hip holsters.

'My escorts have arrived,' said Cauldwell. He smiled wanly. 'I hope I've read the runes correctly. I don't want to end up on the wrong side of history.'

'But you meant well.'

'I just love your English irony.'

Catesby watched as Cauldwell disappeared into the late afternoon. Beams of sunlight filtered through the jungle canopy and made the image flicker like the end of an old film.

'I wouldn't mind some of that whisky,' said Lopez.

'I'll get you a clean cup.'

'Nah, I'll use his.' Lopez picked up Cauldwell's cup and wiped it with his shirttail. 'I don't think I'll get syphilis.'

'How did you get on with your fellow American?'

Lopez poured himself a whisky. 'We got on fine. He thinks I'm an asshole and I think he's an asshole.'

'Sounds like the basis of a great friendship.'

'Fuck no.' Lopez laughed. 'You're pretty unsophisticated, aren't you?'

Catesby smiled, but didn't reply. The American upper classes had a self-confident abrasiveness that left you speechless – which was just as well because they wouldn't have listened to your answer in any case.

'Cauldwell's problem,' said Lopez, 'is that he's never come to terms with his social background. Why are you laughing?'

'Because you're so funny. What about yourself? Have you come to terms with your privileged social background?'

'Ah...' Lopez raised his whisky cup. 'Good point. But I don't need to. When I look into a mirror I see that I am not one of them. I'm adopted.'

Catesby wasn't sure it made much of a difference. 'In any case, you and Cauldwell disagree on matters of ideology?'

Lopez shrugged. 'If I was fighting in South America, I might be a Maoist, but not here. After defeating French and US imperialism, the Vietnamese don't want to fall under Chinese imperialism.'

'And Cauldwell doesn't understand that?'

Lopez drank the whisky and nodded. 'Oh yeah, he does understand, but Cauldwell made his choice long ago and can't change it now.'

Catesby realised that Cauldwell and Lopez must have had some long talks. The full tragedy of Cauldwell's dilemma began to sink in. Once you betrayed Moscow, you can't say 'sorry' and go back. What Cauldwell had done was worse than spying for the West. He would never be forgiven for that. And one day they might kill him for it.

'In any case,' continued Lopez, 'Cauldwell began to be an embarrassment. The Vietnamese decided they had to get rid of him one way or another. I can tell you, he is one nervous puppy. Some of the pro-Soviet faction want to bundle him up and send him off as a thank-you card to Moscow. But I think they might be packing him off to China instead. Who knows?'

Catesby realised that Cauldwell had been putting on a brave face during their conversation.

'And I'll tell you something else,' said Lopez. 'The Vietnamese want to get rid of you too. You and Cauldwell might end up handcuffed together on the same flight to Moscow. Thanks for the whisky.'

'Thanks for your help.'

'You need it.'

Left alone, Catesby began to take stock of his own situation. The worst-case scenario was the Donskoi crematorium; the best case was drinking himself to death in a gloomy Moscow flat with Kim Philby. Hanoi's decision came sooner than he expected.

»»»»»

'You fucking bastard. You fucking cunt bastard.'

It wasn't the first time Catesby had been woken in the middle of the night by a woman swearing at him, kicking his bed and pounding him with her fists. The last time he had deserved it. It had been a selfish betrayal of someone who loved him. But he had never met this woman. Catesby held his arms in front of his face to protect himself as she kept hitting. She finally stopped pounding with her fists, only to aim a foot at Catesby's crotch which he deflected with a raised knee. Her attack suddenly came to an end. Catesby listened to her breathing hard, tired by the onslaught. Finally, a torch was flicked on and aimed at his face.

'I am sorry,' he said, 'if I've done something to hurt you.'

'*She* sent you, didn't she?' The word 'she' was uttered with particular contempt.

'No, I can assure you you've got that wrong.' It was too dark to see her face, but Catesby assumed it was Miranda and that she was referring to her mother, Lady Somers.

'You're a lying fucking bastard.'

'But I'm not lying about that. Someone sent me to find you, but it wasn't Lady Somers. Anyway, *you* seem to have found *me*.'

'You're not funny, not funny at all. Who sent you?'

Catesby mentioned the name of the French journalist who had taken him to Cu Chi and also Huynh. He then added, just to make sure that the PAVN base camp on the Laotian border wasn't full of women with upper-class English voices, 'You are Miranda?'

'Of course I fucking am. But I still don't believe you. I am not stupid. *She* sent you.'

'Listen, Miranda,' Catesby tried to sound calm, 'that isn't true. I've never spoken to your mother about you.'

Miranda gave a bitter laugh. 'Then you're an idiot. You know fucking nothing.'

Catesby stared at the dark shadow in front of him. There was something odd in her voice and manner.

The torch started to fade and Miranda shook it. 'Crappy Russian batteries.'

'There are matches and candles on the table – and, by the way, the torch batteries are Chinese. Like useless backyard iron smelting, a product of the Cultural Revolution.'

'I don't need your commentary.'

A match scraped and there was enough yellow light for Catesby to see Miranda's face. Her hair was dark and straight like her mother's, but the most striking thing was the pallor and tiredness of her face. She was in her twenties, but already a burnt-out case.

'What are you doing?' she asked.

Catesby had picked up his tunic and trousers, which were on the ground beside the bed, and began to pull them on under the green camouflage waterproof that served as a sheet. 'I'm dressing.'

Miranda gave a hacking laugh. 'I thought you were having a wank.'

The way her upper-class voice became inflected with the tone of the street was something that Catesby had noticed in other posh women. Sometimes it was an affectation – they were slumming it – but in Miranda's case it was genuine. She had been dragged through the gutter and the dirt had become ingrained.

Catesby sat barefoot on the side of the plank bed. The surreal irony of the scene seemed to crackle in the candle flame. Catesby, a high-ranking British intelligence agent, and she, the daughter of the head of the British Ministry of Defence, were both dressed in the field uniform of the PAVN, a Communist army at war with the West. And it wasn't a fancy-dress party. In the near distance, the thunder of American bombs pounded into Asia. The tremors shook the table and made the candle shadows jump like frightened cats.

'Just like the Blitz, eh?'

Miranda remained impassive.

'But, of course, you're too young to remember that.' Catesby felt his bare ankle brush a bottle beside the bed. It was the vodka that had been playfully sent by the Soviet Embassy. 'I wouldn't mind a drink. What about you? Even if the Russians have betrayed the revolution, they still produce good vodka.' Catesby laughed. 'Maybe the two facts are related. I am sure your Maoist friends are much more focused and puritanical.'

'You talk too much.' As she spoke, Miranda raised the candle to look for cups. She found them and held them out for Catesby to fill.

'Sorry, it isn't chilled.'

Miranda drank thirstily. As she did so, Catesby noted the needle marks and burn-like scars from heroin injection on her inner arms. She had done it all. He poured her another drink and she seemed calmer.

'Why do you think I'm here?' said Catesby.

'It's obvious, isn't it?'

Catesby paused and waited. It was a good interrogation technique. You waited for the subject to answer their own question.

'You've been sent to bring me back to England.'

Catesby nodded. It wasn't why he had been sent, but he decided it might be useful to play along with her idea.

'So it's true?'

'That is one of the reasons they sent me.' Catesby poured her more vodka. 'How did you find out?'

Miranda brushed a lock of hair from her eyes. 'Someone from Hanoi, I think he might have been a general or something. He said that I had to leave Laos and then leave Vietnam too because my presence was not in the interest of the Democratic Republic of Vietnam. I asked him why, but he couldn't or wouldn't tell me. His French wasn't very good and his English was worse. He then sent for Huynh to help translate.' She paused and her eyes squinted with bitter anger. 'Huynh is a useless cunt. He won't stand up to anyone.'

'But did he help translate, explain what was going on?'

Miranda drank the vodka, but more slowly this time. 'There was a lot of jabbering in Vietnamese – which consisted largely of Huynh nodding agreement. Huynh then summarised. Apparently, Hanoi and London have reached some sort of deal – secret, I bet – in which I'm to be repatriated to the UK.'

'And did Huynh say I was sent to fetch you?'

'No. All this happened two days ago. I talked to Jeffers about it – and he said they were throwing him out too.'

'You worked with Jeffers Cauldwell in London and Brighton?'

Miranda looked away shyly and perhaps slightly ashamed. 'You might say that – but what we were doing was essential for the liberation of the Third World.'

Catesby was tempted to say that Cauldwell was her honey-trap pimp, but held his tongue.

'I asked Jeffers where he was going. He said, "Peking."'

'If he's lucky,' said Catesby.

'He will be. The Chinese have much to be grateful for – he helped them get the Freedom Bomb.'

'Is that what you call it?'

'That's what it is. It frees the People's Republic of China from attack or blackmail by the USA and Moscow. In any case, I asked Cauldwell if he could arrange for me to go to China with him instead of the UK. He promised he would try.' She sighed. 'It kept my hopes up. And then Huynh and a Vietnamese official came to see me this evening. They said that I was leaving for Hanoi tomorrow with an Englishman who would be accompanying me to London.'

Catesby breathed a selfish sigh of relief. It looked like he wasn't going to Moscow after all. He began to try to piece together what had happened. The big boys in Hanoi had weighed up the advantages of staying on good terms with London as opposed to just sucking up to Moscow – and had decided on being nice to London. And then reckoned they could bundle Miranda and himself into one package.

Miranda looked at Catesby. There was pleading in her eyes. 'I'm sorry I hit you and swore at you. I can't go back to London. I just can't.'

Catesby could see that she was desperate not to be sent back. It was a bargaining chip, but one that he had to play carefully. Miranda was the Holy Grail of information that he had been sent halfway around the world to tap. It was all there, in reach.

Miranda reached out and ran her hand up Catesby's thigh. 'I'll do anything for you. I can't go back.'

He lifted her hand away, but held it. 'Look, the damage has

already been done. China's got the bomb and nothing you can tell me can take it away. But you've got it wrong. I haven't been sent here to bring you back; I've been sent to interrogate you.' The truth was easy and made the lies sound even more convincing. 'My bosses in London aren't interested in court trials and prosecutions. That's the last thing they want. But they do want to find out what happened so it can't happen again.'

'I won't go back. There's too much history; too many bad things happened there. I'll kill myself first.'

Catesby squeezed her hand. 'If you tell me what happened, I'll tell the Vietnamese that London definitely doesn't want you back. That we don't want messy trials and publicity,' Catesby smiled, 'that reveal the intelligence services are shit. And,' Catesby gently touched her heroin injection scars, 'even if you think it was for a good cause, you've been horribly used.'

The tears, pent up for so long, came in a flood. Catesby put an arm round her and held her tight. He felt sweet pain as if he were her parent. 'Listen,' he said, 'you don't have to tell me anything.'

'I want to – and I need you to listen.'

It all poured out. A list of dates and names and places. Sordid hotels with camera peepholes and stately homes with stately peepholes. Catesby had never realised there were so many taboos to be transgressed. He had always known that the sexual tastes of the upper classes were bizarre, but had never realised quite how bizarre. Their behaviour was more Aleister Crowley than Kinsey Report. But Miranda's most valuable honey-trap victims were the nuclear scientists at Harwell and officials at the MoD. She introduced them into a dangerous world in which they became willing players. But as Miranda told her story, there was one name she still hadn't mentioned.

Catesby wasn't sure how to ask her. He began indirectly. 'Were you happy as child?'

Miranda frowned and shook her head.

'I suppose that was a stupid question.'

She gave a twisted smile. 'It was a stupid question.'

'You realise, you must realise, that your mother is suspected of passing on secret information to the Chinese.'

Miranda laughed out loud. 'Then she must be doing it through a spiritual medium, from beyond the grave.'

'I didn't know that. I'm very sorry.' Catesby was confused. Why hadn't Miranda mentioned it before? 'When did your mother die?'

'Why don't you shut the fuck up? It's none of your business and I don't want to talk about it.'

Catesby knew that he was getting close to something. Miranda was upset, but he had to play hard as well as soft. 'If you don't talk, they'll put you on a plane back to London and I won't be able to help you.'

'I swear I'll kill myself first.'

'I don't want you to do that.' Catesby touched her scarred arm. 'I care about you.'

'Leave me alone.'

'Okay.' Catesby stared past Miranda into the black night and counted the seconds. He counted three minutes. Two minutes were enough for a subject to calm down and an extra minute meant they started thinking of other things. 'I can do a deal with the Vietnamese if London will back me. Are you listening?'

Miranda nodded. It sounded like she was crying.

'But you need to tell me everything about your mother.'

Miranda shivered and wiped her eyes. 'She died twenty years ago.'

Catesby was confused again. He supposed Miranda was either talking figuratively about a living mother who was 'dead' to her – or about a nanny, a much-loved Malaysian or Chinese *ayah*. 'You must have been very young.' Catesby offered more vodka and assumed she meant an *ayah*. 'You regarded that person, rather than Lady Somers, as your real mother.'

'She *was* my real mother.' Miranda laughed again and shook her head. 'You don't understand, do you?'

Catesby shook his head, but a tiny pinpoint of light was beginning to pierce through. The final piece of the puzzle was about to fall into place.

Miranda looked directly at Catesby. Her eyes shone damp and hurt in the candlelight. 'That's always been the problem. Don't you see?'

'I'm beginning to.'

'Lady Somers,' Miranda rocked back and laughed. It was a braying laugh that pierced through the thatched roof and jungle forest, rocking the night around them more than the American bombs. 'Lady Somers isn't my mother; she's my father.'

Catesby smiled. 'Your father is a very beautiful woman.'

'Isn't she just?'

'How many people know about this?'

'Practically no one. Her Swedish surgeon died long ago. It's her best-kept secret – her most important secret. You can't imagine how fierce she is about it.'

'And you used it against her?'

Miranda finished the vodka in her cup. 'Yes.'

'How did it happen?'

'She used to bring work home. I was astonished by how secret some of it was. She thought it was safe in her house – and there was a wall safe too.' Miranda held out her cup.

Catesby poured the vodka.

'I don't want to get too pissed; I'm not proud of what I did.'

'Was Jeffers involved?'

'Partly. He gave me the camera and showed me how to use it. But even if it hadn't been for him, I still wanted to pass on the information – and I was in such a good place to get it.' Miranda stared into her cup. 'But I'm not a very good spy – and she found the camera in my knickers' drawer. She wasn't looking for a spy camera; she was looking for my drugs stash. Funny, isn't it?'

'What is?'

'She was relieved to find that I'd given up shooting heroin for spying for China. I was, in fact, clean at the time – but I came back to it. We still had a big row about the camera.'

It reminded Catesby of the spy's dilemma. Which is the bigger crime: betraying your country or betraying the person you love?

'There was no question,' continued Miranda, 'that she was going to turn me in, to have me arrested. But she said that both of us might get arrested and go to prison. I made a little joke of it and said: "Where would you go then, *Mother*, Holloway Women's Prison or the Scrubs?" She didn't like that. And, when it was just the two of us, I always called her Pen, short for Penelope. Sometimes we could be like two girls together – talking about clothes and hair.' Miranda smiled. 'But we couldn't swap clothes – she's so much taller than me. And doesn't she have beautiful legs?'

'Indeed.' Catesby remembered how the cops on the gate at the Admiralty used to eye her up as she clicked past on her stilettos.

'Pen wanted to know for whom I was working and what I had already photographed. She thought she could do a cover-up and shift the blame elsewhere. I am sure what she wanted to do was roll up Jeffers' spy ring in such a way that she and I wouldn't get in trouble. But it didn't take her long to realise I wasn't playing that game. The neighbours must have heard us shouting, but they probably thought it was about me and my lifestyle again.'

'Until then, Lady Somers was totally innocent of any espionage activity?'

'Absolutely, completely. Pen was a totally loyal servant of the British state. She is, of course, a great admirer of Chinese culture because of her upbringing. But she would never have betrayed Britain for China.' Miranda laughed again, but this time it was a gentle warm laugh. 'I suppose you could say that Pen is a very complex woman. And, as Whitehall mandarins go, slightly to the left. She votes Labour and thinks she's an anti-imperialist.'

Once again, Catesby remembered the MICE rule. The four ways you recruited an agent: money, ideology, coercion and ego. In her daughter's case, it was ideology; for Lady Somers, it was coercion. 'But you forced her to work for you and Jeffers?'

'You got it in one, Mr Catesby. You must be the star of the Secret Intelligence Service.'

Catesby smiled. Miranda had finally begun to sound a little drunk.

'As I said, Pen is a loyal Brit. But there are two things that she loves more than her country. One is being a woman and the other is me. And she didn't want to lose either of those.'

'So you blackmailed her?'

'You are *so* astonishingly brilliant. You are definitely going to be head of SIS. Sorry, I get sarcastic when I'm pissed.'

'I suppose...'

'If you suppose that Peking gave a shopping list to Jeffers Cauldwell and that Jeffers passed it on to me, you are absolutely right. I then took the list into her study and said, "Pen, if you don't get this information asap, every tabloid in the country will be headlining your story." You could imagine the fun: *Lady – question mark – Somers; Ministry of Defence in Drag Act; MoD Still Awaits its First Woman Boss*. And that would have hurt her more than being called a traitor. At first, I hated doing it. But Pen got used to it – and that made it easier.'

Catesby understood only too well. Being a double agent becomes a habit at first and, after a while, an exhilarating habit like a drug.

'Pen started to joke about it. It was almost as if she enjoyed playing the game. We had ideological arguments, but they were good-tempered.' Miranda lowered her voice. 'And I can tell you another secret about my reserved distinguished Whitehall mandarin of a parent – a most odd secret.'

'Go on.'

'She loves The Beatles. She used to use them against me in our political rows. Pen, particularly after a bit to drink, would dance about singing lyrics from *Magical Mystery Tour*. You know the bit about flaunting pictures of Chairman Mao and freeing your mind.'

'The Beatles,' said Catesby, 'seem to prefer Moscow.'

'And Pen used to sing that one too. All that stuff about being back in the USSR and how lucky you were.'

Only in Britain, Catesby thought with national pride, only in Britain would a pop group take sides in a complex ideological split between two forms of Communism. 'It sounds,' he said, 'as if the two of you got along fine.'

'Sometimes.'

'Do you love her?'

'Yes, of course I do.'

'Then why have you betrayed her?'

'Because she took me away from my first mother.'

'And you can never forgive her for that?'

'I can now. That's why I had to tell you the truth about her. I've settled the account. Now I can love her freely.'

The first person Catesby met at the British Embassy in Hanoi was the Soviet ambassador, who wanted help in translating one of his poems into English. Once again, Catesby felt he had crashed through the looking glass into a surreal world of March hares and talking sheep. Just to make sure that his Vietnamese driver had, in fact, dropped him off at the right embassy, Catesby glanced through the large open window to make sure that it really was the Union Flag fluttering from the flagpole. It was.

The patched white stucco building at 31 Hai Ba Trung was the scruffiest British Embassy he had ever seen – but, with its shuttered windows and dark red roof tiles, it did have the faded charm that always clung to French colonial architecture in the tropics. Catesby half-expected to see the ghost of Albert Camus chatting to Graham Greene. But in this case, the writer in the white linen suit was a Russian ambassador who fancied himself as a poet.

Catesby had briefly met Ilya Scherbakov at embassy functions in Germany and France, but wouldn't have recognised him if Scherbakov hadn't recognised him first. The Russian, of course, had been expecting Catesby to turn up and knew all about what he had been up to.

'I believe,' said Scherbakov clutching a few sheets of longhand written verse in Cyrillic, 'that you understand Russian?'

'Yes, but I'm not fluent.'

'But you look like a man with the heart of a poet.'

'I have the heart of a poet. I keep it in a jar of formaldehyde above my writing desk.'

'Was he or she a famous poet?'

'No, it was only a joke.'

'Ah, I see.' Scherbakov seemed a little disappointed that Catesby didn't have a piece of Shelley or Keats or Christina Rossetti in his study.

'Sorry.'

'But I hope,' said the Russian shaking his poem, 'that you will be so kind as to have a look at this. I have a meeting with Daphne and I want to read it to her.' Scherbakov smiled. 'She is, I believe, "Your Man in Hanoi"?'

'Daphne,' said Catesby without batting an eye, 'is Consul-General.' It was, however, pointless to pretend that she wasn't a spy. In places like Hanoi, diplomatic cover stories were polite fictions that no one believed. Daphne Park was, as Catesby well knew, one of the bravest and most competent officers in SIS.

Catesby took the poem and spread it out on the reception desk. The title translated as: 'I Want the Snow to Fall.' It was a poem about homesickness. About how the Russian soul, languishing in tropical Vietnam, longs for snow, cornflower-blue skies, frosty air, iceflowers on window glass, birch trees, endless snowfields and so on. Catesby borrowed a pen and quickly added to and altered a rough translation that the ambassador had already begun. The poem ended: 'Oh dearest Homeland! How can the Russian soul live in Vietnam!'

As Catesby handed back the poem, Scherbakov asked, 'Do you like it?'

'It combines the lyricism of Pushkin with the sad longing of Chekhov.'

Scherbakov laughed and shook his finger at Catesby. 'I think you are making fun of me.'

'Of course not. It is a good poem and Daphne will love it.'

Scherbakov nodded. As he put the poem in a jacket pocket, someone entered the foyer.

'Look,' said the Russian, 'here comes Jock the Sock.'

Catesby was a little abashed that Scherbakov knew the nickname of Murray MacLehose, the Glasgow-born ambassador. It was a nickname only bandied about by FO and SIS insiders. But there was no ill feeling, for MacLehose and Scherbakov warmly embraced.

'Great to see you, Ilya,' said MacLehose. 'Daphne's waiting for you.'

As the Russian left the room, Catesby called out, 'And thanks for the vodka.'

'Speaking of which,' said MacLehose looking at Catesby, 'why don't you come up to my office for a wee dram.'

»»»»

The ambassador's office had French windows leading on to a balcony that overlooked a small overgrown garden with a scum-covered pond.

'We used to have ducks,' said MacLehose looking down from the balcony, 'but I'm sure they ended up in someone's pot.'

Catesby picked up his whisky and went out to join him.

'Don't lean against the railing, it's unsafe. As a matter of fact, I'm not sure about this balcony. Not sure it will support two of us. Let's go back in.'

Catesby and the ambassador sat facing each other in rattan chairs while wall lizards raced across the crumbling plaster.

'You probably think we're too cosy with the Sovs,' said MacLehose, 'but they're our only joy. The Vietnamese are not treating us well. They probably think we are too close to the Americans. The government minders are especially beastly to Daphne. They won't even let her have a bicycle or language tutor.'

'They must know she's an intelligence officer.'

'It's more than that. They find her intimidating.'

'Don't we all?'

'Quite. But the Vietnamese aren't used to it. The Russians, on the other hand, adore her.'

'Especially Scherbakov. He's reading her a poem about his Russian soul this very moment.' Catesby gave a sly smile. 'I don't suppose...'

'No, William, there is absolutely nothing romantic. But she is using Scherbakov just as much as he is using her. You chaps are no longer just spies, you're back-channel diplomats. Ilya tells Daphne what's happening in the corridors of power in Hanoi and Daphne passes on gossip from Washington. And, by the way, she saved your bacon.'

'How did she find out my bacon needed saving?'

'Scherbakov told her. The Vietnamese wanted to shoot you.' MacLehose reached for the whisky. 'Top up?'

'Yes, please.'

MacLehose poured the whisky. 'The ice, if you want any, is safe, made from bottled water.'

'Thanks.'

'Don't want to drink it neat in this weather. As I was saying, you were headed for an unmarked shallow grave until Scherbakov intervened. He and Daphne worked out an alternative way of dealing with you that the Vietnamese would find acceptable. It is also meant they could get shot of the girl, whom the Vietnamese find an embarrassment.'

Catesby couldn't share all his thoughts because MacLehose was not in the 'need to know' loop. The Russians knew that Miranda was part of a spy ring that had sent nuclear secrets to Peking. But the Sovs didn't know that the spy ring had been busted. On the contrary, Moscow was certain that secret technology was still being passed to China because the Chinese were still making such rapid advances with nuclear weapons. Moscow's dilemma was that they couldn't ask Hanoi to send Miranda to Moscow for interrogation because they knew Hanoi could not risk offending China. So sending Miranda back to London was the second-best option. Catesby's speculations were interrupted by the loud braying ring of Ambassador MacLehose's office telephone.

'Hello … He says it's urgent? … I suppose you'd better ring Daphne first to make sure it's okay with her for him to come up.' MacLehose put the phone down and looked at Catesby. 'That sounds a bit ominous.'

'What's happened?'

'A Second Secretary from the Sov Embassy, almost certainly KGB, turned up and said he had an urgent message for Scherbakov that had to be delivered immediately. Reception said the guy was sweating and in a bit of a panic.'

'Let's hope Comrade Ilya hasn't been recalled for a little chat at the Lubyanka. Maybe he gave too much away.'

'I doubt it. He's too cunning and careful – the message is probably about something here in Hanoi.'

'In any case,' said Catesby, 'there is something I need to tell you. It's about Miranda. I promised her that she wouldn't be sent back to the UK. She's terrified of being repatriated.'

'That's a difficult one, William. I'm not sure you should have promised that.'

'We have discovered that she has family in Malaysia. I was hoping we could work something out.'

MacLehose looked thoughtful, 'We'll have to…' There was an urgent knocking at the door. 'Come in.'

Catesby looked up. It was Daphne Park. She seemed upset. That was unusual. Daphne was never upset, not even when confronted by a machete-wielding mob baying for blood. She nodded a terse greeting at Catesby, then looked at the ambassador.

'You look pale, Daphne,' said MacLehose. 'What's wrong?'

'Miranda Somers is dead. She died of an overdose of heroin.'

'Where did it happen?'

'At the Foreign Ministry. The Vietnamese were keeping her in a guest room under guard.'

'Why,' said Catesby, 'were the Russians informed first? She's British.'

'No one has been informed, William. Ilya runs a string of Vietnamese agents. If it wasn't for him we might have never found out. I need a drink.'

Daphne poured herself a whisky and sat in a cane chair apart from the others. Catesby stared at a wall lizard. There was a long silence punctuated only by the gentle susurrus of a slow-turning ceiling fan.

The White House: 1969

There were only three of them in the Oval Office: the President, the Director of Central Intelligence and a shadowy figure who was taking notes. It was a very private and secret meeting. The DCI looked at the man taking notes.

'This is, Mr President, our most closely held secret.'

The President caught the nuance. 'Richard, I would prefer that,' the President said the name of the note-taker, 'remains so that he can hear what you have to say.'

The DCI stirred uneasily. 'Yes, Mr President, if you think it wise.'

'I do. Carry on.'

'The policy began during the Kennedy administration when Allen Dulles was DCI.'

'The bastard who fucked up the Bay of Pigs.'

'That's right, Mr President. Dulles's idea was based on the old military precept that our enemy's enemy is our friend. It was a very risky policy, but one that Kennedy endorsed.'

'Let it never be said that Dick Nixon was too cowardly to take the same fucking risks as Jack Kennedy.'

'Yes, Mr President. The policy in question began when we realised that the rift between the Soviet Union and the People's Republic of China was deep and permanent – and the two countries were sworn enemies.' The DCI paused and looked at the third person. 'I'm not really certain, Mr President, that I can continue. This is a top secret and highly sensitive matter which has serious ramifications both internationally and domestically.'

'And that's why I want,' he nodded at the note-taker and said his name, 'to hear about it.'

The DCI sighed and closed his briefing folder.

'Perhaps, Richard,' said the President, 'I can continue where

THE WHITEHALL MANDARIN   349

you left off. It has for some time been one of the wonders of the world how a nation of barefoot peasants, who couldn't even manufacture their own bicycles, managed to develop atomic and hydrogen nuclear weapons more quickly than the Soviet Union and the United States. What's your theory? You're supposed to be head of the fucking CIA.'

'I think, sir, you already know the answer.'

'And it is totally fucking shocking. I've half-suspected it for years, but I never believed it could be true. I cannot believe that previous US Presidents and Directors of the CIA conspired to provide Red China with nuclear weapons. Do you realise, Richard, that those actions amount to fucking treason? You have given lethal weapons of mass destruction to an enemy of the United States of America! Weapons that may one day vaporise San Diego, Los Angeles and San Francisco – if not the whole of the USA.'

'It was, Mr President, a policy that had already been imple-mented before I became DCI. There was nothing I could do to reverse it or...'

'I don't want to hear your self-justifications.'

'It was not, sir, a policy that I would have condoned.'

'What on earth were they thinking?'

'The purpose of the policy was to threaten the Soviet Union on two fronts. Remember that Russia has a land border with China that stretches over 2,700 miles. Confronted by a hostile and nuclear-armed China, the USSR would never be able to contemplate war or expansion into Europe or anywhere else. And, perhaps, that policy will one day fatally weaken the Soviet Union and lead to its downfall.'

'But there are risks.'

'There certainly are.'

The President nodded and frowned. 'It seems to me the biggest risk, aside from Chinese nukes landing in California, is disclosure. How are we able to disguise the fact, cover up the fact, that we provided this information to China? If it ever becomes public, it will be lethal.'

'We helped set up a pro-Peking nuclear spy ring in Britain.

The idea being that we could always blame poor British security for leaking nuclear secrets to China.'

'I hope,' said the President, 'there are no fingerprints that could implicate the CIA.'

'No, Mr President, we made use of a Communist spy named Jeffers Cauldwell, whom we turned. Cauldwell was a US diplomat who had originally been a spy for the Soviet Union. At some point, he decided that Maoism was the true Holy Grail of Communism and the USSR had sold out. Not long after his conversion to Maoism, we arrested him and held him secretly in solitary confinement. After eighteen months of interrogation, Cauldwell finally broke and agreed to work for us. We allowed him to escape to Cuba.'

'So in the end, Cauldwell became an American hero.'

'No, Mr President, he remains to this day a committed Maoist. His agreement to do our bidding in England was what he called a "Faustian pact with Satan". Cauldwell believed working in collaboration with us was a price worth paying to enable China to gain access to nuclear weapons.'

'*Realpolitik*,' said the shadowy figure with the notepad.

'I think, Henry, that the damage has already been done. We can't put the genie back in the bottle.' The President paused. 'Since we can't reverse the Chinese policy, perhaps we should take it further.'

'What have you in mind, sir?' asked the note-taker

'As we have armed China, maybe the time has come for us to befriend them. We have left them in the cold for too long. Can you start planning an official visit? One that will shake the world.'

London: October, 1969

Catesby was given the address by Henry Bone. The house was located on a quiet street in Chelsea between King's Road and the river. It wasn't the sort of place where Catesby had expected Lady Somers to live. He would have imagined Kensington or Knightsbridge to be more her taste. Chelsea certainly was an expensive neighbourhood, but one that was becoming more and more inhabited by wealthy pop stars, film types and artists.

Catesby hated what he was going to have to do. But he had been thoroughly briefed by the head of Five as well as his boss at SIS. He had also had a meeting with the Secretary of State for Defence. Catesby tried hard not to stare at the Secretary's marvellously bushy eyebrows, like an overgrown hedgerow. He half-expected to see nesting robins darting in and out. The message from everyone Catesby spoke to was the same. It wasn't going to be a pleasant business. But he had to do it.

There was a car and driver at his disposal, but Catesby opted for the Circle Line to Sloane Square. It was a short hop, but he emerged into a completely different universe from the bowler hats and rolled brollies of St James's. Catesby wasn't wearing a bowler, just a black lounge suit, but he still felt like an alien being as he surfaced into the sunlight and youth of King's Road. It was a heaving blur of bright colours, Vespa scooters, mini-skirts, boots and bobbed hair. It was Miranda's world, but she wasn't there to take it in. Catesby passed a boutique with the name 'Granny Takes a Trip'. A heart-shaped psychedelic message on the window puffed: 'Granny Sells Clothes To Wear Before You Make Love'. He was tempted to go in and buy something for his sister, but lost his nerve. Maybe, he thought darkly, he should get something for Lady Somers instead – but not from there. Catesby continued walking and passed an art house cinema showing Lindsay Anderson's *if....* The film poster posed the question 'Which side will you be on?' Indeed, thought Catesby. Indeed. The film was set in a ridiculous public school and ended with a pitched gun battle between the boys and masters. It was a film about rebellion, but Catesby much preferred the tale of the borstal boy in *The Loneliness of the Long Distance Runner.* Catesby had cried a bit at the end. He was a long-distance runner too, whenever he had some time off, and he knew the pain and loneliness of the sport.

Catesby realised that he was sauntering and wasting time. He was trying to put off doing what he had been sent to do. Maybe he wouldn't do it; maybe he would disappear into the crowds of the fresh new Britain that swirled around him and never go back to the grey repression of Century House and the Secret State. Granny of the love clothes shop didn't sound too young; maybe he could get something going with her. He'd let his hair grow and serve behind the counter in a bright rainbow-coloured jumper with his OBE ironically draped around his neck. Catesby laughed out loud and drew a few stares. Maybe he would wear his OBE next time he made love. But, he thought, it wasn't much of a joke. A lot of toffs did wear their gongs while they were doing it. But not ironically. Unlike them, Catesby approved of the new liberated outrageous Britain that was thumbing its nose at authority. But he feared it wouldn't last. He knew that the heavy black boot of conservatism and control was poised and ready to stomp. Before he had been dispatched to South- east Asia, Catesby had thought rumours of a military coup were as preposterous and silly as UFOs. Now he wasn't so sure. And that was another reason why he had better pay his visit to Lady Somers. Catesby passed a shop advertising psychedelic love and checked his watch. There was still time to buy her a present. He remembered what Miranda had said about her.

»»»»»

The house was a perfect example of London Georgian. It ticked all the right boxes from the cast-iron railings with pointy spikes that guarded the cellar entrance to the plain Hepworth chimney pots with roll tops. And, unlike the vulgar brass door furniture of its neighbours, Lady Somers' front door had cast-iron fittings painted gloss black, including a lion head's knocker. According to Henry Bone, brass door fittings on a Georgian house are always the sign of a parvenu. Catesby lifted the heavy cast-iron ring that passed through the lion's jaws and knocked firmly.

When Lady Somers answered the door she was wearing a cardigan and black trousers so her famous legs were not on display. She put out one hand, while the other pulled her cardigan tight around her as if it were armour. Catesby shook her hand. It was cold as ice.

'I've been expecting you,' she said. 'Would you like coffee, tea – or a drink?'

'Please don't go to any trouble.'

'I was going to have tea myself. It won't be any trouble.'

'Thank you. Tea for me would be fine.'

'Any particular sort?'

'Darjeeling, please.'

Lady Somers suddenly seemed a little flustered.

'If you haven't got Darjeeling, any sort of tea would be fine.'

'No, it's not that. Why don't you go up to my study? It's on the second floor. We'll talk there. It's much nicer. I'll bring the tea.'

As Catesby mounted the stairs, he took in an impressive collection of art that ranged from eighteenth-century English oil paintings to ancient Chinese lithographs. The most unusual was of a man with a shaved head being tortured on a rack. The other odd and incongruous thing was an oar from an Oxford Eight. A brass plate indicated that the oar belonged to The Right Honourable Guy Louis de la Croix Somers. It took Catesby a second to realise that it was Lady Somers' oar. That must have been her former name and she had been an Oxford blue. Catesby kept glancing around as he made his way to the study, but there was no sign of the famous Poussins.

It was a large study with armchairs covered in loose chintz and a coffee table. Lady Somers' desk faced west over a garden with espalier fruit trees. You could see the river and Battersea Bridge, but not the power station. It was a nice place to work – and a nice place to photograph nuclear secrets. For a second or two Catesby thought he could hear Miranda's ghost clicking away with Cauld-well's spy camera, but then realised it was only the click of china as Lady Somers mounted the stairs with a tea tray.

As she came in, she closed the door behind her with a deft flick of ankle and heel. 'Please sit down.'

Catesby sank into an armchair and placed the present he had bought her on the floor beside him, leaning upright against the chair.

'What have you got in that bag? Handcuffs?'

'No, just a token something.'

She began to pour the tea. 'I've already written my resignation letter. But I suppose that's very wishful thinking. I am sure it's going to involve far more than simply asking me to resign.'

'There is, Lady Somers, going to be a full series of interrogations – debriefings if you like – but there is no intention of putting you under arrest.' Catesby paused and fidgeted. His hand shook and he rattled the cup against the saucer as he sipped his tea. 'But that's not primarily why I'm here. I'm not here for plea bargaining – or anything like it.'

Lady Somers looked at him. Catesby looked away. Lady Somers put down her teacup and examined the veins on the back of her hand.

Catesby closed his eyes, which felt strained and moist. He had been given some awful jobs in his time in the service, but this was one of the worst – the worst. How do you tell a parent that her only child is dead? Catesby felt a wave of self-loathing. He shouldn't be feeling sorry for himself; he should be feeling sorry for the woman opposite. He opened his eyes. She was staring directly at him.

She spoke in whisper. 'What is it?'

'Miranda is dead.'

There was no shock on Lady Somers' face, no disbelief, just numbness. Finally, she buried her face in her hands.

Catesby decided to break with the script. He wasn't going to play their game. He reached forward and touched her hand. 'Do you want me to leave you alone? I think I should leave.'

She looked up. The tears had come and her mascara was

smeared. Catesby picked up a napkin and passed it so she could wipe her eyes.

'Thank you,' she said.

'Can I do anything for you?'

'Please tell me what happened.'

Catesby told the story.

When he was finished, Lady Somers got up and looked out the window with her back to Catesby. He could tell that she was crying because her back was shaking – and that the tears were bitter ones. At last, she came back and sat down again.

'Miranda never forgave me.'

'No, she did forgive you.'

'She killed herself to punish me.'

'She didn't kill herself. The overdose was an accident.'

'You don't know that.'

'Not for sure. But I do know that, in the end, Miranda loved you – believe me.'

'But she would never believe me.' Lady Somers raised her voice, almost to a shout. 'I did not take her mother away from her. Penelope took herself away.' She lowered her voice again. 'But what's the point of self-justification now?'

'It might help you understand yourself and your daughter.'

'Did you like her?'

'Not at first, but I grew very fond of her.'

'A lot of people would say that. She was so much like her mother.'

'What happened to her?'

'It is odd, isn't it? Penelope never loved me. To be honest, I'm not sure she ever loved Miranda either. Maybe it was because I was the father. I was shocked when she agreed to leave Miranda behind in London. She was only two.'

Lady Somers was talking about something to which Catesby had been denied access. The war-time files on both Lord and Lady Somers had either been destroyed or put in a hundred-year folder.

Catesby leaned forward and whispered, 'What happened?'

'Towards the end of the war they were looking for agents

with local knowledge for clandestine missions behind Japanese lines in Malaya. Penelope, to my surprise and chagrin, volunteered. We were both landed by submarine on the western coast – a husband and wife SOE team – to rendezvous with a Chinese resistance movement that was fighting the Japanese. Penelope, of course, was a brilliant agent because she spoke all the Chinese dialects of Malaya and knew the country so well. It was, perhaps, inevitable that she would fall in love with Li. She never forgot him. When the Malayan insurrection began in 1948, Li became a key leader in the Malayan National Liberation Army. Penelope went off into the jungle to join him – not just because she loved him, but because she believed in the cause.'

'Did Miranda know this?'

'She did and admired her mother's idealism – and in some way I became the villain. Perhaps I should have gone off to fight alongside Penelope and Li. But who would have looked after Miranda? I couldn't leave her behind again. She was five years old and needed a mother.'

'And you became that mother?'

'Yes – and that is what I always wanted.'

'What happened to…' Catesby didn't know which name to use, 'to your then wife.'

Lady Somers smiled. 'It's okay – call her Penelope. That was her name. Penelope was badly wounded in a British ambush. She later died, but her body was never found. Few, of course, know that any of this happened. The cover story was that Penelope had run off to the South of France with another man and disappeared during a drunken late-night swim – once again, no body. A few of her family knew what had really happened, but found the truth more distasteful than the cover story. They were typical colonial plantation owners and traders – fabulously wealthy. Penelope hated them. In any case, I became Penelope and I brought Miranda to England to begin again.' Lady Somers smiled. 'In a sense, both of us became Penelope.'

'But some people must have known?'

'Of course, but our secrets were never revealed beyond a

select few. The British upper class may not be stiff-lipped, but they are incredibly tight-lipped.'

Catesby sat in silent reflection. There was a certain symmetry between mother and daughter, but also between both of them and Jeffers Cauldwell. Inherited wealth often carried a host of inherited diseases. Arrogance and cruelty were two, but guilt was another. And yet, there was something about Lady Somers' story that did not ring completely true. But it no longer mattered.

'I'm really going to miss Miranda,' she said, with hot tears rolling down her cheeks. 'Sweet Miranda, you were all I had.'

Catesby had done the worst bit, but there was more to follow. He was back on script. 'Miranda told me that you had a secret pleasure, a love of The Beatles.' He reached for the package beside the armchair. 'So I have brought you something to remember her by.' Catesby took the LP out of the bag. John is barefoot and conspicuously dressed in white as the four walk across the zebra crossing.

Lady Somers accepted the album with a faint smile. 'Thank you. How kind.' She touched the cover gently and handed the album back to Catesby. 'Would you please put it on the phono-graph for me? Your hands are steadier.' She pointed. 'It's over there under the bookshelf.'

Catesby turned on the record player and gently put the needle in place. He turned up the volume full. The lyrics were about loneliness and cold and winter. The lines were simple and moving. Years had passed, but there was still hope.

He walked back to where Lady Somers was sitting. She was crying and swaying in time to the music. Catesby put his hand inside his jacket and took the 9mm Browning out of the shoul-der holster. He placed the gun on the coffee table in front of Lady Somers. He leaned over and gently kissed her and then left the room and closed the door behind him.

Catesby stood on the landing and leaned against the banister. He was sick inside with cold sweat rolling down his spine. He looked down the staircase and waited and listened to the song. The smiles were coming back. Years had passed, but the sun was coming back.

»»»»

The shot was a quick sharp bark.

»»»»

The sun had come, but it would never be all right.

Afterword

I try to weave my fiction into an historical background that is accurate and well researched. This is sometimes difficult or impossible because key historical records are missing or have been suppressed. The great enigma of the present time is the rapid rise of China into an economic and military superpower. No one has adequately explained how this happened – and for years no one seemed concerned. The lid began to lift in June 1995 when a walk-in agent turned up at the CIA office in Taiwan and handed over an official People's Republic of China document marked Top Secret that contained design information on all seven of America's nuclear warheads. Further revelations led to the creation of the United States House of Representatives Select Committee on U.S. National Security and Military/Commercial Concerns with the People's Republic of China, better known as The Cox Committee. The complete findings, known as the Cox Report, are still classified, but a redacted version was released on 25 May 1999 blaming China for espionage. This simplistic explanation does not stand up to scrutiny. In December 1999 four Stanford University professors (Alastair Iain Johnston, W. K. H. Panofsky, Marco Di Capua, and Lewis R. Franklin) released a report rebutting the Cox Committee: 'The language of the report, particularly its Overview, was inflammatory and some allegations did not seem to be well supported ... Some important and relevant facts are wrong and a number of conclusions are, in our view, unwarranted.' A number of other reports, including one from the National Academy of Sciences, reached similar conclusions. In any case, the Cox Report concentrates on alleged covert operations which occurred in the 1980s and 1990s. But no report explains what happened in the 1960s. It took the United States seven years and three months to proceed from A-bomb to thermonuclear H-bomb. China made the same technological leap in two years and eight months. When the trail of historical evidence disappears, the novelist has permission to speculate. But it is important that the novelist offers speculations that are probable and rational. I hope I have done so.

A number of real historic events are mentioned in this book and real places are mentioned, but I would like to emphasise that this book is a novel. There are echoes of the Profumo affair, the Portsmouth spy ring and the running of Oleg Penkovsky as a double agent. Consequently, a few real names are used, but no real people are portrayed. This is a work of fiction. When I have used official titles and positions, I do not suggest that the persons who held those positions in the past are the same persons portrayed in the novel or that they have spoken, thought or behaved in the way I have imagined.

Finally, I would like to point out that most of the characters in this book are completely fictional and bear no resemblance at all to anyone living or dead. Lady Penelope Somers, her daughter Miranda, William Catesby, Henry Bone and a host of minor characters are totally the product of my imagination.

Acknowledgements

The core of this book was written while I was recovering from a badly shattered right wrist – 'mush' as my excellent saviour of a surgeon described it. Warmest thanks to Julia who looked after me with loving care during a time when I was unable to drive or do domestic chores. Likewise, thanks to all the staff in the orthopaedics department at James Paget Hospital and to my physiotherapist at Cutler's Hill who also helped me keep writing in adversity.

My agent Maggie Hanbury has once again been a valuable source of guidance and good sense. Thanks also to Henry de Rougement and Harriet Poland at the agency.

A very special thanks to my publisher, Gary Pulsifer. It is a privilege to have a publisher who genuinely loves good writing and does so much to promote it. And a fond thanks to Arcadia's Karen Sullivan for her contagious enthusiasm and to Piers Russell-Cobb for valuing me as an author.

Thanks again to Angeline Rothermundt, who has now polished four of my books into shape, for her flawless proofreading. Gill Paul was the perfect copy editor. Her eye for detail and accuracy is remarkable. Finally, a most grateful thanks to my editor, Martin Fletcher, who was absolutely fantastic. Martin is the ultimate professional. His advice on structure, always accepted, was insightful and creative.

In my attempt to recreate the espionage world of the 1950s and 1960s, I am particularly indebted to Gordon Corera for his *MI6: Life and Death in the British Secret Service*. Corera's book is the best and most readable history of post-war British intelligence that you are likely to find. I would also like to single out Richard Davenport-Hines's *An English Affair: Sex, Class and Power in the Age of Profumo*, a book that perfectly captures the mood of the time. Both books were also a treasure trove of names and places that led the way to further research. I am also indebted to Nora Nickerson for 'A Poem to Paul Tibbets'. The poem explores the mind of the man who dropped the A-bomb on Hiroshima. It is a disturbing poem, but one that I urge everyone to read.

Bibliography

Aldrich, Richard J. *The Hidden Hand: Britain, America and Cold War Secret Intelligence*. The Overlook Press, Woodstock and New York, 2002.

Carter, Miranda. *Anthony Blunt: His Lives*. Macmillan, London, 2001.

Corera, Gordon. *MI6:Life and Death in the British Secret Service*. Orion Books Ltd, London, 2012.

Davenport-Hines, Richard. *An English Affair: Sex, Class and Power in the Age of Profumo*. William Collins, London, 2013.

Deustcher, Isaac. 'Maoism – Its Origins, Background and Outlook' from *The Socialist Register 1964*. The Merlin Press, London, 1964.

Hermiston, Roger. *Greatest Traitor: The Secret Lives of Agent George Blake*. Aurum Press, London, 2013.

Leigh, David. *The Wilson Plot: The Intelligence Services and the Discrediting of a Prime Minister*. William Heinemann Ltd, London, 1988.

Miliband, Ralph; Saville, John. *The Socialist Register 1964*. The Merlin Press, London, 1964.